THE LOST GIRLS

THE LOST GIRLS

PETER LERANGIS
get it started · last call

PATERSON NESBITT
after hours

The three works in this edition were previously published with the author pseudonym Morgan Burke

Simon Pulse
NEW YORK LONDON TORONTO SYDNEY NEW DELHI

This book is a work of fiction. Any references to historical events, real people, or real places are used fictitiously. Other names, characters, places, and events are products of the author's imagination, and any resemblance to actual events or places or persons, living or dead, is entirely coincidental.

SIMON PULSE
An imprint of Simon & Schuster Children's Publishing Division
1230 Avenue of the Americas, New York, New York 10020
This Simon Pulse paperback edition April 2015

For information about special discounts for bulk purchases, please contact Simon & Schuster Special Sales at 1-866-506-1949 or business@simonandschuster.com.
The Simon & Schuster Speakers Bureau can bring authors to your live event. For more information or to book an event contact the Simon & Schuster Speakers Bureau at 1-866-248-3049 or visit our website at www.simonspeakers.com.
Cover designed by Regina Flath
Interior designed by Hilary Zarycky
The text of this book was set in Dante.
Manufactured in the United States of America
2 4 6 8 10 9 7 5 3 1
Library of Congress Control Number 2014946176
ISBN 978-1-4814-2902-3
ISBN 978-1-4391-2092-7 (*Get It Started* eBook)
ISBN 978-1-4391-2091-0 (*After Hours* eBook)
ISBN 978-1-4391-2069-9 (*Last Call* eBook)
These titles were previously published individually by Simon Pulse.

CONTENTS

get it started

PART ONE

PROLOGUE

I've been waiting.

That's right.

Waiting right here all this time.

Watching every move you make.

Searching for the right moment.

Oh, I've been so good.

I've been sooooo UNDER CONTROL!

But I knew it couldn't last for long.

No, it couldn't.

Because I SAW you.

I saw what you DID!

And you have no idea, do you?

No idea what's about to happen next.

What's about to happen to YOU!

It's an art, really.

To be this undercover.

To be sooooo gooooood.

Do you really think you can run wild, just like that?

Do you? DO YOU?

Well, it will all end soon enough, won't it?

Because I'm about to throw a party.

1

"No, I didn't *see it,"* seventeen-year-old Kirsten Sawyer told her friend Samantha Byrne.

"Come on. Admit it, you looked. I *know* you," Sam said, her hazel eyes sparkling in the dimness of the Party Room as she stood under a sign that said DRINKING AGE 21 and screamed ignore me.

Ignore was what Kirsten desperately wanted to do to Sam right then. It was Friday—a crisp October night and, *hello*, the bar was open. But Sam was her best friend of all time, and Kirsten couldn't ignore her. Well, okay, no one could—friend or foe, male or female. Sam was like a weather front. Whenever she entered the Party Room, the music volume seemed to jack up and the brick walls vibrated. Distracted boyfriends sized up Sam's Scandinavia-perfect cheekbones, shoulder-length platinum hair, Maxim-ready figure, and killer fashion sense. Suddenly every girl was thinking that maybe she should have done more with her makeup or worn that push-up bra—*anything* to offset the pull of Sam's eyes. The eyes that could take a boy's free will and fry it to a crisp.

Even Kirsten would admit that she could fry some wills of her own, with her superlong chestnut-colored hair, *America's Next Top Model*–length legs, and a smile that had inspired more than a few love poems. Okay, bad ones mostly, but hey, it's high school and what really counts is the thought. Sam and Kirsten were both, after all, part of New York City's exclusive Woodley School in Riverdale—the Bronx really, but don't tell anyone. A group that defined what it meant to be hot and young and rich at the center of the world in the twenty-first century.

Tonight, Kirsten could see that Sam was in a state, with her eye on her used-to-be boyfriend Brandon Yardley, and her mind set on major-tease mode. Kirsten did not, at that moment, care to focus on the place Sam was eyeing. Not after having spent three grueling hours at a last-minute Kaplan review class followed by forty-five minutes of coaxing the life back into the two pools of brownish mud formerly known as her eyes. "Okay . . . yeah," Kirsten said, humoring her. "You're right, Spammie, it's a sock. I mean, it's definitely not real."

"Wait. It's moving!" Sam's eyes were as wide as softballs. "Kirsten, it's alive!"

That did it. Now Kirsten *had* to look, couldn't *help* looking. Brandon Alexander Yardley, slouched against the bar with his unlit cigarette and strong jaw and the faded outline down the front of his jeans that obviously did wonders for his self-esteem. Yes, it *did* look like there was some extra enhancement in there, but no, it *wasn't* moving.

Just the idea that she was checking it out forced Kirsten to release an involuntary giggle, which wasn't exactly a stellar move. Because here on the Upper East Side of Manhattan, where the value of your seven-figure apartment matched the size of your trust fund, where *everyone* who was *anyone* had already seen *everything* that meant anything (or so they say), getting embarrassed over ogling a guy's, um, *equipment* was far from cool.

Like right now. Like when the subject of your ogle ogled back . . . with great manly pride. "Hey babe, you like what you see?" Brandon called out, thrusting his hips forward a little.

"Oh, please," Kirsten said, trying to sound unaffected and unembarrassed. "I didn't bring my microscope. So why don't you turn your sorry-ass piece of false advertising back toward the bar, where it belongs."

And wonder of wonders, Brandon's never-before-seen modesty burst from hiding and, face turning red, he did as he was told.

Sam let out a whoop. "You go, girl! I didn't know you had it in you."

Kirsten shrugged. She wasn't normally quick with the

comebacks the way Sam was, but this time was different. "Brandon puts to rest any doubts that the human race was descended from barbaric apelike beings," she said.

"That's why we're celebrating my Liberation from Brandon Day, right?" Sam nodded and slung her arm around Kirsten's shoulders and led her to the dance floor.

"Right," Kirsten said, looking around to see who was there tonight.

Kirsten spotted the short and sassy blond haircut of her other best friend, Julie Pembroke. She floated by in her usual neck-to-toe black, with a tight knit shirt that accented her best assets, and of course had drawn a following of five guys in various stages of drool control. "Sorry-ass piece of false advertising?" Julie said. "I've got to remember that one."

"Hi, Kirsten!" shouted Sarah Goldstein, the Cheerleader with the Heart of Chocolate who could spend a week on one food group—sweets—and still look as if she could work a runway. She, as always, was entertaining her own Circle of Male Life, and teasing them with a flip of her wavy auburn locks.

Kirsten waved to her, and to Carla Hernandez, a.k.a. Carla the Geek, who disproved the conventional wisdom that a person who understood I.T. could not be H.O.T. Carla's skirt flared as she danced, revealing a body more lethal than an attachment with executable malicious code, whatever that meant.

As Kirsten moved to the beat, she felt her cares flying away. She had been *dying* to dance. "What did you see in Brandon, anyway?" she asked Sam. "I mean, aside from the fact that he's hot."

"Well, first of all," Sam replied, "what you said about the microscope—it isn't true."

"Really?" Kirsten asked, glancing back at him.

"Tape measure, sister-girl," Sam said with a slow, sly grin. "Or . . . barometer? Isn't that what measures *pressure*?"

Kirsten grinned. "You are so, *so* bad."

Sam threw back her head and laughed, long and deep. "Well, okay . . . seriously? I loved the way he got mad when I called him Brandy Alexander, for one thing. When he's not drunk or stoned or depressed or pissed off, he can be funny and fun to be with. Sexy, too. And—don't faint—*once* . . . I think it was August ninth at three forty-seven . . . he was actually kind. I mean it. Not that you'd want to spend your life with him. He's great for someone with a short attention span like me. The problem is Woodley. The more boyfriends you ditch, the harder it is to avoid them all."

It was true. Woodley was a small place. And not exactly modest. Depending on the newspaper you read, it was "the A-list alma mater of movie stars, heiresses, and a good chunk of the Ivy League" or "a Depraved Preppy Sex Den," but frankly, Woodley girls were much more likely to make the Style section than the gossip column.

On a Friday like this, with the school week over and the night young and the East River breeze wafting past the open doors of the Upper East Side bars, people knew you went to Woodley. It was kind of funny, really. The shopkeepers beckoned you inside, eyes on your well-stocked Prada handbag. The salivating boys shouted from BMWs with New Jersey MD plates or MY SON IS A GREAT NECK NORTH HONOR ROLL STUDENT bumper stickers. Last month's rap hits blared from the speakers. As for the public-high-school crowd, well, let's not go there.

They all knew who you were.

And you just. Didn't. Care.

You headed to the Party Room, where your friends were waiting, the bartender was pouring, and the world was perfect.

"His masculinity threatened, the brooding priapic young Brandon pretends his ex-girlfriend does not exist," said Sam in her best news-anchor voice as Kirsten swam her way through the crowd, pulling Sam toward the bar.

Kirsten looked over her shoulder. "Priapic?"

"Definition at eleven," Sam replied. "Fortunately, tonight Sam is sniffing out a real man, not a Goat Boy with a five o'clock shadow who reminds her of her new stepfather, the dreaded Rolf from Düsseldorf."

"Uh, Rolf doesn't *have* a five o'clock shadow," she reminded Sam.

"Exactly." Sam sat at the bar, waving toward Scott, the bartender. "I have a new policy: No hooking up with high-school boys who look older than Mom's husband. Rolf still gets *carded*, Kirsten—plus, he speaks *German*. What do they *talk* about? What do they have in common? I mean, one minute they're pumping iron at the gym together, the next minute they're pumping each other."

"Uh . . . ew!" Kirsten said, trying to fight off the mental image of Sam's mom, Bobbi Byrne, doing it with her German trainer. Then she flashed a sudden Whitening Strip smile at Scott the bartender, who had finally turned her way. He was an early Tom-Cruise-by-way-of-Justin-Timberlake-with-an-extra-dose-of-testosterone type, perfect eye candy when the dance floor was not enough. And a really nice guy too. "I'd like the usual," she said, winking. "A Shirley Temple."

"The same for me, Scotty," Sam said.

Scott smiled that crooked, sexy little half-smile, which, if he could somehow make it transferable to other guys, would make him a fortune in licensing deals and a lot of girls very happy. He was also famous for having the fastest hands on the East Side, and in moments two martini glasses filled with fresh pinkish-amber drinks appeared on the bar top.

"To freedom," Sam said, holding up her drink, careful not to spill.

Kirsten clinked her glass with Sam's and downed her drink. Definitely not a Shirley Temple. She ordered another one. "No worries!" she said, taking a sip.

"Good. Because we're young, gorgeous, *and single*!"

Drink high in the air, hips moving, Sam danced her way onto the floor. "Come on, Kissyface. Let's go shake our tail feathers!"

Sam was the only person in the world allowed to call Kirsten "Kissyface." And if anyone aside from Kirsten called Sam "Spammie," she'd better hold on to her self-esteem for dear life.

The throbbing pulse of an old-school Jay Z track began to take over the room. Kirsten was feeling so great, she kicked off her Manolos, which were killing her, and cut loose with her friends.

Sam's white-blond hair was flying all over the place, catching the light and drawing attention to her antique silver earrings, shaped like slender, delicate, hanging grapes. Kirsten loved those earrings—along with Sam's matching bracelet, both one-of-a-kind gifts from her grandmother that Sam hardly ever took off. She smiled at Kirsten, then reached into the pocket of her D&G jeans and held out a tiny white pill.

"Want to share?" Sam asked. "Brandon gave it to me last week, but that was before I dumped him. I don't think I'll be getting anything like this again."

Kirsten hesitated. She was kind of gone already. *Oh, why not?* she thought. *It's a celebration!* She took the pill from Sam, turned, and bit it in half before swallowing.

Soon her Kaplan class faded into memory, lost in a

blur of arms, torsos, legs—sometimes Sam . . . sometimes others . . . the usual Woodley crowd . . . also Leslie Fenk, blond and irresistible in a Scarlett-Johannsen-meets-Julia-Stiles way, known as the Woodley Bitch by the boys (and girls) she had seduced and dropped . . . and there in the corner, in his last year at Woodley before taking his drop-dead gorgeous butt to Princeton, was Gabe Garson, a.k.a. Gay Gabe, who was dancing with Emma "Get a Life" Lewis.

Uh-oh, Kirsten thought. It was only a matter of time before Emma saw them. The girl had some kind of weird Sam radar. *Four . . . three . . . two . . .*

Julie spun away from the three guys she was dancing with to give Sam a warning. "Orange Alert," she said, just as Kirsten saw Emma's eyes light up.

The Woodley junior with the mousy brown hair waved at them, then started to dance her way over, her moves totally mimicking Sam's. Poor dull Emma idolized Sam, which in itself wasn't *so* unusual, but the girl, unfortunately, was a little like a hangover: She came on hard and lingered way too long.

Sam groaned. "Oh, God. You've got to get me *away* from her."

Kirsten laughed. "Come on. She's annoying, yes, but all in all she's pretty harmless."

"Kind of like the plague," Julie added with a grin.

Sam shook her head. "You guys wouldn't think it was so funny if you were the one she was obsessed with. I mean, she copies everything I do. One day she's going to make all of you into her best friends, then bump me off so she can take over my life."

"What's up, homey?" Emma chirped, which was something Sam used to say a lot, like, a decade ago.

"Ahhh-chooo!" Sam pretended to sneeze. "I'm fine. Just at the beginning stages of a highly contagious deadly flu."

"We're already infected," Julie said, "but you still have a chance." With that, she pulled Sam away before Emma could leach on to them for the night.

Kirsten gave Emma a weak smile and a shrug, then followed her friends to the other side of the dance floor. Sweeping past a table, she put down her drink and really started to move to the beat of the awesome song blaring over the bar's sound system. She felt her body take flight. Hips, elbows, shoulders—going on their own power.

Soon the dance floor was clearing.

"Showtime!" Sam shouted.

It was just Kirsten and Sam and Julie now. The rest circled around. Watching. Shouting. Cheering. Kirsten caught glances. Guy-glances. They wanted her . . . maybe . . . which was cool, totally cool—but at the moment, she didn't care. All that mattered was the motion and the music and her friends . . . her friends for all time . . .

Click.

A flash went off to Kirsten's right. Near the bar.

Click.

Kirsten looked over, expecting to see the Style Section guy from the *New York Times* or the greasy pervert from the tabloids. But it wasn't either.

It was Brandon.

"Take *this* . . . ," Sam said, pulling up her shirt and showing a nanosecond of breast.

Click.

Too late.

Click. Click.

Now Brandon was dancing with them, bouncing to an unidentified beat, wobbling and breathing heavily. Kirsten made a mental note to be grateful she didn't have to smell that breath. He circled around Sam, leaning close to her face, zeroing in on different parts of her body with his camera.

Click!

Sam leaped back, making it look like part of the choreography, and Kirsten stepped between them. "Enough, Brandon," she said.

"Hmm-MMMMmmm," sang Sam, the *I-am-OUT-of-here* tune that she and Kirsten had used since All-Souls preschool. Then, showing the form made famous in Madame Baudry's fourth-grade ballet class, Sam *chasséd* across the floor—away from Brandon.

Kirsten followed, but she couldn't match Brandon's experience running through a backfield of prep school gridiron kings. "Yo!" he shouted, lurching through the crowd (or maybe he was dancing). "Where you going?"

"As far away from you as I can," Sam called back. "You photographed me on my bad side."

"Come *on,"* Brandon mumbled, his voice slurred and a notch too loud. "You know you want me. Admit it."

"You're right, Brandy Alexander, oh . . . *oh* . . . *OH,* I soooo want you . . . ," she said breathlessly, *". . . to go away!"*

"Don't be a tease, Sam. You know I don't like it." Brandon grabbed Sam's arm, but she shook him off and ran.

"Kirsten!" she cried out, heading for the door.

Brandon sprinted after her.

Kirsten tried to follow. But the Party Room was full of gawkers, and the crowd closed in. *"Out of my way!"* she called out, elbowing through.

She heard a scream. A slam. A chair falling and skittering across the room.

And then Sam's voice.

"Let me go!" she cried. "Stop it! *Help! Somebody help me! He's hurting me!"*

2

Kirsten grabbed Brandon by the shirt collar. Julie, racing over with her entourage close behind, got the waistband. They both yanked hard.

He was a big guy, but he was drunk and stoned and he stumbled backward, his thick hands letting go of Sam's arms. She fell against the door while Brandon thrashed about, finally tripping on his own feet and tumbling to the floor.

The worst part was, no one was helping. No one was doing a goddamn thing!

"What's going on here?" Scott the Bartender said, pushing people aside.

Kirsten and Julie rushed to Sam and helped her up. "Are you okay?" Kirsten asked.

"Never been better," Sam said loudly and angrily, brushing off her clothes. "You know, I think the floor is, like, mahogany or something? That's what we did our floors with at home. Isn't that *interesting*? Being with Brandy Alexander is so educational. You see things you never would have seen with a human boyfriend."

"You're such a bitch!" Brandon said, staggering to his feet.

Sam opened her mouth, and then closed it. If Kirsten didn't know better, she'd have thought Sam was kind of upset by Brandon's not-so-original remark, which was weird because it certainly wasn't the first time Sam had been called a bitch.

Scott pulled him up the rest of the way. "Out of here, Yardley. Go home, sleep it off, and explain it to your mom and dad in the morning."

"I'm not going anywhere." Brandon staggered back a couple of steps, pointing a finger at Sam. "Nobody makes an ass out of me and gets away with it. I'm going to get you back, Sam. . . . I'm going to be your worst night-muh-muh . . ." Brandon could hardly stand up now. He barreled to the front door. The crowd parted like the Red Sea to let him out.

Scott handed Sam some napkins from the bar. "Are you okay? Do you want me to call you a cab?"

"I didn't know you cared." Sam smiled. "No, seriously, I'm okay."

"Brandon isn't," said Josh Bergen, a senior from Talcott Prep who had been part of Julie's inner dancing circle. "Five bucks says he's facedown in some Upper East Side Shitzu dog doo. Any takers? Let's go have a look, shall we?"

Talcott was Woodley's rival school, and Josh definitely had a Talcott sense of humor.

"That's disgusting," Kirsten said, walking Sam back toward the tables with Julie. The music had changed to a slow, sexy Beyoncé song, and the crowd was beginning to dance again.

As Kirsten and Sam sat at a table in the corner, Julie headed to the bar for drinks.

"I can't believe he did that," Sam said. "I can't believe he *attacked* me. Look at my hands—they're shaking."

Kirsten took hold of her friend's hands and tried to calm her down. "He's a creep, Sam. I always thought so, but I just never admitted it to you. I guess I should have."

"No. This is partly my fault, Kirsten. My big mouth. It's like, I'm off him but there's still a connection. Why can't I just break up like a normal person?"

"Um, give me a minute, let me guess. Maybe because *he's* . . . a pig?" Kirsten replied.

"But that's the thing. He isn't. Not really. I mean, I *did* choose to go out with him, right? He's only like this at parties when he gets high." Sam picked out the cashews from the snack dish on the table. "*See*, I think Brandon does drugs because he's insecure about being a country boy. He grew up in Iowa. Idaho. Ohio. One of the O states. You know what his favorite hobby is? Duck hunting. With his dad."

"You're kidding me, right?" Kirsten asked.

Sam nodded and smiled, twirling the ends of her hair with a finger. The girls were both quiet for a moment, and Sam looked as if her mind were a million miles away.

"What are you thinking about?" Kirsten asked, even though she knew the answer.

"What else?" Sam shrugged. "You know, I try to be all tough and make fun of Brandon, but . . . I really liked him, Kirsten. I did. It was just too intense—what he was getting into was—"

"Getting into?" Kirsten said. "Meaning the drugs? Was he going hard-core or something?"

The question went unanswered. Sam dipped her hand back into the snack dish on the table, lost in some thought and staring vaguely in the direction of the bar, where Julie was picking up three delicious-looking pinkish drinks.

Then, suddenly, Sam smacked the table. "Forget it. I'm glad I dumped him. A person has to break from the past, Kirsten. If you do the same things all the time, your brain gets all, like, spongiform. Right?"

"Uh, right."

Spongiform? Kirsten made a mental note to look that one up too.

"Screw the same-old, same-old!" Sam stood up from the table and shouted out loud: "*Screw* the same conversations and the same gossip—and the Upper East Side and the Junior League and the Ivy League—and Mom's Nazi husband. I'm sick of my life! *I want to do something wild and unexpected!*"

She pulled open a button on her blouse. And she leaped across the dance floor, landing somewhere between a bump and a grind, and dancing like this was the last day of her life.

Julie came back with three drinks and set them on the table. "Who plugged her in?"

"You know . . . it happens every few weeks, whenever she breaks up with a guy," Kirsten said.

"Soon, there aren't going to be any guys left for her," Julie said, sitting down. "I give my boys at least three weeks. Then the flush."

Kirsten smiled. Under the tight sweaters and do-it-to-me-now shoes, there was a shy girl in there *somewhere.* Yeah, right. "I don't know, Jules. I think this one's really hard for her. It hasn't been easy breaking away."

"Oh? Are you sure?" Julie was looking out to the dance floor, her eyebrows raised.

A new guy, someone Kirsten had never seen before, was dancing with Sam. A hottie wearing skinny Levi's and a classic Phish T-shirt. He was tall, had scruffy red hair, and a chiseled, rugged face. And he seemed a little older, like maybe he'd wandered into the wrong bar or something. A junior or senior in college, Kirsten figured. This Phish shirt was odd because he was more than a little dangerous looking. . . .

And totally Sam's type.

Here we go again, Kirsten thought, taking a sip of her drink. Mmm . . . a pomegranate martini. Just what the doctor ordered. "Who's the Viking?" she asked Julie.

"Never seen him before," Julie replied.

"Well, she's found hers. I guess it's time we found ours." Kirsten threw back half her drink. "Come on, let's dance and look irresistible."

The floor was body-to-body now. As Kirsten made her way across the room, she could see Sam was weaving among the hordes, her new guy following her like Erik the Red charting a course to the New World.

The Party Room was hot tonight.

Really hot.

Kirsten tossed her head back and drank it all in. *Same-old same-old?* Nah, She loved this place. On the Upper East Side, where a hundred brushed-steel Euro trash and décor-of-the-month clubs lined First and Second Avenues, full of suburban kids seeking other suburban kids, the Party Room was something from another time. Just an old brick building with no name, no markings, no window—as if the last guy who lived there put on his hobnail boots and left two hundred years ago, and the house was still waiting for him.

A historical plaque near the corner said it was a stop on the Underground Railroad or something, but if not for that you'd never look twice, never think of entering—unless you *knew.* Because when you went down the creaky stairs and stepped through the thick oak door, warped by its own weight and age, you entered a kind of Alice in Wonderland world that was neither basement nor ground floor, a world of brick walls and recessed lighting, polished oak bar and plasma TV screen, floors worn smooth by centuries of foot traffic, and monster speakers whose sound somehow barely filtered up to the street—and you knew you were part of a secret, an address passed from class to class, hardly ever straying from the Woodley fold.

And judging from the fact that the management never spent a penny on advertising, they must have liked it that way too. The Party Room was forever old, forever new. And always hot, hot, hot.

Scott, she noticed, was no longer at the bar. She glanced around and saw him talking to a cop in the open front door. Once in a while the neighbors would call in complaints. Loitering, trash talking, kids peeing against the building walls. Like it was such a *shock* to New Yorkers that a place called the Party Room actually had parties? Hello?

The officer didn't seem to care. Dozens of kids, mostly Woodley students, passed him by, shouting, laughing at the top of their lungs, many of them saying hi to Sam as she made her way toward the door with Erik the Red.

"That was a fast recovery from heartbreak," Julie said, dancing with Kirsten and Gay Gabe. "I think it might even be a record."

"She's got good taste," Gabe said, practically drooling over Sam's new guy.

Sam let out a tuneless blast of singing. Normally she had a great voice, which meant only one thing. "She's all done," Kirsten said.

"Kisssyyyyyfaaace!" Sam called out from the door. "Don't leave without me!" She put her right hand to her ear, thumb and pinkie extended, and mouthed, *I'll call you.*

Kirsten took her cell phone from her pocket and looked at the time.

12:09 a.m.

She changed her ringer setting to High and waved good-bye to her friend.

3

"So long, farewell, au revoir!" Julie sang out.

"You're wasted . . . ," Kirsten sang back, "and also very flaaaaaaat."

"Wasted, yeah." Julie straightened up. Her size 36Ds smartly saluted the sleeping denizens of Park Avenue. "But flat? I don't think so."

"Can you make it home by yourself?" Kirsten asked.

"My girls will point the way." She turned her breasts up East Eighty-Fourth Street. Yodeling, she wove her way home on the rain-slicked pavement. "God, Kirsten, all these houses look the same, don't they?"

Kirsten waited until Julie let herself into the cozy confines of her brownstone town house—the correct one—then closed her jacket tight and turned to walk home.

Scott's martinis were still whirling through her system too, and her feet slipped and slid off the heels of her fabulous Manolos. She thought about hailing a cab, but the cool night air felt good against her face, especially after the muggy closeness of the Party Room. Besides, it was starting to drizzle and you could never get a cab on the East Side in any sort of precipitation whatsoever. Especially if you needed one. It was some kind of municipal law.

Her footsteps clattered on the sidewalk as she headed toward Park Avenue. She felt like that actor in the old movie *Some Like It Hot.* The one who dressed as a woman but couldn't handle heels. Jack Lemmon. That was his name.

The walk was short, and so familiar, she could do it in her sleep. Left on Park, three blocks downtown to East Eighty-First, then right to Fifth Avenue. Her apartment building was on the corner. Across the street from the Metropolitan Museum of Art and familiar to the world from the hundreds of movies filmed in front of her building. Hector would be on front-door duty tonight. He was the nicest doorman ever, as opposed to the creepy night guy in Sam's building.

Sam.

Where *was* she?

Kirsten stopped walking and pulled out her cell and checked it for the fourth time since Sam had left the Party Room.

Texts . . . none.

Voice mail . . . nothing.

Missed calls . . . nothing.

Received calls . . . her own phone number, three times. The times Mom had called to screech.

The phone's screen said 2:41 a.m.

Kirsten sighed. *Don't leave without* me, she remembered. That's what Sam had said. Right, Kirsten had heard that one before. But Sam also said she'd call. And lately she was pretty good about that. By now, she usually checked in.

But Sam had lost track of time.

The last time this happened was a total disaster, the night Sam ended up in a Vassar dorm room passed out on the floor with four college guys and an unopened magnum of Dom Pérignon. She attempted to sneak it out at 4:00 in the morning only to catch her heel on the doorjamb and smash the bottle to bits in the hallway.

That was the night Kirsten tried to set a limit: 2:00 a.m. for cell-phone-check-in time. Which was kind of dumb, like something a parent would do, so of course she didn't push it.

Still, Kirsten was pissed. Mainly, she had to admit, because she wanted details about Erik the Red.

Kirsten turned around, deciding to take the long way—back over to Lexington, around to East Eighty-Third. There she would pass the brownstone of Ambassador Reynault, whose Yale-sophomore son, Julian, had been Sam's summer fling. Maybe Sam had ended up there tonight. If so, the light would be on in the basement room, affectionately known as Julian's Den of Delights.

But 141 East Eighty-Third was dark, top to bottom, like

every other brownstone on the block. Everyone asleep in the middle of the City That Never Sleeps.

As she passed Number 127, she heard footsteps behind her.

Clup . . . clup . . . clup . . . clup . . .

She turned quickly. The way she'd been trained. The instinct every New York girl cultivated. The idea was to face the person, meet him eye to eye. If it's just a nobody, he won't care. If it's an attacker, you'll catch him off-guard, show him you're a person with a will of your own—and he's more likely to back off.

But there were no eyes to meet. Three doors down, a figure slipped into the shadow of a basement entrance.

"Hello?" Kirsten called out.

Nothing.

Kirsten's heart thumped harder in her chest. *Stop being paranoid,* she told herself. *Stop messing with your own head. You're almost home.*

A set of headlights appeared two blocks away, but the car turned down Lex, leaving the whole street empty down to the river. Definitely, at this point, a cab was the best idea. Maybe she'd have better luck with them on Park. She turned and began walking fast.

Clup, clup, clup, clup . . .

Shit, Kirsten thought.

She crossed the street, and the footsteps crossed too.

She stopped, and they stopped.

Screw the mind games. Focus, Kirsten. Straight line. Park Avenue ahead.

Her ankle twisted in her shoes, and she leaned down to slip them off without breaking stride, but the right one was stuck and she smacked against a scrawny maple, turning around in time to see a pair of shoulders, a coat, legs running toward her, and she didn't want to look, didn't want to attempt the eye contact thing because she was scared now and she *needed a cab*! And so she stopped thinking altogether and ran, ran full speed, barefoot, clinging to the shoes and watching the amber lights of Park Avenue coming closer, the cabs gliding past the center median, uptown, downtown . . .

Clup-clup-clup-clup . . .

"TAXI!" Racing onto Park, she shot into the intersection too fast and too scared to notice the livery cab screaming toward her, uptown, trying to beat a yellow light.

SKREEEEEEEE . . .

Kirsten jumped into the street, toward the median, and the car barreled by her, careening through the light, barely missing the line of parked cars on the other side of the street, and Kirsten kept running, across the intersection, left on Park, ignoring the stream of Spanish curse words that spewed from the cab and thrusting her arm out like a crazed bird hoping to flag a real cab, going her way, but there was nothing, *nothing,* as if the drivers had planned to shun her on purpose.

She veered west on East Eighty-Second Street—familiar

territory, high brownstone stoops—and ducked into the sunken area behind the steps leading to a basement rental apartment. In the sudden stillness, her violent heartbeats felt like fists to her chest. She crouched down in the shadows and willed herself quiet, listening for footsteps.

A truck rumbled up Madison. A horn blared on Park. But East Eighty-Second was silent, as silent as New York could be.

He was gone. She could make it home by herself. Lesson learned. No harm done.

Stand. Breathe. Move.

Kirsten stepped out from the stoop and onto the sidewalk. She looked left and right and began to walk, peering carefully into the slanted shadows of the rising stoops.

Three blocks to home.

At the corner of Madison Avenue, she turned left—

And felt a hand grab her by the arm.

"Noooooo!" Kirsten screamed, kicked, and fought with all her might.

"Ahhh! Ow! Stop it!"

The hand let go.

Brandon Yardley stumbled away. "Jesus, what is *wrong* with you?"

"Oh my God." Kirsten was hyperventilating. She couldn't see straight. "You asshole."

"Holy shit, Kirsten, that hurt," he said, rubbing his leg. "And what the hell are you screaming about?"

"That *hurt*?" Kirsten spun around on her bare feet and walked down Madison. "You follow me like a pervert, you make me run into the street where I almost get killed, then you attack me. *Now take a wild guess what I'm screaming about!*"

Brandon walked with her, and Kirsten could smell the beer on his breath.

"I wasn't following you," he said. "I just saw you come around the corner. I wanted to ask where Sam was. That's all."

"Sam?" Kirsten turned to face him. "What do you want with her?"

"We have some unfinished business," he said, staring at her with a kind of desperation in his bloodshot eyes. "It's personal."

"Look, Brandon. I don't know where she is," Kirsten began.

"Fine. If you don't want to tell me where my girlfriend is, I'll find her on my own." Brandon turned to leave, but Kirsten stopped him. Clearly the guy was losing his grip on reality and she had to put him in check.

"Brandon," she said slowly, "Sam *isn't* your girlfriend. She doesn't want to see you anymore."

Brandon shrugged as if it were no big deal. "It was just a fight," he said. "She'll be back."

Kirsten shook her head. "Uh, I don't think so," she said. "Her mind is made up. She's already moved on with someone else."

Brandon furrowed his brows. "I saw them," he said

through gritted teeth. "I'm going to beat the crap out of that guy just as soon as I find them!"

Kirsten rolled her eyes. She didn't care what Sam had said earlier. Brandon *was* a pig. A Neanderthal. Plain and simple. "Whatever. You do what you want," she said, "but the party is over. I suggest you get a life!"

Brandon gripped Kirsten's arm tightly, surprising her. His face had turned bright red; the veins in his neck and forehead bulged. "She can't treat me this way. And you can't either, Kirsten. You tell Sam that. You tell her *nobody* screws Brandon Yardley."

Kirsten yanked her arm away. She was so done. "Yeah. Least of all Sam Byrne," she said, and walked down Eighty-First Street, onto Fifth Avenue, halfway down the block and through the front door of her building with her shoes in her hands.

Hector, the doorman, bolted to his feet. "Kirsten? Are you okay? Your shoes . . ."

Kirsten ran to the elevators, which were out of sight from the street. "I'm fine, Hector. Thanks!"

The elevator opened. Kirsten stepped in, sank to the carpeted floor, closed her eyes, and rode upward. The doors opened right into the front hall of her penthouse apartment, which was dark. Good. That meant Mom and Dad had gone to bed.

Kirsten padded into the dark living room, flicked on a

light, and sank into the goose-down sofa. She inspected her throbbing arm. She was starting to get a bruise where Brandon had grabbed her. Great.

Why do you even bother, Kirsten? she wondered. *You should know better than to get involved with one of Sam's heartbroken beasts.* She glanced at her arm again. *Look where it gets you.*

She stared out the bay window at the darkened museum across the street, at the string of streetlamps snaking into the park toward the reservoir, and sighed. Somewhere out there Sam was with a cute guy, in some state of substance abuse and/or undress, most likely having the time of her life.

And where was Kirsten?

Kirsten was alone in her apartment, having been chased down and threatened by her best friend's latest castaway. "Wait till I get my hands on you, Sam," she said softly. "You are *so* dead."

4

The vibration in her pocket awoke Kirsten the next morning.

In her dream she had been running through the neighborhood streets, but instead of Brandon chasing her it was rats, big disgusting sooty subway rats—the animals she hated worst in the world—

DZZZZZZZZZ.

She screamed and sat up with a start, fumbling for her cell phone. *That's* what the vibration was.

Her four-poster bed came into focus. She was still dressed in her clothes from last night. And she felt as if someone had peeled open her head and dropped in broken glass. This was going to be one gigantic hangover. How had she gotten from the sofa to her bed? Was last night—the whole horrible thing—one long, bad dream?

She pulled out the phone, flipped it open, and saw Sam's home number on the screen. The time was 10:42 a.m.

DZZZZZZZZZ.

"So," she said, putting the phone to her ear, "what's it like to do it with a Phish head?"

There was a pause at the other end. "Hello? Is this Kirsten?" Bobbi Byrne asked.

Shit. It was Sam's *mom*! Open mouth, insert filthy, New York City–grime-encrusted foot. "Oh! Hi, Bobbi! What I meant was—"

"It *is* you, thank goodness!" Sam's mom said. "Kirsten, would you tell Sam I need to speak to her right away?"

"Sam?" Kirsten repeated.

"Yes, Kirsten. I've been trying her and you all morning. Last night Sam mentioned that she might be sleeping at your house. Would you please put her on the phone?"

Kirsten took a deep breath.

This was bad form for Sam. Really breaking the Code, which was—more or less—(1) Always complain, always explain (2) Keep in touch (3) When in doubt, cover your girlfriend's butt.

The problem was, you couldn't do (3) very well if you didn't do (2). And you couldn't do any of it well with a raging hangover.

"Well, um . . . ," Kirsten said, "as a matter of fact . . . I can't put Sam on right now. . . ."

"Oh . . . I see," Bobbi said. "I suppose she's with the Fish boy?"

"F-Fish boy?" Kirsten said.

"Kirsten, darling, I heard what you said. Fish Head. I wasn't born yesterday. That must be Spencer Fish's nickname, right? The boy in Model Congress? Is that who she's with?"

Image assault.

The thought of Sam Byrne with helmet-haired Spencer Fish, whose nose looked like a pork roast and whose wardrobe was JCPenney clearance, nearly made Kirsten fall off the bed.

In the background she heard a groggy male voice saying, *"Do ve need to call nine-von-von?"*

Rolf from Düsseldorf. With his Teutonic sense of the world, which, if Kirsten didn't handle this situation right, would curdle in a minute. From the way Sam described him, Rolf *would* be the type to call the cops. And that would be a catastrophe of Olympic proportions. Every sweaty, pencil-chomping, taped-together-eyeglasses reporter in New York City was salivating at the chance to find dirt on a New York Society girl. "Woodley Coed Home After a Two-Day Bender"—*that's* what Rolf's meddling would lead to, because at the moment Sam was probably passed out on the floor of some friend of a friend of a friend in Brooklyn Heights or Scarsdale and wouldn't be awake until half-past lunch. Only there was *no way* Kirsten would tell that to Bobbi and Rolf.

"I meant—she's not with me because she . . . got up early and left," Kirsten said.

"So she's not with the Fish boy?" Bobbi asked.

"I don't think so," Kirsten said. "She's probably on her way home right now . . . or maybe she stopped to get some breakfast or something. Her cell phone is dead, that's probably why she hasn't called you," she continued. She was on a roll. Sam and Julie would be proud.

"Oh," Bobbi said. "Okay."

"Don't worry," Kirsten added. "I'm sure she'll be home any minute . . . if not sooner."

"Thanks, Kirsten," Bobbi said. "I wish all her friends were like you."

Oh, they are, Kirsten wanted to say. *They've been covering for her for years.* "No problem. Talk to you soon. Bye!" She hung up, sank back on the bed, and tapped out Sam's number. Oh, the girl was going to owe her big for this. Maybe brunch at the Plaza—that sounded nice.

"Hello, um, yeah. Sam here. Go ahead and talk, but make it fast. And if you can't make it fast, make it funny. . . ."

At the beep Kirsten said, "I won't be fast or funny. Where are you? I just got off the phone with your mom, and my nose grew six inches. She thinks you're doing it with Spencer Fish. I told her I'd buy him condoms because it never occurred to him he'd need any. Ha-ha. Just kidding. About some of it. How was Erik the Red? Details, you owe me details. You owe me a lot more, but we'll talk later. Call your mom ASAP, she's getting on my nerves. Good night."

Kirsten hung up and tried to get comfortable on her bed, but the urge to sleep had passed. Her brain still felt like it was in a bowl of broken glass.

A shower was called for. Head function in the morning simply did not begin without something minty and expensive on one's face. Kirsten stood up, slowly. She peeled off her clothes, put on her robe. Then she inched her way into the hall toward the bathroom, one foot at a time.

From Mom and Dad's bedroom at the other end of the apartment she heard a rustling of bedsheets, a snore or two. They'd be good for another hour. She flicked on the bathroom light, then flicked it off. Too bright. Everything was too bright. The night-light would do just fine.

As she closed the bathroom door behind her, she spotted a blinking light on the answering machine in the front hall, by the elevator.

Had that message been there when she'd arrived home? No. It must have come in sometime after 3:00 a.m. or so. But Sam wouldn't call her *house* phone. She always used the cell.

Still, Kirsten tiptoed out of the bathroom and into the front hall. The answering machine sat on an antique table, flashing a "1" in Mailbox 3. *Kirsten's* mailbox.

She pressed play.

CHHHH . . . SSHHHHH . . . WRONNNN . . .

Great. It was a butt dial. In the background were a car horn and some distant, garbled voices.

Whoever had done this must have had Kirsten's number on speed dial. She knelt and cocked her ear closer to the machine. Someone was yelling or laughing, it was hard to tell which and impossible to recognize the voice, which was obliterated by the roar of a passing bus and the screech of a car's tires. When that noise died down, Kirsten heard footsteps and the fragment of a conversation.

". . . is this place . . ." were the only words she heard clearly. They could have been from Sam, but it was hard to tell. She turned up the sound and heard the voices continue. One voice was female, that was for sure. The other voice was too hard to tell, too quiet.

". . . doesn't make sense . . ." Yeah, that was Sam, she was fairly sure. There was something about the rhythm. She seemed aggravated about something. *Not aggravated enough to make a real call to her best friend,* Kirsten noted.

The footsteps were quickening now. The voices had stopped, and so had most of the traffic noise. Kirsten heard a thump and a kind of strangled gasp.

And then, piercing through the speaker, clear and sharp, was the knife-edge sound of a scream.

"No . . . NO . . . NO-O-O-O-O-O!"

Kirsten jumped back, and the tape abruptly ended.

It *was* Sam. There was no mistaking the voice.

What had happened? Who was she with? WHERE WAS SHE?

5

"And then I erased it," Kirsten said on Monday morning. "I was so freaked out, I pressed the wrong button and I erased the entire message! I can't believe I'm such an idiot!"

"Wait. You *heard* Sam scream?" Carla Hernandez asked. She was sitting next to Kirsten at a lab table in Mr. Costas's third-period biology class. "Or you *thought* you heard her scream? Maybe it wasn't her."

Sarah, Julie, and Leslie pulled up their stools around Kirsten in a circle. Today's experiment was the dissection of a fetal pig, which had been pinned to a lab tray on its side and was at the moment totally ignored by the group except for Leslie, who let out a little "Ew . . ." before pulling her stool the farthest away.

"I'm *sure* it was her," Kirsten said. Gazing down at the bio specimen, she felt her eyes blur with tears. Normally dissections didn't bother her, but this shriveled little pig, eyes squeezed shut, feet crossed in an oddly dainty way, made her want to cry. Everything today made her want to cry.

Sam had been missing since Friday night. She hadn't called all weekend, hadn't shown up anywhere. And the scream was playing over and over in Kirsten's brain. "There was a lot of background noise," she went on, "buses and cars. So I couldn't hear what she was saying. It sounded as if she was arguing, but I couldn't tell."

"Who was she arguing with?" Julie asked.

"I don't know!" Kirsten shot back. "I couldn't even tell if it was a guy or a girl. I probably could have figured it out, if I'd heard it again. I still can't believe I erased it!" She looked around at the girls at the table. "That's when I started calling you all—and I'm sorry, I know I didn't explain myself, but I didn't have time. I had to keep calling and find out if *anyone* had seen her."

"What did you find out?" Carla asked.

"Roger Cohen and Elissa Mackey saw her near Canal Street and the Hudson River—and Gina Reese says she was dancing at a club in the meatpacking district," Kirsten said.

"I asked Dan Christensen, and he swore she was at a club on Avenue B," Julie admitted with a sigh.

Kirsten nodded. "And Trevor Royce thought she was at Sarabeth's Kitchen Saturday morning. The message was obviously left Friday night—so if she was at breakfast the next morning, she's probably, okay, right? So then why hasn't she called? Why would she be in town and not call any of us or her mom?"

"Maybe she was eloping after breakfast," Leslie said, poking around the pig fetus with a forceps. "Um, what are we supposed to do with this piggie? Cut it up? I'm not in the mood for moo shu pork."

"Leslie, why are you in our group?" Julie asked.

"Let's get started, girls," Mr. Costas said, circulating around the room with a little smile on his face and a tweed jacket whose bottom hem was losing the battle with gravity. "And, er, don't *hog* the lab equipment."

Across the room, Jason Wolfe cackled. "Good one, Mr. C!" It was safe to say that he'd probably win the distinction of being chosen Class Kiss-Ass at the end of senior year.

"Bobbi called me about a hundred times over the weekend," Kirsten went on, absently fingering the handle of the scalpel, "and I kept stalling. But I finally had to admit that I had no idea where Sam was."

"Oh my God, is that its *thing?*" Leslie said, taking a feathered clip out of her hair and putting it on a little flap of skin protruding from the fetal pig's abdomen. "It's cute."

"It's an *umbilicus*," Carla said, "not a *thing*. It says so right on the diagram."

"How can you possibly ever use that clip again?" Sarah asked.

Julie spread out the lab instructions. "Well, I'm worried.

Really worried. I mean, the last time we saw Sam, she was leaving the Party Room with that strange older guy."

"He wasn't strange at all," Sarah said. "Hot, yes. Would I have gone with him? Yes. Might I have run off with him, forgetting to call my folks for a few days? Most definitely."

Leslie laughed. "You know, guys, this is *just* what she wants."

Julie glared at her. "What are you talking about?"

"Uh, is this Sam, or what?" Leslie replied. "Like, *shameless grab for attention*? Come on. When we were kids, like, when my little brother Jordan was a month old? One day Sam and I are playing in the living room—and the baby monitor's in there too, connected to the little microphone thingy in his room, so you can hear him? So Sam sneaks up to Jordan's room, goes right up to the thingy, starts making baby noises and then choking noises and then horrible little screams, like, 'Get me out of here!' in this baby voice. Well, my mom comes into the living room at that moment and thinks it's Jordan and *totally freaks*—"

Mr. Costas sidled up behind them. As always, he wore a Harvard bow tie, which was kind of sad when you imagined that he must have once had great potential but ended up teaching biology at a prep school and doing lame stand-up comedy on Monday nights at clubs nobody had ever heard of. And to which none of the students ever went, of course. Very theatrically, he cleared his throat. *"Mademoiselles?"*

Carla batted her eyelashes. *"Pardon, le débauché de la mère."*

"Ah, oui," said Mr. Costas, looking a bit confused.

The girls huddled over the pig and tried to look terribly engrossed.

"What did that mean?" Julie asked.

"Motherf—" Carla began, but cut herself off as Mr. Costas turned back to them.

Kirsten forced herself to pay attention to the experiment. *Make first incision along dorsal side.* Following her lab notes, she picked up a scalpel and tried to figure out what *dorsal* meant.

"Hey, wasn't Sam doing it with some Yale guy?" Leslie whispered. "I'll bet he took her to, like, New Haven, Connecticut, or something."

"Julian's home for the semester," Kirsten said. "So yeah, anything's possible, but I doubt it. He was just a summer Nantucket thing. Sam got tired of Rolf saying she had a 'boyfriend in Jale,' and broke it off."

"Can we get off this topic?" Leslie said with a groan. "She's fine. If it isn't a prank—or even if it is—so what? Face it: We're all Woodley Bitches. It's not the first time Sammy Byrne spent the weekend shacked up with some hottie, and it won't be the last."

Enough.

That had crossed the line.

"You're the only *bitch* at this table, Leslie. So shut up,"

Kirsten growled, stabbing the scalpel into the pig's side. *"Just shut up!"*

Julie, Carla, Sarah, and Leslie all stared at her, mouths agape.

Mr. Costas came running.

"Uh, Kirsten . . . ?" Julie squeaked.

"Is everything all right, girls?" said Mr. Costas, peering into the lab tray. "Who did that to poor Arnold?"

"It's the samurai dissection technique," Leslie said. "Kirsten got carried away."

Mr. Costas folded his arms. "Well, Kirsten, uh, we do prefer a more conventional lab technique at Woodley, but it looks like you won't be required to do it for the moment. I just received a note about you. The headmaster would like to see you in his office, right away."

Kirsten's mouth felt dry. She looked around at her friends. This was not good. Mr. Cowperthwaite never called you into his office unless there was a huge problem.

"Pig-stabbing infraction," Leslie said, but no one laughed.

"See you," Kirsten said, gathering her books. She stood and headed out the door and down the hall.

The Woodley School bio labs were in the new wing, actually the latest of four wings that had been added to the school's original somber Gothic building. It was built shortly after the Civil War by a financier named Alexander Chester Woodley III. The new buildings were attached to the old one in a kind of wheel with spokes, giving the school a feeling of, depending on who you talked to, a fortress (adults) or a prison (students). The playing fields were some of the only undeveloped land in the Bronx, and they lay just beyond a gentle hill with a small pond and a willow tree that had to be trimmed each year because its hanging branches hid more action than most of the clubs on West Street.

The principal's office was on the first floor, near the entrance to the old building, which you entered via a ramp that was like a tunnel back in time, into narrow hallways whose walls were lined floor-to-elbow-height with dark-stained oak and festooned above with commemorative plaques.

Mr. Cowperthwaite was standing outside the office, leaning against the wall, arm in its permanent crooked position as if still holding his beloved pipe that had been banned from school at least two decades ago. Next to him was a man in a navy blue suit, his eyes blue and half-lidded, sort of a Brad Pitt on a high-carb diet. And behind him were three New York City cops.

"Ah, Kristen," Mr. Cowperthwaite rasped, having never learned her name correctly after ten years. "This is Detective . . . uh . . ."

"Peterson," said Brad Pitt, flashing a badge. "Sorry to interrupt your day. We just wanted to ask a few questions about the disappearance of Samantha Byrne. Her parents filed a missing-person report this morning."

Kirsten swallowed. "Have you . . . found out anything?"

"Well, one lead so far," Peterson said, his blue eyes pinning her. "According to her parents, Ms. Byrne was last seen at your house."

6

Kirsten sank into a red leather armchair that let out a slow, faintly fartlike hiss. Being in the headmaster's office without Mr. Cowperthwaite was bizarre, to say the least. When Kirsten was little, she thought he lived there. She still suspected it.

But now it was just she and the cops. Detective Peterson sat behind the tall oak desk, putting his worn-out brown Florsheims up on the ink blotter. He grinned, breathing in the scent of leather, wood-polish, and ancient pipe-tobacco. "Nice school. Hard to believe it's the Bronx."

Behind him two of the cops sat on the padded seat in the window alcove, overlooking the willow-draped slope of Woodley Hill. "*Da* Bronx," one of them corrected Peterson.

Cop humor, Kirsten figured. The guy was trying to lighten the mood, which she appreciated, sort of.

"It's actually Riverdale," Kirsten said. She hated this room. Just stepping in here made her feel as if she was in trouble. Of course, the fact that she was being investigated by the police didn't help.

"Let's cut to the chase, Kirsten," Peterson said, leaning forward. "I know you're nervous, so I'll make this short. Where exactly did Sam go after she left your house Saturday morning?"

Shit.

Shit, shit, shit.

All of Kirsten's lies were coming back to haunt her. Everything she'd told Bobbi.

Peterson was looking at her steadily. Professionally. Like he did this all the time and expected results. *If anyone can find Sam, I'm the man,* his gaze seemed to say. That part was a relief. A big relief. Even if Leslie was right, even if it was a prank, Kirsten's gut was telling her something *was* wrong.

The problem was Saturday morning.

What was she supposed to do—lie, and say that Sam had stayed at her house? Tell the truth, that she'd gotten stoned and drunk *(Yes, Officer, I am underage)* and then let her best friend walk into the night with a stranger? Either way, she was toast.

Okay, Kirsten, this guy is gathering information, she reminded herself. *The point isn't me. The point is Sam.*

She could fudge the rest.

"I—I personally don't know where she went Saturday," Kirsten said, "but I called some other Woodley kids, who said they saw her. . . ."

As Kirsten detailed each of the sightings, Peterson wrote them down on a legal pad. "And you began to suspect something was wrong when . . . ?"

"I heard this scream on my answering machine. It sounded like Sam, but I erased it by mistake—"

"Which was when . . . ?"

"Saturday morning."

Peterson leaned back, tapping his pencil on his chin. "So let me piece together the time line. Sam leaves your house Saturday morning after sleeping over. It must be fairly early, because that same morning, presumably after she's been out and about for a while, she calls and leaves a scream of terror—and even though you're home, the call goes to the answering machine. At some point you go to the machine, hear the message, and erase it—and you call other kids, who tell you they've sighted her at clubs. And these sightings all happen on Saturday morning, too, because after all, she's been at your house until then. Now, I'm kind of an old guy, so I don't know—are the clubs really open that early? Or, shall I say, that late?"

Kirsten gulped. She could see it now. Leg irons and stripes. Tearful visits with Mom across a Plexiglas barrier. That's where she was headed.

She swallowed again. This was insane. This was all her fault. If she *hadn't* covered for Sam, if she hadn't stalled for the *whole weekend*, Bobbi and Rolf would have called the police earlier and maybe Sam would be in school right now, in bio lab with Kirsten, all their friends, and the fetal pig.

Slowly, her head sank, her hair covering her face. "Okay, about Friday? Sam wasn't exactly at my house. She . . . didn't wake up there Saturday morning. . . ."

"I see. So . . . you were trying to keep her parents from freaking out? And that's why you lied?"

She peered up. Peterson's head was framed from behind by the huge Woodley grandfather clock, which now struck eleven, momentarily startling her but not affecting him one bit.

"Yes," she said, taking a deep breath. "Sam didn't come home with me . . . she wasn't at my house at all. I just . . . I assumed she was asleep at some friend's house . . . and all I had to do was make a few calls to find her. I didn't want to tell Bobbi the truth. I thought she'd get all upset and . . ." Kirsten's voice trailed off.

"And what?" Peterson said. "Call the police?"

All Kirsten wanted to do was cry. Like a fourth grader. "Yeah."

Peterson stood up. The other officers shifted to look at him as he came around the desk and knelt by Kirsten's chair. "Hey, you're not under arrest, Kirsten. I'm not interested in what you did at what party and at what time. And I don't care about the lies—covering to your friend's mom is not a crime. But it's not a good idea for your friend's sake, either. Trust me. You think you're doing her a favor, but you're not. You just get wrapped up in bigger and bigger lies. And before you know it, you're involved."

Kirsten was beginning to feel cold—cold and very alone. "*Involved?* In what?"

"Bad choice of words. Nothing yet," Peterson said. "Look, I'm just gathering information. My job is to get your friend back, that's all—so *we're on the same side*, okay?"

Kirsten nodded. *Involved*. The word was so ugly. "Okay . . . there was this guy at a bar, red hair, kind of cute, sort of rugged, wearing a Phish T-shirt, which seemed kind of strange because he wasn't the type. None of us had ever seen him before. He looked older, like college-age. Anyway, Sam was dancing with him, and then they left together—"

"She left the place, just like that, with someone she'd never met before?" Peterson asked.

Kirsten didn't like the implication. Sam loved to have fun, but she was *not* stupid, and despite what Leslie said, most definitely *not* a whore. "Sam and her boyfriend had just broken up, and she'd been upset, so maybe she wasn't totally her normal self. I think she was kind of glad to have someone new. And all they did was go outside. . . ."

Peterson scribbled something down. "Was he there—this boyfriend?" he asked, not looking up from his pad.

"Brandon? Yeah. Earlier. But he was gone by then. He was kind of loaded."

The detective looked up. "How did their relationship end? Was it mutual?"

Kirsten thought back to that night. "Not exactly," she said. "In fact, they had a huge fight on Friday. Brandon got a little carried away and freaked out on Sam."

Peterson was writing steadily. "So . . . have you ever talked to Brandon about this? Has he told you about his feelings? Would you say he has a grudge against her?"

"Sure. I mean, *she* was the one who broke up with him. He followed me home that night. Scared me half to death. He was mad crazy upset about the breakup—and about that guy she left with."

Peterson wrote some more, and then began pacing. He gazed out the window a moment, watching a couple—Winnie Forbes and Trey Gladstone, it looked like—walking slowly, lip-locked, across the field. "Tell me, Kirsten," he finally said, "was Sam unhappy at home?"

"Well, her dad left her mom for a Buddhist quilt-maker. They live in Vermont. Wouldn't that make you unhappy?" Kirsten shifted in her seat. Was he implying that Sam's home life would push her into self-destruction? That was absurd. "I mean, a lot of kids come from divorce, and they don't all disappear. What does her unhappiness have to do with it?"

"Just gathering background," Peterson said, scribbling a little more. "Is there anything else you want to tell me?"

Kirsten thought a moment, then shook her head. "Just

one question, I guess. Do you get a lot of cases like this? And do you usually, like, *solve* them?"

Peterson stood, putting his notepad in a briefcase and signaling to the cops, who began heading for the door. "I'll be honest with you. Most missing-person cases tend to be runaways. They leave home, upset about something, camp out with a friend, sleep in a park, whatever. Then, when they're tired of the rough life, it's back home to Mom and Dad. Especially in cases like this, where there's just some minor family dysfunction. It's a classic scenario."

"Well, thanks, I guess," Kirsten said.

"Thank *you*, Kirsten, you've been a great help." At Peterson's signal, the uniformed officers went for the door. As they left, Peterson extended his hand to Kirsten. "Between you and me, I think your friend will show up in a couple of days."

Kirsten tried to smile. He seemed convinced. She wished she were too.

But the sound of the answering machine message kept replaying over and over in her head . . . the sound of that scream. . . . Why didn't the police think it was important enough to consider?

Peterson followed the other cops out. Kirsten heard them talking in muffled voices to Mr. Cowperthwaite in the hall. She waited. The last thing she wanted to do was see them again. The second to last thing was go back to the fetal-pig dissection.

She hung her legs over an arm of the chair and glanced

out the window. It was a clear day, the pond rippling, the grass swaying gently. A flock of geese soared overhead, steadily south.

She caught sight of someone coming over the horizon—staying more or less hidden by the crest of the hill, probably cutting class. Kirsten liked to do that herself sometimes, just walk and walk in the fields without a care.

It was a girl, she could tell that, although she didn't know who. Silhouetted in the sun, the girl stopped and looked up, the morning light bouncing off her long platinum-blond hair.

She recognized the cut, just below the shoulders, and the confident flip of the head as the girl turned away and continued walking, downhill now, with a familiar stride, ever so slightly swaying at the hips.

Kirsten came slowly out of her chair and walked to the window for a better view. "Oh my God," she whispered when she realized who the girl was.

Suddenly a smile burst onto Kirsten's face.

There was no mistaking any of it. This whole conversation with Peterson, the entire sleepless weekend, had been totally unnecessary.

Because her best friend was back!

Sam Byrne was back!

7

"Sam? SPAMMIE!" Kirsten cried.

The window was heavy. Like lifting her Gucci overnight bag on the way to a weekend in the Hamptons. Yes, Kirsten laughed at her own stupid thought. Stupid thoughts were great. Sam was back, making the world safe for stupid thoughts.

She squeezed under the sash, fell onto the grass below, and began running.

There she was. Wandering across the crest of the hill. iPod in her pocket, headphones on, swaying to the music. Picking dandelions and blowing on them.

So *Sam.*

So incredibly, wonderfully *Sam.*

Here at Woodley.

Where had she been? Why the hell hadn't she called? Was this her idea of a joke—making everyone crazy and then showing up one afternoon like Julie Andrews running across the Alps?

Kirsten ran up, stumbling over her own feet, not knowing whether to laugh, scream, or cry. She wanted to throw her arms around Sam, lift her in the air, and squeeze her to make sure she was real.

And *then* kill her.

Sam was looking in the other direction, lost in her music. Her outfit rippled in the wind, the dress they had picked out together at the Marc Jacobs show during Fashion Week.

Kirsten paused, catching her breath. Then, gently, she tapped her best friend on the shoulder. "Spammie, where the hell have you been?"

"Huh?" Sam turned around slowly, as if she'd expected Kirsten all along.

And Kirsten's smile fell. For a moment she couldn't say a word. It was as if someone had played a cruel joke with Sam's face, distorting it somehow. Her eyes were wrong, her mouth a little too big, the grin some kind of mockery.

"That is so funny you said that," the girl said.

Finally the voice connected with the facial features, knocking Kirsten into reality, making her realize that it wasn't Sam at all.

Not by a long shot.

"Emma?" Kirsten said, not wanting to believe it.

"Did you really, like, mistake me for Sam?" Emma giggled. "That is so weird. I guess it's the look, huh? Robert Swensen Salon. You *have* to go to him, Kirsten. He's expensive, but he's worth every penny." She twisted her newly dyed platinum hair around her fingers—the same way Sam always did.

Kirsten didn't know what to say. Emma's makeup was exactly the way Sam did hers: just a touch of pale pink lip gloss for daywear, her eyebrows plucked just so—enough to give them arc, but way short of the Martian look favored by the Long Island South Shore crowd. Again, Sam's exact technique. But the worst part was that Emma had gotten the *hair* right—the same blond shade, cut exactly to Sam's just-over-the-shoulder length.

And the sight of it made Kirsten short of breath, torn between the urges to cry, scream at Emma, or slap her.

But she did none of the above. She felt numb. This was just too weird.

"Emma, I'm sorry, but it's like you *copied* her," Kirsten said.

Emma shrugged. "It's just a look."

Okay, the girl had always been a little obsessed with Sam, but this was way over the top. "I think it's a little more than that," Kirsten told her. "How can I say this . . . do you really think that by doing this you'll magically be just like Sam? Because that's what it looks like. I mean, come on—you're *Emma Lewis*, okay? What's wrong with Emma Lewis?"

Emma turned in a huff, walking down the hill. "God, what grouch pill did *you* take this morning? I thought you, of all people, would *like* this look. Maybe you're just jealous. I'm sure Spammie won't mind when she sees me. She'll probably think it's cool."

"*You* don't call her Spammie," Kirsten snapped. Emma was totally over the line, and being polite was out the window. "Only her best friends do, and that will never in a million years be *you*. The least you can do is respect the fact that she's missing and not look as if you're trying to take her place!"

Emma stopped. She faced Kirsten with a blank, befuddled, very *Emma* look. "Sam is missing?"

"Open your eyes, Emma. Sam isn't in school today. She hasn't been seen since Friday night, when she left the Party Room. The police are here asking questions. Bobbi Byrne has filed a report. *I haven't slept in two days!*"

"Oh no! Oh my God." Emma dropped slowly to the grass as if her knees had given way. She started to cry. "No! Not Sam! No, please! Anybody but *her*!"

To say the least, it was not Oscar night.

Kirsten looked at her watch. She was not about to comfort Emma. She was going to go back to class, trust that Peterson was on the case and that Sam would be back soon.

"We're all broken up, okay, *really* broken up—all of us who *care* about Sam," Kirsten said, starting back to class. "So if you know of anything, call the police precinct and ask for Detective Peterson."

"I . . . I do," Emma said, her voice tear-choked and small. "I *saw* her, Kirsten."

Kirsten stopped in her tracks. She looked warily into Emma's eyes. Her patience for attention-grabbing was less than zilch. "You saw her? You saw her *where*, Emma? Did you see her after she left the Party Room?"

Emma smiled—an odd, far-off, private kind of smile. "I saw her in a dream. Saturday night. She had met some people. I couldn't tell who they were—nice people, traveling across the country, having adventures wherever they went. I don't know how they made a living or anything. Maybe they didn't have to. But Spammie was with them and having the greatest time. And just when I woke up, she turned to me and said, 'Tell them not to worry. Tell them I'm fine. I'll always be fine, and I'll always be thinking of them. . . .'" Emma raised her sleeve to her forehead dramatically, like something out of an old black-and-white movie. "And then it was over," she said with a sigh. "What do you think it all means, Kirsten?"

Kirsten was at a loss for words. She didn't believe in dreams coming true, especially Emma's insane dreams.

And at the moment, her eyes were on the shiny silver bracelet Emma was wearing on her wrist, which looked very familiar. In fact, it looked exactly like the antique bracelet Sam always wore—the one she'd inherited from her grandmother.

"Can I see that bracelet?" Kirsten asked.

Emma retracted her hand, hiding the jewelry. "Um, why? Why do you want to see it?"

"It's so beautiful," Kirsten said. "It also looks familiar."

"It's mine," Emma shot back. "It's *my* bracelet, and you can't have it."

Kirsten took a deep breath. "You stole it, didn't you?"

Emma's face reddened. And then she began to run.

Kirsten caught up with her halfway down the hill and spun her around. "How could you do that?"

"It's *my* bracelet, Kirsten," Emma insisted. "You want to take it, don't you? Well, I won't be talked out of it, and I won't sell it! You know how hard it was to find this?"

"It must have been really hard," Kirsten said. "What did you do, sneak into Sam's house at night? It's one of a kind, Emma. She told me that a million times. And she would *never* have given it to you."

Emma pulled back, looking at Kirsten as if she were crazy. "I bought it at East Side Jewelers. I can shop for jewelry too. I was looking for one exactly like Sam's. Is there anything wrong with that? Um, Kirsten? Are you, like, losing it?"

"You're dressed up as Sam, wearing Sam's jewelry, talking about your dreams of Sam—and accusing *me* of losing it?"

"The news about Sam is *very* stressful," Emma said. "You could see my dad, you know. He's a traumatic-loss specialist. When his patients get like this, he says—"

Kirsten didn't wait to hear the end of the sentence. As far as she was concerned, she'd be happy never to see

Emma's face again. And if her dad was a famous shrink, it was no wonder the Upper East Side was so screwed up.

She ran down Woodley Hill and circled around the building to the main entrance. First period was just letting out. As she rounded the hallway to the science wing, Carla, Sarah, and Julie were rushing down the hall.

"Are you okay?" Julie asked.

"Fine, for someone who's just spent the last half hour with a psychopath and a police detective."

"Did they find Sam?" Sarah added.

Kirsten shook her head. "He just asked some questions. Bobbi filed a report. Detective Peterson is on the case, but no, they haven't found her."

"They will," Carla said. "Or Sam will just show up on her own."

"Who's the psychopath?" Carla asked.

"Emma. I think she stole Sam's bracelet." Kirsten sniffed the air. Something smelled funky. "What's that stink?"

"Eau de Raw Pork," Sarah said with a look of disgust. "It's all over us."

Julie made a face. "And formaldehyde."

"Come with us," Carla said. "We'll have a ritual wash and some smokes to get rid of the stench."

Kirsten followed them into the girls' room, her brain straining with worry over Sam, anger with Emma, and a mixture of dread and hope over what Peterson would find.

She didn't smoke cigarettes. This morning, however, she would make an exception.

After school, Kirsten met Julie outside the old building in the Woodley courtyard. Cell phones weren't allowed in school, so no one had called Sam's house since lunch. Once you were outside, though, it was wireless heaven.

"Everyone's talking about Peterson," Julie said, moving away from the noise of the hundred or so conversations. "He kind of sucked the air out of the school. There are all these rumors about Sam."

Kirsten nodded. She'd heard them too. Sam was involved in a religious cult. She'd run away with a Norwegian prince. She'd wandered into Penn Station and fallen asleep on the Amtrak express to the West Coast. "Mr. Cowperthwaite looks like he's aged ten years," Julie said. "He told me Peterson had called in some other kids to the office, but he wouldn't say who."

"Yeah, well, Leslie wasn't one of them. She wishes she were, though. She wants to marry Peterson and have tough little boys who will be movie stars and cast her as the sexy mom."

"Leslie is pissing me off almost as much as Emma." Kirsten took out her cell phone and began to tap out Sam's number. "Let me try her one more time," she said, even though deep down she knew that she wouldn't get an answer.

She'd just finished when Brandon rammed into her from behind.

"Ow. That *hurt*, you asshole!" Kirsten said.

"Nice vocabulary," Brandon muttered, looming over her like a sweaty bear. "I like a girl who talks dirty. Did you talk to Peterson that way?"

Kirsten gave Julie a look. Brandon's eyes were bloodshot, as usual, but he was also pale, and his navy blue Woodley uniform was wrinkled and kind of dirty—as if he'd been sitting in the fields smoking weed all day instead of being in class.

"Peterson called you in too?" Kirsten asked, backing away from him. She didn't like the way he was staring at her.

"Ohhhh, you're so surprised, aren't you?" Brandon said mockingly. "Think back. Remember what you told him about me. That I abused and threatened Sam. *Of course he called me in*. You made me sound like a freaky pervert!"

"I would never do that. It would give perverts a bad name." Kirsten put the phone to her ear, wanting him to just go away.

"I'm talking to you!" Brandon yelled, knocking the phone out of her hand.

Kirsten jumped away from him.

"Stop it!" Julie cried. "Brandon, you're wasted."

"So what?" Brandon said with a guttural laugh. "I was wasted on Friday, too. But that doesn't make me a murderer. Does it, Kirsten?"

"Who said anything about—" She stopped.

Brandon lurched forward, backing Kirsten against a wall. Julie tried to push him away, but he was too strong. "You know what I think?" he said. "I think you two did it. You're her best friends. You let her leave there with that guy. You killed her."

"Sam is *not* dead!" Kirsten cried. "Don't even joke about that!" He was crazy. Kirsten looked around for help, but the phone callers were gabbing away on the other side of the building, and there were no faculty members in sight.

And now Brandon was pushing her—pushing her around toward the side of the building, behind the old hedges that badly needed trimming.

"Brandon, knock it off," Julie said, "or I'm going to get a teacher."

But Brandon's eyes were on Kirsten. "Yeah, good. Go ahead, Julie. You do that and leave us alone."

"Julie, don't!" Kirsten cried. She was shaking inside, but she tried to seem tough. She fixed her gaze on Brandon. "You lay a hand on me and you're dead."

"You don't scare me," Brandon said, his voice lowering to a whispery rasp. With every word, Kirsten could feel the puff of his hot breath on her cheek.

She tried to back away some more, but her heel caught on a crack in the pavement. She fell back, gasping, onto the asphalt of the faculty parking lot.

Brandon stood over her, his face a black shadow in the setting sun. "You'd better watch your back, Kirsten, because I'm going to do what you did to me. I'm going to trash your life. And when you least expect it, when everything seems to be going your way, you're going to pay. . . ."

8

There was something slow and sleepy about the Party Room on a Monday night. It was a nice feeling, usually. But tonight, Kirsten thought, it felt sad and weird and empty, even with all her friends there.

Without Sam, the Party Room could never feel right.

Kirsten was still shaking from the afternoon. Brandon's threats echoed in her brain, scaring her, making her think about Friday night, about what he might or might not have been capable of doing. And then there was Emma, who was also a freak in her own right.

"Here, this will make you feel better," Julie said, bringing a small cork-lined tray full of drinks to Kirsten, Sarah, and Carla at their table.

Julie had been the one to suggest coming here tonight. At first Kirsten had said no, but the alternative was moping around the house in a state of panic. Mom and Dad were walking around like zombies, talking about Sam in hushed tones as if they really believed that Kirsten wouldn't be able to hear them. But she could, and she didn't want to. Anything was better than that.

"I can't believe you didn't nail Brandon," Carla said. "You should have kicked him where he lives."

Kirsten sipped her drink. It felt warm and soothing going down. "*You* try thinking of that when he's hovering over you."

"I never saw him like that before." Julie shook her head. "It was as if something inside him just . . . snapped."

"Really?" Sarah said.

"Don't cross him . . . ," Kirsten said almost to herself. "I mean, he wigged out just because I mentioned him to Peterson. Imagine how angry he must have been at Sam when she broke up with him."

"Do you think he could have . . . ," Sarah said, her voice trailing off.

"Brandon?" Carla swallowed a sip of her drink. "But I thought he loved her. That's why he was so upset when they broke up, right?"

Kirsten flinched, remembering Friday night all over again. Why hadn't she told Sam's parents the truth? Why hadn't she called the cops herself after Brandon had acted like such a basket case?

Because she was covering for her best friend, that's why. Sam would have done exactly the same thing for Kirsten.

"I don't want to think about it anymore," she said, and downed the rest of her drink.

"Yeah, hey, let's not get morbid about this," Julie said. "Detective Peterson told Kirsten that Sam probably just ran away. He's a pro. He knows. He has experience. And face it: Sam *is* unpredictable. So let's give him a chance. He's only been on it a few hours."

Carla finished her drink too. "You know, I'm thinking about Sam right now—about what she'd say if she saw us here like this. She'd laugh in our faces and tell us to get up and shake it!"

She got up from the table and began to groove, right there, all by herself, to the hip-hop song booming over the sound system.

Kirsten stood up too, eyeing the door. Someone walked in, a guy she'd never seen before. "What if he shows up tonight?" she murmured.

"Brandon?" Sarah said. "If he does, we do to him what we did to Arnold."

"The fetal pig," Carla explained, slashing with her hand, *Psycho* style. "Eee, eee, eee, eee!" she screeched.

Sarah and Carla were not exactly the Sopranos, but it was nice to have someone covering your butt.

They all headed to the dance floor, but Kirsten's heart wasn't in it, and after a few minutes she left her friends and went to the bar. Hot Scott was there as always, polishing the already shiny wood. "Don't worry," he told her. "I'm sure they'll find her."

"Thanks." Kirsten nodded. "Hey, it's Monday after the weekend. Don't you ever get a day off?"

Scott smiled. "I need the cash. But I think I'll knock off Wednesday. Hump Day."

If Sam were here, she'd have something really smart to say about that, maybe involving the word *priapic.* "How about a pomegranate martini?"

"ID?" Scott asked with his trademark half-smile, and Kirsten flashed the lame card she'd bought as a joke in Times Square with Sam and Julie last July. Scott didn't even bother to look.

Yes, we love Scott, Kirsten thought as she watched him shake a mixture and pour it into a pretty glass. But no matter how much she tried, she couldn't get Sam and Brandon and all of it out of her mind—not even for a minute.

"Hey Kirsten, so who was the guy dancing with Sam that night?" Scott asked, writing out a tab. "The tall one with the red hair."

Kirsten shook her head. "Don't know much about him. Just that he left with Sam, and the police don't seem to think he had anything to do with her disappearance."

"I don't know, there was something about the guy that I didn't like," Scott said as he cleaned a few glasses. He paused. "Probably the Phish shirt."

Kirsten smiled. Leave it to Scott to lighten the mood a little. "Maybe you're right," she said. "Who likes that band, anyway? Granola heads."

"Well, I'll keep an eye out for him—and nail him if he comes in here again." Scott gave her a long look, then quietly picked up the tab he had just written and ripped it in half. "This'll be on me, Kirsten. For all of you. On the house."

Kirsten's cheeks suddenly felt hot. "Thanks."

"Hey, I know how you feel. I had a friend like that once—would disappear, sometimes for weeks. High school guy. Always came back, with a cowboy hat from Wyoming or a pound of weed from Mexico—never knew how he got to those places without a driver's license, but hey, he had a good time. We figured he wouldn't last through age twenty-five." Scott laughed, a sexy deep-chested guffaw. "Now he's the president and CEO of a Silicon Valley tech company."

"That makes me feel better. Maybe Sam will give me a job after college." Kirsten took a sip of her drink. It went down smooth. "Okay, I'm alive again."

Next to her, a soft male voice said, "I want what she's having."

Kirsten glanced to her left. A couple of barstools away, a guy sat down, all dressed in black. Silk shirt, cotton pants. He had dark brown hair, beautiful upward-arching eyebrows, and a nose that was so perfect, it had to have been sculpted.

"And one more for her," he added, smiling at Kirsten.

"You could be arrested for that," Kirsten said.

The guy smiled again. "Corrupting a minor? Well, I guess I'll just have to hold you here until the effects wear off. I'm Kyle."

"As in MacLachlan?" Kirsten cringed as the actor's name came out of her mouth, because first of all he was old and gray and not that good looking, in her opinion, and second of all the only reason she knew him was because she'd been forced to watch *Blue Velvet* by her film-freak ex-boyfriend, Max Danson. Fortunately, Max had graduated, but unfortunately, he was last seen trying to get college girls to appear nude in a so-called student film. And third of all, *Blue Velvet* sucked, and this Kyle was much, much, *much* cuter.

"He's made some really good films. Didn't love *Blue Velvet,* though," Kyle said. "And you are . . . ?"

"Kirsten."

"As in Dunst?" he asked.

Kirsten could live with that. "I guess so."

"She wishes she looked like you," he said, his smile spreading impossibly wide across his face, giving it a sort of sweet and tender openness.

"So does the other Kyle," Kirsten said.

"Wishes he looked like *you*?"

Kirsten blushed. "No—!"

"I didn't know this about him," Kyle went on, teasing her. "What magazines do *you* read?"

Kirsten laughed. *Laughed!*

Scott's back was to the CD jukebox, and in a moment a very slow romantic ballad was playing. Whistling softly, Scott began wiping the bar. He looked up at Kirsten and winked. "Great dance tune."

Kyle was already getting up from his stool. He reached out to her with just the right amount of confidence. He held her gently, body-to-body, as they danced across the floor.

Out of the corner of her eye, Kirsten could see Carla, Julie, and Sarah huddled together and smiling at her. She closed her eyes and let thoughts of Sam and Brandon and Emma recede just for a moment. She hadn't felt this good in such a long time.

"Do you live around here?" Kyle said in a voice soft and clear and delicious on the ear.

"Of course," she said. "I go to the Woodley School—well, maybe that doesn't mean anything to you. You're not from around here, are you?"

"What makes you say that?" Kyle asked.

"You're a guy, you're smart, and you're nice. They don't make them with that combination around here. I hear there are a few in, like, Wisconsin or something."

Kyle laughed. "Actually, I was born and raised here. Upper West Side. Sorry—I know to you Woodley girls that knocks me down a peg."

"So do you go to college or something?" Kirsten asked. This guy was way too cool and mature to be in high school.

"Uh, Bowdoin College," he said. "You know . . . in Maine?"

"My mom thinks I should go to a college down south, so she can be warm when she visits," Kirsten admitted. "What's it like at Bowdoin?"

"Well, at this time of the year, when the sun is still high in the sky, you can walk through Brunswick in your shorts and T-shirt, the heat on your face and the snow crunching under your feet—and it makes you feel so alive."

God, he was a poet, too. "You must be an English major."

"Political science," Kyle replied. "Actually I'm doing research on a seminar project. It's called 'A Marxist Analysis of Manhattan Elitist Society,' and I'm going to examine all the cultural tropes that signify class distinction and serve to stifle social mobility. Basically it's *Lifestyles of the Rich and Famous* for credit."

Smart. That was good. Kirsten liked smart.

As the song ended, Julie danced up close. "Hi, I'm Julie. Uh, Kirsten, I have to leave at ten? I think Carla and Sarah are going too. You can stay if you want. Are you okay?"

Kirsten nodded. "I'm fine." She could see Carla and Sarah standing near the door, looking on approvingly. Carla gave a subtle thumbs-up.

"She's cool," Kyle said, watching Julie walk away. "Is she your best friend?"

"Well, one of them . . . ," Kirsten said. Her friends were

walking out now, and Kirsten imagined Sam with them. Sam would adore Kyle. If she were here, she would have made sure that Kirsten got every bit of contact information by now. If you didn't have at least one guy's contact info by ten, it promised to be a loser of a night, in the World According to Sam.

In two hours it will be midnight. Almost Tuesday. Soon Sam will have been gone for three days, she thought.

"Kirsten . . . ?" Kyle said, touching her shoulder with concern.

"I'm . . . sorry," Kirsten said, looking up at Kyle, at his big, soft, basset-hound eyes, but all of a sudden she couldn't focus as tears spilled from her own.

"Are you okay?" Kyle asked. "Kirsten?"

She couldn't bring herself to put together the coherent explanation, because nothing made sense, the world had been turned upside down. So she followed her instinct and did the only thing that would make her feel better, which was to wrap her arms around his broad shoulders and kiss him, long and deep, so that someday, when everything was all right again and Sam had been found, she'd still have a good memory of this night.

"It's not you, Kyle," she said when they parted. "I just need to get out of here . . . alone."

Kyle reached into his back pocket, pulled out a pad of paper, tore off a page, and scribbled something on it. "Here's my cell. Call me, okay?"

Kirsten took the paper and put it in her pocket. Kyle was so wonderful and sweet and sexy, but she wasn't sure if she would ever call him. She was just too messed up right now. Too confused. She needed Sam back safe and sound, and she couldn't think about anything else until that happened.

And then she was running across the floor, flinging her weight against the metal door latch, rushing out into the cool night to the sound of a deep snap that may have been the door opening or, just possibly, her soul breaking.

9

"I don't know his last name," Kirsten said into the cell phone. As soon as she'd entered her building that night, she'd immediately called Julie, who was now pumping her with millions of questions as she rode up her elevator. "Just Kyle from Maine."

"Sounds like a toothpaste," Julie's voice replied. "I can't believe he's from so far away. He looks familiar."

"Actually, he's originally from New York City," Kirsten said.

"See? I never forget a face. I just don't know from what."

"Well, if he *has* been around New York, I don't know how I ever missed him." With a barely audible *ding*, the "PH" indicator lit up at the top of the polished-oak elevator panel. "More tomorrow," Kirsten whispered. "I'm home."

"Sweet dreams. *Really* sweet, if possible. But don't do anything that requires the changing of sheets. Your cleaning lady already came."

"Shut up," Kirsten said. "Good night."

"Hey, Kirsten? Are you okay? Really? Because if you get lonely or sad, my mom's happy for you to sleep over—even in the middle of the night."

"Thanks, Julie."

She loved Jules.

Kirsten hung up just as the elevator door slid open. Mom had left a light on and a note:

DETECTIVE PETERSON CALLED TO LEAVE HIS DIRECT NUMBER. TURN THE LIGHTS OFF, PLEASE! ☺

The depressing mention of Peterson was almost made up for by the amusing idea that in a home that could fetch $9 million on the open market, Mom was worried about an extra three cents on the Con Ed bill.

Kirsten took the note, checked the answering machine—zilch—and sneaked through the house. Her room had been freshly made up by Marilena, the housekeeper, with new Ralph Lauren sheets turned back just so. A slight hum confirmed that Kirsten's iMac was still happily running on her antique desk.

Kirsten quickly undressed and, needing sleepwear appropriate to her desired mood, took out her slinky LaPerla negligee.

No, that wouldn't do.

Back in the drawer it went, and out came her soft flannel L.L. Bean jammies, the ones Marilena had bought her for Christmas last year. With a yawn, she checked her phone, which now had a cascade of texts, mostly people asking about Sam. She was in no mood to talk now, so she ignored them.

Now she only had to deal with her e-mail messages. She hadn't checked them in a few days, so there were one hundred and fifty-seven messages, mostly the usual stuff, cheap Vlagr@, penl$ enlargement, breast enhancement, triple XXX chat rooms . . . *delete delete delete delete delete delete delete delete delete delete delete delete delete delete delete* . . .

Message one fifty-six had a familiar "From" address—one that gave her a pang in the chest: bYrNiNgBuSh@gmail.com.

It was Sam's address. Probably one of the fifteen or so lists of jokes and weird Web site links Sam had sent last week.

Kirsten squinted at the date on the message, her finger poised to delete again, but she froze.

It was today's date. The message had been sent early this morning.

"That's impossible," Kirsten murmured. "Sam's been gone since Friday. . . ." Then she gasped. "Unless Sam is really okay!"

Her hand shook as she brought the cursor to the message and wondered *why*? Why the hell hadn't she called? *Why e-mail?*

It didn't matter. She clicked on Sam's address. Instantly the message blinked onto the screen.

```
From: spammie byrne (bYrNiNgBuSh@gmail.com)
To: kirsten sawyer
(lesbiches326@gmail.com)
Subject: hey there babes!
hey kissyface, wazzup!!!! evrything fine wid
me so dont worry . . . like that guy
singz . . . dont worry b happy . . . u no the
one with the dreds whashisname i foget?? ;O
whatever! lol not home now, will be
sooooon . . . dont tell Bobbi yet ok.
cu & ttfn!!!!
xxxxxxxxxoooo spam
```

"I don't BELIEVE it!" Kirsten shouted.

She leaned down and kissed the phone screen.

Sam was okay!

She had to talk to her right now. She tapped Sam's number.

"Kirstie?" Mrs. Sawyer called. "Is that you?"

"Yeah, I'm home!" Kirsten called out.

"Are we forgetting, tomorrow is a school day!"

No kidding, Kirsten did not say. "Okay . . . sorreeeee. G'night."

Two. Three. Four. Mom was asleep.

Sam's line was ringing now.

"Hello, um, yeah. Sam here. Go ahead and talk—"

Voice mail. Damn.

Kirsten waited and said, "I got your e-mail. We need to talk—mucho madness. Call me!"

Just to be sure, she answered the e-mail:

```
From: kirsten sawyer
To: spammie byrne
Subject: Re: hey there babes!
WHERE R U??????????????? :(
```

As the message went off into cyberspace, Kirsten waited and watched.

For the first time ever, she wished she were a geek. Carla would have been able to look at the headers, or whatever they were, and find out exactly where this message came from, what time Sam wrote it, and what she was eating.

Kirsten scanned Sam's message again. Having her words, right in front of her, was so comforting.

Her words . . .

Something about them was funny. Kirsten read through the message again, and her excitement began to lose its edge. It was the right address, so it *had* to be from Sam—but something was off. Something in Sam's words.

The third time through, Kirsten's heart began to sink. She had exchanged a million messages with Sam, give or take a few. And she knew all Sam's tricks. All the ways she expressed her Sam-ness online. Yes, this message was from Sam's e-mail address, all right.

But . . . it wasn't from Sam.

10

"Settle down, kids," Mr. Costas said at the beginning of the next day's bio lab. "Get into your lab groups and be serious. No *hamming* it up!"

Kirsten was in no mood for bad jokes about fetal pigs. She dragged herself to the lab table, where the shriveled little specimen awaited them. Sarah, Carla, Leslie, and Julie gathered around her.

She was feeling raw. She'd hardly slept again, getting up several times in the night to reread the message, hoping she'd change her mind, hoping to find a sure sign that Sam *had* written the note. But she just became more and more convinced that it was a forgery.

Why? The question haunted her. What kind of person would forge an e-mail message from Sam?

Julie spread out the experiment's instruction sheet on the table. "Keep telling us about the e-mail, Kirsten," she said, eyeing Mr. Costas as he walked away. "I can listen and do this stuff for the report. . . . 'Examine aqueous contents of eye.' This ought to be fun."

Kirsten lowered her voice to a whisper, continuing a conversation they'd begun before class in the hall. "Well, I realized the message *couldn't* have been from Sam, and I forwarded it to Detective Peterson. He called me right back on the cell. I couldn't believe he was awake. He asked me all kinds of questions that I didn't know the answers to, technical stuff. He said he wants to see the headers or something, so I told him I'd ask Carla."

"Just a minute." Taking a scalpel, Julie carefully lanced the pig's eye.

"Ohhh . . . ," Sarah groaned, holding her stomach. "Someone call PETA."

"How can you do that?" Leslie asked, turning green.

Kirsten looked away. "What confuses me is that it comes from Sam's e-mail address—but Peterson says it's possible to steal an e-mail address. Is that right, Carla?"

Carla nodded. "Just a matter of setting up an account with your own POP and SMTP protocols but spoofing the reply-to. Anyone can do it."

"In my sleep," Sarah muttered.

"But . . . 'kissyface'?" Julie said. "No one but Sam calls you that."

"True, but people have ears—someone else could *know* about it," Kirsten replied. "It was the other stuff, in the subject line and at the end of the note. Sam *never* calls me Babes. And all the emoticons—she wouldn't be caught dead using those."

Sarah frowned. "Wait. Why?"

Mr. Costas sidled by, looking over Carla's shoulder. "Very good. And remember, the sagittal section of the fetal pig is *not* the Central Pork. . . ."

Carla rolled her eyes.

Mr. Costas smiled proudly, and Julie read the next part of the instructions. "'Open thoracic cavity and remove organs for examination, as per instructions . . .'"

As Julie went to work, Kirsten looked away. "I dreamed about Sam all night," she said. "I just couldn't figure out *who* would do something like steal Sam's e-mail address—and *why?* It's perverse. And so I'm thinking about this over breakfast and reading the Metro section of the *Times,* page three, and I see this article—something like 'Upper East Side socialite daughter reported missing after late-night carousing at notorious teen gathering place. . . .'"

"That sucks," Sarah said.

"Maybe not," Carla replied. "The more people who know about Sam, the more who know what she looks like, the better chance of finding her."

"Did they really say 'gathering place'?" Leslie asked.

"Peterson says the press coverage can be bad news,"

Kirsten added. "The runaways know they're being chased, so they go further undercover."

"Well, *I* saw it on the local morning news," Sarah said. "They mentioned the mystery man. Gave a description, too. Red hair and all, even the Phish T-shirt."

"Do you think she married him in Vegas, like Britney?" Leslie asked brightly.

"You are sick," Julie told her as she made incisions through the aorta and pulmonary artery, reached in, and carefully lifted out the pig's heart. "Could you hold this for me?" she asked, turning to Leslie.

"Mglfff!" Leslie clapped a hand over her mouth and ran from the room.

Kirsten stared at the little rocklike organ in Julie's gloved hand. It didn't look revolting at all, just small and tough.

"Guess the little piggy doesn't have to worry if its heart will ever be broken," Emma's voice said softly from behind.

Kirsten, Carla, Julie, and Sarah turned. Emma was standing there with a little smile, in all her wannabe-Sam glory.

"You decided not to cut class today?" Kirsten asked.

Emma nodded. "Don't mean to interrupt, guys," she said, drawing her perfect platinum hair behind her ears. "I just wanted to say I'm sorry, to Kirsten. I didn't mean to yell at you."

Kirsten noticed that Emma's wrist was bare. "What? No bracelet today?"

"I didn't want to get into an argument. I've had enough of that. Look, we're all in this together now—you, me, all of you guys. I mean, we were always in different circles, but sometimes you have to look past that. I'm sad too. We've got to be like sisters at a time like this."

Julie set the heart down, and the girls looked at one another uncomfortably. Emma sat on Leslie's vacated stool, but no one had the urge to tell her to go.

"I'm having trouble with the lab," Emma went on. "I don't know, I guess I'm not cut out for dissection."

"That was a bad joke," Carla said dryly. "'Cut out'?"

"Ugh. I didn't mean it like that," Emma said. "It's just gross. And the smell."

Kirsten sighed. "I think it's disgusting too."

"Well, today's your lucky day," Emma said. "I told Mr. Costas that I had a religious objection to the dissection. The teachers are trained to take that kind of thing seriously. Even Mr. Comedy Central. So he said that if anyone wanted, we could get together and do a report with diagrams instead."

"Fine with me," Sarah said.

Emma was smiling, and in the white-green reflection of the overhead fluorescent lights, her makeup was a little too pale, her hair color a little too fake. But Kirsten had gotten used to that by now.

She was kind of weird, yeah, and Sam had always disliked the girl, but frankly, all of their lives Kirsten had felt a little sympathy for Emma. She was clearly messed up, without a sense of self, blah blah blah, but until now totally harmless. So, what if she was telling the truth? What if she had bought a close knockoff of Sam's bracelet? What if this psycho obsession was just a phase, on her way to some other obsession, with Elvis or Taylor Swift or something? And wasn't there an old cliché . . . something about the better the shrink, the weirder the kid? Emma had that on her plate too.

"Thanks," Kirsten said. "That's nice of you, Emma."

"Hey, anytime, sister-girl." Emma put her arm around Kirsten's shoulders.

Sister-girl? Kirsten turned. Another phrase that was signature Sam.

No one made a move to go off and write that separate report. Instead, they all watched as Julie held out the instruction sheet and read aloud the next step in the lab: "'Removal and inspection of joints . . .'"

Emma made a face. "Well, Doctor, I'm out of here. Kirsten, come join me. I'm going to the library to start research."

"I'm with you," Sarah said, looking ambivalent but glad to get away from Arnold.

"You're abandoning me?" Julie asked.

"I'm going to be an English major," Sarah said. "This is irrelevant to my education."

"I'll stick around," Carla said.

Kirsten laughed. "Me too. As long as I can stand it."

"Okay, well, see you later!" Emma said cheerily.

As the two girls left, Kirsten felt uncomfortable. Sam had said something Friday night that had stuck in her head. Something about Emma. *"One day she's going to make all of you into her best friends, then bump me off so she can take over my life."*

It had been a joke. No one had taken it seriously, of course. But as Emma headed for the door, Kirsten noticed something new. A pair of earrings that looked like intricate little antique grapes dangled from Emma's ears.

Kirsten had seen them before too. Sam had a pair. They matched her grandmother's bracelet.

"I just wanted to say I'm sorry," Kirsten said to Kyle from across a table at Jackson Hole on Second Avenue. She nervously unfolded her napkin and placed it on her lap. "For running out on you at the Party Room, I mean."

Julie had finally convinced her to call him after school that day—saying that Kirsten would always be wondering "what if?" if she didn't. Which was true. So she did, and there they were. Kyle had suggested meeting at this place, and now Kirsten was feeling weird and embarrassed for having run out of the Party Room like some crazy and dramatic lunatic.

But he didn't know about Sam, so he couldn't have understood her mood that night. He deserved an explanation. Although the clatter and bustle of a burger joint was not exactly an intimate setting, and the background music was the third inning of a baseball game from the wide-screen TV above the bar, it was okay. Jackson Hole was always full of Woodley kids. And they served cheap pitchers of beer.

Sarah was sitting with Trevor Royce in the back, and a table full of kids from the debate team were noisily discussing foreign policy or something near the door. Jackson Hole was right up there with the Party Room in the home-away-from-home category.

Kyle was wearing a baseball cap and dark glasses. He smiled curiously. "I was alone on an elevator in an office building once. Big, roomy elevator, and I was in the back. The door opens, and there's this woman—like, maybe in her early twenties. She runs in, really quickly, and goes, 'Sorry!' And I'm like, 'That's okay.'"

"And . . . ?" Kirsten said.

"And . . . I'm thinking, what was she sorry about? We were doing exactly the same thing, using the elevator to get down to the street. So . . . I was wondering, do you think that it's a chick thing—you know, to apologize all the time? Like, you've been trained to automatically think of the other person's comfort?"

"A *chick* thing?" Kirsten repeated.

Kyle blushed. "Sorry, I didn't mean to be offensive. My theory is that guys go too much in the other direction—always looking after themselves first. Oh God, I'm alienating you. I get nervous when I'm around beautiful, smart girls and I don't have any idea what to talk about. Okay, what I *meant* to say was, no need to apologize. I wasn't offended. Not even a little."

Kirsten had to laugh. Kyle was cute when he was nervous. She instinctively reached across the table and touched his hand reassuringly. How could he think she minded a guy actually taking the time to think about how a *girl* thought? "Monday night, I was . . . not in the greatest mood," she said. "Some really bad personal things have happened."

Kyle's face darkened. "I'm sorry . . ."

"Maybe you've seen the news reports about the missing girl," Kirsten said.

Kyle winced. "You knew her?"

"She's my best friend," Kirsten said.

The waitress swooped down, placing plates in front of them. "Kaluba burger . . . Woulia Boulia salad . . ."

As they began eating, Kirsten spilled the whole story to him—the details of Friday night, the scream on the answering machine, the weekend of back-to-back phone calls, Peterson's interrogation, Emma's weird behavior, and Brandon's threats.

Kyle listened. He was a great listener, looking at her with

rapt attention, asking gentle questions, his eyes still and sympathetic. Kirsten hardly knew him, but she felt she could talk to him about anything. "No wonder you were feeling so bad, Kirsten," he said. "That's a lot to deal with . . . so much uncertainty."

Kirsten sighed. "I'm worried about *everything.* That strange guy she left with . . . I mean, no one's ever seen him, before or since. But then there's Emma, and I don't know if she's a harmless dweeb or a psycho thief. Who knows? She could have Sam tied up in a spider hole, feeding her mice while writing a ransom note—*I don't know!*" Kirsten took a deep breath. She was going overboard. It was the lack of sleep. And the uncertainty, Kyle was right about that. "I'm sorry, Kyle, I didn't mean to go off like that."

"Hey. Apologies not necessary, remember?" Kyle looked up. "Someone's waving to you. Over by the door."

Kirsten turned to see Emma waving and grinning a Sam-like grin and wearing a jacket similar to the one Sam had bought at Barney's last month. She was arm in arm with some guy, blocked from Kirsten's view at this angle, who was now whispering into Emma's ear. Summoning up all her good manners, Kirsten waved back, and it occurred to her that since Sam's disappearance, Emma was the only girl who had seemed consistently in a good mood.

The waitress pointed Emma to a table at the opposite end of the restaurant, and as the happy couple turned toward it, Kirsten saw who Emma's partner was—*Brandon*.

She felt ill—as if she was going to lose it right into her Woulia Boulia salad. "That's Emma . . . *and* Brandon," she told Kyle. "This is so sick. Brandon didn't know Emma existed! She must have jumped on him. She's stolen Sam's look, and now she's trying to steal her boyfriend—I mean, her ex-boyfriend."

"Bizarre," Kyle said, jockeying in his seat for a clearer look at the couple.

The baseball game suddenly gave way to the sharp trumpet blare of a special news report. *"Good evening,"* an anchorman said. *"Tonight we have the latest on the Missing Preppy Case. . . ."*

There, above the bar, in full life-size color, was Sam. With that megawatt smile, frozen in time on the day they'd taken the school pictures in Central Park. The image faded, and a new one took its place, a drawing this time.

"Samantha Byrne was seen leaving an uptown club with a man who looks like this," the reporter announced. *"Persons with any knowledge are urged to contact the New York City Police at once."*

It was a police sketch. A man with fat cheeks, a scraggly beard, heavy eyebrows, and red hair.

Totally not right. *So* not right.

Kirsten shook her head. "No. He didn't look like that at all. He was younger. Thinner and better looking. I gave Peterson a description of that guy—it wasn't at all like that. . . ."

More Woodley kids were in the restaurant now, and Kirsten could see their faces, all around—staring at the screen, eyes red, looking at Sam, looking at her—all the pity, the whispers, the attempts to figure the identity of a man who was not the right guy . . . and in the background, the sound of Emma's voice, chattering away, talking about Sam, Sam, Sam.

It was too much. Too much talk and hand wringing and misunderstanding. She had to do something. Sitting back and waiting for the cops to bring Sam home wasn't enough. She stood up from the table, averting her eyes from Kyle's bewildered glance. "Sorry, Kyle," she said, "but I have to get out of here."

"But where are you going?" he asked.

"The police are looking for the wrong guy. I'm going to call Peterson and give him the description again. And then I'm going to look myself. I know the places Sam likes. I'm going to go to every one of them and search in every dark corner until I find him."

Kyle stood. "Kirsten, I know you're upset, but I don't think that's a good plan. It could be dangerous."

He looked so concerned. She was leaving him again, just the way she'd done at the Party Room. "I can't *not* do it," she said softly. "I owe it to Sam. I can't just stand by anymore."

"I'll go with you," Kyle said.

She thought about it briefly, but shook her head. At this

point, her trust in fellow human beings was at an all-time low. "No," she said firmly. "I need to do this alone."

Kyle took a deep breath and nodded. "Okay. I understand. But promise me you won't do anything crazy when you're out on your own."

Kirsten nodded and attempted a smile. "I won't. Promise."

As she took her coat and left, she intended to keep her promise. She wouldn't do anything crazy on her own. She would get Julie to go with her.

11

I'm so proud of myself. *Really proud.*

I am keeping my impulses in check.

Control is important.

I will take my time with this one.

Change happens with time. Time and patience.

And control.

Let's face it. It's nice to have someone to talk to at a party.

An intimate conversation among friends. I could get used to this.

"Now, some of the girls I know," I tell her, "they have big mouths. Or they can be sweet, with good hearts, but they are not nice to animals? I don't get it? Do you get it? I bet you think I'm an animal, don't you? DON'T YOU?!

Silly, she can't answer you. She's got a handkerchief in her mouth!

But you do crazy things when you're in a good mood.

And when you're sucking on nitrous oxide to disguise your voice.

To make it sound all squeaky. It's funny.

I think about turning off the TV. The nightly news reports have ended, but you never know when they'll break in again. Got to keep up with the news.

"Now, I have a theory," I tell her. "Want to hear it? Here's what I've learned. Some people think they can get away with treating the animals like crap. But they're cowards! This time they'll learn their lesson. You watch. They'll hover around a little, but ultimately they're too afraid to come inside and join the party . . . because they know if they get too close—smash! Like mashed potatoes."

Mashed potatoes.

There are mashed potatoes in the fridge.

Hmmm.

It is past dinnertime—way past dinnertime. My, how time flies when you're having fun, but the old tummy is rumbling and WHAT KIND OF HOST DOESN'T OFFER A GUEST DINNER AT DINNERTIME?

"Be right back. And . . . don't go away!"

Don't go away. Ha. Right.

A laugh a minute. We are having fun now, aren't we?

There they are. Back of the fridge, in the container.

Into the microwave. Add salt. Mashed Potatoes setting . . .

Another hit of nitrous oxide . . . no use sounding like me. Yet.

"Ah, voilà! Doesn't that smell good?"

Idiot. She still has a handkerchief in her mouth. You put it there so she wouldn't make noise. Well, she can't eat with a handkerchief in the mouth either, Einstein . . .

"Out it comes! Now keep quiet if you want mashed potatoes, made by my mom from a special family recipe!"

"WHAT THE HELL DO YOU THINK YOU'RE DO—"

"Handkerchief back in! Bad girl, Spammie, now breathe . . . two . . . three . . . four. . . . Shall we try again?"

I pull out the handkerchief. Not so glam now. It's a sad sight, really. Her mouth is dry and cracked. A little red at the corners. Maybe it's an allergic reaction to the laundry detergent. Shouldn't use that cheap Arm & Hammer shit anymore.

Ah well, this treatment is temporary. She won't need a handkerchief when I'm through, will she? No, she won't need it at all.

At least she's quiet now.

One spoonful.

"Mmmm. Mmmmm, is it good?" I ask.

"Yes, yes, it's good," she says.

She likes it. SAM LIKES IT!

I bow, which is ridiculous, because she still has the blindfold over her eyes so she can't see me. And clumsy me, I drop a lump of the precious potatoes right in her lap. "Oops. Sorry."

"Those are brand-new pants," Sam says. "I can get the stain out in the bathroom with a little shampoo. It's amazing how that works—"

"Really? OH, REALLY?" I shouldn't get so angry. But she's trying to scam me. She must think I'm a moron. "And what ELSE will you do if I untie your hands?"

"Look, what I'm trying to say is . . . I have to go to the bathroom," she says. "It's an emergency, okay?"

"That's what this pot is for," I say calmly, because I have heard this crap before.

"Well, yeah, that—but there's something else, okay? It's not something you can do for me, and it's private, and you know exactly what I mean—now, you don't have to give me my bag, but if you give me what I need from the bag, I'll take it in and come back and spare your floor from leaking into your neighbors downstairs, who I'm sure would not take kindly to it. Hey, look, I'm not going anywhere, all right? Do you hear me screaming and carrying on?"

Sigh. Oh, all right. I understand. I get closer, pulling my trusty Swiss Army knife from my pocket. "You know what happens if you try anything. . . ."

I reach around and undo the knot, but it's a good knot . . . it's a TOO GOOD knot, and I'm wondering if I just use that knife and get some more rope, but rope has gotten expensive, at least this kind. . . .

"Owwwwww!"

I'm on the floor.

She kicked me.

THE BITCH KICKED ME!

And now she's raising her arms. She's doing it. She's removing the blindfold.

"Oh my God . . . ," she says. "It's you. I don't believe it's you."

Stupid.

How unbelievably stupid.

I push her back onto the chair. She tries to fight back, but she's not as strong as I am and if she had THOUGHT OF THAT IN THE FIRST PLACE, I wouldn't have to do this.

"LET ME GO!" she shrieks.

I'm feeling sad.

She didn't know how to follow directions.

All we needed was some time.

She didn't get that little fact.

JUST A LITTLE TIME, THAT'S ALL.

"I'm sorry," I say. "We would have been a good team if you weren't so OUT OF CONTROL. I can't let you go now. It was too early. You saw my face, and it was too early to do that. ALL I WANTED WAS FOR US TO BE FRIENDS AND TO LEARN A LITTLE SOMETHING ABOUT LOYALTY, BUT YOU SAW MY FACE!"

What can I do? I have no choice now. . . .

12

"That's the place," Kirsten said, looking at the faded remnants of painted letters—cuts—on the wall of a grimy warehouse down the block, under the abandoned elevated freight train in New York's old meat-packing district.

She and Julie had been to four clubs already, dropping a wad on drinks that they either had to chug or leave behind. No luck so far. This was the last place Kirsten could think of, a place Sam went to only in her craziest moods.

They passed couples making out in the old truck docks, and were winked at by a person of indeterminate gender wearing lurid makeup and few clothes. Against the night-black support beam for the elevated train, a rail-thin guy was snorting something from the palm of his hand, and Kirsten thought she saw reflected in the streetlight a hypodermic needle passed among a crowd near a parked Lexus. Beneath their feet the sidewalk was slippery. Once last summer Sam had gleefully explained that the pavement was permanently saturated with the fat left by slabs of beef dragged by truckers across the sidewalks.

Back in those days, though, the pavement probably didn't bounce with a pounding hip-hop beat like it did tonight.

"Sam used to go *here*?" Julie asked.

Kirsten nodded. "As a last resort." It wasn't her favorite place either. She and Julie breezed past a line of less-than-fashionable waiting forlornly behind the velvet rope. They waved at the bouncer, a beefy guy chewing gum, who barely looked up from his paperback copy of *The Fountainhead*. Kirsten had dressed in her tiniest Prada tank, which pretty much guaranteed admittance anywhere, even here, even if the gate people didn't know her.

"We're looking for a college guy with scruffy red hair!" Kirsten yelled over the noise coming from within. "Might have been wearing a Phish T-shirt!"

The guy shrugged, gesturing to the door. "Go on in, if you want. Have a look. . . ."

"Thanks." Kirsten gave him a small business card, her dad's, with his info crossed out and her own name, cell number, and e-mail address written on back. "Please call if you see anyone like that."

Kirsten and Julie descended a black metal staircase that clanked and shook as they walked, down into a dance floor that crawled with bodies. The bass was like a physical assault, like something injected straight into the bloodstream. On any other night it would have been impossible to resist the urge to dance, but tonight Kirsten and Julie elbowed their way through the sweaty, pumped-up crowd. On the walls, which seemed to stretch the length of a football field, vast screens played scenes from *Reservoir Dogs*, *Bonnie and Clyde*, *The Silence of the Lambs*—gun violence, amputation, and cannibalism as background. From the ceiling hung thick metal hooks, chutes, and curved tracks left over from meat-processing days, not used as decoration, and it made Kirsten think of helpless pigs and cows floating through the air on their way to shrink-wrapped meal-sized portions.

"I DON'T SEE HIM!" Julie shouted over the noise.

"COME WITH ME TO THE BAR!" Kirsten replied.

"I'M NOT STAYING HERE. DON'T ORDER DRINKS!" Julie said.

The bartender had massive shoulders that could have been sides of beef themselves. Kirsten caught his attention, leaned over the bar, and once again gave a description of Erik the Red.

"Oh. This is the guy on the TV?" he said.

"Exactly. But he really doesn't look like that—"

"Thinner, right? Younger. Like, twenty-two, twenty-three?"

"Do you know him?"

"Maybe. There is a guy comes here who has this really red hair. Spends a lot on drinks. I think he hangs at Mole, too. Over on West Street near Little West Twelfth. I saw him there when I was subbing one night. Anyway, I'll keep my eye out here, too."

"Thanks!" Kirsten handed him a card.

Mole. She didn't know that place at all, but for the first time, they had a lead. She felt a flicker of hope. "This is great," she said.

Julie slumped onto a stool. "What's so great? There are thousands of guys with red hair. We can't go to *every* club. This is like finding a needle in a haystack. Let's go home."

Kirsten glanced around, surveying the faces that swung in and out of the flashing lights. They hadn't found the guy, true. But she didn't believe the trip was a total failure. They'd planted seeds. Created a buzz. The bartenders and bouncers in all of Sam's favorite places had Kirsten's card and knew how to reach her.

"Hey," said a deep voice behind Kirsten.

She turned to face a guy about six feet five, with sunglasses and spiky black hair and enough hardware pierced into his face to stock a small jewelry store. He grinned wordlessly at Kirsten, until she realized he was holding his hand out to her.

In his palm were three small blue pills. "Free, for you. If you dance with me."

Julie rolled her eyes and grabbed Kirsten's hand. *Out of here,* she mouthed.

They both bolted from the bar.

"Bitch," the guy called out.

They made their way back upstairs and onto the street. "Can we go now?" Julie said, storming into the street to hail a cab.

"Just one more place," Kirsten said. "Mole. It's not far."

A taxi veered over to Julie, and she pulled open the back door, looking tired and exasperated. "Kirsten, I want to find Sam. I want to try to get this guy and ask him questions. But New York is too big to do this kind of stuff. We could be out here all night and still not scratch the surface of all the clubs and bars. I'm heading home. Come home with me, okay? We're not helping Sam by running ourselves ragged."

Kirsten wanted to go home too, but she couldn't. If she didn't look, if she didn't try one last place, she'd never forgive herself. What if he was there? What if she missed him and could have found out the crucial bit of information about Sam?

It wouldn't take long, she promised herself. A quick look, and she'd catch a cab back home.

"It's okay, you go ahead," she said to Julie. "I won't be long."

Julie hesitated, then got into the cab and closed the door. "I don't feel good about this," she said. "I already have one missing friend."

Kirsten smiled. "I'm not going anywhere, not with anybody. I just want to look at the place. I promise, I'll call you as soon as I leave the club."

"You promise?" Julie asked, and Kirsten nodded.

As the cab sped off, Kirsten headed down West Street. It was dark but full of people. Just ahead, the sidewalk was clogged with motorcycles in front of a biker bar. Men with beards and potbellies eyed her as she passed, and a punked-out stoner with a shaved head and a studded color called out, "Peace, you guys!" and started laughing.

At the corner of Little West Twelfth, a couple leaned against a big black Escalade, French-kissing and moaning. The car was nice, and reminded her of the one Brandon drove around whenever his dad let him. . . .

She stopped in her tracks. It *was* Brandon leaning against the car. The same blunt profile and leather jacket, the same wavy black hair.

He came up for air, and Kirsten heard his guttural, low-throated laugh. It was joined by a dreamy cooing noise that sounded a lot like Sam, but Kirsten knew to expect that by now from Emma.

Kirsten veered into the street to avoid them, but it was too late. "Kirstennnn! Hiyeee!" Emma called out.

"Hey, Emma," Kirsten said.

"Look what the wind blew in," Brandon said. "Looking to score some weed, Kirsten? Or are you checking up on me for Peterson? Why don't you stick around awhile, maybe I'll commit a murder for you."

Emma put a finger to his lips. "Come on, Brandy Alexander, be nice."

Brandy Alexander? Kirsten cringed. That was what Sam used to call him. "You don't miss a thing, Emma. Not even a nickname," she said.

Brandon pushed Emma aside and began striding toward Kirsten. "I think you are following me, aren't you? You want to pin Sam's disappearance on *me.* You are one sick bitch, Kirsten. You know that? I don't like people like you. I don't like you at all."

He was moving fast toward her now, nearly jogging. The veins in his neck were taut, his eyes bloodshot. He was reaching into his pocket.

Kirsten backed away, turning her ankle on the curb. She cried out in pain, stumbling into the street.

"Brandon, what are you doing?" Emma cried out. *"Come back here!"*

Kirsten scrambled to her feet and tried to hobble. Emma had grabbed Brandon by the shirt and was pulling him back. "Stop it!" she cried. "Control yourself, Brandon!"

Mole was just across the street. A small crowd stood out front, waiting to get in, and Kirsten limped as fast as she could into their midst. "Hey, are you okay?" the bouncer asked.

"I could use some ice," Kirsten replied.

He let her in and signaled to the bartender. The club was smaller than Cuts, with an air-conditioning system jacked up way too high, professional dancers in G-strings and little else on raised platforms, and couples—mainly same-sex but a little of everything—going at it on the dance floor. A retro mirror ball turned slowly, sending pinpricks of light around the room, and Kirsten limped to the bar, grimacing. Someday she'd sue Brandon.

The bartender, a blond woman, filled a sturdy plastic bag with ice and gave it to Kirsten. "What do you want to drink?" she asked.

"This is fine," Kirsten said, placing the bag on her ankle. "Actually, I'm looking for someone. . . ."

She gave the bartender a description of the red-haired guy, and of Sam, but got the same reaction she'd gotten all night: a blank look.

The numbing cold felt good. Kirsten glanced back to the door, afraid that Brandon may have come in, but he wasn't there.

On the stool next to her, a hunky jock-type guy with a slightly whirly-eyed, just-at-the-verge-of-too-drunk look on his face smiled at her and said in a deep voice, "Standard opening line."

"Excuse me?" Kirsten replied.

"Practiced confident reaction to affect attraction in a desirable member of the opposite sex." The guy laughed. "Sorry. It's a meta-conversation—like, a description of the underlying *meaning* of a conversation, instead of the actual words."

"Oh," Kirsten said. "Pretty geeky."

"Self-deprecating laugh with the realization that because

contact has been established, the line has actually accomplished what it was meant to do." He grinned.

"Uh, sorry, I can't play the game. My ankle hurts, I've had a terrible night, I'm about to go home, and I'm just not smart enough. You must be at Columbia or something."

"A couple of miles to the south." He burped. "I'm at NYU Law now. But don't hold that against me—the burp or the college. I'm Chip, by the way—"

"Okay, Chip by the way, I have a question. I'm not supposed to be asking this. I'm supposed to be heading home, but I might as well ask you, anyway. You know the girl in the news reports? Samantha? Well, she's my friend and I'm trying to find her. She was last seen with this red-haired guy. They gave a police sketch on TV, but—"

"It sucked. Didn't look a thing like him, right?" Chip said.

Kirsten wasn't expecting *that*. "Yeah. That's right. . . ."

"I know the dude. Scruffy red hair, Phish head, good looking, likes to barhop on the Upper East Side. You wouldn't tell it was him from that stupid-ass police composite, but yeah, couldn't be anyone else. I went to Andover with him, but I didn't know him well. He hung with the film crowd. Tim something or other."

"Tim?" Kirsten repeated.

"I'm pretty sure," Chip said. "His picture is in my yearbook."

Kirsten sat upright. Suddenly her ankle wasn't hurting so much anymore. "Do you still have it? The yearbook?"

"Sure. It's at my place."

What incredible luck! Kirsten looked him in the eye. He seemed pretty harmless. "'At my place'?" she said. "Standard come-on line to cute girl? Um, maybe you could go get your yearbook and bring it back? Pretty please?"

Chip laughed. "I live kind of far away. If I go and come back, thereby squandering a week's worth of personal spending money, how do I know you'll still be here? And if you're gone, it means I'll be stuck with a big-ass book full of pictures of prep school kids for the rest of the night. It's not exactly optimal for picking up a cute girl?"

"I can wait," Kirsten said with a smile. "My ankle is in lousy shape, anyway."

"Come with me," Chip said. "My roommates will be there. They never leave. They're engineering students. Even geekier than me."

Kirsten sighed. She'd promised Julie she'd be right home and wouldn't leave with anyone. She'd told Kyle she wouldn't do anything crazy. If she did this, she'd be breaking all her promises.

But if she didn't, she'd never see the photo. Never get Erik the Red's real name. Never come up with the lead that might get her closer to Sam. All for fear of a law student and his engineering roommates.

"I'll pay for the cab," Kirsten said.

• • •

"Only the lobby smells," Chip said, inserting his key in the front door of his building. "It's because of the restaurant next door."

Lobby was a pretty grand name for the miserable dingy cell they were in, with its broken black-and-white floor tiles and dented mailboxes on the wall. And any restaurant that gave off such a god-awful stink had no business serving food to human beings. "So . . . um, what neighborhood *is* this?" Kirsten asked.

"I don't think there's a name for it," Chip replied, "but it's walking distance to Chinatown, Little Italy, SoHo, the East Village, the Lower East Side."

"But not NYU . . ."

"A long walk." Chip grinned. "How do you think I keep my boyish figure?"

From Kirsten's sense of the cab ride, anywhere would be a very long walk.

The door creaked open, and Chip held it for her, which was a good thing because it looked like it weighed about three tons, maybe 50 percent of that being old layers of paint.

Kirsten stepped into the building, and the door swung shut with a loud *thwock* that echoed up the shaft of the stairway. That was about it for the public area—a longish hallway with graffiti-covered walls, three foreboding metal doors, and a sturdy black industrial stairway.

Chip's apartment was on the fifth floor.

He jammed another key into a door that looked like it had been kicked in one too many times, and pushed it open. With a bow, he gestured Kirsten inside. "Welcome to my humble *château.*"

She'd read about "railroad flats" in books about New York, but this was the first she'd seen. The apartment was a string of small rooms; you had to go through each one to get to the next. A living room was at the end.

This was a very small railroad. It had that old-New-York-building smell of decay, which was like nothing else in the world—not exactly a food smell or a human smell, more like a faint cloud of highly concentrated dust, like the grime that collects on things kept in an attic for a few lifetimes.

They walked through door number one, the lone closet . . . door number two, empty kitchen . . . door number three, empty bedroom . . . and finally the living room. Also empty.

"Um . . . where is everybody?" Kirsten asked.

"Good question—they must be out," Chip said. Kirsten glanced around and began wondering exactly how many roommates there were in this very small place, and what kind of extra-close and kinky relationship they must have.

The living room decor was beer cans, empty chips and pretzels bags, and magazines. The place was barely humanized by personal photos in plastic frames on the mantelpiece of a bricked-over fireplace.

Photos of Chip and various friends and family members. Just Chip's family. Just Chip's friends.

"So how many roommates do you have?" Kirsten asked.

Chip was standing in the archway that led out of the apartment to the front door. He was smiling, but his expression had lost that half-drunk goofy geekiness it had in the bar and had turned into something else, something that did not make Kirsten feel all warm and snuggly inside.

With a heavy shrug he said, "Facial expression that translates as a sheepish admission of false pretenses."

Kirsten swallowed hard. "So . . . you lied? Is that what you're trying to tell me?"

"Okay, okay, let's end the game," Chip said. "I have to admit something, Kirsten. I know Sam. I didn't tell you in the bar because I thought you'd freak out—big time."

"Really? You *know* Sam—*and* you know this Tim guy? Do you know where they are?"

Chip leaned against the side of the archway, looking absently at his nails. "I wonder if *you* know Sam as well as you think you do. She's into some, um, wild things. Things you don't know about. I used to see her at a bar way over on Fourteenth, a place called the Leather Vault. Weird crowd there . . . really weird . . . but kind of cool at the same time."

Great, Kirsten, just great, she thought angrily. *You've gotten yourself inside the apartment of a very strange, very large man in the middle of Manhattan's only neighborhood without a name, and he's telling you your best friend hangs out at S&M bars with an Andover guy named Tim who likes Phish and oh, by the way, the only way out is through this doorframe AND HE'S BLOCKING IT!*

It wasn't going to work. He was lying. "Where's the yearbook?" Kirsten asked. "Just show it to me, let me write down this guy's name, and then I'll get myself a cab, okay?"

"Oh, the yearbook . . ." Chip made a half-assed show of looking around the room. "I can't seem to locate it in my personal library. It must have been stolen." He pushed himself away from the archway, eyes locked on Kirsten's, and began walking steadily toward her. "Oh well, I guess we'll just have to think of something else to do."

13

The window?

No. Too high up.

Scream?

Who would give a shit in this neighborhood?

Call the police?

Her cell was dead, and there was no way she could ever find his phone. There was nothing 'real' in this shithole of an apartment.

"You told me it was here, Chip." Kirsten backed away, stepping on things that crackled and crunched, but there was no place to back to. She was against the wall. "You told me you had roommates and that you went to Andover."

"You didn't come all the way here to look at a yearbook, Kirsten," Chip said. "You came because you wanted to."

She could feel his breath now. And his eyes, burning down the front of her like a laser. His hand reached around and grabbed the left side of her butt.

No time to think. She reared back with her right leg, as far as she could, and let loose a sharp knee to the balls.

"Aaaaaggghhhhhhh!" Chip doubled over in pain.

Kirsten shoved him aside and ran. She could hear him fall into a pile of debris, moaning loudly.

The front door was stuck. No, bolted. Three times.

She twisted and untwisted, the tumblers on the locks clicking wildly before the door suddenly shot open and she nearly fell into the stairwell.

A surprised rodent, or maybe an industrial-grade insect, scurried for cover as Kirsten pounded down the stairs. He would recover. He would come after her. How long did it take guys to recover from something like this? Long enough for her to get a cab?

Fourth floor. Doors opening, frightened eyes peering out from cracks, behind small chains.

Third floor. Second floor. Despite her bad ankle, Kirsten jumped half of the last flight and landed in a heap on the ground level. Scrambling to her feet, she body-slammed the ancient outer door and bolted out onto the street.

Chip's building was mid-block, and to the left, a gang of seedy-looking guys lurked on the corner, talking loudly into cell phones.

Not there. She turned and ran the other way, without looking, because there was no time for that, and after two steps collided with someone she hadn't seen.

"Ahhhhhh!" she screamed, and instinctively grabbed his arm, wrenching it hard behind his back. "Leave me alone, you asshole!"

"Ow! Kirsten, it's me. Let go! Please!"

It wasn't Chip. Not at all.

"Kyle? Oh my God, Kyle, what are you doing here?" Kristen asked, releasing him from her death grip.

"Well, I, um, actually—" he stammered.

There was no time. Not here. Not within sight of Chip's apartment.

Kirsten grabbed his hand. "Come on!"

She ran to the next street, pulling Kyle behind her. There were no cabs there or anywhere. A row of metal-gated shops lined both sides of the deserted street, a boarded-up old theater at the end of the block.

They ran to the theater and ducked into the dark alcove under the old marquee. They weren't alone, but the other people were fast asleep under ratty blankets against the door.

"Sorry . . . Kirsten . . . ," Kyle said, catching his breath. "I didn't mean to scare you—I was following you, but I lost track. . . ."

"Following me?" Kirsten said. "Really? Like, *all night*?" She wasn't sure how to react.

"Well, yeah . . . more or less . . . ," he said.

Kirsten was stunned. She'd been out for hours. What had he been doing? Had he been in the clubs? Walking behind her and Julie on the sidewalks? Tailing her in cabs? It was strange. It was *spying.*

"You could have said hello," she said, but she hated the words the moment they came out of her mouth. "I mean, don't get me wrong, Kyle, I'm *so* grateful you're here now—I don't know what I would have done without you—but still . . . following me? *All night?*"

"It was dumb, I know," Kyle said sheepishly. "I just—well, after our conversation in Jackson Hole, I thought you might be headed for trouble. I figured you'd get mad if you saw me, so I kind of stayed low. I missed you when you left Cuts, but heard the fight with Brandon, only by the time I got there, you'd run into Mole. Anyway, I waited outside and jumped in a cab when you took off with that guy. But we lost track of you—the driver didn't know this neighborhood too well—so I've been kind of wandering around, hoping I'd see you. I'm really, really glad I did." He looked at his feet.

Kirsten let out a sigh. He was worried about her, that's all. Actually, when she thought about it, what he did was kind of nice. "I guess I'm glad you found me, too, Kyle," she admitted. "Next time I do something like this, I'll take you along. Okay?"

"Next time?" Kyle asked. "You plan on doing this a lot?"

Kirsten smiled. "Depends on the company."

Kyle leaned close, and all the feelings that had built up over the night—the fear and anger, frustration and betrayal—

began to lift, leaving Kirsten feeling cold and fragile and empty and sad.

She needed a hug. Badly. She threw her arms around Kyle, letting go of the last remnants of the night's sleaze and terror, and she held tightly until her cheeks rested in a warm patch of her tears on his shoulder. "It's my fault, Kyle. You warned me, but I ignored you. I thought I could find her. I thought if I didn't try, no one else would. I was so stupid! And I let this . . . this creep trick me. . . ."

Kyle folded her in his arms. "Hey, it's all right. . . . You're safe. . . . You don't have to explain."

They stood there, saying nothing, rocking back and forth, until Kirsten was feeling calmer, and he seemed to sense the moment it was all right to move. Together they walked to a wide two-way street—Delancey—and flagged down a livery cab driver.

And after a bumpy cross-town ride, they were gliding up the West Side Highway, the black sash of the Hudson River to their left, reflecting the moon and the bright thickets of lights from the high-rises in New Jersey.

Kyle lived on 112th and Morningside, a quiet street on the *way* Upper West Side, near Columbia University. They got out at a dark brownstone on a quiet block.

"Your parents live here?" Kirsten asked.

"No, a friend," he said. "A senior at Columbia. It's student housing. He's letting me crash."

"When do you go have to go back to Maine?" Kirsten asked.

"Shhh. Don't worry about that." Kyle let her into the building and showed her to a small first-floor apartment with a smudged Quik-Erase notepad on the door and furnished with exactly two chairs and a ripped sofa, a TV, a sound system, and a card table. He made cocoa on a hot plate while she sat on the sofa under a soft cotton blanket that he had pulled off a chair.

It was cold and cheaply furnished, and there was dust all over the place, but Kirsten felt absolutely divine.

Kyle put on a slow, sleepy jazz track and kneeled on the floor close to her, next to the sofa. Close enough so that Kirsten knew exactly how she felt inside, that for the first time tonight, for the first time in a long time, there was nothing to worry about, nothing to hold her back. And the shudder of guilt and sadness, the thought of Sam and where she might be at that moment, gave way to a voice in her head that was part Sam's, too, that said being here with Kyle was the right thing to do.

"Are you all right?" Kyle asked, tenderly sweeping her hair away from her face.

She rested her head on his shoulder, closed her eyes, breathed the fading scent of his cologne, and finally relaxed.

When he kissed her, she pulled him gently onto the sofa and knew by his touch that the night, as far as she was concerned, was going to be just fine.

• • •

She awoke to the sound of an ambulance screaming by.

Kyle's eyes flickered open. They were still on the sofa, wrapped in his blanket, and when he moved away, the cold rushed in to chill the warmth their bodies had created. "Sorry about that. The hospital is a block away."

Kirsten looked at the clock on the wall. It was 4:07 a.m. "Oh my God," she said, jumping off the couch and retrieving her things from the floor. "My parents, at the moment, probably think I'm the next Paris Hilton and are ready to kill me."

"I'd better get you a cab." Kyle stood up, reaching for a long-sleeved tee that was hanging over the side of a chair.

A big Grover from *Sesame Street* was printed on it.

Kirsten laughed. "Wearing *that*?"

"If you don't love Grover," Kyle said, pulling the shirt down over his head, "then I'm sorry, there's no future for us!"

They hurried out onto the street, which was absolutely silent and beautiful. Kirsten rested her head against Kyle's shoulder until they reached Broadway, where she prayed there were no cabs, which would force them to go back until the morning—but this was New York, and a taxi pulled up right away.

"Bye," Kirsten said.

Kyle opened the door for her, and she stepped inside.

And she discovered that even after a night like she'd just had, a simple kiss on the street from a twenty-one-year-old guy in a Grover shirt could rock her world.

• • •

"Hey, lady, the meter's runnin'."

When those romantic words awoke her fifteen minutes later, she was sprawled out in the backseat of the taxi. The driver, leaning over the front seat, had the hairiest nostrils she had ever seen.

She gave him a twenty and told him to keep the change, and the guy nearly knocked over Hector in a race to open the cab's back door for her.

She floated into the building, her perma-grin practically blinding herself in the elevator mirror. She knew there were going to be frantic, angry messages on her cell, couldn't check now anyway. She'd get the lecture soon enough, and she figured she'd hang on to the good mood while she could.

Quickly she took off her shoes. Chances were that Mom and Dad had gone to bed, and she could tiptoe into her room unnoticed.

Ding. The door whooshed open into the penthouse.

Kirsten cautiously stepped in, taking care to avoid the floorboard that always creaked.

"Hi, sweetie," came Mom's voice from the kitchen.

Shit, Kirsten thought.

They were waiting, both of them fully dressed and standing at the archway from the foyer to the kitchen. But they didn't look angry.

Mom's makeup was gone, her skin pale and puffy. Dad's

eyes were red, and his mouth drawn in a tight line trying so desperately to be neutral looking that it scared Kirsten. She felt her knees weaken, and she sat on a wooden banquet seat in the foyer. "You have something to tell me . . . ," she said, not wanting to hear it, but knowing that she had to.

Her parents both pulled up chairs from the kitchen and sat close to her, facing her. And she knew exactly what they were going to say before it came out of their mouths. But until the last second she hoped, hoped she wrong, and they were merely going to yell at her, scream at her, *disown* her, any of which would have been fine, anything else but the words that now came haltingly, half-choked, out of her father's mouth.

"Kirsten, I . . . I don't know how to tell you this," he said, "but . . . Sam is dead."

PART TWO

14

Dead.

Sam was dead.

The reality hit her over and over, through the night, through the sunrise she hadn't even noticed—the image of Sam promising to call, the scream that was erased by mistake, the look on her mom's face the night before, the awful news . . .

It always came back to that night at the Party Room, to one simple truth.

Sam was never coming home. *Why didn't I stop her?* Kirsten asked herself. *Why didn't I force her to stay with us that night?*

When the smell of coffee and bacon wafted into her darkened room from the kitchen, Kirsten realized it was morning. The hours of crying had wrung her dry. Her lips were parched, her body achy.

Slipping on her robe and mules, she shuffled out of her

room for some water. In the kitchen, Dad was eating his breakfast alone, already dressed in an elegant gray suit and starched white shirt, as usual, but looking haggard and old. In the background, Sandy Kenyon of WINS radio was delivering the day's celebrity Hollywood news, usually Kirsten's favorite feature, but she wasn't hearing a word, and instead of listening went straight to the fridge to pour herself a glass of bottled water. "They've been talking about Sam all morning," Dad said grimly. "Nonstop."

Kirsten wasn't interested. She grunted an "Oh" and began heading back to her room, when the radio let out a blast like a symphony orchestra, and an urgent voice intoned, *"We bring you the latest on the breaking story of the Samantha Byrne Murder case. . . ."*

Murder.

Kirsten sank into a kitchen chair, feeling short of breath.

". . . In what seems like a grotesque reenactment of a three-year-old news story, a senior from a prestigious New York City private school was found bludgeoned to death in Central Park, in nearly the same location—and by exactly the same method as the infamous Talcott murder three years ago. Samantha Byrne, whose disappearance was reported by her parents after what was by all accounts a typical night of wild partying on the Upper East Side, was found today by an early-morning jogger. Authorities say the teenager was stabbed over seventy times, then beaten repeatedly in the right temporal lobe. Her mouth was found to be gagged with

newspaper, and her hands were bound with a tie—a tie decorated with the symbol of Talcott Preparatory School. . . ."

"Oh my God . . . ," Kirsten whispered. "Oh my God . . ."

"For New Yorkers, the murder recalls that of Carolee Adams, whose convicted killer, Paul Stone, was released earlier this year on a legal technicality. Stone had always maintained his innocence and has not been seen since. . . ."

Kirsten couldn't listen. Forgetting her water, she ran into her room and stood by the window, staring over the trees, over the gray-blue expanse of the reservoir in the park.

Where had it happened? Right outside her room? Had Sam been there, crying for help, when Kirsten arrived home Friday night? Where was the yellow police tape? She didn't see any police tape.

It wasn't true. It couldn't be.

Kirsten tried to remember the details of the Carolee Adams case, but it was all a blur now. She was just fourteen when it'd happened, entering high school, meeting new friends and having fun. At that time, she didn't know Carolee or any of the kids at Talcott. The murder was something so far removed from her life. She never thought it would affect her directly . . . that is, until now.

After Carolee was killed, Paul Stone's photo had appeared in all the papers. Kirsten wished she remembered what he looked like—but she had only a vague recollection: blondish hair, bland expression. She wasn't even sure of that.

And now he was free. *They let him off.* But people who did those kinds of things usually came back to do them again. Everyone knew that. How could they have let him go?

Kirsten pulled her curtains shut, nearly ripping them from their hooks, blocking the view she never wanted to see again. And she collapsed on the bed, feeling sick and hollow.

She wasn't aware of dozing off, but the sharp rapping on her door roused her from an agitated sleep.

The door opened, and Julie, Sarah, and Carla peered in. They all looked like shit, and they didn't say a word, just ran in and wrapped Kirsten in a big, communal, tearful hug that broke through the numbness.

Kirsten held them tight and cried. She couldn't say a word, couldn't bear to believe that the circle of friends had shrunk forever. There were four of them now. All her life there had been five. The playdates, the birthday parties, the homework sessions and all-night IMing—*five.* It had never occurred to her that it would ever be different.

"School was canceled," Julie finally said, her face pink and swollen. "Your mom called our parents and invited us over to keep you company. I—I just can't believe it, Kirsten."

"What are we going to do?" Kirsten said. "How can she be gone?"

"And *murdered,*" Carla said, shaking her head. "It doesn't seem possible. . . ."

"I remember when they let that guy out of jail," Sarah

said. "I knew something bad would happen. I had a feeling. But who would have thought . . . ?"

A Talcott tie. That was what stuck in Kirsten's mind. Talcott was one of the most prestigious schools in the East. She had a sudden realization. "Wait. Didn't Brandon go to Talcott?"

Carla nodded. "He transferred to Woodley freshman year."

"Right after the murder," Julie added.

"He never talks about it," Carla said. "The only time I ever heard him mention Talcott was in the Party Room, when someone else brought it up in conversation. Brandon got all weird. Said he hated the place, didn't have any friends there, didn't even like to think about it. Makes you wonder."

"Oh my God, oh my God . . . ," Sarah murmured.

"I don't know," Julie said. "He is a slimeball, but it doesn't mean he's a . . ."

Murderer?

Kirsten filled in the rest of the sentence, but her mind was racing back . . .

To the night before, when Brandon was following her across Little Twelfth Street. To his explosion at the Party Room on Friday night, and his threats on Madison Avenue. To the day he'd backed her against the wall, outside of school. She could still hear the words he'd said as if he were there:

I'm going to trash your life. And when you least expect it, when everything seems to be going your way, you're going to pay. . . .

When he was on drugs, Brandon was capable of anything. Could he have done it?

Kirsten felt tears welling up again at the thought. What did it matter? Sam was gone. Nothing would bring her back.

But if Brandon laid a hand on her, if he was the one, Kirsten wanted to know. Because he would be the one to pay.

Kirsten buttoned her Burberry jacket against the suddenly sharp wind that evening as she rounded the corner of Eighty-Third and First with her friends.

It had been the longest day of her life. She hadn't eaten when her friends were over. She hadn't eaten after they'd left. She'd tried Kyle on his cell all day but only got voice mail. Mom and Dad were sweet, staying home and holding her and crying with her and getting her to drink tea. But the phone kept ringing all day. Finally she mustered up the energy to go over to Sam's mom's place, which was just the worst. Everyone wanted to rehash and console and cry. And throughout all of it, *Peterson,* bugging her at least five times for more information, all the while insisting that she *mustn't* think it was her fault, which was the most ridiculous thing to say, *because at a time like this, who was thinking about fault?*

Okay, she was. All the time, every minute. How easy it would have been to have pulled Sam back into the Party Room when she was on her way out . . . or earlier, when they'd first walked in and seen Brandon, to have suggested a different bar. Either way, and with a hundred other scenarios, none of this would have happened. And somehow, who knows how it happened, in the middle of all that, she'd somehow agreed with the girls to come to the Party Room, which at the moment seemed like the world's worst idea ever.

Kirsten paused, her knees shaking, as they approached the familiar oak door to their favorite haunt. "Guys, this is really, really stupid. Why are we doing this?"

Julie stopped and turned to Kirsten, taking both her arms and looking her firmly in the eye. "We talked about this, Kirsten, and we all agreed. We've been home all day. We're going to be home tonight and all day tomorrow. The phones, the media, the crying—it's too much. We love Sam, Kirsten. We want to honor *her*, not everybody else's take on her story, everyone else wanting to analyze and figure it out for their own mind. *This* is what Sam would have wanted, Kirsten. Not for us to sit around and cry. For us to *do* something—something crazy and fun."

"But the memory . . . ," Kirsten said. "It was only five nights ago. . . ."

"Think about the other memories," Sarah said. "All the nights we spent with her here."

"This place *was* Sam," Julie reminded her. "Her soul is still here."

Kirsten took a deep breath. She tried to imagine what

Sam would say if she were here—if she were hovering around watching her friends react to her death. She would nod and sympathize. She would be touched that they all loved her so much. But then, after a while, she would smile and push them right through this door. And she would say, *Have one on me.* "Yeah," Kirsten said. "Let's go."

As the girls descended the staircase, the bouncers nodded solemnly. The music was loud, the floor pretty sparse. Not a big Woodley crowd tonight, although members of some of the other classes were here, people who didn't know Sam.

Kirsten was not up for dancing. Not yet. She needed a drink.

Scott was dressed in black, but he was always in black. "Hey," he said gently, "how are you guys holding up?"

Kirsten tried to smile. "I could use some help."

"It's on me," Scott said, sliding a drink across the bar to her. "I've got my eye out for Red. The minute he shows his face in here, he's toast."

Red. Kirsten had thought about him a lot today too. Could he be Paul Stone with his hair dyed? He was probably about the right age. But when she imagined Scott—or Peterson, or anybody—catching Red, it didn't make her feel better. Having Sam back would make her feel better. "I just can't believe this really happened. Why? Why *Sam*?"

Scott sighed. "I've seen so much shit in my life. You never think it's going to happen to you. Never. But the world has a way of knocking you on your ass when you least expect it, and you just have no control."

"But I could have *done* something, Scott!" Kirsten said.

"What? Run over and blocked the door? Pushed her back into the bar? She was a big girl, Kirsten. She had her own mind." Scott put his hand gently on Kirsten's shoulder. "You shouldn't have done anything different. You did what a good friend does. Look at me, Kirsten. *It's not your fault.*"

Kirsten nodded. Out of the corner of her eye, she spotted Emma Lewis floating like a zombie through the sparse crowd. Her hair was limp and unbrushed, her eyes red, her Sam-like makeup all gone.

"Sorry, Scott . . . I'm out of here," Kirsten said, pushing back her barstool.

But she wasn't fast enough. Emma stood in front of her, cornering her between the stools and the bar. "Oh, Kirsten. I—I feel soooo guilty. So totally guilty. Oh my God. Can you ever . . ." Her voice broke, and she began to sob, the words barely escaping from her mouth. "Can . . . you ever . . . forgive me?"

"You're forgiven, Emma," Kirsten said, rolling her eyes. She was not in the mood for this drama. "For whatever. Now would you leave me alone?"

"You don't understand!" Emma blurted out, choking back tears. "I—I *did it. I'm the one who did it!*"

15

Emma was sobbing, the words caught in her throat, and Kirsten had to force herself to breathe because the thought of what Emma was trying to say, the implication in all its bizarreness, was catching her off-guard. "What, Emma? What are you talking about? *Tell me exactly what you did!*"

Julie, Carla, and Sarah, who had been dancing listlessly, came running.

"I'm s-sorry . . ." Emma nodded, gulping hysterically. "It started as a game, but I didn't realize—it's a crime, a serious crime—"

Kirsten held on to Julie, who was stiff, uncomprehending. "Oh, Emma . . . oh, God, don't tell me this . . ."

"I—I didn't even think I was capable of doing it! I learned how to change the Reply-to address. Josh Bergen showed me. It wasn't Sam. I'm *sooooo sorry.* Will you ever forgive me?"

Kirsten let go of Julie, and her knees nearly buckled. "*The e-mail*—is that what you're telling me? You wrote that stupid bogus-sounding e-mail? Is that *all*?"

"Emma, you scared the shit out of us!" Carla said.

"I don't really know why I did it," Emma barged on. "At the time . . . I was convinced Sam was all right. And Kirsten, you had been so upset when I saw you on Woodley Hill. I wanted you to feel better. So . . . I sent the message. I know it was totally crazy. If I had known . . ."

Kirsten leaned against the bar. "Get out of here, Emma. You're really sick."

"I can't believe she's really dead, Kirsten," Emma said. "I've been crying all day, watching the news. Brandon's upset too. I went to his house—you know, to comfort him—I mean, he's the only one who loved Sam as much as you and I did—"

"Brandon never loved Sam," Kirsten snapped.

"You should have seen him. He was acting *so* weird—totally freaked out. Saying all kinds of stuff, not making any sense. He wouldn't even come out of his house! He scared me so much." Her hands trembling, Emma lowered her voice.

Julie, Carla, and Sarah moved in closer.

"I saw something . . . at his house . . . ," Emma said, "something that scared me. I mean, it may not mean anything, so I don't want to say it. . . ."

"What?" Julie insisted. "What are you talking about?"

"Brandon keeps a Talcott tie pinned to a dartboard in his room," Emma whispered. "Today the tie was missing."

Oh God. Kirsten closed her eyes as her mind whirred. Suddenly things were beginning to connect. Brandon was a Talcott student three years ago—when Carolee was killed. And the guy they put in jail, Stone, no one really knew if he'd done it. He was released and there *had* to be a reason for that—which meant that the killer would still be out there. . . .

Was it possible? Kirsten wondered. No, it was a crazy idea. Brandon was only fourteen back then, and why would he do it? Why?

But she *did* know why he might want to hurt Sam. Maybe even . . . kill her?

"The moment I brought it up," Emma went on, "he told me to get out."

Kirsten shared a look with her friends. Whether Brandon was a murderer or not, it was clear that he was unstable and dangerous.

"Emma, does he know you're here?" Carla asked.

Emma nodded. "I'm worried."

"Stay away from him," Kirsten said. "Don't let him know that you told us. You'll have to tell Detective Peterson about this."

"Help me, Kirsten," Emma said, tears falling down her cheeks. "I'm scared. He's mad at me now. What if he . . . ?" Her voice trailed off as she nervously pushed her hair back behind her ears.

Kirsten noticed that her earrings were off and her bracelet was missing. "Emma, what happened to your jewelry?"

Emma stiffened. "It's at home. Why?"

"You've been wearing it every day."

"It—it reminds me of Sam. It makes me sad, Kirsten. Why do you ask?"

Kirsten didn't know the answer. Except that it seemed strange. It just seemed strange. "You're not trying to be Sam anymore—why, Emma? *Why aren't you trying to be like Sam?*"

"Kirsten . . . you're scaring me . . . ," Emma said. "Sam is dead. I don't want to be like Sam anymore! You can't make me!"

Scaring *her*? Kirsten couldn't imagine *anyone* being more frightened than she was—or more confused. And for once she didn't think that her friends could help her sort this whole thing out. She needed to talk to Kyle—now. "You know what? It really wasn't a good idea for me to come here. I've got to go."

"But we just got here," Julie said.

"I know, but I'm not feeling well." Kirsten was walking fast now, practically jogging to the door.

"Where are you going to be?" Carla called out.

Kirsten put her hand to her ear, thumb and pinkie outstretched. "I'll call," she said, before running through the door.

And her stomach did a flip-flop. That was Sam's exact gesture, on her way out of the Party Room Friday night. On the way to her death.

Kirsten bolted upstairs and caught a cab to the Upper West Side. On the way, she tried Kyle at least ten times on the cell, but just got his message.

The taxi dropped her off at Kyle's West 112th Street apartment, and Kirsten saw that the light in the first-floor apartment was off.

Fine. She would wait. He had to show up sometime.

Some of the apartment windows were open, and from the floors above, it seemed as if Eminem were trying to out-shout Missy Elliot.

She walked up the stoop and pressed the buzzer.

A college kid, wearing headphones and dressed in head-to-toe Fubu, came barreling through the door. He held it open, releasing a smell of frying burgers and burnt tomato sauce.

"Thanks," Kirsten said to him.

"I'm in 3C, babe," the guy said as he left, not giving Kirsten the chance to kick his ass.

Okay, so maybe I won't wait for Kyle in the building. I could write him a note and hang out at the corner Starbucks. There has to be a corner Starbucks around here somewhere, she thought, rushing up to Kyle's apartment. She reached for the Quik-Erase notepad—and noticed that the door was ajar.

"Kyle?" she called, pushing it open wide.

Her voice echoed eerily in the dark, and she fumbled for the light switch.

Click. The light came on. And Kirsten let out a gasp.

The chairs, the ripped couch, the sound system, and TV—all were gone.

She ran into the kitchen alcove and pulled open the cabinets, checking each one for signs of life. Nothing. Not even a single macaroni-and-cheese package.

Then she rushed to the bedroom and pulled open the closet—only to find a bunch of old wire hangers inside. That's it.

The apartment was empty.

And Kyle was gone.

16

Kirsten's mind raced. Kyle's friend was a student. Maybe his semester was over. Maybe he was kicked out of school and had to leave right away—and so did Kyle?

She heard the clatter of footsteps in the hall and ran to the door, startling another guy, this one dressed top-to-toe in crisp Abercrombie and Fitch.

"Did you see what happened here?" she asked.

The guy peered into the room. "Whoa . . . so *that's* what all the noise was about. Guess the dude moved out."

"Did you know him?" Kirsten asked.

"Nope. Kept to himself." He leaned against the doorjamb and smiled. "That sucks. You have no date tonight, huh?"

Kirsten barged past him and ran out of the building. She pulled a stick of gum from her backpack and popped it into her mouth, chewing nervously. Head down, she headed for Broadway.

There had to be an explanation. People didn't just vanish. *He'll call,* she told herself. *He probably spent the day moving. Maybe his cell died. It's not his fault. He'll apologize and invite me to his new place.* She checked her cell again. No messages.

At the corner of 112th and Broadway, Kirsten tossed her gum wrapper into the trash. It slid down the front page of a discarded *New York Post,* neatly folded over, which had a headline so huge and hysterical, you could practically hear it screaming.

DID TALCOTT KILLER KILL AGAIN?

Under the headline, just above the fold, was a photo—the top of someone's head. Kirsten gave the paper a quick once-over for banana peels and spit, but it was spotless, so she carefully fished it out and let it drop open.

It was a mug shot. A face staring directly into the camera, almost defiantly, eyes half-lidded. His hair, kinky and blond, was piled thickly on his head, and his scraggly beard hung from his chin like wet moss.

She caught a glimpse of the caption: PAUL STONE.

She remembered him now. How the newspapers and TV reporters had always described him as a bland-looking guy, totally nondescript.

But it wasn't true. It was just the expression on his face—dull and lifeless. Under those drugged-out lids his eyes were dark and piercing, and the beard obscured a jaw that was clearly fine-boned and chiseled. If you imagined the beard gone, the hair tamed, the eyes wide open, and some weight loss, he wouldn't be half bad looking.

It took a few seconds to sink in before she realized something else. Something important.

She knew Paul Stone.

She knew exactly who he was.

"Oh my God . . ." Kirsten's hand shook. She had to balance the newspaper on the rim of the trash can just to read the article.

> NEW YORK, LATE EDITION—
>
> New York City's declining crime rate may have its mayor bragging about "the safest city on earth," but don't tell that to the students of the prestigious Woodley School in Riverdale—or to their parents. "Letting Paul Stone out of jail was a travesty of justice," said Dr. Richard Fenk, plastic surgeon and father of a Woodley senior. "He should be in jail for life. And now the bastard is out—scot-free. As a father, what am I supposed to do now—keep my daughter under lock and key?"
>
> On a blustery fall day, when Woodley would normally be filled with the chatter of teens comparing notes, fashions, and fancy vacations, the

> school was vacant. Three blocks away, the victim's mother, socialite Barbara "Bobbi" Knauerhase, formerly Byrne, waved reporters away as she left her luxurious Park Avenue apartment, too distressed to talk. Her husband, personal trainer Rolf Knauerhase, vowed that "this subhuman piece of garbage will soon be crushed."
>
> Rumors have been circulating that Stone, now 21, has adopted a new identity—perhaps, speculates Dr. Fenk, with the aid of plastic surgery. According to a spokesman for the New York City Police Department, Detective Norman "Pete" Peterson . . .

Kirsten couldn't continue with the article. The photo kept staring at her. Daring her to look. It was the face of a killer.

She aged the face in her mind, colored the hair brown, imagined it calm and happy and smiling. At first glance, no, it wouldn't have been obvious. But it was clear when you knew what you were looking at.

The shape, the tilt of the head, the slightly forward slant of the forehead—it had to be him.

But it couldn't be him.

She held on to a slim hope that there might be something—a scar, a birthmark, a crossed eye—something that would give away the fact that they were different people.

But the more she looked at it, the more obvious it became.

Leslie's dad was wrong. Paul Stone hadn't had plastic surgery.

A razor. Dye. Age. That was all he'd used.

A new identity.

Kyle had never told her his last name. Never mentioned much about his past.

But now it made sense.

Paul was Kyle.

Kyle was Paul.

Kirsten was in love with a murderer.

Sam's murderer.

From the depths of the night she heard a muffled howl. Only when people began to stare did she realize it was coming from her own throat.

17

Kirsten wasn't sure how she made it home to the familiar confines of the Upper East Side. One minute she was sick, hovered over a city garbage can accepting a crumpled napkin from some homeless woman so she could wipe her mouth. Then, as if by magic, she found herself climbing the familiar steps of the Metropolitan Museum of Art.

She slumped in the darkness next to one of the museum's old fountains and glanced at her watch. Three hours. She had been walking the city for three hours, thinking about her best friend's murder. Thinking about how it might have happened. How scared Sam must have been when she'd realized it was all about to end—right before her skull was cracked open.

Kirsten shuddered, imagining Sam's last few minutes of torment. And it had all happened practically right outside Kirsten's bedroom window—in the park where their nannies had taken them every day as kids, the place where she and

Sam would sneak away to smoke cigarettes and talk about boys and about their dreams for the future. They were supposed to share an apartment in TriBeCa and go to NYU and after they graduated they had planned to spend a few years living in Florence so they could drive the Italian boys wild and go a little crazy themselves before they finally decided to get serious about their careers.

But now Sam was dead.

And then there was her murderer. Kyle . . . or Paul . . . or whatever his name was.

Kirsten's stomach lurched when she remembered their tender night together, how happy and giddy she was . . . how she didn't want to leave him, that night or ever. She closed her eyes, and the image of his cold, blank mug shot appeared before her. *Did he know I was Sam's friend before he'd even met me? He said he wanted to help me find Sam's killer. Was it all part of some weird, disgusting plan? How could I have been so stupid?*

"This whole thing is sick!" she screamed, not caring if the socialites out for an evening stroll with their overmanicured puppies thought she was crazy. She let the tears stream from her eyes. She let all of her emotions bubble to the surface.

Finally, Kirsten took a deep breath and decided to head to her apartment across the street, her only solace that now she knew the truth and that she'd tell the police about Paul Stone first thing in the morning.

On the corner of Eighty-Second she saw the shadow of

a man slumped against a building, homeless and poor, and it struck her that on the other side of the wall of that building, *her* building, was someone else living in the midst of the greatest wealth per square foot in the country. She had the urge to give the guy everything she had. She reached into her pocket, fumbling for cash. "Here," said Kirsten, holding out a fistful of bills. "Take this."

He reached out, and his face came into the light. "Kirsten—"

Kirsten froze and stared at the face of Sam's killer, his eyes shadowed by a long-brimmed baseball cap. "Kyle," she said, wanting to run but too scared to move.

"I've been waiting for you." He stepped forward and pulled her into an embrace.

He doesn't know that I know, Kirsten realized. Her stomach churning, she forced herself to hug him back. But it wasn't the same, and Kyle noticed.

"Hey, what's wrong?" he asked, pulling away. "Have you been crying?"

Kirsten didn't want to talk. She just wanted to get out of there. She glanced at her building's entrance at the center of the block. "I—I've got to go," she said, starting for the door.

"No—wait," Kyle said, gripping her wrist tightly. "We have to talk." He started pulling her in the opposite direction. "I've got something . . . important to tell you. It's kind of about Sam."

Kirsten began to panic. It was just like every thriller movie she'd ever seen. First, the killer explains how he murdered your best friend. Then, he murders *you* because you know too much! "No!" she said. "No, please!"

"Shhhhhh!" Kyle pushed his right hand over her mouth and pulled her back . . . back . . . down the street and into a darkened service entrance.

She kicked and fought to get away. But Kyle was just too strong. With one arm he turned her around and pinned her to the door. And then she saw it—a Talcott tie dangling from his hand! "No, please. Don't kill me. Don't kill me!" she cried.

18

"What? No . . . Kirsten . . . I wanted to show this to you. My Talcott tie." Kyle loosened his grip on her.

"So what?" Kirsten said. "Anybody could buy a Talcott tie. It proves nothing."

From above, a window opened. *"Hey, what's going on down there?"*

Mr. Federman—the celebrity defense lawyer and the father of Frankie, who was the likely candidate for Woodley valedictorian. One word to him, and the police would appear instantly.

"Kirsten, you don't understand," Kyle whispered, breathing heavily. "I have a tie, but that doesn't make me a murderer. You're right. It's so easy to get one of these ties. I didn't kill anybody. You have to believe me."

"How can I?" Kirsten said. "You lied about your real name, *Paul.*"

"Please. Don't call me that," Kyle said softly. "Paul died

when they locked me up. Those bastards ruined my name and destroyed my family."

"Do you kids know what time it is?" Mr. Federman yelled down. *"I'm calling the police!"*

Kyle's eyes burned through the darkness, steady and intense. He wasn't moving, wasn't running. "If you want to tell him, go ahead. If you want to leave, fine—but I've been in jail for two years for something I didn't do. That's why I came back—to clear my name so I can be free, have a normal life." His voice faltered, and he hesitated as if he wanted to say more but wasn't sure he should.

"What?" Kirsten said, trying to process it all. He sounded so sincere, so confused and hurt. "What did you want to say?"

"Just that when I met you . . . after all that's happened to me . . . you made me realize that I could still open up to people. I trust you, Kirsten. Please, try to trust me."

Kirsten looked away. *Trust?* The word ripped her apart. He was reaching inside her, right into her soul, to the place where she could be hurt the most. She wanted to trust him, but she wondered if that was part of the plan too, if that was what he'd done to Sam and to Carolee.

When she looked back, she saw that he'd moved aside.

She stepped forward. She was on the sidewalk now. A few steps and she'd be around the corner, on Fifth Avenue.

Home.

She glanced up to Mr. Federman's open window. *"It's me,*

Mr. Federman, Kirsten Sawyer! Sorry about the noise. It's nothing. We'll be quiet, I promise!"

The old man appeared at the window, dressed in a plaid nightshirt. With a nasty grumble, he slammed the window shut.

Kyle smiled. "Thanks."

"Look, I want to believe you," Kirsten said, "but how can I? You're not who you say you are. You disappear from your apartment without telling me—"

"I had to," he said. "My face is so familiar right now. I can't stay in one place very long."

"And the next place I see you is the front page of the *New York Post. You had a trial.* They convicted you, Kyle."

"I was released!" Kyle insisted.

"On a *technicality,"* Kirsten reminded him, "whatever the hell *that* means."

"It means they had no grounds to arrest me in the first place. Inadmissible evidence. It means they nailed me for no reason. They convicted the wrong guy."

Kyle reached for her, but Kirsten stepped back. "I need proof, Kyle."

"Okay. The night Sam disappeared? I wasn't even in New York. I was in the Hamptons. I took the Jitney."

"Who were you staying with?"

"I was alone, Kirsten. At my parents' summer house. I have a key. They don't know I went. Nobody knows. That's my point. If they try to hang Sam's murder on me, I'm dead. I have no alibi. That's why I need you."

"Need *me*? For what? I wasn't there. What could I do?" Inside, she was so confused. Part of her wanted to hate him and turn him in—and the other part wanted to help him, somehow, to help him clear his name and feel once again the closeness they'd shared. She wanted to ride out tonight, escape with him and live cocooned in a cabin somewhere in the wilderness, sipping hot cocoa under warm blankets, far away from the city, the media, and murder. How could she want that, too? How?

"You have to vouch for me, Kirsten," Kyle said. "You have to tell them we were together that night. We were at my apartment, listening to music."

"But . . . but that's not true," Kirsten said.

"You could just say it was."

"You . . . want me to *lie* for you?"

"Not lie," Kyle pleaded, stepping toward her. "Just back me up, in case they come after me."

Kirsten stepped back.

No. That's not the way it worked. What was it Peterson had told her? *Lying for a friend is never a good idea. . . . You just get wrapped up in bigger and bigger lies. And before you know it, you're involved. . . .* "I can't, Kyle," she said.

"But Kirsten, it's the only way. . . ."

He was deluding himself, and she was deluding *herself* if

she believed this would work. If Kyle was to clear his name, if he was going to fight lies and prove his innocence, he had to do it with truth. Otherwise, he was a bad bet for her, plain and simple. He'd be carrying around a whole web of lies that would just continue to grow. And that's if he was innocent.

If he was guilty . . . well, she didn't want to think about that.

"Sorry, Kyle . . ." Kirsten edged down the sidewalk. "I can't. This is too much. Too deep. Please don't come near me. I never want to see you again!"

She turned and ran, down to Fifth Avenue and around the corner.

Barging into the lobby of her building, she tried to hold back the sobbing. Hector must have thought she was a total soap opera nut. "Sorry, Hector," she said, nearly smashing into the elevator panel as she checked over her shoulder. "I'm okay. Really."

"Miss Kirsten?" Hector replied. "Are you sure?"

Kirsten pressed the button, and the elevator slid open. *"Bueno,"* she said as she stepped inside. "Just *bueno."*

The door shut, and Kirsten collapsed onto the upholstered bench opposite the mirror. She looked like shit.

She felt like shit.

About as *bueno* as someone who was in love with a killer could be.

19

"Spike it! Spike iiiit!"

The voice of Ms. Gardiner, the Woodley PE teacher, bellowed through the cavernous gymnasium as two teams of volleyball players went at it.

Kirsten felt tired and strung out and about as far from being in the mood for a nice competitive game of volleyball as she could be. Kyle hadn't tried to call her since their fight last night, and she had been reluctant to talk about it with anyone, because anyone in her right mind would tell her to go to the cops right away, to turn him in because her life was at stake. And, of course, Kirsten knew that that was the most reasonable thing to do, but she couldn't. She just couldn't turn Kyle in.

So she told Julie, and only Julie. But all day long kids had been staring at her, whispering behind her back, and Kirsten had the paranoid feeling that somehow the news had gotten out.

On the sidelines, Woodley girls stretched listlessly but picturesquely, waiting to play winners. And Kirsten couldn't help noticing that behind their sad expressions, their devastation over Sam, they were already beginning to come back to normality, to try to establish Life-as-We-Know-It once more, and it bothered her, it cut her to the soul, because it wasn't time yet.

"Do you think Ms. Gardiner is gay?" Leslie asked, strengthening her triceps as she tightened her already perfect ponytail.

"Is the sky blue?" Carla replied with an overacted yawn.

Sarah attempted a sit-up but fell back to avoid developing an unsightly six-pack. "Why do you ask, Leslie—need a date?"

"Hey, I don't take your sloppy seconds," Leslie shot back.

Kirsten stood up and turned away. "I can't deal with this right now," she muttered to Julie.

"Come on, you need de-stressing. Let's work some sore muscles." Julie took her best friend by the arm and led her to a mat in back of the gym. Because Julie was a class leader and a stealth jock, Ms. Gardiner wasn't likely to bitch and moan.

"So, are you going to tell me what happened between you and Kyle?"

"Julie," Kirsten said, "did you tell anyone about what happened between Kyle and me last night?"

Julie looked slightly offended. "Of *course* not," she said.

"But they all *know* about Kyle and me, don't they? How? How did they find out?"

Julie shrugged. "You know you can't keep a secret at Woodley no matter how hard you try."

Kirsten thought back to last night's argument at the side of her building. The old blowhard in the flannel pj's. "I'll bet Frankie Federman let it out. His dad spotted us."

"Could be, but what's the difference, Kirsten?" Julie asked, touching her forehead to her knee. "Look, the important thing is, you told Kyle to step off. That was great."

"I'm nervous," Kirsten admitted. "I mean, he didn't hurt me yesterday, but what if he's really guilty and I let him get away?" She paused. "I noticed a bunch of missed phone calls on my cell when I was in the courtyard earlier. I didn't recognize the number. Do you think it could be him? What if he comes back for me?"

"For one thing, it isn't going to be easy for him now. Everyone knows who he is. Everyone's looking for him. But frankly, as your friend, that doesn't comfort me. I say call Detective Peterson! Like, now. But if you don't want to do that, if you really think that Kyle *wasn't* feeding you a load of crap . . ."

Julie did a halfhearted yoga stretch while keeping an eye on Ms. Gardiner, who was likely to force volleyball on them if they weren't going through some sort of motions. Kirsten followed her lead.

"But you don't know him, Julie," she said. "If you did, you'd understand how I feel. The Kyle I know is not like that mug shot in the newspaper. He's sensitive and thoughtful and kind and . . . he wears a *Sesame Street* shirt, for God sakes!"

Julie stopped stretching and leaned in close. "I hate to say it, Kirsten, but what you're saying sounds *really* familiar. Like every time you hear the news about some shy, sweet geek who turns out to have killed, like, a million people or something. '*Nope, I had no idea Jeff Dahmer was carrying around a human head in his bowling ball case. He was a great guy, the best player in the league! I can't believe he turned out to be a psychopathic killer who ate people!*'" She paused for a dramatic effect. "Serial killers fool people time after time, Kirsten. How do you think they become *serial*?"

There was no way Kirsten could concentrate on her classes. For the rest of the day she kept thinking about what Julie had said in gym, then what Kyle had told her last night, then back to Julie's advice. Then she started thinking about Brandon and his missing tie, and then Emma and how weird she had been acting lately too. By the end of eighth period she was more confused than ever. To make it worse, she had received two more mystery calls on her cell, which she ignored, but as she pulled her stuff out of her locker, she felt as if the phone were burning a hole in her pocket.

She was tired and cranky. Her math book was wedged

on the top shelf underneath a pile of magazines. She gave a good, hard yank—and everything came crashing to the floor. *"Shit!"* she cried out.

"Gesundheit," Brandon replied from behind her. He was smiling—smarmily.

Kirsten rolled her eyes, ignoring him. She knew that Brandon had heard the rumors about her and Kyle—by now, everybody at Woodley had—and he was probably looking forward to an opportunity to rub her face in it. Kirsten wasn't in the mood. She shoved the magazines in, took her math book, and split.

"What's the hurry?" Brandon said. "Got a date?"

"Screw you, Brandon." Kirsten hurried down the hallway, but Brandon was faster. He ran around her, blocking her way.

He looked awful: hair greasy, chin unshaven, his eyes dilated . . .

"I hear you were at the Party Room last night, but you bounced," he said. "Guess you recovered from Sam's death pretty quick, huh? I hear Emma was there, too, crying on your shoulder." He leaned closer, which gave Kirsten the opportunity to get a whiff of his rank breath. It had to be at least 100 proof. "I know that bitch said something about me. What did she tell you? What?!"

He had this crazed look in his eyes that kind of scared her, but showing fear was not how you handled Brandon Yardley. He was like a dog—once he knew you were afraid of him, he'd hunt you down and rip you to pieces. "Why don't you ask her?" Kirsten said. "And be sure to be just as charming as you are right now. I'm sure she'll open right up. She always does, for you."

"The cops came to my house last night, Kirsten. They asked all these questions," Brandon admitted. *"What did she say?"*

"If they came to your house, then *they* told you what she said, and you already know," Kirsten said. "And frankly, I'm glad they came. It shows that they're still thinking about the case, Brandon, that they realize Sam's killer may not be the obvious suspect."

"What the hell is *that* supposed to mean?" Brandon said, his eyes gaining focus and heat. A crowd was beginning to gather now, but Brandon didn't care. "You're such a bitch, Kirsten. You don't care about anybody else, do you? Just yourself and your goddamn clothes—and all the stupid-ass guys you think you can twist around your finger. That's the way it was with you and Sam, wasn't it? You were laughing at me Friday night. You think you're really hot. Well, okay, you asked for it. *You asked for it!"* His face turned a deep crimson as he reached into his jacket pocket.

What is he pulling out from his jacket? Kirsten backed away slowly, her heart thudding hard in her chest. "Brandon, everybody's watching," she said. "What are you doing?"

"It's your fault, Kirsten," he told her, stepping forward.

"You're making me do this. But that's what you wanted, isn't it?" He pulled his hand out quickly—holding a picture. A four-by-five photo.

And Brandon was leaning into her, waving the image in her face. "See . . . that's who you *really* want, isn't it?"

Kirsten struggled to control her frantic heartbeats. She recognized the image right away. Brandon had taken it Friday night at the Party Room. There was Kirsten and Julie. And Sam.

Look at her, look at Sam. . . . She was dancing. They all were. It was the moment after she had flashed Brandon, taunting him, and he was shooting photos continually. She looked irritated, mocking—but *alive,* so incredibly alive—and Kirsten remembered how it felt, how in-your-face Brandon had become that night.

Why is he showing this to me? she thought, turning away. *How did it happen? How did everything go so wrong?* She wanted to go back in time, to jump into the photo and change everything. . . .

"Look at it!" Brandon thrust the picture inches from her face. "Go ahead, look at every face and tell me who you see!"

Kirsten took the photo from Brandon and held it close, her eyes scanning the faces of her friends and the more blurred faces at the edges—Josh Bergen and Frankie Federman, Trevor Royce . . .

But there was another face, staring at the camera but not

exactly *in* the crowd. It was a reflection in the mirror over the bar. Peering out from the gawkers, the face happened to have caught the glare from Brandon's flash, and his features were sharp and bright.

Kirsten put her hand to her mouth. She knew the face. She hadn't seen him there Friday night, hadn't suspected he'd been in the same room, but back then she hadn't known him. And it dawned on her that in all their conversations since, he hadn't told her he was there, in fact he had *lied*—had said he was in the Hamptons!

"Recognize your boyfriend, Kirsten?" Brandon asked. "Recognize Paul Stone?"

20

"He was there *Friday night,* Julie," Kirsten said, leaning over a drink at the Party Room that evening, still reeling from her earlier run-in with Brandon. It was just she and Julie tonight. As much as she loved the rest of her friends, she didn't need a crowd right now. She needed one sympathetic ear and mind, to help her sort things out. "Kyle was in the Party Room," Kirsten went on. "I saw his face in Brandon's picture, reflected in the mirror. But last night Kyle told me—right to my face—that he was in the Hamptons on Friday. He *lied* to me. And the worst part was, he wanted me to give an alibi. He wanted me to cover for *his* lie!"

Julie put a hand gently on Kirsten's shoulder. "This must be so hard, Kirsten. You really fell for him, huh?"

"I'm just so confused, Jules. I mean, Kyle was so convincing. He showed me his Talcott tie. He still has it. And Brandon is missing his. And with all Brandon's rage and violent behavior . . . I just thought maybe . . ."

"Come on." Julie put a hand on Kirsten's shoulder. "You do know Kyle could have gotten another tie anywhere . . . right?"

Kirsten nodded and took a slow sip of her drink. She knew that she was grasping at straws, but she couldn't help it. What was wrong with her? Why was it so hard for her to fully commit to the idea that Kyle was Sam's killer?

"I—I don't know, Julie . . . I just have this . . . *feeling*," Kirsten said. "It's hard to explain. I know Kyle lied, and I know it looks really bad . . . but against all reason, something inside my gut is telling me that he didn't do it."

"But Kirsten, his face was in the picture," Julie said. "He was there. He lied. Why else would he have lied if he wasn't trying to cover something up?"

Kirsten shook her head and stared into her drink. "Last night, I tried to put myself in his shoes . . . tried to imagine I'd been accused of something I didn't do, that I'd been put in jail and then released. I tried to picture life with this cloud over my head, and then finally making up my mind to come back to the scene of the crime to prove my innocence—only to have another horrible murder happen, *which is exactly like the one I'd been accused of before.*" She glanced at Julie. "And I asked myself, would I tell the truth if I knew people would place me near the scene of a crime that I didn't do, which matched the *other* one I didn't do—would I be tempted to lie?"

Julie listened silently, mixing her drink.

"All we know is, Kyle was *there*," Kirsten went on. "Just like you and I were there. We don't know that he left with Sam. It hasn't been released that Friday was the night Sam died. It could have been Saturday or Sunday or even Monday. The picture may not mean anything. There are still so many other questions, Julie. Like, what did Brandon do after I saw him that night? And that red-haired guy—no one's heard from him at all."

"I guess he should have contacted the police when he heard the reports," Julie said quietly.

"Yes," Kirsten said, "if he was innocent."

"He might have been able to help," Julie admitted. "He was the last person to see Sam alive."

"We're not even sure of *that* . . . ," Kirsten replied, taking a final sip and emptying her glass.

Scott walked over with a concerned expression. "How's it going? You guys look pretty serious over here. Can I get you anything?"

"You're the best, Scott." Julie looked at her watch. "I've got to go, though. My parents don't want me to stay out so late anymore. If we leave now, we can walk home. It's beautiful out."

Going outside sounded great to Kirsten. She was feeling a little claustrophobic. "Thanks, Scott. See you soon."

"Feel better, guys," he said.

Kirsten and Julie walked out of the bar and into the clear

night. Kirsten pulled her cute little cashmere blazer closed against the dry chill in the air, which hinted that winter was just around the corner. Walking up Second Avenue, she could smell distant burning fireplaces, and then it occurred to her why Julie had suggested the walk. Partly for the fresh air and weather, but also for the memories.

On every street was some story, sweet or funny or painful, that involved Sam. In a way, recalling those stories felt like a good way of saying good-bye.

"Sam loved this farmers' market," Kirsten said, gesturing to a corner stand covered for the night by a corrugated-steel gate. "She said it was because of the fresh fruit, but really it was because they always gave her free candy. The owner was in love with her."

"They all were," Julie said with a laugh.

The girls passed bar after bar, each with its own memory, until they got to Eighty-Third Street, where they would turn to go home. There, on the corner, was a brand-new club called Janus.

"Oh God, you know what Sam would have said about this," Kirsten said.

Julie howled. "Sure: 'What happens if the "J" light blows?'"

"Then it becomes a different kind of bar," Kirsten remarked, checking out the entryway.

The décor was totally from the 1980s, with lots of

brushed steel and black-and-white surrounding the door. Kirsten gazed through the big plate-glass window to the left of it. Inside, people were dancing, but there was a small crowd of Dalton and Spence preparatory kids surrounding a high table, drinking beers and eating nachos. Then she saw a shock of red hair only briefly, moving behind the window crowd.

Kirsten stopped. It was impossible to tell for sure, but the cut seemed similar, and the height was about right. "Did you see that?" she asked. "The red hair?"

Julie raised an eyebrow. "Kirsten, a lot of people have red hair. Let's go. It's getting late."

No. Kirsten couldn't leave without checking. She wouldn't have been able to stop wondering. "Let me just take a look, okay? Just wait here a second. If it's him, I'll come tell you. We can call Peterson."

Julie looked at her watch. "Make it quick, okay?"

Kirsten entered the club and made her way to the bar. The techno-pop house music irritated her, echoing harshly off the polished black floor and metal ceiling. She slithered among the dancers, looking for the red hair but not seeing it.

Oh well, she thought. *At least I tried.* She turned to head back, and noticed that there was another room off to her left. She peeked into the room and breathed in a thick cloud of marijuana smoke. She should have figured. When the cloud lifted she noticed a stoned-looking Goth girl slouched on a fuzzy black chair, holding her hand underneath a low white table.

On the other side of the table was a man with red hair pulled back into a ponytail.

Kirsten moved closer as he told a joke that failed to amuse his partner.

He smiled, and it was the smile that did it. The same smile she'd seen at the Party Room.

The same smile he'd given Sam, before leaving with her for the last time.

Purely by accident, Kirsten had found Sam's mysterious red-haired man.

21

"Hello?" Kirsten said. "Excuse me?"

The guy stopped talking to the Goth girl and stared at her through bloodshot eyes.

Yes. It was him. Definitely. The choice of partner was an interesting twist—about as different from Sam as could possibly be—but the profile, the ruddy skin, the strong features and jaw were dead on.

He nodded at Kirsten. "What's up?" he said through a smirk.

"Can I talk to you for a minute? About my friend, Samantha Byrne?"

The guy squinted. "What? Who?" he said.

"Last Friday night . . . the Party Room? Long blond hair? Really beautiful? You left with her." Kirsten shrugged at the guy's companion, who was chewing gum with her mouth open. "Sorry, but he did."

"I don't know what you're talking about," the guy drawled.

"Sam Byrne—you know, the girl in the news, the one who was . . ."

They were both looking at her blankly, as if neither of them had watched TV or picked up a newspaper all week. She hated having to spell it out, to say the words. "She was killed. In Central Park. They haven't found the murderer, but you were with her the last time she was seen in public, so I thought you might know something."

"Do you have . . . a picture?" the guy asked, his voice a little slow and drawn too, and Kirsten realized he was probably stoned out of his mind, and it would take a lot to get him to focus.

Kirsten pulled out her phone and scrolled through photos. "Sure. Let me take a look. . . ."

The guy leaned forward, rising from his seat, peering at Kirsten's phone. Kirsten glanced at him for a second. He was tall, about six one, and seemed a little shaky. She kept searching and finally found a shot of the two of them mugging for the camera on Woodley Hill. God, she missed Sam.

"Here," she said.

But when she looked up, he was gone, darting among the dancers toward the bar.

Kirsten took off. She ran after him, getting to the bar as he disappeared behind it, and followed him into a narrow hallway that led past the kitchen and the bathrooms. At the end of the hall was a metal door with a sign that said FIRE EXIT—DO NOT OPEN, ALARM WILL SOUND.

Kirsten pushed it without any alarm sounding and emerged into a dark alley. To the left, the alley ended in a brick wall. To the right was a line of trash cans, leading to East Eighty-Third Street. The guy was past the cans already, his sneakers thumping the concrete, and he turned left, up Eighty-Third toward Third Avenue.

Kirsten could hear the clamor of club-goers around the corner, on Second Avenue. Julie would be there, waiting, but there was no time to get her.

She raced to the street and looked to the left, up the block. It inclined upward to Third. On the uptown side, the air-conditioning unit to some institutional building belched hot air onto the sidewalk. The downtown side, just past a construction site, was a wall of tenements and old brownstones.

But the sidewalks on both sides were empty.

This guy was fast, incredibly fast. The distance to Third Avenue was huge, a long cross-town New York City block. It seemed impossible to get so far so fast. Especially for someone stoned.

Kirsten was racing now, running up the block without thinking, her feet barely touching the pavement, her eyes burning, her mind struggling with the possibility that this guy—a total stranger, a stoner no one had seen before, who had happened into the Party Room one night, maybe for the first time—might have singled out Sam.

As she reached the end of the construction site, she slipped on some concrete dust, against a stack of cinder-blocks. In the shadow of the blocks, a shape moved. Kirsten was off-balance, unable to react fast enough.

As she struggled to right herself, it sprang toward her.

Screaming, Kirsten jumped aside. The red-haired guy sped past her, out to the sidewalk, and began to run.

He was clumsy, flat-footed. Kirsten regained her balance and took chase. He ran like someone who had been smoking dope, and despite the fact that Ms. Gardiner, the gym teacher, had nearly flunked Kirsten in track and field, she was gaining on him.

She could hear his labored breathing as they both approached Third Avenue, and she jumped, arms extended, closing them around his legs as she fell to the sidewalk.

He stumbled down with her, and they rolled to the right, landing against the wheels of a gray Toyota parked smack against the curb—and she held him, tightly. She had run him down. After days of being beaten about emotionally by Brandon and Kyle and Emma, she was on top this time.

"What . . . what the . . . ?" he stammered.

Kirsten scrambled forward, sitting on his chest. "What happened that night?" she demanded. "Where did you go with Sam?"

"Out, that's all," he said.

"What's your name?" Kirsten demanded.

"What's it to you?"

"You went to Talcott, didn't you? Talcott Prep. You had the tie!"

"Freeport High School. A long time ago." He fixed an icy stare on her, and a creepy chill ran down Kirsten's back. "You'd better get off of me before I get angry," he said. "You don't want to get me angry."

"Kirsten?" Julie's voice called from behind her. "KIRSTE-E-E-ENNNNN!"

Kirsten turned. "Over here!" she cried, waving a hand.

The red-haired guy pushed. Kirsten lost her balance and fell back. He slipped away, jumping to his feet, and ran.

Kirsten took chase again, but he was in the street now, waving down a taxi, which had to swerve to avoid him.

As Kirsten squeezed between parked cars and into the street, he was climbing inside the back of the cab. She grabbed the handle of the door as it shut, and the taxi peeled around the corner, leaving her behind.

"Oh my God," Julie said, running up to her, out of breath. "Kirsten, are you okay? What happened? How did you get here? What did he do to you?"

"Nothing," Kirsten said. "I pinned *him*."

"You did? How? *Why?*"

Kirsten caught her breath. She'd had him. She'd almost

gotten his story. *Almost!* "He ran when I asked him about Sam. He was wasted, Julie. That was the only reason I could get him. I got the feeling he gets wasted a lot. He admitted going somewhere with Sam, but wouldn't tell me where. He said he didn't go to Talcott, and knows nothing about a tie."

"Thank God you're okay, Kirsten," Julie said, taking out her cell phone. "But you shouldn't have done this alone. I'm calling the police."

Brushing off the sidewalk gravel from her knees, Kirsten wondered what good she'd done. She hadn't gotten the red-haired guy's name. She wasn't any closer to knowing who Sam's killer was. And she made someone who may have killed Sam pissed off at *her.* Nothing about tonight made Kirsten feel better.

As Julie tapped out the number for Peterson—a number they all knew by heart—Kirsten slung an arm around her friend's shoulders, and they both started home.

She kept a wary eye on her surroundings, though, because she had the oddest feeling. A feeling that she was being watched . . .

22

I never imagined I'd bring HER into this, but this one has a big mouth, doesn't she. I don't like all the talking.

"NO TALKING!" I tell her.

I have to stop it, or they're all going to suspect. It may be too late. They may ALL think I'm involved, and how's that for trying to stay under the radar, trying to be in CONTROL and failing.

Aw, look. She's starting to cry. So sensitive. So sweet.

"You know you brought it on yourself," I say nicely, but I don't have much patience for her sniveling.

"NO SNIVELING!" I say.

It's late. I'm tired. Well, of course. I didn't go out and get her until two a.m. And with that, I was lucky. What a surprise to find her.

Now, where did I put those special pills?

It was hard to get so many of them. Ah. Here . . .

Ten little pills . . . twenty little pills . . . cute ones, grind 'em up good, put 'em in the milkshake. WHIIIRRRR goes the blender, smells like fruit smoothie, tastes like fruit smoothie. These will fit nicely into that BIG MOUTH!

She's shaking now. Good. Maybe she'll think next time. NEXT TIME. Ha-ha.

Up goes the hankie, off the mouth. So easy. Well, that's what happens when you flirt with them and get them drunk.

No need for nitrous oxide tonight. She can hear my voice. I don't care, she's not going anywhere after this.

"Open up," I tell her. "It's to give you strength, come on, you have an empty stomach . . . remember—scream and you get NO FOOD. Here. That's it, open wide. . . . You'll need it. It will help with the BIG headache you're going to have."

Ha-ha. I'm so funny today. It won't help her headache. Nothing can help. But THAT'S WHAT YOU GET WHEN YOU HAVE A BIG MOUTH AND MAKE PEOPLE GO SNOOPING INTO MY BUSINESS!

Come on, hold still. There. There it goes. Down the hatch.

The hard part is over.

Oh. Yes. Almost forgot . . .

Now where oh where did I put that tie?

Shit. Shit shit shit. I used it.

Well, then, I'll need something else, won't I. . . .

PART THREE

23

"I looked at the mug shots for hours, but I didn't see anyone who looked like Red," Kirsten told Julie over the phone. It was almost noon, and she'd just returned home from the police station. "They obviously don't have a thing on this guy. Last night they called Janus and the owner said no one had ever heard of him. They asked about the girl who was with him, too, but she was long gone. Peterson says he went around to every bar in the neighborhood, from Ninety-Sixth to Seventy-Second, but had no luck. It's like this guy doesn't exist, Julie. Like he's a phantom."

Kirsten shifted down the length of her mattress, propping her feet on one of the posts of her four-poster bed. She wanted to forget this morning's interview. It had been the worst way to begin a weekend. Peterson hadn't taken her into a private room this time. She had to talk about Sam's death and possible murderer right in the main part of the station house, with cops walking in and out, walkie-talkies blaring—Kirsten had never seen so many Dunkin' Donuts take-out bags in her life. "Well, I did the best I could. It was weird. Kyle's picture—the old Paul Stone shot from the *Post*—is all over the walls."

"You told Peterson about Kyle, too, right?" Julie asked. "About what happened the other night?"

Kirsten cringed. She knew Julie was going to ask this. And Kirsten had come close to telling Peterson, but somehow she just couldn't. She had a bad feeling. The news reports were full of attacks on the police, saying they botched the arrest of Paul Stone two years ago by destroying evidence and not following procedure and all that. Kirsten knew the cops wanted Kyle badly, and maybe it was for all the right reasons or maybe they wanted to hurry up and get him in jail so that all the negative press would go away. Somehow she couldn't be the one to deliver him to them. . . . "No. I didn't tell him."

"You *didn't*? Kirsten, what's the matter with you? You still think he won't be treated fairly? *That's not for you to decide!*"

"I know. I know, Julie. It may be the stupidest thing I ever didn't do—" Kirsten was interrupted by the beep of an incoming call. "Sorry. Talk later, okay? Gotta go. . . ." She pressed the Call button. "Hello?"

For a second, no one answered. And then a soft male voice said, "Kirsten, it's me. Kyle."

Kirsten sat up. "Kyle?"

"It's so good to hear your voice. Listen, I can't talk long. I have to see you. Right away—"

Kirsten was shaking. She didn't know why. No, she *did* know why. It was relief and happiness and fear and resentment and anger and mistrust, all of them mixed together in her mind, held inside and making her want to burst. "You . . . you lied to me, Kyle. You weren't in the Hamptons Friday night. You were at the Party Room, weren't you?"

There was a long pause. "Yeah, I was. I was hoping you wouldn't find out before I had the chance to tell you. That was one of the things I was calling about."

She wanted to believe him. She was so eager to believe that he was trying to be honest, that at least he had *planned* to come clean, that she had to take a deep breath, slow herself down, and force her mind into some rational, obvious, right-brain thinking: *She* had mentioned the lie, not him. Maybe he *hadn't* been calling to admit he'd been at the Party Room. Maybe that was another lie. "Kyle, how can you expect me to trust you? How can I know what's the truth and what isn't?"

"I've been thinking a lot about those things—about lies—ever since we . . . talked. And I realize I can't do it anymore. I can't keep it up. You're right, the more I try to run from this, the worse it gets. I can't live a life built on lies. I know that. I'm going to the police tonight, Kirsten. I'm going to tell them the truth—all of it, even if I know they won't believe me. I wanted to clear my name, but now, with Sam's murder, I don't think it's possible. I wish I could find out who did it, but I can't keep going on like this. I can't keep running."

"I found the red-haired guy, Kyle," Kirsten said. "The one who left the Party Room with Sam. I saw him at a club last night. He's creepy, Kyle."

"Really?" Kyle sounded hopeful. "Did the police pick him up? Who is he?"

"I don't know," Kirsten said. "He got away from me. And the police don't have any leads on him yet."

"Well, it's a start," Kyle said slowly. "It means there may be a chance for me after I turn myself in."

He was still going to go to the cops. He wasn't going to back out. It was a good decision, a truthful one. "Good luck, Kyle," she said.

She heard Kyle sigh. "Which means, Kirsten, I may not see you for a long time. Forever, maybe. I'd like to see you now. Is that all right? Will you meet me?"

His voice was soft and vulnerable, and she went down the mental checklist of all the things that made her mistrust him—there had been so many lies. But maybe he really had figured it out: that, in the end, the truth was all you had. He hadn't proven himself yet, but she was willing to give him the benefit of the doubt. For now. "Okay, Kyle," she said. "But I'm nervous."

"I understand," Kyle replied. "We'll meet in a public place. Before dark. Like, in front of the Met."

"Too close to home," Kirsten said. "Let's do it by the Alice in Wonderland statue in the park, near Seventy-Second Street." There would be little kids around, nannies with big mouths and cell phones—just in case. She looked at her watch. "Fifteen minutes. See you there."

Fourteen minutes later, Kirsten was winding her way down the footpath toward the statue. Clouds were gathering overhead, but the park was packed with people. Through the trees she saw the masts of radio-controlled miniature sailboats gliding across the pond. The official Parks Department name for it was Conservatory Water, but it was really the Stuart Little pond, of course. When she was a kid she had spent hours looking for him—Stuart—on all the little sailboats. Her first unrequited love. A boy born as a mouse. How simple life was back then, before she'd discovered what she knew now: that boys couldn't be mice at all, but they could grow up to be rats.

"Would you like to join me for tea? Pull up a mushroom." Kyle was sitting on the tiny bronze mushroom seat of the Alice statue, leaning over the bronze mushroom table, across from the Mad Hatter. He was dressed in a black flowing cotton shirt that accentuated his shoulders, and his soft hair picked up the light of the setting sun.

She was toast.

Although a hundred loud voices in her head still said, *Get out while you can,* she listened to the rising chorus of, *Go for it.* She went to him, slowly at first, and he stood. "I guess you must be pretty scared of me," he said softly.

And he was right, a part of her was scared, but when she looked at his uncertain, questioning smile, the notion of being *scared of him* evaporated from her mind, and she suddenly found herself in his arms, holding him and not wanting to doubt or think at all.

This was why she had wanted to see him in public, she realized. Not because she was afraid of him. Because she was afraid of *herself.* Because she knew she'd want exactly what she wanted right now. Something so private that their meeting had to be out in the open for her own good.

"I missed you," Kyle said.

"Kyle," Kirsten said, "I need a promise from you. That as long as we're here, it's all truth between you and me."

Kyle nodded.

"I want to say I've missed you. I have and I haven't. If you disappeared right now, my life would be so much easier. Can you understand that?" He looked wounded, and she snuggled her head on his shoulder. "But we're supposed to tell the truth, and the truth is, I *don't* want you to go. And against my better judgment, and my friend's advice, I want to give you a chance. But we have to take this slow, Kyle. Very slow."

A few yards away, a face-lifted mom grinned at them.

"We were like that once," she said to her buttoned-down-and-balding husband, who looked as if his memory chip suddenly needed replacement.

"Um, maybe we should get out of here," Kyle said, glancing around.

Kirsten laughed. "Okay. I guess we're setting a bad example for the kids."

She took Kyle's arm, and they wound their way uphill, farther into the park, away from Fifth Avenue and the pond. They took the tunnel under the car road and made a right around the Boathouse, continuing upward on a steep path that led into the heavily wooded part of the park. To their left, on a patch of dirt just off a footpath, Kirsten spotted a huge leathery snapping turtle sitting on her eggs. A light drizzle, which began as they walked up the hill, became a steady rain when they reached the top. Looking down the hill, Kirsten could see people rushing into the Boathouse and toward the park exits. She heard the phone ring in her pocket but ignored it.

Just up the path was a landscape construction site. An unmanned backhoe was parked next to a corrugated construction shed. As the rain pounded their heads, Kyle took Kirsten's hand. "Come on!" he cried.

He pulled her around to the front of the shed. A thick padlock hung uselessly from the broken hasp of the door, so he pulled it open. Inside was a collection of rakes, shovels, rolled-up fencing, metal posts, buckets, and thick rolls of bright yellow CAUTION tape.

Not exactly the Plaza, but dry.

The rain pelted the metal rooftop, sounding like kettledrums, and Kirsten thought she heard her phone again, but Kyle was now offering her a seat next to his, on two overturned buckets.

They sat, arms around each other, listening to the rain. And after a while, Kirsten pulled out her phone. 2 new messages.

"Sorry, Julie's been trying to reach me," she said, calling her voice mail. She held the phone tight to her ear and listened to the recorded message:

"Kirsten . . . Kirsten, oh my God, where are you? Why can't you be there?"

"What's up?" Kyle asked.

"Shhh . . ." Kirsten had to put her finger in her outside ear to block the sound of the rain.

"Did you hear the news?" Julie was crying hysterically. *"Oh, this is so horrible!"*

Kirsten stiffened. Julie was never this out of control—not even at Sam's funeral.

"It's Emma . . . she's dead, Kirsten. They found her. Her head was beaten in, and she was tied up just like Sam was! But the killer didn't use a tie—he used T-shirt. With, like, Grover on it. Is that sick or what?"

It was sick. Really sick. Kirsten wanted to scream and cry

out, but she didn't. Instead, she glanced at Kyle. He had worn a Grover shirt the night she'd been at the dorm. He'd worn it all the way down 112th Street.

Kirsten pulled the phone away from her ear, putting her other hand over the earpiece to keep Kyle from hearing the voice.

As she hit the stop button, he was smiling at her curiously. "Everything okay?"

"Fine," she said, and she worked hard not to show her growing, numbing panic. She stood up and began to back away, as far away from Kyle as she could, toward the wall of the shed.

"Kirsten?" Kyle said. "You look upset. Are you sure everything's all right?"

Tied with a Grover T-shirt . . . she thought, *a Grover T-shirt!*

"Kirsten, what's wrong?" Kyle asked. "Did something happen to Julie?"

He'd promised to tell the truth and had made her promise too. But how could she tell him the truth about what she'd heard? That Emma had died, strangled by his shirt? Because it *was* his shirt. At some point, you had to stop believing in coincidences. She'd allowed him to fool her about the Talcott tie—but what could he possibly say about a *Grover T-shirt?*

What did the truth mean to Paul Stone?

She'd been a fool. He'd tricked her totally. The red-haired

stoner hadn't killed Sam. Neither had Brandon or Emma—Kyle had, *Paul* had.

"Kirsten, talk to me." He rose from the seat, stepped closer to her, and now, even the *sight* of the door was obliterated, and Kirsten realized that she had let herself be led into a shed in the middle of nowhere, into what must have been the only *isolated public spot* in New York City. He was six foot one and strong, and he was between her and the door. She wouldn't stand a chance.

"Well, um, actually, Julie's having some . . . homework problems," Kirsten said, hating the lameness in her own voice. "S-so I should probably go help her out. . . ." She tried to sidestep around him, but the shed was narrow and its walls were crammed with tools and boxes, jamming them both into a kind of narrow corridor, and the *only* way she could get by him would be somehow to squeeze past, which at the moment seemed about impossible.

"The rain will let up in a little while," Kyle said. "Can't you wait a couple of minutes?"

She was instinctively walking toward the door, toward him, which seemed a stupid thing to do to a killer, but he was backing away. Closer to the door. And she realized maybe as long as he kept backing up, this would work. When he was close enough, she could leap by him.

Kyle tilted his head with concern. "You're shaking, Kirsten."

"I—I am?" Kirsten said.

"The truth . . . remember? We have to be honest with each other."

"I know." Kirsten said. "Okay."

He was now a few feet away from the exit. "Julie told you something, didn't she? Something you don't want me to hear. What is it, Kirsten? Can't you tell me?"

Kirsten lunged away, but Kyle was between her and the door. Her foot slipped on the rain-slicked floor and she fell, crashing into a stack of flowerpots. Her cell phone flew out of her hand, and Kyle picked it up.

"It's about me, isn't it?" Kyle asked, staring at the screen. "I need to tell you the truth. Did she say something about me?"

"No," Kirsten said. "I just—I have to go."

Kyle's eyes had lost their strength and sharpness. He was scared, Kirsten could tell—but not as scared as she was. As he began punching in numbers, Kirsten realized he was *replaying her voice mail,* putting her phone to his ear and listening to Julie's voice.

"No!" Kirsten sprang upward and tried to take back the phone, but he held her away, and his face, as he listened, slowly grew red. "Oh my God . . . *ohhhhhh, no . . . no, no, nooooo!*"

He let the phone drop and turned around as if lost, as if trying to find his bearings. "So you think . . . because of that . . ."

"Just give me the phone, Kyle," Kirsten said, "and step away. Please. Let me go."

Suddenly, with an odd, strangled-sounding cry, he reared his arm back and punched the wall of the shed, and Kirsten cringed.

Kyle's face lost its color. "I'm dead!" He yelled. "They're going to send me to jail for the rest of my life! I'm dead!" He smashed his fist against the opposite wall.

While he wasn't looking, while there was an inch of space, Kirsten scooped up her phone and made a break for it, pushing Kyle aside and barreling into the door, shoulder first.

It swung open, letting in the cool rain. Her feet slipped on the debris, and she stumbled, reaching out with her arms to steady herself.

Kyle held her back, taking her by the arm. "Where are you going? Can't you see? *This* is what happens when you try to tell the truth. Someone has to be out to get me. Somebody wants to ruin my life! How can I tell the truth, Kirsten? I was so stupid to think it would work!"

"Let me go!" she shouted.

Kyle pulled her back and yanked the door shut. "You can't go," he said. "I need you. They found the shirt. The damn *Grover shirt*, Kirsten. They'll lock me up forever. Oh God, you have to back me up. You have to tell them you were with me last night. That I was nowhere near Emma."

"I *wasn't* with you last night. *I won't lie!"* Somehow, Kirsten had found the courage to say it.

"You have to see what's going on. It won't work if you

don't stick with me—just this time. Just so I can get away. I need you, Kirsten. Will you do it? Will you?"

This time, she didn't feel it. She didn't feel the tug of his personality, the instinct that made her want to give in, to trust him. All she felt now was another instinct, the will to survive against a killer, against someone who was deluded or evil or both, and she made a sudden desperate break for the door again.

Kyle slammed it shut. The roar of the wind became muffled.

Kyle took her by the shoulders and pulled her deeper into the shed. In the closeness of the space, his perspiration was steaming from his shoulders, dissipating into the cool air. "You will say yes, Kirsten," he said, "if you want to leave this place."

24

"Yes."

Kirsten heard herself speak, but it didn't feel like a word; rather, a reflex from some other part of her body, like the sudden jerk of a hand away from an electric shock.

"What did you say?" Kyle asked.

"I said yes," she repeated, consciously now. "I'll lie for you."

Kyle loosened his grip, but not by much. He was still scared, his eyes wild. "We can't think of it as a lie. It's just buying time until we can build a case—because that's what we have to do, Kirsten. The cops won't, even though it's their job. We have to come to the table with another story. Tell me more about the red-haired guy. Did he jump you? Did he pull a knife or anything?"

"No, he just ran away. *I* jumped on *him*, but he escaped when I turned to signal Julie."

Kyle nailed her with his eyes. "He threatened you. He dragged you into an alley and said he was going to kill you.

He had a backpack and he started to pull something out of it—you couldn't tell what it was, but it looked like a long, rolled-up piece of clothing—when all of a sudden, Julie called you. She came running up the street with a bunch of other kids, and he realized he was outnumbered, so he ran."

"Okay." Kirsten swallowed her disgust.

"Give him words. He said, 'You saw me that night at the Party Room. You got a good look at my face. So you're next.' Something like that."

Kirsten nodded, silently, but Kyle seemed to grow more tense and irritated.

"The cops will believe you Kirsten. They'll give you the benefit of the doubt. And we'll be able to find the real killer on our own. I know we will."

All Kirsten could do was stare at him, thinking over and over, *He's insane . . . completely insane. . . .*

Kyle pulled her farther into the shed, gesturing for her to sit on an overturned bucket, and she did, leaning forward, keeping the weight on her feet in case she had the chance somehow to bolt.

"You have to understand what the last two years have been like." Kyle was speaking so fast now, he nearly tripped over his words. "It wasn't only me. After I was released, my parents were getting death threats over the phone. They had to quit their jobs and move. You wouldn't believe what they had to pay Randall Luis Gringer to take my case. It nearly bankrupted them. We won, but what good did it do? The media angle was: The cops blew it, and the court let off a killer on a technicality. So not only did everyone assume I was guilty, the cops were embarrassed. We showed them up, Kirsten. And now they're pissed. They want revenge and they're just waiting for me to stumble, and *the real killer knows it*. He's using me to get away with murder!"

The idea that Kyle had been represented by Randall Luis Gringer—a.k.a. Gold-Plated Gringer, Counsel to the Stars, Lawyer of the Loophole, with his custom-designed suits and personal fleet of private jets—didn't impress Kirsten, because Gringer could get anyone off. But the intensity of Kyle's emotion struck her like a cold slap, because he didn't realize how crazy he sounded. He thought he sounded logical, like a rational person hurt by circumstances beyond his control, and it dawned on Kirsten that he *believed* he was innocent, that he'd created this whole story to hide behind, to deny the things he'd done—that, to him, they weren't lies because *he really thought they were true.*

She knew she had to appeal to that logic. "Kyle, a minute ago you said you were going to go to the police to tell them the whole story, the truth—"

"A minute ago I didn't know they'd find a Grover shirt on Emma's body!" Kyle said. "Here's the truth, Kirsten: *I didn't do it*. It's not lying if it's to protect the truth. Is it?"

He was standing firm, legs apart, his right foot almost

touching the battered scoop of a sturdy shovel, its handle resting upright against the wall. It was angled forward from Kyle, within reach of Kirsten.

She leaned forward slightly.

"The point is," Kyle said, "someone killed Sam, and since it wasn't me, it had to be the red-haired guy. We all saw him leave the Party Room with Sam. You said he was a creep. He's the only one who could have done this. So how can we let him get away with it? We tell them he attacked you, and afterward you called me, and we were together all night, including the time that Emma was killed. It's not all about truth, Kirsten. It's about justice. It's about keeping this guy from doing anything bad ever again."

Outside, the wind sent a sudden blast, sending the fallen branch of a tree against the side of the shed with a sharp *smack*.

Kyle jumped, looking toward the noise.

And Kirsten found herself leaping up, grabbing, her fingers closing around the shaft of the shovel handle.

"What the—" Kyle said.

But he didn't have time to finish, because Kirsten was swinging, twisting from the hips, throwing her weight into the sweep of the shovel blade through the air until it made contact with Kyle's lower back.

He lurched forward with a startled grunt and fell to his knees, then forward onto his chest. "Kirst—"

Kirsten dropped the shovel and ran for the door. She

tripped over cans, nearly invisible in the stingy light of the shed, and grabbed the door handle.

It was stuck. Kyle had pulled it too hard and had jammed it.

"Ohhhhh . . . ," came Kyle's voice.

She glanced behind her. His shoulder blades were rising. He was pushing himself up. Kirsten banged on the handle, pounded on the door with her shoulders and hips. "Help! Help me! Somebody! Help!"

Behind her, she heard Kyle stumbling to his feet. And before she knew it, Kyle's fingers were around her collar and he was pulling hard, choking her, making her lose her footing as he dragged her into the shed.

He released her, and she fell against a machine, a spreader of some kind, tucked into the farthest corner from the door. She looked around for something, anything that she could use to defend herself.

Kyle was stepping toward her now, his eyes wide with a mix of emotions that Kirsten couldn't quite read, and his mouth was moving as if he was trying to say something.

"Let me go, Kyle," she said. "You don't want to do this. You know that, right?"

"You're going to betray me . . . ," he replied, his voice barely more than a whisper.

Kirsten grabbed on to a nearby rake and held it in front of her. "I don't want to hurt you, Kyle. But I will. I'll use this unless you push that door open."

He wasn't answering and he wasn't afraid; instead, he calmly reached over to the wall behind him, where a spool of yellow tape hung on a hook. It was the plastic tape used to cordon off construction sites, and he was unwinding a length of it, twisting it as he did until he had at least thirty feet, then ripping it from the spool and doubling and tripling it.

He was doing it so matter-of-factly, as if making a tourniquet or repairing a piece of equipment. "This won't hurt," he said.

Kirsten swung the rake, hard. Kyle jumped back, calmly timing her swing. And as her momentum pulled her around, he lunged, grabbing her arms and quickly wrapping, wrapping the tape around her wrists.

"STOP!" Kirsten shrieked. *"POLICE! POLIIIIICE!"*

The sound was muffled. Pathetic. With the rain pounding the roof, she had trouble even hearing herself, and Kyle was working fast, pushing her down onto an old wooden seat, threading the tape around her thumbs and binding her fingers together. "Does this hurt?" he said. "I don't want it to hurt."

"YES, IT HURTS!"

It hurt like crazy, but it hurt even more knowing he was going to kill her, and she looked around frantically because now everything around her, every object, was a potential weapon she could use to kill him first, if she could get up somehow, if she could break through the plastic tape . . .

"I don't want to do anything to cause you pain, Kirsten," he said, making a knot. "I just needed to buy time. I thought you understood that. But you were fooling me, pretending to go along. You lied. That's the ironic thing, Kirsten. We were talking about justice and truth, and you *lied*!"

At that last word he gritted his teeth, pulling the knot tight. "Just one more step," he said, and he grabbed the spool and unrolled the tape around her legs, binding her to the seat. "This will be so much easier for you if you don't struggle."

"YOU CAN'T GET AWAY WITH THIS, KYLE! HELLLP!" She tried to kick him, but he was too strong, and when her legs were secure he stood and wrapped the tape around her upper arms. His shoulder was against her chest now, and she could feel his breath and see the raindrops on his hair, matting it into brown clumps.

His left ear was inches from her mouth.

She thrust her head forward, her teeth clamping around the ear, and she bit. Hard.

Kyle shrieked and reeled backward. "God *damn* it! *Shit!* You're an animal! You're a fucking animal!"

She yanked on the tape, but she was stuck. He'd done his work well. She was bound to the chair, neck to ankle. She lurched up and down, the chair banging noisily on the floor.

Kyle stepped forward. His ear was bleeding, dripping onto the floor, pooling with the rainwater, but Kirsten wasn't watching him. She was only moving, pulling, jerking, working the tape, *yes,* it was coming loose and she strained even harder. . . .

"You're making me do this, Kirsten," he said, standing over her now, bent at the waist, keeping his upper body safely distant from her. "I didn't want to. I never would have dreamed of it. But you were going to betray me. . . ."

Then Kyle stretched a length of tape between his hands and looped it around Kirsten's neck. . . .

25

"No!" she cried out, feeling the rough edge of the tape touch the back of her neck. "NO-O-O-O! *Don't kill me, too!* You said you loved me, Kyle. How can you do this to someone you love?"

Kyle paused, his hands on either side of her, the tape pressing against her neck. "Kill you, too? My God, you really *believe* them, don't you?" He knelt, looking into her eyes.

"No, I don't," Kirsten said, lying through her teeth. This was all about survival now. "I just got scared, that's all. I'll help you. I'll do whatever you want."

Kyle shook his head. "I can't trust you anymore. Don't you see what just happened? We had it all planned out. It would have worked. Don't you see how bad it is to screw things up with a lie? Sorry, Kirsten."

His hands drew together, bringing the tape around front. And Kirsten did the only thing she could think of doing.

She spat in his face.

Kyle flinched, and Kirsten leaned into him, tilting forward on the chair's legs. She went over, taking him with her, making him fall into the blade of a backhoe. He yowled in pain and collapsed, moaning.

On her side, Kirsten wriggled her legs until she was able to work the tape over the bottoms of the chair legs. She pulled her legs free, the tape going slack, and was able to stand. As she yanked her body from side to side, the chair swung until it fell away.

Legs free, hands free, she ran for the door.

Behind her she could hear Kyle struggling to his feet. This time she propped her foot against the wall to the left of the knob as she pulled. The added leverage worked, the door flew open, and she ran.

The rain had let up somewhat, but the sun had set, and through the trees she saw red tail lights turning away from the small field where she was. "HELLLP!" she screamed, running.

It was a police car, Central Park precinct. Even before she reached it, two cops had jumped out and were rushing toward her. *"There's a murderer in the shed—over there!"* she screamed, pointing.

The door to the shed was wide open.

The younger of the two officers seemed frightened. "Is he armed?" he asked.

"No," Kirsten said.

The older partner, gray-haired and overweight, stepped forward. "Let's find him." They were on a blacktop path, and he stepped off it and onto the soggy field, trying to see into the shed. As he crept past a thick hedge, it moved.

Kyle jumped out, knocking into the officer, throwing him off-balance. He tussled with him on the ground while the other partner ran forward, shouting, "FREEZE!"

But Kyle was running now, sprinting across the field, through a row of bushes and into a parking lot. The younger officer took pursuit, but he was loaded down with equipment and was no match for Kyle.

Kirsten watched Kyle disappear over the hill and out of sight. Then she went over to the older officer, who was drenched from his fall onto the waterlogged turf. "Are you okay?" he asked. Then he reached down to his holster. "Son of a bitch. He took my pistol."

CRACCCCK!

Kirsten flinched at the sound just over the hill. It was a gunshot. Kirsten had never heard one before, but it sounded like fireworks—that's how people always describe it—and it could have been Kyle's gun or the cop's, but *someone* had been shot at.

From the officer's belt, a walkie-talkie squawked, "Request backup!" He took off in a run, and Kirsten followed.

They crossed the road, approaching the crest of a hill,

and Kirsten braced herself, wondering if Sam's murderer was now dead.

The young officer, who was trudging toward them, looked shaken. "No one was hurt," he said. "I thought the guy didn't have a gun."

"He took mine," the other man said.

The younger cop looked toward the east edge of the park, and Kirsten followed his glance over the stone gate, into the ribbons of light along Fifth Avenue, and along the amber rectangles of apartments coming to life with preparations for dinner. And she knew that, somewhere, Kyle was running hard, making plans to escape again and to lie low, wrapped in a fantasy of lies that, this time, she hoped would come crashing around him. She would make sure she did whatever she could to make that happen.

"Motherfucker," the young cop said, staring off into the distance.

Kirsten smiled a weary smile. *"Le débauché de la mère."*

"Huh?"

"Never mind," she replied. "It's a Woodley joke."

Epilogue

"I would put vitamin E on those suckers," Scott the bartender said as he examined Kirsten's wrists in the dim light over the Party Room bar.

After two days, her wrists were still red from the tape. It had been good for plenty of attention at school, but Kirsten didn't really want that. Sam's and Emma's deaths still hung heavily over everyone, but Kirsten's story had been, in its own way, a bright light—a life saved, a culprit discovered.

She'd been interviewed on-air four times, shown her wrists to a nationwide audience. She'd even gotten Brandon to give his picture of Kyle to the media, and it was televised, too, enhanced for clarity.

Over the last twenty-four hours, other photos of Kyle had surfaced, from his friend at Columbia and from old Talcott schoolmates. They all claimed that Kyle was a nice guy, and that it was unimaginable he'd do this.

The two police officers, Percy Charles Randolph (the

younger one) and Walter Schmidt (the older), had become heroes, the theft of Schmidt's gun conveniently not mentioned in the news reports—though Percy had found it in the park right where Kyle had dropped it, where it had accidentally discharged a round.

Kirsten's parents had taken her out to a subdued candlelight dinner last night, the celebration of gratitude for Kirsten's life tempered by prayers for Sam and Emma.

It was Kirsten's idea to spend tonight at the Party Room with Julie, Carla, and Sarah. There had been more tears than laughs tonight, and Kirsten had heard a million times how relieved everyone was that she'd been spared.

Kirsten appreciated that, but at night, when she had to fall asleep, she couldn't help wondering what it had been like for Sam and Emma the nights they'd died and how they must have felt when they'd known they wouldn't escape.

That was the hardest thing of all, and she didn't know if she'd ever get over it.

Julie danced over, looking gorgeous in her new Stella McCartney number, and of course bringing along a crowd of guys. "Aren't you going to dance?" she asked.

"Later," Kirsten said.

They'd talked it over before, she and Julie. The days had been so full of tears, and it was important to honor Sam's *and* Emma's spirit by living life, by doing the things they loved to do so much.

But it wasn't easy.

Bleeeep.

The bar phone rang, and Scott snatched it up. "Party Room, Scott speaking . . ."

Kirsten turned and watched the action on the floor. The Woodley lacrosse team had arrived, and by the looks of their dance moves, they still thought they were out on the field.

"Who?" Scott was nearly shouting to be heard over the racket. "Yeah, you bet she is . . ." He held out the phone to Kirsten. "You're the popular one tonight!"

Kirsten pressed the phone to her ear, covering her other ear against the noise. "Hello? *Hello?"*

She heard a voice at the other end, but it was only a mumble. The lacrosse guys were blotting out even the dance music. She hopped off her stool and crossed behind the bar to the hallway that led to the bathrooms. It was a little quieter there. "Sorry. Try again—and speak louder!" She pressed the phone closer to her ear.

This time she heard the words clearly.

"It's me," the voice said. Kyle's voice. "It isn't supposed to be like this. We'll see each other again. I'm coming back as soon as I can."

Her fingers went slack. She let the phone fall.

But Kyle had already hung up.

after hours

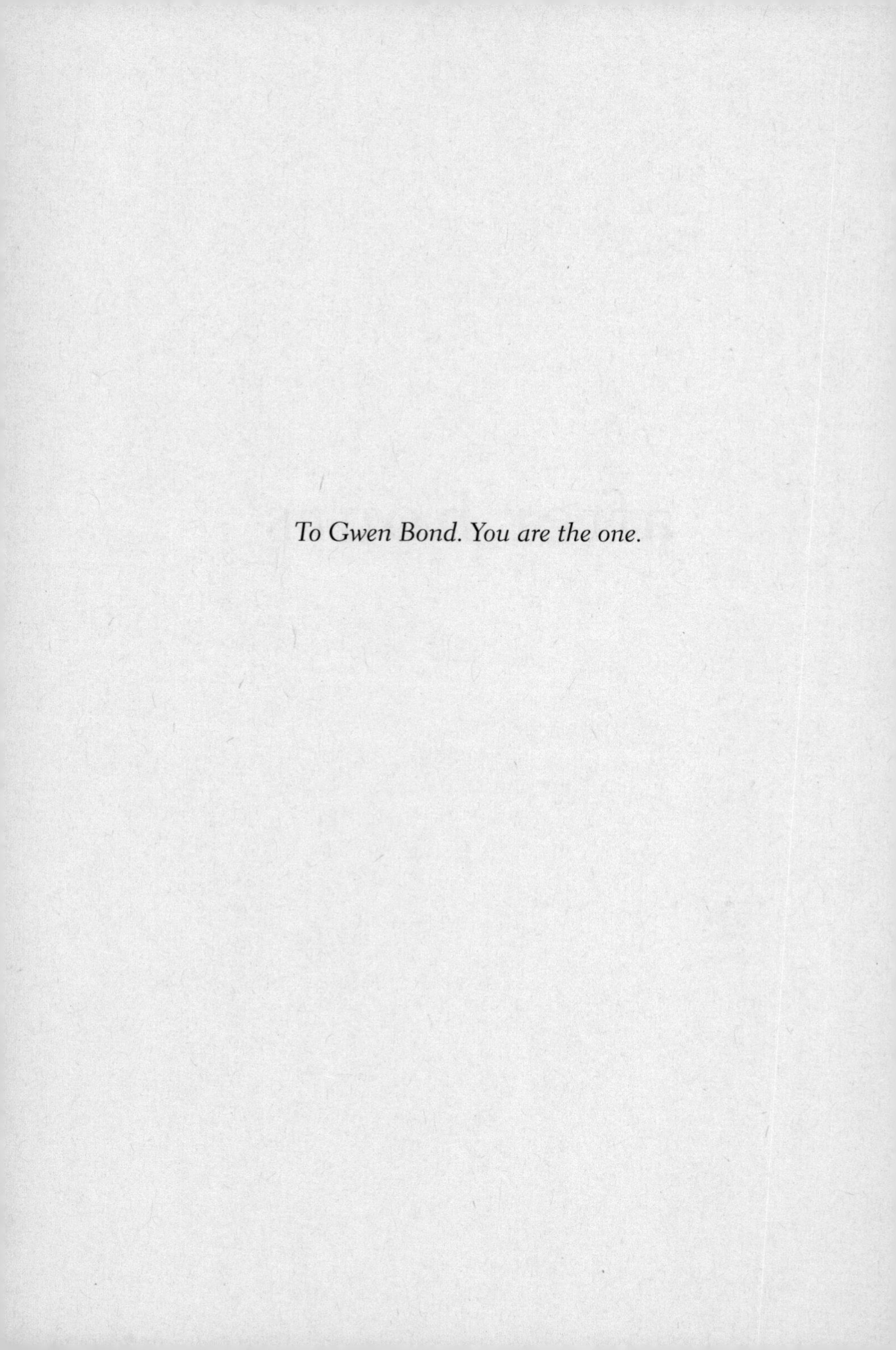

To Gwen Bond. You are the one.

PART ONE

PROLOGUE

Don't worry. I haven't forgotten about you. No, not at all.

Your turn will come. . . .

Oh, it hasn't been easy, this waiting. It takes a lot of patience and control.

And practice. . .

But my technique is perfect now.

Yes, you heard me. Killing Samantha Byrne and Emma Lewis was PRACTICE!

And it was fun.

I liked hearing them scream and beg. I LIKED IT!

I was almost sad when it was over. The lifeless look in their eyes. The blood running from their heads and out their mouths.

I thought wrapping Sam's hands with a Talcott tie was a nice touch, didn't you?

Oh. Of course you didn't.

I know, I know . . . so sad . . . so, so sad. . . .

But I'm coming for you. Do you hear me?

I want to see YOU gasp for air. I want to see YOU choke on your own blood. I want to be THE LAST THING YOU SEE when you take your final breath.

No, I won't let you get away.

It's time . . . IT'S TIME!

1

"I still see him," seventeen-year-old Kirsten Sawyer told her best friend, Julie Pembroke. She ran a shaky hand through her super-long chestnut-colored hair as she paced Julie's Victorian bedroom.

"Who?" Julie croaked from underneath a pile of covers on her bed.

"Kyle . . . I mean, Paul Stone . . . or whatever his name is," Kirsten said. She thought back to that day last October when she'd first met him and he'd told her his name was Kyle. He was so sweet and understanding when Kirsten told him how upset she was. That her best friend, Samantha Byrne, had been missing for days. Of course he was. It was later when Kirsten found out that Kyle was really Paul Stone, a convicted killer.

"You couldn't sleep again?" Julie asked.

Kirsten shook her head. "Every time I close my eyes, it's like he's on the inside of my eyelids. I even thought I saw him at the Party Room last weekend, Jules. It could have been him, right? He said he'd be back, remember?"

"Kirsten, think about it. There's *no way* he'd come back to the city. The police are looking for him big-time." Julie sat up in a sea of frilly designer sheets. Her hair was a mess of cropped blond bed-head, and two dark circles underneath her blue eyes were just waiting for some concealer. "Don't forget, he was convicted of killing Carolee Adams three years ago. And he's the major suspect in *two* new murder cases, Emma Lewis and—"

"Sam Byrne! I know!" Kirsten snapped. "How could I forget? She was our best friend! And she wound up dead in Central Park—practically right underneath my bedroom window. Kyle killed her. Wrapped her wrists in his Talcott tie before he bashed her head in and stabbed her and—"

"Stop it!" Julie cried. "This is sick. You can't keep reliving it. You know Sam wouldn't want that. Why can't you . . . just . . . stop?"

"How could we know what Sam would have wanted?" Kirsten asked. And how could Julie expect her to ignore the pain? She pulled a well-worn snapshot out of her jeans pocket. *The Three Amigas*—Julie, Kirsten, and Sam—hugging each other on the front steps of their old high school in Riverdale, The Woodley School. It was taken on the first day of senior year. They looked so happy then. So excited about their future after high school, only . . . Sam didn't graduate, did she?

Now that high school was over and done with, Kirsten and

Julie were going to spend the summer between Manhattan and Julie's house in the Hamptons before they began college in the fall. Their other two friends, Sarah Goldstein and Carla Hernandez, had already left for a summer in Tuscany. Then they were off to college at Barnard for four years. Who knew if Kirsten would even see them again? That's how much things had changed.

It was weird. The five girls had been inseparable all through grammar school, junior high, and high school. Through first dates and first drinks and first loves. But then Sam died. Now Kirsten and Julie were hardly friends with Carla and Sarah. They'd barely hugged at the Woodley graduation ceremony, and they only occasionally e-mailed one another.

They couldn't handle it anymore, Kirsten thought. *Carla and Sarah wanted to forget what Sam went through—and they did.*

"Just try to relax a little, okay?" Julie said.

"It's useless," Kirsten muttered, shoving the photo into the pocket of her Coach tote bag. She glanced out the window. "Plus it's late." Last night they had stayed out until ten . . . in the morning. Then she'd spent the rest of the day tossing and turning in Julie's bed. Now it was night again. It was time to go out—or maybe even go home.

"After the party, there's the after-party," Julie sang groggily, and made a goofy face at Kirsten, but Kirsten didn't smile.

"I've got to go, Jules," she said, suddenly feeling claustrophobic in the enormous room. "I'll call you later, okay?"

she said, grabbing her pink Coach tote and slipping into her matching Manolos. She opened the large oak door that led to the rest of Julie's sprawling town house.

"Wait, Kirsten!" Julie said. "Why don't you just stay over? I'll have the cook make us something sinful and we can have a movie marathon or something."

But Kirsten hurried out of the room. Out of the house. Out onto the hot, blustering street, the hot, balmy June air coating her arms and neck as she walked down Eighty-Fourth Street on the Upper East Side of Manhattan.

It was dark outside, and Kirsten couldn't believe she had wasted an entire day in freak-out mode. *It's ridiculous,* she thought. *Maybe Julie is right.* She glanced at her watch, but the face was blurry. She blinked. *Last night was rough, but I didn't think it was* that *rough.*

A garbage can lid clattered to the sidewalk behind Kirsten, and she whipped around. Nothing there.

Of course there's nothing there, Kirsten scolded herself. *Stop being so jumpy. Stop thinking people are out to get you. Just stop it!*

But still, every house seemed foreboding—every alleyway dark and scary.

New York isn't my city anymore, she thought as she hustled down the empty street. Her home hadn't been the same place ever since the last time she saw Kyle—the night he tried to kill her, and she'd escaped. Kirsten used to love the vastness of Manhattan; it felt like a big, anonymous playground. But now each stairwell, each unknown intersection, each shady building was just another hiding place for a murderer.

"Come inside, baaaa-bbbby."

Kirsten gasped and spun around again to see an elderly woman coaxing an overgrown shih tzu into a Bentley.

"Stupid, Kirsten," she muttered, resolving to make it home without suffering another breakdown. She hugged herself as she hurried down Eighty-Fourth Street, nearing Lexington. Then, unmistakably loud and clear, Kirsten heard heavy footsteps start off on the pavement behind her. She glanced back, spotting a scruffy older man with graying hair across the street.

As nonchalant as Kirsten tried to be, she could feel the muscles in her neck contract. *Calm down, freak show. He's across the street—besides, people are allowed to walk around at night,* she told herself, but her stomach began to tighten as the man suddenly crossed to her side of the street. His footsteps quickened.

So did Kirsten's. What if it *wasn't* all in her head? She tucked her purse under her arm and started hustling around the corner of Eighty-Fourth and Lexington. Tearing across the street, she headed uptown, toward a busier Eighty-Sixth Street, instead of heading to her building, which was on Eighty-First and Fifth. There was a subway there, and shops.

The footsteps kept coming as Kirsten raced toward the entrance. He was getting closer! Swerving through Eighty-Sixth Street's traffic, barely dodging a crosstown bus, Kirsten booked across the street. There was nowhere to go except down into the subway station.

Taking three steps at a time, she stumbled down the urine-soaked stairwell, falling to her knees.

"Owww!" A shock of pain ran up Kirsten's leg. A deep cut crisscrossed her knee. Then Kirsten saw her pursuer bounding down the stairs! She jumped up and darted toward the platform entrance and hopped the turnstile, ignoring the shouts of a Jamaican Metrocard-booth guy behind her. She hopped onto a local train just as the doors were slamming shut.

Finally safe, Kirsten stared at the man through the train's scratched-up window. He was running toward another woman on the platform now. When he reached her, he gave her an enormous hug and a kiss on the cheek. *Oh my God. He was rushing to meet his girlfriend or wife or something.*

She felt like a total idiot. Again.

"What the hell is wrong with me?" Kirsten muttered as the train screeched out of the station. She collapsed onto a gray bench and caught her breath, each gasp stinging her overworked lungs. She glanced around the empty subway car. *Not a good thing,* she thought.

Kirsten stood up again and decided to move to the next car, where she hoped she would see some people. But as she pulled open the metal door at the end of the car and walked into the next one, the overhead light flickered, then went black. A high-pitched sound of metal grinding on metal pierced her ears, and the train suddenly stopped, tossing Kirsten into the next car.

Someone must've pulled the emergency brake, Kirsten thought. She felt her way in the dark for a bench to sit on to wait for the conductor's announcement. Clearly there was no one in this car either.

Her arms outstretched, she turned and slipped on something, falling to the ground. The floor was slick for some reason. Wet. Sticky. And there was a stale metallic smell in the air. She tried to pull herself up, reaching blindly for a door handle, when the lights came back on.

Kirsten gasped. She was sitting in a pool of blood! Thick, gooey redness seeped into the fabric of her skirt. Hands and legs were slick and shiny and red. Slathered with blood. Covered with blood!

"I *told* you I was coming back," a voice said.

Kirsten looked up. Kyle, wide-eyed and manic, stood at the other end of the subway car! Kirsten tried to scream, but nothing came out of her throat.

Kyle walked slowly toward her, holding out a blood-stained tie. A *Talcott* tie! "I've come for you, Kirsten," he said, "just for you . . ."

The lights dimmed as Kyle broke into a run, his eyes piercing her mind, paralyzing her limbs.

"Save me!" Kirsten screamed. "Someone save me!"

2

"Save me," Kirsten said again, and opened her eyes.

She was lying on a black leather reclining chair in an ultra-modern Midtown office. No books. No warm pillows to cry into. Just a lone Calder print looming on the wall, herself in that chair and a concerned Dr. Helen Fitzgerald, Psychiatrist, staring at her from across the room. Somewhere, water was straining through a Zen rock garden.

"And then I woke up," Kirsten added. "Just like last time. The dream is always the same. It starts off with a normal conversation about Sam, and then it gets freaky and I end up covered in blood. Just before something really awful happens, I wake up," she sighed, not bothering to make eye contact with her newest psychiatrist.

"And then you can't fall back to sleep," Dr. Fitzgerald said.

Kirsten rolled her eyes. "Ding, ding, ding! Ten points for the psychiatrist in the blue suit."

Dr. Fitzgerald stiffened in her chair and smoothed a strand of short brown hair into place. She was Kirsten's third psychiatrist in as many months. *What's she going to say or do that's any different?* Kirsten thought as she looked the woman over.

Kirsten had already made a string of assumptions about her newest doctor: Fitzgerald was a forty-ish spinster whose Moderne taste was merely a cover-up for an ultra-boring lifestyle. She probably lived with fifteen cats and hoarded price-saver coupons.

"You've got to have patience, Kirsten," Fitzgerald assured her.

"But when am I going to stop freaking out over *nothing*?" Kirsten replied. "I mean, every minute of every day? Come on. And don't give me that psychobabble about having post-traumatic stress disorder. That doesn't help me."

"You've been through a lot." Fitzgerald crossed her legs and stared into Kirsten's eyes. "Don't deny yourself that. Don't try to speed through some quick-fix recovery."

"A quick fix is *exactly* what I need!" Kirsten yelled, though not really meaning it. She could be a bitch when she wanted to.

"That's bullshit, Kirsten, and you know it," Fitzgerald snapped back. "Stop hiding from the *real* issues."

Whoa. Hello. Kirsten jerked into a sitting position. *Maybe this one isn't like the others.*

"I'm here to help you," Dr. Fitzgerald added in a softer tone. "I'm not going to sit here and watch you suffer."

"I . . . feel . . . so . . . *guilty*," Kirsten heard herself confess. Her voice didn't even sound like her own. It was high-pitched and tentative, like a little girl's voice. She felt nervous sharing this deeper thought, but somehow, Fitzgerald's blunt honesty had made her seem trustworthy.

"How so?" Fitzgerald asked. Attentive. Clear. *Interested.*

No one wanted to hear about Kirsten's stresses anymore. She was a broken record. A record most of her friends and family wanted to store in the attic and forget all about. Even *Kirsten* was tired of going over the same memories—it had to stop. But how?

Fitzgerald stared into Kirsten's eyes with a warm, inviting smile that said, "It's okay. . . ."

"I can't help thinking that if I hadn't lied to Sam's parents and the police about where Sam was the night she vanished, maybe they could've found her in time. Before Kyle got to her," Kirsten admitted. "And . . . maybe if I had never met Kyle . . . or never attended Woodley . . . or never *existed*, maybe Emma would still be alive too!" Kirsten stared at Fitzgerald, tears streaming from her eyes. "It's *my* fault they're dead . . . *my* fault!" Kirsten sucked in a deep breath and went silent, clasping her shaking hands and waiting for the doctor to say something.

But she didn't—not for a while.

"Well, Kirsten," Fitzgerald finally began. "In psychiatric terms, when someone follows you in your dream world, it usually means that you're actually *looking* for someone. To save you. Because—"

"You are everyone in your dreams," Kirsten finished her sentence. "Freud."

"Ding, ding, ding! Ten points for the woman in the five-hundred-dollar shoes." Dr. Fitzgerald cracked a smile.

Fitzgerald definitely didn't have fifteen cats, Kirsten decided. "Sorry," she said. "I just want to be normal, you know?"

"And you deserve to find that normalcy," Fitzgerald replied. "You've been through hell and back, and now it's time to regroup. To regain the power over your life, to get some strength."

"Or just some *rest*," Kirsten added. "I'd be happy with just one good night of sleep."

"This should help a little," Fitzgerald told Kirsten as she scribbled out a prescription. "Just don't take more than one sleeping pill per night."

"Thanks." Kirsten smiled.

"But more than anything, Kirsten, the only way for you to feel better is to stay busy. Stay positive."

"Easier said than done," Kirsten replied.

"Well, for starters, your mom told me that you're working at a radio station this summer. WXRJ?"

"Interning," Kirsten corrected her.

"Pay or no pay, it's a great way to start dealing with life. Healthy distractions can offer a positive way to deal with loss."

"I guess you're right," Kirsten said. "If I keep obsessing over the past, why would the present get any better?"

"Exactly!" Fitzgerald smiled as she handed Kirsten the small white prescription note.

Kirsten tucked it into her purse.

And with that, Fitzgerald closed her notebook and stood up. "It's time to start your new life, Kirsten. It's time to move on."

3

"I don't get it," a male voice said from across the phone line.

"Because once you love *yourself* and really understand *why* you are interesting and unique, Maury, then you'll feel confident dating other people," Kate Grisholm replied.

"Ohhh, *now* I get it," Maury said.

Kirsten cracked a smile as she watched her boss give advice to a caller on her radio show. Two weeks into her internship at WXRJ and Kirsten was already fielding calls and monitoring the radio feed from where she worked in a room with computers they called the tech room. She knew working on *Love Stinks, with Kate Grisholm* would be interesting, but she'd had no idea that she'd be doing so much with the live show. She loved the sense of responsibility her job gave her.

Out in Studio Five, Kate gave Kirsten a thumbs-up sign and transferred the call back to Kirsten.

"Thanks for calling *Love Stinks*," Kirsten added before letting the caller go.

"No—thank *you*," he replied. "From now on, I'm gonna say, 'Maury, you're the man!'"

"Exactly! You're the man, Maury!" Kirsten hung up and laughed to herself.

"What's so funny?" a guy behind her asked.

Kirsten gasped, startled. She spun around in her seat—to see a total hottie looking out from a tangle of blond hair and holding a stack of manila envelopes.

"Whoa. Sorry. I didn't mean to scare you." The hottie smiled. Cute.

"You didn't *scare* me," Kirsten lied, trying to regain her cool factor, which was not going to be easy.

"I'm Brian."

"Kirsten."

An awkward pause.

"I'm a mail," Brian stated proudly, breaking the silence.

"I can see that." Kirsten smirked. Okay, maybe seeming cool to this guy would be easier than she'd thought.

"Oh . . . no, um, I'm a *mail intern* is what I meant to say," Brian added, nodding at the envelopes in his hands with a shy grin. "Today's my first day."

"I can see that, too," Kirsten couldn't help teasing him.

Brian's face flushed. He was cute. Very cute.

"I mean, in a perfect world, I'd be down in Cape May surfing or whatever," Brian loosened up, leaning against the doorway. "But as far as work goes, radio's pretty cool, you know?"

"So you're not from the city?" Kirsten asked, even though it was obvious that he wasn't. He had "I'm-not-from-Manhattan" written all over him. Wild and wavy blond hair, extremely loose Ocean Pacific pants, and granola-boy sandals. She liked it.

"Me? No way. I'm from New Jersey." Brian chuckled and looked at his feet.

"Well, I'd be happy to show you the ropes, Jersey Boy." Kirsten winked and looked him over again. He seemed nice. Different. It was refreshing to talk to a guy who was a little shy—not like the guys she was used to being around.

"Really? That'd be great because—"

Just then, Kirsten noticed Kate Grisholm taking off her headphones and closing down the main studio. The show was ending.

"Shit!" Kirsten shouted. She turned back to the phones, transferring the waiting calls to the sign-off tape that told them to call tomorrow, "even if Love Stinks!" Kate was a tough boss who expected everything to run like clockwork, and Kirsten didn't want to mess up this opportunity. "Earth to Kirsten," Kirsten joked, turning back to Brian. "I totally spaced out for a second. . . . Long weekend."

"That's cool." Brian grinned as he tucked a ringlet behind his ear. "I space out all the time."

"Really?"

"Mmm-hmm . . . ," Brian said.

Again, silence butted its way into their conversation. This time, however, it was kind of sweet.

"Well, it's very nice to meet you, Kirsten," Brian said finally.

Back out in the main studio, Kate rapped against the glass partition and mouthed *good night* to her interns.

"Oops," Kirsten said, jumping up to clear out the studio before the next show.

"Oh. I'm getting you in trouble," Brian realized. "Let me get out of your way. . . . Um . . . okay, then . . ." Brian frowned slightly, shrugged his shoulders, and walked out.

"Wait. Brian?" Kirsten looked up, realizing she might have seemed a little rude, but Brian was already halfway down the hallway with his pile of mail. "See you around!" she called out, trying to salvage her first interaction with the only cute guy her age at WXRJ.

Kirsten turned back to her work, straightening Studio Five WXRJ, when the phone rang. *That's weird,* she thought. *The calls aren't supposed to come into the studio after the show's ended.* She looked at the digital readout, but there was no flashing caller ID number. The phone kept ringing. After a few more seconds of hesitation, she answered it. *"Love Stinks,"* she said in her best professional voice.

"I know," a guy replied.

Kirsten's hands began to shake. It sounded like . . . *him*. Like Kyle. But it couldn't be, right? It couldn't! "Caller, can you please identify yourself?" she asked.

"It's me, Kirsten," the voice said.

Kirsten almost fell out of her chair. It was Kyle. She'd recognize his deep, breathy voice anywhere. Just the very *sound* of it started to constrict her lungs. This *has to be a dream,* she told herself. *Another nightmare!*

"I need to speak to you," he said. His voice sounded urgent, upset.

"How did you know where to find me?" she asked him, starting to panic, wondering *where* he was calling from. Was he back in New York? Could he have gotten into the station somehow?

"I—I just want to talk," he said.

Frightened, Kirsten looked around for Brian. Maybe she could get him—or anybody—to walk her out of the building. But Brian was gone, and the studio seemed strangely quiet.

"How did you get this number?" Kirsten demanded again.

"I couldn't risk calling your cell," Kyle explained. "I found out where you were through Woodley's intern program."

Kirsten felt her stomach flood with acid. Not even one of the most prestigious schools in the country could protect her privacy. "Leave me alone, Kyle, I mean, *Paul*!" she screamed, and grabbed her purse off a desk.

"Don't use that name!" he yelled back. "And I told you. I

just want to talk. You don't have to be afraid of me!"

Yeah, right. That's what he said the last time I saw him—right before he tried to kill me! Kirsten slammed her headset on the desk and bolted out of the studio, knocking over a stack of DAT tapes on her way out.

As Kirsten fumbled with the keys to Studio Five, she heard a door open somewhere down the hallway; she shuddered with desperation. She found the right key, jammed it into the lock, and booked it down the long hallway. She'd make it to security on the first floor and stay there all night if she had to.

Kirsten rounded the corner and slammed into a waiting elevator. She must've pressed "L" a hundred times as she waited for the door to close. *Almost there, almost there . . .*

Then, just as the brass door began to swish closed, a hand slipped through the opening!

It's him! Kirsten thought, squeezing her eyes shut. *He said he'd come back for me—and here he is!*

4

"Where are you rushing off to?" Kate asked, shifting her large leather bag onto her shoulder.

Kirsten opened her eyes as the elevator door closed. She was now alone with her boss for the first time and she was acting like a crazy person!

"Are you all right?" Kate asked.

"Oh . . . I, uh . . . I have an appointment," Kirsten said, trying to come up with something believable. "A doctor's appointment." A line of sweat beaded across her forehead.

Kate frowned. "At night?" she asked. The lie wasn't very good.

"What?" Kirsten said, racking her brain for a better excuse. Nothing.

"You have an appointment *at night*? You must have a great doctor," Kate added.

"Yep. It's part of a new health plan at Sinai," Kirsten said as they arrived at the lobby and the elevator door opened.

"See you tomorrow!" She bolted out of the elevator and through the main lobby.

As Kirsten ran into the pedestrian traffic of Times Square, thoughts of Kyle slammed back into her head. She looked around frantically, trying to find him in a sea of faces, but Times Square was too bright and too busy. A garish electronic billboard flashed obnoxiously on the side of a building, illuminating the people with shades of greens, blues, browns. *Kyle could be anywhere!*

Kirsten pushed her way up Broadway, but she had no idea where she was headed. Her parents were off antiquing upstate somewhere and wouldn't get back until tomorrow. And Kirsten didn't exactly want to go home to an empty apartment right about now. Then she realized there was only one place she wanted to be at a time like this—one place where she'd feel safe, at least for a little while.

Kirsten rooted through her purse, found her cell phone, and punched in a number as she jostled through the people and made her way toward the Upper East Side of Manhattan. One ring, two rings, three rings . . .

Come on. Come on! Kirsten thought.

"What's up, baby?" Julie answered.

"Meet me at the Party Room!" Kirsten said.

"Sounds like you handled it well," Scott, the infamous bartender at the Party Room, yelled over a pack of giggling

Woodley School sophomores as he handed Kirsten one of his trademark mojitos.

The Party Room's elegant oak bar was packed tonight, with the usual crowd of soon-to-be power players in the business world, fashion world, publishing world . . . or *any* world they wanted, really. In other words, an elite group that defined what it meant to be young and rich in New York City, *and* who knew how to work it. Oh, there were a few faces missing, probably already summering in Provence or wherever their families liked to summer. Others, like Kirsten, were biding their time in the city, working at amazingly fortunate internships and making the trek out to their family's twenty-eight-room summer "cottages" in the Hamptons on Long Island every Friday night.

"Come on, Scott," Kirsten said. "I broke out into a cold sweat and Kate *knew* I was lying. It wasn't pretty, believe me! Now my boss is *sure* I'm a lunatic."

"Well, so what?" Scott said. "You had a right to freak out. You got a call from a *murderer.* Give me a break!"

"Yeah, about that call . . . ," Kirsten began. "I was so *sure* it was Kyle, but now . . . I don't know. Maybe I was just imagining it. Maybe I just freaked out again." She took a long sip of her drink, suddenly feeling exhausted from the whole ordeal.

Scott ignored the b-boy who was standing at the bar, waiting for a refill of Guinness, and rested a brotherly hand on Kirsten's arm. "You're going to be okay," he said, "but I don't want you to be taking any chances with this guy. He's a maniac. If you think he called you, I believe you, Kirsten. Don't doubt your instincts."

"Thanks, Scott-land," Kirsten said. Over the past few months he had become a real friend. When most of her other friends had begun to doubt Kirsten's sanity, Scott had always been there to support her, making her feel comfortable and safe. She didn't know what she'd do without him.

"And don't worry about the elevator thing with your boss," Scott continued. "Kate Grisholm probably didn't even notice it."

Forever busy, Scott turned to help the giggling girls and the b-boy. The sophomores ordered their requisite draft beers, and when Scott leaned over to get some glasses, they literally gasped at the view of what could quite possibly be the world's most perfect ass.

Desperate much? Kirsten thought. Giggly sophomores were so hilarious, but she couldn't blame them, really. Scott was a major hottie, for sure—kind of like a young Tom-Cruise-meets-Justin-Timberlake type, only taller and nicer and with a smile that could melt a heart from a thousand miles away.

Kirsten smiled for a moment. She and her friends had been just like that back in tenth grade. To them, every night they were able to get into the Party Room was another night they'd spent leaning up against the bar, licking their lips as seductively as they could, angling to score some free drinks from the hot bartender.

Kirsten laughed out loud. She felt a rush of alcohol swirl in her brain, so she steadied herself on her barstool.

"What's so funny?" someone asked.

Kirsten smiled and spun around. "Jules! I'm so glad to see you!" She immediately sprang forward and hugged her. As she squeezed Julie tight, Kirsten felt a swelling in her throat, the kind that promised tears.

"Um, good to see you too," Julie said. "What's up, Kirsten?"

"I just really need a friend right now. I—I think he called me today," Kirsten confessed, pulling back.

"Who?" Julie clearly had no idea why Kirsten dragged her out tonight.

"Kyle!" Kirsten cried. "Who else?"

Julie rolled her eyes. "Oh."

Kirsten tilted her head. What was that all about? Then she realized. "Oh my God," she murmured. "Not you, too, Jules. . . . You don't believe me!"

"No, sweetie . . . sure, I do . . ." Julie paused. "Well, at least I *want* to. It's just that there've been so many times when—"

"When *what*?" Kirsten demanded. She was getting angry now. Sure, it was okay if Kirsten doubted herself at times, but Julie was her *best friend*; someone who was supposed to be there—through good times and bad.

"Nothing. Forget it," Julie said. She sat at the bar, and Scott poured her her usual pomegranate martini.

But Kirsten wasn't finished. She wanted to know what Julie was really thinking. "Say it, Julie!"

"Okay!" Julie shrugged. "It's just that you've been kind of . . . extra *sensitive* lately . . . and . . . um . . . I'm not sure when you're experiencing something real or just *thinking* it's real." Julie put a hand on Kirsten's shoulder. "Like the other day, for instance. Remember when you thought someone was chasing you and it turned out to be just some guy rushing to meet his wife?"

Kirsten nodded. The comment hit her like a punch . . . because it was true.

"I mean, how do you know it was Kyle?" she asked. "Did he say, 'Hi, it's Kyle'?"

Kirsten thought back. "No, not exactly," she admitted. Did she freak out over nothing again? Did Kyle really call her, or was it all in her head? Her head began to swirl, thinking about it all.

Julie sighed and looked at the bar. "Look, I didn't mean to—"

"No." Kirsten sighed. "You're right." She stared into Julie's eyes. "I'm losing it."

And this time, Julie hugged her back. They embraced for a long time at the bar as people looked on.

"That's what friends are for!" sang a sarcastic voice behind Kirsten and Julie.

The two girls simultaneously turned around to find

themselves face-to-face with Leslie Fenk, otherwise known as the Woodley Bitch.

"You guys gonna get out of the way or what?" Leslie slurred.

Julie smirked at Leslie's slutty Gaultier dress. With her platinum-highlighted hair pulled into a messy-on-purpose ponytail, Leslie looked like a bad version of Paris Hilton tonight. "Take *my* seat. All of a sudden I feel sick." Julie hopped off her stool and leaned into Kirsten's ear. "Gotta go to the bathroom," she whispered. "Hold Leslie off until I get back."

Kirsten laughed as Julie hurried off through the crowded bar.

Leslie tilted her head. "Do you have something to share with the rest of the class, Ms. Sawyer?" she quipped sarcastically.

"You know what, Leslie?" Kirsten sighed. "I'm not in the mood today." She drained her glass and tried to get Scott's attention. He was swamped, so she'd have to suffer through more alone time with Leslie until Julie returned.

"What happened to poor little Kirrrrrrsten *this* time?" Leslie pressed, swaying back and forth. She was loaded.

"Life happened," Kirsten found herself saying.

"Amen to that, sister," Leslie slurred heavily as she plopped down on the stool next to Kirsten.

"SISTER"? Did Leslie Fenk just call me "sister"? The night

was getting weirder and weirder. The two rivals sat quietly for a moment as they both strained to get Scott's attention.

"Know why everyone thinks I'm such a bitch?" Leslie suddenly asked, making sure her neckline plunged deep enough for Scott.

"I don't know." Kirsten rolled her eyes. "Why?"

Leslie laughed to herself and then faced Kirsten with a smile. "'Cause I am!" she cheered. Leslie was in rare form tonight.

As hard as she tried to remain icy, Kirsten felt a smile creep across her own face.

"I just can't help it," Leslie added. "It's like people with Tourette's syndrome, or whatever it's called. They bark out all this weird stuff every now and then, even if they don't want to, even though they *wanna* bottle up all that stuff and just . . . be . . . normal and nice-y, nice. . . . I mean, if someone's wearing double denim or has a reeaallly vicious panty line or something like that," Leslie continued, "it's only so long before I have to say *something* about it, right? Like, 'Howdy buckaroo!' Or, 'Are you wearing Depends?'"

Kirsten broke into a laugh. *At least Leslie is funny. I could use some comic relief.*

"Do I make any sense at all?" Leslie asked as she leaned into the brass railing that lined the bar. She was cashing out. Big-time.

"Maybe." Kirsten shrugged.

"Hey, pep up!" Leslie said, poking Kirsten in the arm

several times. "I feel like I'm talking to a brick wall."

Kirsten rolled her eyes. "Sorry to disappoint you, Leslie, but I *told* you I'm not in the mood for fun and games."

"Okaaaaay, okaaaaay," Leslie said, holding up her hands. Then she let out a big exaggerated sigh and opened her tiny leopard Gucci party purse. "Look, I was going to save this for myself, but *obviously* you need it more than I do." She pulled out something and shoved it into Kirsten's palm. "Don't say I never gave you anything."

Kirsten looked at the two iridescent green pills in her hand.

"A little pick-me-up!" Leslie said. "Go for it." And with that, she slid off the barstool, kissed Kirsten on both cheeks, and slunk off to a posse of frat boys.

Did that just happen? Kirsten asked herself as she watched Leslie flirt. Then she glanced at the pills. *I've been a real drag lately. Maybe I do need a little help.*

Julie returned from the bathroom. "So did you tell her off?" she asked Kirsten.

Kirsten discretely downed the pills and chased them with Julie's drink. Then she turned to face her friend. "Totally," she lied.

Julie sat back down and slung an arm over Kirsten's shoulder. "Let's just forget about Kyle altogether tonight, all right?"

"You're right," Kirsten agreed. "I don't want to think about him ever again."

5

Think it's that easy? Think you can just snap your fingers and wish me away?

I hate this place. Too hot in the summer. Stinks like urine, rotting garbage, horse crap.

It blows my mind how naive you can be.

You can't run away from me.

I'm just growing stronger. Smarter. Bolder. All the time keeping my control, though.

I won't give you the satisfaction of losing my temper again. Everything I do is cool. Cold. Frosty, even.

You see, I'm whistling while I work!

Hot, hot heat. It's boiling inside. Shit!

You WON'T slip away this time! You can't HIDE FROM YOUR FATE!

You've just been lucky. That's all. But luck changes just like everything else. Just like you've changed. Just like my life changed when you entered it.

Well, now it's time to leave my life. Get out for good.

YOU GOT THAT!?

Too hot.

Can't breathe.

Got . . . to . . . breathe. That's all. Just . . . find . . . some . . . space.

It's only a matter of time.

And I've got all the time in the world. . . .

6

"See you next time!" Kirsten hugged Scott as she stumbled out of the Party Room.

Her friend was closing up inside, and the smell of stale beer drove Kirsten to the street. Scott had let her stick around until she was the last person standing in the bar. Or almost standing, as the case may be.

Julie was long gone already. Kirsten vaguely remembered her friend leaving the bar around midnight. Something about how she'd rather watch *Sex and the City* reruns in her town house than be "the latest cautionary tale of 'debutantes gone bad.'"

Now what? Kirsten wondered. She was a little drunk, but so totally awake, and she still didn't feel like going home. But what else was there to do? She stepped off the curb and jutted a hand into the air to flag down a taxi.

An enormous stretch Hummer screeched alongside, almost hitting her. "What the hell!" she cried, stumbling back onto the sidewalk. "You almost ran me over!"

Leslie Fenk popped her head out of the sunroof, grasping a glass of champagne. "Nice ass!" she cried, checking out Kirsten.

Kirsten snapped up and smoothed out the back of her miniskirt. "That's sexual harassment, Fenk!" Kirsten joked. "I'm getting a lawyer!"

"Ohh, I'm sooooo scared," Leslie played along.

"What's up?" Kirsten shouted as the Hummer idled loudly next to her.

"See for yourself." Leslie let out a low, trucker-size burp. "Get your butt in here!" she added before a hand reached up and pulled her down inside the car. Leslie screamed and laughed, then popped her head back out of the sunroof. "There's a hot deejay spinning at Vinyl tonight."

"You mean *this morning*?" Kirsten said.

"Yeah. Now. Whatever." Leslie apparently wasn't much for details. "He's got some kind of French name, so you know it's going to be tight. You coming?"

The door to the car opened, and Kirsten could hear the loud thumping of a vicious techno song. *Why not?* she thought. "Move over!" she said, and climbed into the car. As she slid into a plush leather seat, she was literally enveloped by a cloud of pot smoke. A crew of bug-eyed, chuckling Talcott boys were getting stoned as Leslie Fenk lay across their laps.

A kid in a black hoodie—red eyes peering out—shoved a

short brown blunt in Kirsten's direction. Without even thinking, Kirsten took a long drag.

"Damn, Leslie!" one of the boys shouted. "You got more hot friends like this?"

The kid gave Kirsten a sinister smile, but she didn't care. She took another long drag, letting the pot smoke sting her lungs. As she coughed out smoke to the delight of the other bombed-out passengers, the Hummer screeched back to life and tore downtown.

Two songs later and the Hummer skidded to a halt outside the front doors of Vinyl. Kirsten and the rest of the crew poured out onto the street, laughing and shouting. Immediately, Leslie worked her flirtatious magic with a thick bouncer outside the club. Within seconds, Kirsten found herself being swept up inside the velvet curtains.

The club was hot. Very hot. Break beats clacked through a vast deep-blue room.

Kirsten couldn't make out any faces yet—but she didn't have to. She knew who was there. Vinyl's regulars were a crazy mix of hip-hop heads from private schools, NYU kids on E, and strung-out performance artists from Williamsburg, Brooklyn.

Leslie's posse spread out into the jamming crowd, and Kirsten fought her way to the bar. "Anything strong!" she shouted to a sexy bartender over a pulsing Jungle track.

A shaky hand slapped a twenty down on the marble bar next to her. "It's on me."

Kirsten turned around to see Brandon Yardley, another recent Woodley graduate, looking, well, terrible: half-moons under his full-moon pupils, a ratty beard, his nostrils red and raw. It looked as if he'd been through hell and hadn't quite made it back yet.

Kirsten was definitely not in the mood to talk to him. He used to go out with Sam—and recently he'd gone from being a heavy drug user to a *really* heavy drug user. He was obnoxious and very aggressive, so much that he'd threatened Kirsten on several occasions after Sam's death. Now, looking at him wobbling and blinking, trying to make his eyes look "not so bloodshot," Kirsten didn't understand what Sam ever saw in him. Actually, she never understood it back then, either.

Brandon stared at Kirsten for a long time, as if he was waiting for something.

"You look like a million bucks, Brandon," Kirsten finally cracked. She took a sip of a purplish concoction as the bartender made change for Brandon.

"Funny." Brandon's dead expression didn't change. "You don't look so hot yourself, Kirsten."

Good point.

"Thanks for the drink," Kirsten muttered, shaking her head and turning away.

"Wait. I want to tell you something. Something about Sam." Brandon grabbed her arm, stopping her.

"Just don't, Brandon," Kirsten warned. The last thing she

wanted to do was talk to him about Sam. She remembered the last time he had gotten her alone and wanted to talk about Sam. It was on the last day she had seen Sam alive—after a late night at the Party Room. Sam had left early with some guy, and Brandon was jealous. In fact, he'd practically accosted Kirsten on the street, wanting to know where they were so that he could bash the guy's face in!

Then Kirsten noticed tears welling in Brandon's eyes. He let go of her arm and swiped them away. "Remember when we were all friends? You . . . me . . . Sam?" he asked. "You remember that, don't you? When everything was good?"

Kirsten nodded. She vaguely remembered a couple of times when they had all gone out together. It was fun. But that was before Sam broke up with him. Way before.

"I miss those times," he said. "You and I . . . we should be . . . I don't know . . . *friends*," Brandon added as he brushed a curl out of Kirsten's face. "*Close* friends. Don't you think Sam would have wanted that?"

"NO!" Kirsten cried. "You must be tripping on something serious tonight." She tried to move away from him, but Brandon stopped her.

"Listen to me for a second!" he yelled. "We *both* lost Sam. And I lost Emma, too! I'm messed up, and I need to talk to someone. Is that so much to ask?"

Kirsten felt the tears coming back too. Why couldn't she get away from the pain for one night? Just one night! Kirsten pushed past Brandon, but he reeled her back in with no thought to his strength versus her slight frame.

"I know things, Kirsten!" he said, his eyes drugged out and wild. "You have to listen to me! I went to Talcott. I—"

"I can't do this, Brandon!" Kirsten winced. She could smell the whiskey on his breath. "No more! Please!"

Suddenly, Brandon's expression darkened. "Maybe you're right, Kirsten. I guess we can't be friends." His fingers crept slowly across Kirsten's chest, up her neck, around her throat.

"Get. Your. Hands. Off. Me," Kirsten said through clenched teeth. She reached down into her pocketbook and slowly found her keys, ready to stab. No one around them seemed to notice or care about their standoff. *You have no idea, Brandon,* she thought, feeling the rage swelling in her chest. She was tired of being a victim.

Brandon leaned into Kirsten, but right before she was forced to fight back, Leslie Fenk came to the rescue.

"Kirsten's *my* date tonight, Brannnndon!" Leslie chirped, nuzzling her cheek next to Kirsten's.

Brandon stepped away, shocked.

Kirsten relaxed, and added on to Leslie's game. "You didn't know about us, Brannnndon?"

"Whatever," Brandon slurred. "I'll get you later, Kirsten."

"Good luck, asshole!" Leslie shouted. "She's all mine!"

Although Leslie was quite possibly the craziest person Kirsten had ever met, at that moment, crazy seemed like the only way to be. Before her mother's voice could find its way over the thumping bass lines, Kirsten leaned over and kissed Leslie fully on the lips. "Thanks, Leslie. You saved my life."

"Woodley sluts unite!" Leslie screamed, and dragged her new pal toward the crowded dance floor.

As they fled, Kirsten managed to swing her head back to see Brandon one last time before a couple of girls dressed in vintage 1960s minidresses and rocking out to their own tune blocked her view.

The girls continued toward the dance floor, and Leslie handed Kirsten a small red pill with an "xxx" stamped on both sides. "Here," she said. "We're going to be here all night." Leslie swallowed an identical one and then twirled into the crowd with her hands in the air. "Now let's party!" she cried.

Kirsten swallowed hers and joined Leslie. As she let her body free, a flash of strobe lights went off through the club and the room started filling with white smoke. It rolled in thick, and soon Kirsten couldn't see anything around her.

Leslie squealed with joy as multicolored lasers pulsed through the smoke. "This is so crazy!"

A few minutes later, Kirsten began to feel a little woozy. She reached out for Leslie but couldn't find her anywhere. A cold gust raised the hair on the back of her neck, and Kirsten realized that she was alone.

In the center of a crowded, pulsing club, but completely alone.

7

BEEP! BEEP! BEEP! BEEP! *BEEP! BEE—*

THWACK! Kirsten slammed her fist against her Hello Kitty alarm clock, knocking it to the floor. "Shit! I'm late!" she cried out. She blinked several times, but the bleary pain in her eyes wasn't going anywhere.

When she sat up in bed, Kirsten's head split open with pain. A series of images flashed through her mind: crashing on a couch in a back room of the club, someone strong dragging her back into the Hummer, a bumpy ride, more smoke filling her lungs, stumbling past José, her morning doorman.

Kirsten looked down at the alarm clock, still wailing on the floor.

12:16!

She was late. Very late. After the elevator run-in yesterday, Kirsten knew she couldn't afford to make another bad impression on Kate Grisholm.

She downed two of the pills Leslie had given her this morning and swallowed a lipstick-y glass of stale water, then scrambled to get dressed. No time for a shower. No time to worry about looking cute for that surfer boy, Brian.

No time to care, Kirsten reminded herself, and sprinted out of the apartment, down onto the street.

Summer in NYC was oppressive. It was already steamy outside when Kirsten raced out of the lobby. She broke into an immediate sweat as José hailed her a cab.

"You all right, Ms. Sawyer?" José asked.

"I'm fine, José, thanks," Kirsten blurted, sopping up the stream of sweat running down her back.

"I've known you for a long time, Ms. Sawyer," José surprised her by continuing to stand by her side. He furrowed his brows and looked Kirsten up and down. "I've seen you grow up. . . ."

"Yep!" Kirsten replied absentmindedly, still scanning the streets for a cab.

"And I have never seen you look so—" José cut off as a cab pulled in front of the building. He opened the door and waited for Kirsten to climb inside.

"What?" Kirsten turned back to him before getting into the taxi. She was curious now. "What is it?"

"Well, I've never seen you look . . . so . . . lost," he admitted. "Are you sure you're okay?"

Kirsten nodded, but her heart sank. She felt like total crap at that moment. For some reason, her doorman's opinion shook her deeply. She slipped into the cab and mumbled WXRJ's address to her driver. As the cab sped away, Kirsten felt a pit in her stomach. The man who had been calling her cabs for the last seventeen years had summarized Kirsten Sawyer in one word: *lost.*

Kirsten pulled out a mirror from her purse and looked at her reflection: She looked awful. Her once sparkling brown eyes were now sunken and blank. Her shiny hair had lost its luster. Her skin was pale and pasty. She *did* look lost.

Kyle had invaded her dreams, her thoughts, and now, even her soul. Tears began to stream down her face. *That's it. No more!* She pulled her cell phone out of her purse and quickly dialed a number.

"Precinct!" a shrill voice announced over the line.

"Detective Peterson, please," Kirsten pleaded between sobs. "I have new information on Paul Stone."

Kirsten sank into the backseat, wiped tears from her eyes, and tried to collect herself. It was the millionth time she'd called Detective Peterson, the young cop in charge of the Sam Byrne murder case, but this time Kirsten had something real.

"Homicide," Peterson rasped. His voice sounded tired, overworked.

"Hey. It's Kirsten," she said.

"How can I help you today, Ms. Sawyer?" Peterson asked.

Kirsten could hear someone was shouting in the precinct. She imagined Peterson standing next to the booking desk, taking time out of his crazy schedule to field yet *another* call from that psycho teenager.

Screw it, Kirsten told herself as she pressed on. *I've come this far. . . .*

"I think Kyle called me," she said.

"You think?" Peterson asked.

Kirsten wondered if he believed her at all. She looked outside the cab and shook her head. Her taxi was crawling through Midtown traffic. At this rate, running would get Kirsten to WXRJ faster.

"I imagine he didn't reveal any information about his *whereabouts* did he?" Peterson asked.

"No," Kirsten admitted.

"And did he threaten you in any way?"

"Not really, but—"

"Did he line up a place to meet with you, or another time he'd call?"

"No," Kirsten confessed. She was starting to feel stupid for calling. What new information did she really have, anyway?

"Listen, Ms. Sawyer," Peterson sighed. "I'll make a note of the phone call, and I *assure* you that my guys will continue to work on this. But until we have a more substantial lead, there's not much more I can do right now."

Kirsten stared at her face in the compact once more. She just wished it could all be over already. But unlike movies and dime-store thrillers, real life didn't wrap up conveniently. And, apparently, young detectives didn't always save the day. "Thanks, anyway," she said, but Peterson was already off the line.

Stuffing her cell phone back into her purse, Kirsten looked out of the greasy cab window. She was still five blocks away from work, and now they were stuck behind a garbage truck.

Kirsten gave the driver a twenty, opened the door, and ran the rest of the way to work. When she finally arrived at Studio Five, Kirsten was literally covered in sweat. And, much worse than that, Kate Grisholm was already in there, preparing to start the live show.

Kirsten ducked low behind the glass-paneled wall and sped through the hallway, barely evading her boss. Rounding the corner, she quietly slid into the tech studio and closed the door. *Close call,* she thought.

But then she heard him!

Brian. Even though it wasn't his job, he was setting up the phone log, checking Kate's computer. He was covering for Kirsten!

"Look what the cat dragged in," Brian kidded, looking up through his blond curls.

"Alarm clock didn't go off," Kirsten said, and immediately got to work. "Thanks for covering for me." She took over the task of getting the phone bank ready to start fielding calls.

"No problem," Brian winked as he moved out of her way and opened the door to leave.

Kirsten smiled at a curious Kate Grisholm out in the studio and gave her the thumbs-up signal.

"So, I'll see you—"

"Love Stinks," Kirsten interrupted Brian as she answered the first caller. She mouthed *sorry* to him as she typed the caller's name on her computer.

Checking to make sure Kate wasn't looking, Kirsten finally looked back at him. "I'm going to make this up to you," she whispered as the theme music to *Love Stinks* piped through the studio.

"I hope so," Brian said smiling.

Is he flirting? Kirsten wondered.

"There's a party this weekend out in the Hamptons. You should come," she said. "As my official invite. As a thank-you."

"Really?"

"Really," Kirsten said as she switched to the next call.

"That sounds cool," Brian said, smiling back. "Actually, I'm staying out there on the weekends, anyway. Over in Amagansett. Surfing."

"Well then, it's a date," Kirsten said.

"Is it?" Brian teased. He then moved to grab the envelope he'd left on the phone bank. He lingered as he reached right past Kirsten.

He smelled good. Really good.

Still close to her, Brian turned and whispered, "I like you, Kirsten."

"I thought you were an innocent Jersey Boy." Kirsten smiled.

"I *am* from Jersey, but I never said I was innocent." Brian winked again as he walked out of the tech room.

Wow. He really is cute, Kirsten thought with a slight grin as she sifted through a pile of prerecorded commercials. She liked Brian, too. She liked him a lot. But was she ready for feelings like these?

The Zen fountain in Dr. Fitzgerald's office bubbled as usual. Kirsten found herself getting lost in its tranquil sound.

After a long, stressful day at WXRJ, Kirsten lay back on the sleek black leather recliner and poured out her thoughts. "Brian's obviously sweet and nice and all that, but—"

"But *what*?" Dr. Fitzgerald smiled.

And Kirsten smiled too. She couldn't help it. Doctor Fitzgerald had found a way to win her confidence, and now Kirsten felt as if she were gossiping with a friend—to a point. She wasn't about to tell Fitzgerald about how she'd been partying nonstop for the past few weeks.

"I'm just not ready to get involved with another guy," Kirsten said. "Not yet."

"Fine. But I'm just saying you should keep your options open," Fitzgerald replied. "A little romance might be a nice distraction."

"With my luck, Brian will end up being a psychotic killer too!" Kirsten cracked.

"What if he's not?" Fitzgerald continued. "What if he's just a really good kisser?"

"Is this *The Bachelorette* or something?" Kirsten shot back. "Why are you so hot for me to start dating again?"

"It's not just about dating, Kirsten. It's about *living.* I'm just trying to get you to loosen up a little. Life won't move on until you *let it* move on."

"But how can I do that if I can't stop thinking about Sam?" Kirsten countered. Just mentioning her friend's name made her feel a lump in her throat.

"Have you visited Sam's parents since the murder?" Fitzgerald suddenly asked.

"No, not after the funeral," Kirsten admitted. "I haven't been able to bring myself to see them. I mean, come on. I lied about Sam staying over with me the night she was killed! Then I protected Kyle."

"You know, sometimes comforting someone else can be the best comfort for yourself," Dr. Fitzgerald said. "Maybe it's time you paid them a visit."

Maybe I should, Kirsten said to herself. It was a good idea—one that she hoped she had the courage to actually go through with. "All right." Kirsten looked at her watch. The hour was up. "If I'm going to move on, I'd better get a move on."

Dr. Fitzgerald tilted her head. "See you in a few days," she said.

Kirsten walked out of Dr. Fitzgerald's office feeling lighter. Maybe relaxed for the first time in a while, even a little confident. She exited back onto Park Avenue and headed up Eighty-Third Street, almost jogging with her newly found energy—until she slammed into someone.

"Whoa!" It was Scott, looking alarmed.

"Oops! Sorry!" Kirsten said. "What are you doing?"

Scott shrugged. "I'm just doing a little favor for my kid sister. How about you?"

Kirsten frowned. She didn't want to tell Scott that she was seeing a psychiatrist, even though she knew he'd be cool about it.

"Hey. You all right, Kirsten?" Scott asked. "Did Kyle call you again or something?"

"No, no . . . nothing like that," Kirsten said. "Let's change the subject. What's up at the Party Room?"

Scott broke into a grin. "Well, we're having a tiki theme tonight. It's a little weird, I know, but I'm making awesome piña coladas. The manager is actually buying *real* coconuts this time!"

Kirsten recalled what Scott's mojitos had done to her the other night. "Sounds like fun."

"So will I see you there, or what?" Scott asked, playfully punching her in the arm.

He didn't have to ask twice.

"Beam me up, Scotty!" Kirsten smiled. "I'm there!"

8

Later that night Kirsten lit a joint that Leslie had given her and inhaled deeply as she listened to the rain hit the roof of her penthouse apartment. Her parents had long since gone to sleep, and she needed something to take the edge off. She was sick of Dr. Fitzgerald's sleeping pills, and after a crazy night of partying, she needed something to help her relax. She exhaled the smoke into a sheet of Downy fabric softener to mask the scent. An old boarding school trick Julie's older brother, Chad, had taught them before heading off to military school.

Kirsten relaxed into the thick down covers of her bed, letting the air-conditioning blast her into oblivion, and rehashed another night at the Party Room. She could still see herself and Julie learning how to hula dance, surrounded by a pack of salivating guys and laughing between sips of Scott's fresh piña coladas. Kirsten also remembered Brandon Yardley wearing a stupid yellow lei and trying to corner her all night.

Thank God *he left early,* she thought as the pot started taking effect. Her eyelids became heavier as she listened to a distant siren out on the street. *Chill,* she kept telling herself. *It's time for some* real *sleep.*

Kirsten finished the joint, smudged it out in a Diet Coke can, and waved smoke out of the air. She rolled out of bed and took off her slinky red Marc Jacobs dress. *I looked good tonight,* she thought as she let the raw silk curl to the floor. She yawned and opened the door to her walk-in closet.

She stepped inside and reached to flick on the light, but it was already on. *Weird,* she thought. *I never leave the light on in my closet.*

Then Kirsten heard a hanger drop near the back of the closet. Out of the corner of her eye she saw some clothes move! She gasped and backed up in a frenzy of motion. Clothes seemed to grab at her as she fought her way out of the closet.

As fear ripped through her, Kirsten ran out of her room. The hallway lights were off, but she didn't stop for a second. "Aghh!"

"What's going on?" Gil Sawyer grumbled, coming out of the master bedroom. Daddy wasn't exactly the nurturing type. He smelled of pipe smoke and NyQuil. Kirsten's most consistent childhood memory of her father was sitting outside his study, waiting for *permission* to give him her latest scribbled artwork.

"In my room!" Kirsten screamed at her father.

Kirsten's mother, Susan, rushed out of the bedroom. "What's wrong, Kirsten?" she cried.

"Someone's in my room!" Kirsten shivered.

"Oh my God!" Mrs. Sawyer grabbed her daughter and held her as tightly as possible.

"You sure?" Mr. Sawyer asked.

"Go check, Gil!" Mrs. Sawyer snapped, shoving her husband forward.

Mr. Sawyer sighed in annoyance and marched toward Kirsten's room. He never believed Kirsten, and nothing could get his heart rate above two beats per minute, anyway.

"Careful, Dad!" Kirsten held her breath as her father walked down the long hallway and disappeared into her bedroom.

"Dad?" she called out after a few minutes of silence. After a few seconds of Kirsten imagining the absolute worst, however, her father shuffled back out of Kirsten's room.

"Couldn't find a thing," he said with a frown.

Kirsten felt her body go weak as her father shuffled past her, back to sleep. *I really* am *going nuts,* she thought. Well, she was also stoned, so maybe it was just paranoia.

"I know what you need, sweetie," Mrs. Sawyer said. She took her daughter's hand and led her into the kitchen. She sat Kirsten down on a stool and hummed softly as she boiled a pot of water.

"You've been going to all of your therapy sessions, right?" her mom quietly inquired. She sounded like she was talking to a scared fifth grader.

"Yes," Kirsten said, feeling totally pathetic since it was clear that her mom *and* her dad thought she was nuts too.

"Here. This will calm you down," Kirsten's mother said warmly as she handed Kirsten a cup of cocoa.

Cocoa. Mom's cure for everything.

"Thanks. This will definitely help." Kirsten played along and took a small sip from the cup. Maybe this made her mother feel better, but Kirsten knew what *she* needed to really calm down.

"How about some nice graham crackers?" her mom asked. When she walked into the pantry for a moment, Kirsten rushed into the library—to the liquor cabinet—and poured a generous helping of Ketel One into her drink and headed back to her bedroom.

She couldn't deal anymore. How could she? She was seventeen years old and she had already lost her mind. Maybe she should just buy the straitjacket now and be done with it. She bet she could get something in a nice shade of purple from Prada's fall collection.

Kirsten drowsily entered her bedroom. She shut off the light and collapsed on her bed, sighing. Just before drifting off to sleep, she rolled over and noticed that her closet door was still open and the light was still on.

Kirsten huffed as she stumbled to her feet. She walked into the closet and reached for the string that led to the overhead light. As she stretched to pull the cord, she lost her balance and fell into her winter clothing rack.

Whoa—spins, Kirsten thought, sliding down the wall of the closet to the floor. She leaned over and rested her head on the plush mauve rug. *Better. . . much better.*

And then she saw it—right in the center of the carpet.

A fresh muddy footprint.

Someone *had* been there!

9

That's right!

Be afraid. Be very afraid.

I don't care if that's a cliché.

I don't care about a goddamn thing right now, as a matter of fact.

All I care about is keeping control. Keeping my head on straight. Keeping my plan in sight.

I've got you right where I want you!

Are you FREAKING BLIND?

God, I could use a drink. But I won't. I won't weaken myself like you do. I'll keep strong. And wait. For the perfect chance.

Perfect.

Yeah, right!

I remember I used to believe in perfect. A happy family. Christmas glee—the whole phony package. I used to actually believe that there was right and wrong out there in the world.

Now I realize there's only hot and cold—living and dying.

I could care less about my own life at this point. This isn't about me! Can't you see that? Hello!!!!!

The only reason I stay alive—stay breathing—is so that I can MAKE YOU FEEL what I feel every day.

Why am I even wasting my breath on you?

Like you give a shit.

You probably think I'm the villain. You probably still believe in heroes just like everyone else.

Well, here's a news flash: Batman and Robin were into S&M. Superman was a perv in a costume, flying around looking for hot chicks to nail.

Heroes are dead.

And so . . . are . . . you.

I'm still cold. Still in control. Calm, even. Ahhhh . . .

Sure, we might've had a close call or two, and sure, my hands might be shaking all over this goddamn page, but trust me:

It's because I'm excited. Exhilarated!

The end of this story is already written.

And I have the pen. . . .

10

"Way to go, Sawyer!" Julie cheered as she moshed to a White Stripes song blasting through the Hamptons party. "Go for it! Brian's a total hottie!"

"Chill, Julie!" Kirsten blushed. "I'm not ready yet."

The two girls stood in the center of Clark Gansevoort's summer rager—the house party to end all house parties that his parents let him throw every year despite the thousands of dollars it cost them in puke stains alone.

"Not ready?" Julie teased. "What're you talking about, slut? You're the one who invited him!"

"I just need some time," Kirsten whined, pushing Julie away. She knew why Julie was so juiced up in the first place: She had a plan to hook up with Clark at least once this summer. Her beefcake crush had just graduated from Talcott and was headed for Harvard on a football scholarship.

As Julie continued to dance circles around her, Kirsten watched Brian from across the crowded room, nursing a beer and nodding his head to the music. He didn't quite fit with the Richie Rich kids who made out on antique wicker furniture, did keg stands in the vast *Architectural Digest*-like kitchen, snorted coke in the master bedroom, and tried on Mrs. Gansevoort's tacky golf outfits. And he didn't seem to know anyone—except Kirsten, who at this point in time was kind of feeling like a freak and wondering why the hell she'd invited him there, anyway.

"Come on, girl!" Julie pressed on. "You need a *healthy distraction*! Isn't that what your shrink keeps saying?"

"You mean my *psychiatrist*?" Kirsten corrected Julie. Her best friend was cruising for a serious bruising tonight.

"You say tomato, I say to-maaaahh-to," Julie sang.

"Ugh," was all Kirsten could get out as she slammed a glass of wine.

Too embarrassed for words, Kirsten stalked off into another room, avoiding Brian altogether. *Smooth move,* she chided herself as she searched out the bar.

And no surprise whatsoever, Leslie Fenk was already there. She was dressed to kill—Versace everything—flirting with Clark's two older brothers. Kirsten remembered them from last year's bash. They were both Harvard boys, too, and their names were Chauncey and Reginald, or Mortimer and Tanner or something equally WASPy.

Kirsten snuck up behind Leslie and slipped her hands over her eyes.

"I smell Dior," Leslie said, playing detective. She reached up to touch Kirsten's hands. "That could only mean one thing," she hummed. "It's a Woodley girl!" Leslie spun around and gave Kirsten a big hug and a kiss, lingering a few seconds with her arms around her waist.

Slow down, Fenk, Kirsten thought as Clark's brothers drooled. She backed off a little. She remembered the last time that she went out with Leslie. Pretending to hook up to avoid Brandon Yardley was one thing, but being Leslie's latest plaything was altogether something else.

The brothers Gansevoort high-fived and left Kirsten and Leslie alone.

"Glad to see you," Leslie purred. She reached into her handbag and found two tiny tabs of Ecstasy. "Take both at once and call me in the morning," Leslie joked.

"Now we're talking!" Kirsten cheered.

Kirsten had taken E only once before—with Sam. She knew exactly what it did: It made you all hot and tingly—every sensation was bigger and better. Kirsten winked at Leslie, placing both pills on her tongue.

An hour and a bottle of Cristal later, and Kirsten stumbled outside to the pool area. As she watched a splashing and shouting chicken fight in Clark's Olympic-size pool, she laughed out loud. Her head swam with a warm liquid sensation, and a giddy shiver crawled across her chest.

God, I feel gooood! Kirsten thought as she looked around

for Brian. *Time to find my crush.* She giggled. She spotted Brian dancing next to the pool. An Outkast song blared from a set of enormous loudspeakers. Kirsten could literally *feel* the beat on her skin.

Brian looked much more comfortable now that he was dancing to a hip-hop track. In fact, he had great rhythm. Kirsten licked her lips. A huge grin spread across her face as she approached him.

At first, Brian didn't see Kirsten walking along the side of the pool. He was busy dancing with two Chapin Prep girls, keeping both of them plenty interested while also keeping a respectful distance. Kirsten wondered if Brian was too good to be true.

"Brian!" Kirsten yelled out, swelling with courage. She made her way to him, gently edging the Chapin sluts out of the way, and started dancing with Brian.

Closer and closer.

Kirsten felt the music grow louder. She felt amazing. When Brian grabbed her hands and started swaying with her, Kirsten felt a wave of tingles run up her arms.

The bass line seemed to appear in front of her eyes, rattling the world in a melodic, magical way. As the deejay mixed in another song, something Kirsten didn't recognize, Brian grabbed her by the waist.

Hello.

They dipped to the music, moving in lazy, hip synchronicity. Kirsten knew they looked good together. Taking things to the next level, she ran her hand up the back of Brian's neck, grabbing at his blond curls. He didn't seem to mind at all.

Then Kirsten stepped back so that Brian could watch her moves. She raised her arms above her head, swaying her hips and moving in sync with the beat. She spun around and—

"W-w-w-whoa!" Kirsten's arms flailed in the air as she lost her balance and teetered by the edge of the pool. She reached out for Brian's hand, but before he could snatch her up, she crashed backward into the water with a big splash.

As Kirsten surfaced in her now-ruined dress and gasped for breath, everyone broke into laughter. She slammed her fist into the water and glanced back at Brian, totally humiliated.

He reached out his hand to help her, but he was laughing right along with the others.

"Screw you guys!" Kirsten cried. She wasn't really mad at Brian or the partygoers. As the warm fuzzy feeling from the Ecstasy gave way to a burning sensation of embarrassment, she waded out of the pool and rushed back inside the house.

"Hey, Kirsten! Wait up!" Brian called to her, but she ignored his shouts and scanned the house for Julie.

Time to GO! Kirsten felt trapped under her skin. Everyone seemed to be staring at her, but she didn't stop racing from kitchen to living room to master bedroom to home theater. *Where the hell are you, Jules?*

Kirsten almost ran into Brian as she approached the basement door.

"Kirsten! Are you okay?" he asked, trying to slow her down.

"Not okay," Kirsten said, pushing her date out of the way. She opened the door to the "off-limits" basement and ran down the steps. She lost her footing halfway down, slipped, and slid down the rest of the way. "Shit!"

Eight ball, corner pocket.

Or was that right leg, side pocket?

On top of the Gansevoorts' antique pool table, Julie lay underneath Clark's linebacker body, making out and feeling him up without a care in the world.

Kirsten glanced around the room: Neon beer signs flickered in the corners. Budweiser Girls winked at the NASCAR drivers posing on the opposite wall.

Pulling herself up and massaging her bruised ass, Kirsten coughed, clapped, stomped, and snapped for two full minutes, but Julie and Clark weren't about to be interrupted. Finally Kirsten screamed, "I've got to get out of here, Julie!" and her friend looked up.

Julie's face was a smear of makeup, and Clark cursed to himself as he stared daggers at Kirsten. Julie winked at Kirsten and mouthed *please?* as Clark began kissing her neck again.

However bad her friend's taste was, Kirsten knew that

Julie wasn't going anywhere—probably for the whole night.

Ugghh! Kirsten could have screamed, but instead, she bit her tongue. She knew that her friend had wanted to get with Clark for a long time. Simply put, Julie Pembroke was a selfish bitch when she was "getting some."

Kirsten gave up and hurried back up the staircase. Her dress was cold and wet and it stuck to her legs as she ran.

Once again, Kirsten rushed by Brian, unable to deal with her growing embarrassment. To make it worse, she was starting to feel a little woozy. And Kirsten *did not* want to be known as the girl who fell in the pool, then puked after she saw Julie and Clark practically *doing it* in the basement. Out of options, frustrated and angry, Kirsten booked through the marble foyer and burst outside the front door.

As tears welled in her eyes, Kirsten stood on the expansive Gansevoort lawn and remembered something. She reached into her sopping-wet Gucci purse and fished out Julie's car keys. Julie didn't have any pockets, so she'd asked Kirsten to hold them.

Stumbling toward Julie's parents' new Porsche Cayenne, Kirsten fumbled with the alarm until the SUV beeped open. Just as Kirsten reached the vehicle and climbed-fell inside, a deafening bolt of thunder rippled through the sky.

In the rush to get inside, 'cause she wasn't wet enough already, Kirsten dropped the keys under the front seat. "Stupid!"

After spending the next few seconds scrambling for the

keys, Kirsten started up the Porsche. It roared to life as rain started hammering against the windshield.

Even with a storm falling all around her, Kirsten couldn't think about anything except that look on Brian's face as he'd laughed at her. "I'm pathetic!" she said as she jammed the SUV into reverse and skidded across the driveway.

Barely missing a wrought-iron statue standing guard at the entrance to the Gansevoorts' driveway, Kirsten gained control of the Cayenne just in time to swerve onto the main road, demolishing the corner of Clark's large front hedge.

Just get away, her mind spun. *Get home.* The tears came faster now. *I made a total ass of myself. I'm a total screwup!* She swerved as she wiped snot from under her nose. She was sobbing now. *A wreck. A total wreck . . .*

Kirsten slammed on the gas and took off faster into the stormy night. *Forget Brian! Forget ever dating at all!* Lost in her head, she ignored the angry honk of a driver whizzing by her in the opposite lane. Her tears started to flood her eyes, making it harder to see.

Rain. Lightning. Wind.

The storm was now right on top of her. Kirsten swerved again as a strong gust brought a sheet of rain across her window.

Feeling the tug of fear, Kirsten downshifted the Porsche. The gears whined as the SUV jerked into a slower pace. *I don't want to die tonight,* she thought.

But just as Kirsten started to travel at a more reasonable pace, another lighting bolt crackled right in front of her.

Kirsten screamed out and swerved again. This time she struggled to gain control of the vehicle. Her sight returned to her—just in time to see a U-Haul truck coming right at her.

"Noooo!" Kirsten yanked the steering wheel to the side as the truck squeezed by her left, barely missing the driver's side mirror.

Behind her now, the U-Haul swerved safely back off the shoulder of the road where Kirsten had carelessly forced it. Adjusting her rearview mirror, Kirsten breathed a sigh of relief, shook her head, and watched the truck disappear around a curve in the road.

Then she turned her attention back to the road ahead.

"Oh my God!" she yelled. Something was standing right on the yellow stripes, not five yards in front of her! Kirsten slammed on the brakes with every living ounce of energy she had.

SCREEECH!

11

A deer stared peacefully at Kirsten through the rain-splattered windshield. After a few moments, a knobby-kneed fawn caught up to its mother, and the two animals bounded off the road.

I could've killed someone. . . . Kirsten's stomach churned at the realization. *I could've killed myself!*

Fully stopped now, Kirsten turned off the Porsche and buried her head in her hands. She started to sob. Hard. Harder than she had in months. Kirsten's ribs hurt as she gasped for air.

After a long while, Kirsten started the SUV again and pulled it to the side of the road. She was way too messed up to drive. Getting behind the wheel in her state was quite possibly the stupidest choice she had ever made.

Just as Kirsten pushed her seat back and prepared to pass out right there on the side of the pitch-black roadway—a bright light illuminated the inside of the Porsche. She quickly ducked down in her seat. *What if it's the cops?* The last thing she needed was a DWI.

When Kirsten heard brakes slamming on behind her, however, she shot up in her seat. *Now what?* she wondered.

A dark figure ran toward the Cayenne through the heavy rain.

Kirsten ducked again, hoping whoever it was might think the car was empty. When the mystery person tapped lightly on the window, waited, and tapped again, however, Kirsten slowly found the courage to sit up and look through the tinted glass.

"Need a lift?" Brian asked, smiling.

Kirsten let out a breath. *Thank God it's Brian,* she thought. *Wait a sec, wasn't he the one I was trying to get away from in the first place? Oh yeah. He was.*

Her face instantly began to flush as the whole embarrassing scene at the party flashed in her brain.

"I saw you leave the party. Are you okay?" Brian added as Kirsten rolled down the window.

"I'm just resting," Kirsten said. *God, that was lame,* she thought.

"Let me drive you home," Brian insisted.

However embarrassed Kirsten might've been, she wasn't about to get behind the wheel again that night. And Brian insisted on driving the Porsche to Julie's beach house and walking the two or so miles back to get his car.

When Brian pulled into the Pembrokes' driveway, he hopped out of the Porsche and opened Kirsten's door for her. He escorted her up the cobblestone pathway right up to the wide farmhouse entrance, then they both stopped outside.

Kirsten felt her face turn red again. The tingle of Ecstasy was still working through her bloodstream. She knew she looked horrible, and she felt even worse now.

He must think I'm a total loser, Kirsten thought as Brian stared into her eyes.

"You can dance, girl," Brian said, surprising her. Then he made some kind of surfer signal with his hand.

"What are you doing?" Kirsten laughed.

"Hang loose, yo!" Brian flashed her the sign again.

Kirsten did her best to imitate the gesture, but her version came out looking more like a broken garden trowel.

Brian laughed, took Kirsten's hand, and showed her how to make the sign. "Like this," he whispered, close to her ear.

"Oh," was all Kirsten could say, his voice sending delicious shivers from her ears all the way down to her toes. But then Kirsten remembered the pool again. "Listen, Brian. I want to apologize. I got way too messed up tonight, and—"

"Stop, Kirsten," Brian gently interrupted her. "You don't have to say anything."

"Yeah right," Kirsten exhaled, moving away from Brian. "I thought I could handle myself, and instead I—"

"Went pool hopping!" Brian smiled again. "It's cool,

Kirsten. I only laughed because it was a funny moment. I wasn't laughing at *you*."

"Really?" Kirsten asked, still feeling a little less defeated. "I'm glad, because—"

Then Brian leaned in and kissed her. A tender and passionate kiss. Kirsten enjoyed his soft lips for a moment, but then slowly pulled away.

"Oh . . . sorry." Brian frowned. It was his turn to flush with embarrassment. "I thought . . ."

Kirsten's mind scrambled to find the right words. "No. It's not you, Brian. Really," she assured him. "I just can't . . . *do this* right now." She really liked this guy, but she had too much other stuff that needed to be sorted out before she could be with anyone. She wasn't ready. She knew that now. "I need to clear my head first. Right now I'm just too confused."

Brian's face sank.

So did Kirsten's. She didn't want Brian to take it the wrong way, but it would be impossible to explain the whole situation. "It's not like I don't *want* to . . . I just—"

"It's cool," Brian said. Rubbing the back of his neck, he turned to leave.

Kirsten didn't want to see him go, but what could she do? "I'm not trying to mess with your head or anything!" she called out.

Brian turned back to face her one last time. "See you at work," he said flatly, and was gone.

Kirsten shook her head and slowly opened the front door to Julie's place. Things hadn't worked out the way she had planned. But then again, what *was* working out these days? Once inside, Kirsten shut the door and leaned against it. She rubbed her temples and let out a long sigh.

I'm lucky to be alive, she thought as she locked the door. Images of passing cars and skidding tires flashed through her mind. She tossed Julie's keys onto a couch in her living room and crossed into the kitchen. Turning on the overhead light, she pulled a teakettle from a top shelf and filled it with water.

Kirsten thought of her mother's cocoa. She hadn't even tasted it before spiking it with vodka. She set the kettle on the stove and then searched through the cupboards above the sink for tea. Nothing.

Kirsten then turned and walked over to the Pembrokes' English pantry.

She pushed the swinging door open and let out a piercing scream.

Kyle! He stood just two feet away from her, waiting in the dark.

12

Kirsten screamed again as Kyle advanced toward her. His eyes looked wild and desperate. His wavy brown hair was drenched from the storm.

I'm trapped! Kirsten's mind screamed.

She bolted out of the pantry and slammed right into the stove. The teakettle toppled off its burner, splashing steaming water all over the floor, spattering Kirsten's legs with pain. "Get away from me!" she cried, running into the living room. "I'll call the police!"

Kyle followed, not saying a word and staring at her with hard and angry eyes.

Kirsten raced to the door and fumbled with the locks. *Have to get out of here!*

"Who was that guy?" Kyle finally spat out. He was angry. Very angry. He must have been lurking outside when Kirsten returned home with Brian.

Kirsten turned and faced him, her back against the door, "N-n-no one!" she stammered.

"Was that your boyfriend?" Kyle demanded.

"No, it wasn't. Please, Kyle!" Kirsten was crying now—couldn't hold it back any longer. She was all alone in a house with a killer. The wind was whipping outside. For a moment, Kirsten thought of Brian, but he was long gone by now.

Then she reached for the doorknob and twisted it and yanked open the door. *Run!* she thought. *Run, Kirsten, run!*

But before she could get five steps, Kyle grabbed her and squeezed her tight in his strong arms. Desperate, Kirsten bit Kyle on the arm and tried to knee him in the groin. Kyle screamed out in pain, but he was simply too powerful.

He dragged her, kicking and screaming, back into the farmhouse, slammed the front door shut, and locked it. Then he turned around and faced her.

Flooded with panic, Kirsten fell back against the couch and tensed her whole body. She closed her eyes. *It's going to happen. He's going to kill me right now!*

But then there was a pause.

A long pause.

Kirsten could hear Kyle breathing. He was just waiting for something.

For what? Kirsten thought as she slowly opened her eyes.

Kyle was now sitting on the floor, exhaling deeply. He

wrung his hands and looked at her, clearly trying to figure out what to say.

Kirsten jumped up and made a run for the back door. She was fully crying now, screaming, "No! No! No!" over and over again.

Kyle leaped up from the floor and gave chase. He caught up to her in the kitchen and didn't let her go this time. "I'm not going to hurt you!"

The wind rushed out of Kirsten's lungs. She felt beaten, broken.

"Just listen!" Kyle pleaded in desperation. "Please."

"Why should I?" Kirsten shouted back.

"Because I'm innocent!"

"Bullshit!" Kirsten cried, sobbing harder now. "You've lied to me from the start."

Kyle held on as she kicked, clawed, and pushed her way around the kitchen. "Just . . . just don't . . . be afraid," he said. "I just came here to tell you the truth."

"No . . . ," Kirsten repeated herself, weakening in Kyle's arms. She slowly stopped struggling. "I can't . . ."

"If you still don't believe me after what I tell you, then you can turn me in, okay?" Kyle added with a tired voice. "I won't fight it."

Alone in the middle of nowhere, surrounded by howling winds and empty roads, Kirsten knew that there was nowhere to go. Kyle must've been following her for days, waiting for the perfect moment to show up. She remembered the footprint in her closet. God only knew how he got into her white-glove building, much less her penthouse apartment.

But now that he was here, she saw something . . . tender in his eyes. He looked fragile and vulnerable.

There was nothing else to do but listen, Kirsten decided. She would hear Kyle's story and hope that he remained calm. At this point, the best and only path was the one of least resistance.

Kirsten pulled back from Kyle's grasp and leaned against the kitchen counter. Avoiding eye contact, Kirsten crossed her arms and waited for an explanation. "Okay, Kyle," she finally said. "What?"

Kyle sat against the kitchen table, brushed the overgrown bangs out of his eyes, and began: "The truth isn't pretty, but it's *true*." He cleared his throat before continuing. "I was in love with this girl, Carolee. I'll never forget her. . . ." Kyle swallowed, clearly affected. "Carolee Adams was my first love, my high school sweetheart."

Kirsten softened her stance and started to listen. Something about the calm, honest tone in Kyle's voice was setting her at ease.

"I saw her at the first dance of sophomore year. Carolee was this amazing, cool, smart freshman, and as soon as I met her, I knew she'd be my girlfriend."

Kirsten caught herself smiling slightly. Kyle was a romantic at heart.

Kyle then sat down in a chair next to the table. He took off his drenched flannel shirt; an undershirt clung to his muscular frame. "Now it's my senior year, okay? I'm an all-state point guard on the basketball team with a 3.7 GPA. I'm a lock for a full ride at Brown. I've been dating Carolee for three years and I am practically married to her by now. Life is cool. Better than cool. Honestly, I thought I was living the high school fantasy . . . until one night . . . the night that changed my life forever. . . ."

As Kyle told her his story, Kirsten could picture the night in question three years ago—back when Kyle was Paul Stone . . . a senior banquet . . . a beautiful spring night . . . hanging out with close friends . . .

How could things have gone so wrong . . . ?

PART TWO

13

Kyle is Paul . . . Paul Stone.

And Paul Stone is walking across Seventy-Ninth Street, heading to the Zoo with his boys.

Not a kid's zoo. *The* Zoo: the tightest hip-hop club on the Upper East Side.

It's Friday night, right after Talcott Preparatory School's Senior Banquet. It's the last weekend before graduation, and therefore, the last weekend to *rage*.

As he and The Crew—Moyer, Goldstein, Willett, and Schloss—hurry down Lex, sharing not-so-furtive swigs from a bottle of Captain Morgan, Paul laughs as his friends rip on one another's mothers:

"The bitch is *so* fat." Willett jams a finger into Schloss's back. "She jumped up in the air and got stuck!"

Everyone laughs, giving Willett pounds.

"Oh yeah?" Schloss says. "Well . . . your mom is dumb!" Schloss has *no* skills playing the game.

"Schloss," Paul teases, "is that the best you can come up with?"

"That's what your mom said last night!" Schloss counters, shoving his friends as he laughs.

In the middle of chugging rum, Paul breaks into laughter, spraying the sticky liquor all over himself. "Wait. What the hell does that even *mean*?" he asks, scrunching up his face. "You're saying that my mom took one look at your shriveled-ass thing and kicked you out of bed?"

"Damn, Paul!" Moyer sucks his teeth. "Quit overanalyzing the mother jokes!"

"Yeah, bro!" echoes Goldstein. He always copies Moyer. "You're not in AP English right now, bitch!"

The guys always bust Paul about being a nerd. But though he knows he's different from the last-name-only guys he rolls with, Paul Stone is loyal to the core. Ever since making varsity as a sophomore, Paul's been inseparable from his b-ball crew.

Paul smiles as they walk down the street. It's a big day of celebration. Four years of Talcott and soon he'll be free.

The only thing I'll really miss at that place is Carolee, he thinks. Paul can't wait to see her at the party. They've been planning this night forever. He thinks about dancing with her, holding her, kissing her and, eventually, taking her home.

Even though Paul's going to be in Rhode Island next year, he plans on driving back every weekend. He'll make the relationship work no matter what.

Finally, The Crew arrives at the Zoo. As expected, a huge line snakes out of the entrance. Every single high school girl in America waits outside, dressed in hip huggers, Tommy Girl skirts, and far too much makeup. But lucky for Paul, Moyer knows the door guy. Without so much as a moment's hesitation, he and the others slip inside.

On the other side of the velvet curtains, Paul enters a dark black-lit club thick with smoke and overdone bass. As Jay-Z vibrates, he weaves his way through a wall of wannabe thugs near the entrance.

Although someone leans into his shoulder, trying to start something, Paul simply bounces off and keeps on walking. He could care less about fighting tonight. *Tonight is all about Carolee.*

Paul makes his way into the heart of the club and looks around. The place is packed with Talcott seniors. Everyone is tossing back drinks, screaming out, "Seniors rule!" and dancing with reckless abandon. They're letting out the stress they've accumulated over four years of essays, late-night studying, and five thousand extracurriculars.

"Pretty hot, huh?" Willett bumps into Paul with shots of Patrón.

"Hell yeah!" Paul agrees as he slams the drink with his friend. He rocks backward and then slings an arm around his friend. Paul's happy to be out. Happy to be celebrating. Happy to be alive.

The only thing missing is his girlfriend.

Where is she? Paul wonders. He's starting to get nervous. He always feels better with Carolee by his side. She takes care of him. She makes him feel loved, special—all that greeting-card stuff. For Paul, a relationship is more than just sex. "Where is she?" Paul finally shouts.

"Who?" Willett asks through a long burp.

"Carolee!" Who else would he be looking for? "She was supposed to meet me near the entrance."

"Right over there." Moyer moshes into his two friends, then stretches out an arm and points across the dance floor.

At first, Paul can't track where Moyer is pointing. It's too dark to see. A strobe light blurs his vision.

When the lights flash bright red, however, Paul sees her. Carolee's right in the middle of the dance floor, wearing a backless nothing, grinding with some guy!

What the hell?

And then it gets worse! Seemingly having the time of her life, Carolee laughs and whispers into the guy's ear. And the guy grabs Carolee around the waist!

As his friends start to laugh, Paul's face contorts. *It's our night!* his mind screams. A searing streak of anger runs through Paul as he rushes into the mob of partiers.

"Watch it, dude!" someone yells as he plows through, stumbling from his last tequila.

Without thinking, Paul yanks the pair apart, grabbing

Carolee forcefully by the arm. "What do you think you're doing, Carolee?" he screams, attracting everyone's attention.

Carolee's face flushes red as she spins away from Paul.

From anger? Guilt? What?

"Stop it, Paul!" she shouts.

"What the hell are you *doing*?" Paul reaches for her again, mad-dogging the guy she's been dancing with.

"Just calm down!" Carolee yells back, clearly tipsy. She looks as beautiful as ever: milky skin, blond hair, green eyes. But now Carolee's beauty infuriates Paul.

As much as Paul loves his girlfriend, he hates her in that moment.

"Who the hell are *you*?" Paul shouts at the guy as he rolls up his sleeves, ready to go right then and there.

Before the guy can defend himself, Carolee jumps between the two boys. "Steve's just a friend!" she stammers, pushing against Paul's chest.

Something about Toronto, something about camp and "catching up," but Paul's barely listening. He's too busy grilling Carolee suspiciously. "Why didn't you tell me you had a visitor?" Paul pushes.

"I don't know!" Carolee cries out "Just chill, okay? I guess it slipped my mind or something! Is that a crime?"

Why is she being so defensive?

"You want to see a crime?" Paul yells as he shoves Steve. He imagines Steve's skull splitting on the sidewalk outside. Blood covering his new Jordans. An ambulance.

Steve careens into a group of girls, falling to the floor. He looks pathetic, and—*damn it*—innocent!

What's happening to me? Paul thinks. He never loses control like this.

Finally Steve gets up: "Hey, buddy. Sorry about this. We're just camp friends."

And to Paul's burning embarrassment, Steve has a thick Canadian accent. "Steve," he adds, extending his hand for an international treaty.

Why's he have to be so goddamn nice? Paul thinks. He feels like a total asshole now.

Carolee stares daggers at Paul. She's been moody lately, but Paul always assumed it was because he was leaving for Brown soon.

"Welcome to America," Paul mutters as he walks off angrily to the bar. His neck feels hot with embarrassment. But even if Carolee and Steve are just friends, what's with this dirty dancing?

Got to get a drink, Paul thinks. Even though he usually knows his limits, tonight he's going to drink right past them.

At the bar Moyer stops harassing yet another girl for a moment and turns to his friend. "You're gonna let Carolee play you like that?" Moyer shouts, already on his second shot of Jägermeister. "She's too hot to trust, son!"

Paul takes off his Talcott tie and tosses it onto the bar.

He slams a shot of Jäger, but then turns back toward Moyer. "Wait. What'd you just say?" Paul asks.

Moyer isn't paying attention now. He's too busy staring at Carolee on the dance floor.

"Oh! I get it!" Paul pushes Moyer. "You're into her too, aren't you?"

"What?" Moyer laughs it off. "Bros before hoes, man!"

Am I going crazy? Paul asks himself. He's overreacting again. "Sorry," he finally says, and tries to calm down. *Carolee's just upset about my leaving. She still loves me. She's . . .* Paul's thought trails off as he looks back across the dance floor. *Carolee? Where's Carolee!*

She's not on the dance floor anymore. And neither is Steve!

Leaving Moyer at the bar, Paul hurries through the club. He scans everywhere, but doesn't find them. Then Paul remembers the downstairs section of the Zoo—the almost-pitch-black basement where he and Carolee sneaked off the last time they were there.

Paul finds the back stairwell and hurries down into the dark storage area. He stumbles through stacks of champagne crates and empty kegs, seething with anger.

How could Carolee play me like this? Paul thinks. *On my biggest night of the year!*

In the distance there's a soft light glowing from behind a large, opaque glass door. Paul hurries forward and pulls on the handle. It's locked.

Just as Paul turns to leave, he hears a giggle on the other side of the door.

Carolee!

Paul yanks on the door again, but it doesn't budge.

More giggling.

Paul loses it. He jams the butt of his hand directly through the glass!

Shards spray everywhere. Blood spiders across Paul's fist as he steps through the doorway, searching for a light. He throws on a switch to find Carolee, *his* girlfriend, hooking up with Steve!

They're sprawled across a table, pawing each other in a large, empty room.

Paul can't believe his eyes. *How could I be such an idiot?* he thinks, running his bloody hand through his hair.

Carolee and Steve just freeze, like two rats caught raiding the trash.

Trash! Paul bounds toward them.

Steve, slight but sober, dodges Paul's first charge and sends him flying into a stack of chairs.

"Paul!" Carolee screams as her boyfriend makes a second lunge at Steve.

They start to wrestle, cracking through the Sheetrock walls as they whirl about.

After a few moments of intense struggle and Carolee's constant screaming, people start running into the room from upstairs.

Way past anger, Paul spits blood and tackles Steve into a stand of bar stools. Yanking his hair, Paul lands a few solid punches. His blood mixes with Steve's, a coldhearted crowd cheering them on now.

Finally, two hefty bouncers dive through the crowd. Paul breaks away, but the bouncers grab him anyway. D-Train, the larger of the two giants, gets in a few stomach shots on Paul.

Ooof! Paul sinks to his knees.

Suddenly Carolee lunges toward Paul and slaps him hard across the face. "We're over!" she screams, and then turns to comfort Steve.

Paul tries to make a run for Carolee, but D-Train puts him in a sleeper hold and pushes him to the floor. Then Carolee pulls Steve by the arm and rushes out.

As Paul watches Carolee escape, fixing her slutty shirt, he slams his hand against the concrete floor. "I'll kill you, Carolee!" he screams in front of some fifty witnesses.

And the bouncers put the final hurt on him.

14

Hammered. Really hammered.

The tacky red chili lights in Tropixxx, a seedy bridge-and-tunnel bar down on Fifty-Ninth Street and Second Avenue blur above Paul Stone. He tries to focus on one strand, tries to regain his clarity, but everything's on spin-cycle.

The whole useless world is in constant motion.

It's over, Paul keeps chanting to himself over and over again, keeping upright by holding on to Moyer's shoulder. "I should've strangled that punk!" he says through his teeth.

"Yeah, you should have!" Moyer adds. "But at least you got in some good shots, bro."

"Who even cares?" Paul says. "It's over!" Pain swells in his neck and back and ribs, but that doesn't stop him from slamming another shot of Jäger. He barely feels the burning liquid go down.

It's over, Paul thinks again as he envisions Carolee's last horrible expression before she dumped him. *How long has she been cheating on me?* he wonders.

Next to the bar, the rest of The Crew has cornered a young public school girl on the dance floor. Gina *something* dances carefree with the pack of drooling guys, showing off her exposed midsection and too-tight jeans. Although she's young—just a freshman at a school near Talcott—tonight she looks good.

Gina laughs as the basketballers crudely compliment her moves.

She has no idea what she's starting, Paul thinks as he watches Gina flirt with The Crew. He leans back against the bar, content to just observe the insanity.

Soon Goldstein and Willett try to grab Gina and dance closely with her, but she backs off.

"Come on, Geeena!" Willett whines.

Gina giggles. "Not so close."

But the guys don't exactly respect her space.

Laughing at his friends, Moyer leans into Paul and whispers, "Watch this!"

Paul frowns, knowing just how far his friend can take things.

Moyer jumps into the fray and, without an ounce of caution, pulls Gina in close.

"Get off me!" Gina yells, pushing Moyer away.

Bad idea.

Paul watches Moyer's expression darken. A vein emerges on his forehead. He's a notoriously bad drunk, prone to fits of sudden anger. Realizing he has to stop this thing before it starts, Paul steps forward to hold Moyer back. But he's too drunk and too late.

Moyer reaches for Gina once again, yanking her in close, making the girl wince in pain.

Paul moves again to defend Gina, but before he can say or do anything, Willett holds him back, pushing him up against the bar. As Paul struggles with Willett, Gina breaks free from Moyer and runs out of Tropixxx.

"Game on!" Moyer yells out as he sets off after her.

Goldstein follows.

"Stop!" Paul tries to shout, but it comes out a slurred jumble. Willett and Schloss then grab a hold of him and literally drag Paul out of the club. He's too drunk to resist, and his friends are too rowdy to care.

The Crew piles into Goldstein's souped-up Beamer as he screeches to a halt outside the bar. Paul and the others squeeze into the way-too-small car, like five sinister clowns.

Goldstein then takes off, with Moyer riding shotgun, scanning the streets for Gina.

"Gina? Oh, Geeena!" Moyer sings out as the rest of the guys laugh.

Over the jacked-up sound system, Paul protests again: "Leave her alone, Moyer!"

But Moyer's not having it. And neither is Goldstein as the car screeches down the block.

"Like we're going to take *your* advice on women, Paul!" Schloss teases.

Feeling woozy, Paul leans back into his seat. *Got to get my shit together,* he thinks, grabbing his head to relieve that pounding inside.

The Crew then spots Gina running up Second Avenue, wiping tears from her eyes.

"Poor baby!" Goldstein laughs, and he accelerates toward her.

Paul reaches out, sloppily grabs Goldstein's shoulder, but his friend shrugs him off. Then Goldstein guns the car and pulls next to Gina, almost hopping onto the curb with reckless enthusiasm.

Gina jumps back with a horrified scream.

Willett leans out of a window, reaching toward the frightened freshman. "Get in, Gina!" He laughs. "We just want to be friends!"

The boys cackle.

"Stop following me!" she screams, looking up and down the block, probably for help.

"Seriously, guys!" Paul slurs. "She's scared shitless."

"Shut up!" Moyer says, pushing his friend back against the seat.

"We just want to hold hands!" Willett adds as he high-fives Schloss.

"You'd better leave me alone!" Gina cries, trying to squeeze around the vehicle. "My brother's gonna be here any second and he'll kick your asses!"

"Yeah, right!" Moyer screams, fully enjoying the hunt. "I bet your brother's, like, ten years old or some shit. If you even *have* a brother," he adds, licking his lips.

"No!" Paul shouts.

Gina picks up the pace. The car lurches forward.

"Guys, stop!" Paul is sobering fast.

But The Crew is just warming up:

"Give us a taste, Gina!"

"This isn't funny!" Paul says.

"I love you, Gina!"

"Enough already! Let her go!" Paul screams out, fighting to grab the wheel.

Goldstein turns around and slams a forearm into Paul's chest. "DO NOT touch my car, dude!" he yells.

Suddenly, Gina breaks for it, crossing the street awkwardly in her stilettos.

Goldstein whips back around, realizing he's losing her, and slams on the accelerator. Everyone laughs again, but then they accidentally hit her. They're shocked silent.

"Holy shit!" Goldstein yells as the car screams to a stop and Gina disappears in front of it.

"What the hell?" Paul shouts, searching for the lock to his door. He manages to find the lock and throws the door open.

This is not good! He spills out onto the street and scrambles to stand back up. "Come on!" Paul shouts as he looks back to the car, expecting The Crew to follow. "What?" Paul screams.

They don't get out. They don't even budge! His boys are just sitting there, shocked silent. Four muscle-bound cowards.

Paul turns his head and looks toward the front of the car; he can't see Gina yet, but he can *hear* her moaning.

"Get the fuck out here! We gotta check on her!" Paul insists.

That's when a ghost-white Goldstein slams his car into reverse and takes off.

"COME BACK HERE!" Paul yells out into the night, but his voice just echoes off the buildings.

Now he's all alone.

Shit! he thinks, trying to jog his brain into functioning shape again, then slowly turns toward the moaning. *I hope she just twisted an ankle or something. After all we weren't going* that *fast when we bumped her.*

Ready to apologize to Gina, Paul finally looks down at the girl. "No!" he cries out in horror.

Gina is writhing on the concrete in a pool of blood.

15

Blood spills across the curb in a long stream, finding its way to a nearby storm drain.

Gina's body jerks in frenetic bursts. Her hands reach out to Paul, and she wheezes out a slow, low moan.

"Gina! Can you hear me?" Paul asks. He kneels down and cradles the girl in his arms. *Things are bad. Very bad,* he chants to himself.

"Don't worry, okay? Just . . . stay calm."

Gina just stares at Paul through her tears. She tries to speak, but blood bubbles out from her mouth.

"You'll be okay, Gina. I'll get you help." Paul rips off his jacket and bundles it against the girl's forehead, trying to stop the flow of blood.

It isn't working.

Blood like a river.

Paul breathes out slowly and steadily as he fishes his cell phone out of his pocket. He immediately dials 911, but as he presses talk, he notices that the display on his phone is shattered—probably from the fight with Steve.

Trying to keep his cool, Paul holds Gina's hand. Her palm is growing cold, lifeless. Her eyes shut as she barely whispers something.

"What did you say, Gina?" Paul asks. "Can you say it again? Just once more? Please!"

But she says nothing. A few more twitches jolt Gina's body, and then she lies still.

This is not happening! Paul collapses inside. *Why did my boys leave me like this?*

Everyone is abandoning me!

Left with no alternative other than all-out yelling, Paul calls out, "HELLO! HELP!" His voice sounds hollow against the concrete landscape. "Somebody fucking *help* me!"

Paul knows that Sixty-First Street is a quiet, sheltered block, but maybe *someone* is within earshot.

No one comes, however. For a while . . .

Paul looks back down at Gina.

Wait! No!

Her chest is still. The wheezing sound has stopped altogether.

SHE'S NOT BREATHING!

"No!" Paul yells in terror. "Gina!"

Paul leans over Gina's body and presses his lips to hers.

He took a lifeguarding class in Nantucket the summer before and still remembers the basics.

Pumping Gina's chest, Paul blows air into her lungs, but nothing happens.

Nothing!

Paul wipes blood from his face and hangs his head in utter misery. A stupid joke . . . and now a girl is dead!

He tried . . . he tried to stop their teasing, but not hard enough.

Now it's too late. Too late for Gina.

Too late to help.

Paul's head spins.

Too late for me? My future? Brown?

Too late to do any good . . .

Slowly and unsteadily, with regret echoing in his head, Paul stands up, backs away from Gina, and heads straight for the subway.

Blood never washes out, Paul thinks as he stands in his bathroom, staring at the red splotches on his face, arms, and hands. He scrubs off as much of it as he can, frowns in the mirror, and shuts off the bathroom light.

A girl is dead! Paul closes his eyes and sees her bloody corpse again. He walks toward his bed as tears well in his eyes. "And I left her there . . . ," he whispers, crawling into bed, aching everywhere. He closes his eyes, but the images of Gina and Steve and Carolee loop through his brain.

A girl is dead. . . .

As Paul lies in his bed, staring blankly at the swirling ceiling fan above, he's startled by a knock on his bedroom door.

A heavy knock.

Maybe Paul's dad heard him come in. Usually he just ignores his son's late arrivals, but tonight, for some reason, maybe Kirk Stone was feeling unusually *involved*.

Paul tries to ignore the knocking, but that's when the pounding starts. "What the hell do you want?" Paul shouts out.

No one responds. Just more banging.

Finally Paul gets up, hurries across his room, and yanks open the large oak door.

It's the police! Three cops in uniform, hands resting on the barrels of their guns!

Gina! Paul's mind shouts. *Good-bye college. Good-bye future. Good-bye everything!*

"Paul Stone?" one of the officers asks.

"Yes . . . ," Paul responds. He feels the acid boiling in his stomach. His scrubbed body burns.

"Senior at Talcott, right?" another says.

Paul feels the moisture in his mouth vanish. He tries to speak, but he can't form the words.

And for a split second, he closes his eyes and waits to hear Gina's name.

The first officer pushes past Paul and begins to search his room. The second one follows suit, while the third keeps an eye on Paul, grilling him up and down.

Just say it, Paul thinks. *Tell me why you're here. Say it out loud!*

"Carolee Adams . . . ," the third cop starts.

Paul furrows his brow. *What?* Carolee?

"Your *girlfriend*?" the cop continues, staring at him with hard, focused eyes.

"Yes?" Paul nods his head and relaxes a bit. *Maybe they* didn't *know about Gina.*

"She's dead."

"Huh? What?" Paul says in a panic, not sure he heard right. Don't they mean *Gina*?

"We found her in Central Park," the stone-faced cop continues. "Murdered."

"No, but—" Paul is swimming in confusion. He feels vomit welling in his throat.

WHAT THE HELL IS GOING ON?

"Carolee Adams is dead!" the officer shouts.

"No!" Paul screams, anguish twisting his face.

As Paul sinks to his knees, the cop suddenly wrenches his arms behind his back and slams handcuffs on his trembling wrists. "And we're arresting you for her murder."

16

"Oh my God," Kirsten mumbled, her head weary as the early morning light streamed into the kitchen windows of the beach house. *Two girls,* she thought. *Two brutal deaths. . . .*

Thrust back into reality, Kirsten stiffened and pulled farther away from Kyle as she remembered Sam—and how her last moments of life had to have been just as terrifying.

"I did *threaten* Carolee that night, but I didn't *kill* her," Kyle insisted. "The cops found my fingerprints all—"

Kirsten watched him hold back tears and hug himself with his strong arms. She searched his eyes, trying to process it all. Was he telling her the truth? Or was he just a really good actor? She wasn't sure.

"Someone had tied up her hands with . . . my Talcott tie," he went on. "I must have left it at the bar. It's sick!" Kyle stopped talking and looked away as his tears finally broke through, and he swiped at them with the backs of his hands.

And Kirsten had to fight against the instinct to reach out to him.

Maybe he is *telling the truth,* Kirsten thought.

"My prints were all over her body. Wherever she wasn't . . . cut," Kyle whispered. "And because of our fight at the Zoo and the tie . . . it seemed like an open-and-shut case."

Kirsten shook her head. "But why didn't you tell the *truth*? You had an alibi."

"That's just it," Kyle said. "I went to the guys, and they flat out told me that they wouldn't support me. If they did, they could have been charged with second-degree murder. So my 'friends' let me take the fall. My best friends!" His tears were uncontrollable now.

Kirsten wanted to cry, too, but she didn't. She reached out and touched Kyle's hand.

"My lawyer," Kyle went on, "actually my *dad's* lawyer, said it could be worse if I told the truth. I'd be tried for both crimes! That was the biggest mistake of my life. When my name was released to the papers, Brown revoked my college scholarship. And even though the case hadn't begun, Talcott expelled me for 'tarnishing the school's moral standing in the community' and, worst of all, my *dad* even started doubting me!" His eyes seemed hurt and defeated. "My life was ruined!"

"Calm down, Kyle," she heard herself saying. "It's okay. . . ."

"I couldn't tell the police where I was at the time of

Carolee's murder," Kyle went on. "I was directly involved in another death the very same night! God, that *same night*."

Kirsten had no idea what to think anymore or how to react. She looked down at the kitchen tiles and let out a long, deep breath.

"Believe me, Kirsten." Kyle raised his head, his face stained with tears. "I was ready to own up to what happened to Gina. Take responsibility. But then I realized I'd be killing myself *and* incriminating my friends."

Some friends, Kirsten thought as she looked back at Kyle. He was clearly in pain.

"At least I *thought* they were my friends." Kyle clenched his fists.

"God . . ." Kirsten sighed again. "But if you didn't do it, who killed her? Who killed Carolee?"

"I don't know, Kirsten." Kyle shook his head. "I guess anyone at the Zoo could have found my tie . . . and used it on Carolee. But why? That's the question I've been asking myself every day for three years. I have to find out what really happened," he said. "That's why I came back to New York—to find out the truth and to clear my name. I can't live with this cloud hanging over my head."

There was a long pause. Kirsten stared into Kyle's eyes, hoping that if she looked at them long enough, she would know the truth—know if Kyle was a murderer, or a victim of circumstance. *Why would he tell such a horrible story if it wasn't true?* she wondered. Then she thought of something else.

"What about the other girls?" Kirsten asked. "What about Sam and Emma?" Maybe Kyle didn't kill Carolee, but that didn't mean he wasn't involved in the other murders.

"I don't know. Have you ever heard of a copycat killer? Someone who imitates another crime? Maybe that's the answer, or maybe the murderer is just a nut who likes to kill pretty girls. . . ." Kyle paused and raked a hand through his wavy brown hair. "Honestly, I don't have the answer . . . not yet," he said. "But I *will* find it. I have to. You don't know what it's like in prison, Kirsten. I can't go back there. Will you help me?"

Kirsten heard the pain in his voice. The pain and confusion. She looked at him, *really* looked at him, for the first time in eight months. He was so thin. Kyle looked as if he had lost twenty pounds since she'd last seen him—*at least.*

Kyle seemed so convincing—his pain and anguish so real. Kirsten found herself *wanting* to believe him. She wanted to fly across the table and comfort him and tell him that everything was going to be okay and that she was going to help him find the real killer, and that after this whole mess was behind them, after the truth was finally clear and out in the open for everyone to see, they'd finally be happy. *But . . .*

"I can't do this," Kirsten said. She couldn't put herself out there again. "I've been through too much. This whole thing . . . I don't know . . . it's . . . it's just too hard." She couldn't look at him.

"Kirsten . . . ," he said. "I need you . . . *please.* You're the only person I've got."

Kirsten's eyes welled up. "It's not fair of you," she told him. "You can't do this to me. It's not fair!"

Kyle nodded. "Okay," he whispered. "I . . . I'll—"

"Just . . . get away," she said. "Run . . . far away. . . . I won't turn you in. I won't tell anybody that you were here. Just get away, before it's too late. Get away before anybody finds you."

Kyle nodded. Just as he was about to say something, the kitchen door flew open.

17

Julie stumbled through the kitchen doorway drenched, drunk, and delighted.

Kirsten glanced back at Kyle and relaxed a little when she realized he had snuck away. She hoped she could keep Julie in the kitchen long enough for Kyle to duck out of the front door.

Kirsten turned back to see Julie dancing around the room, ranting about how she was going to make "canpakes!" She pulled out a large box of Bisquick from the pantry and opened it, covering herself in a cloud of pancake mix. "What's up with you, slut?" Julie asked sloppily.

Kirsten rolled her eyes. Even though Julie was wasted, she could still read Kirsten like a book. "Nothing," she lied.

"This is no time to hold things inside, Kirrrrsten," Julie said, and cracked a mischievous smile. "Like your *'psychiatrist'* said. What's wrong? Tell Julie *allllll* about it."

"I said *nothing* is wrong," Kirsten snapped, not meaning to.

Julie shrugged. "Whatever." She rambled on about the

rest of the party, the joy of pancakes, about how hot Clark was, and walked into the hallway bathroom.

Kirsten slumped in her chair by the kitchen table. She stared at the one Kyle had been sitting in not five minutes earlier, and boiled with the truth.

"Ahhhrrrrrggggggh!" Julie screamed from the bathroom. "Hellllllllp!"

Uh-oh. Kirsten jumped up and ran toward the screaming.

"Ahhhhhhhh!" Julie rushed out of the bathroom, arms waving above her head, and she slammed right into Kirsten. Both of them toppled to the floor as Kyle fled into the living room, dragging a shower curtain behind him.

"The phone!" Julie scrambled to her feet, making a beeline for the cordless by the couch in the living room.

Kirsten found herself grabbing Julie and holding her back so that she could get to the phone first.

"What the hell are you doing?" Julie screamed.

"Just wait!" Kirsten pleaded. As the two friends wrestled toward the phone, Kyle bolted out the front door.

Kirsten relaxed as she saw Kyle tear down the circular driveway and leap over Julie's fence.

"Are you crazy!" Julie screamed. "We had him here! Right here in the house!"

"Julie—" Kirsten began.

"We could've turned that psycho in!" Julie continued, and grabbed the phone from Kirsten's hand.

Before she could dial 911, Kirsten snatched the phone from her and backed away.

"Give me that!" Julie yelled, swaying in her drunkenness.

"He didn't do it!" Kirsten blurted out. She raised her hands to her mouth, trying to trap the words back inside.

Julie's face sank. Her arms dropped to her side. "No. You can't be *serious*, Kirsten . . . right?"

"I am," Kirsten replied. "Very serious. He came here to tell me the truth."

"Wait." Julie was stunned. You *knew* he was here? I cannot *believe* you, Kirsten! He could've killed you. . . . He could've killed *me*!"

Kirsten turned bright red. It was true. She *had* risked Julie's life by not warning her. "But . . . he told me what really happened," Kirsten mumbled as guilt and confusion closed in on her.

"And you fell for it," Julie muttered, suddenly sober. "You know, you amaze me more and more, Kirsten. How could you be so *stupid*?"

Stupid? Kirsten thought, finding herself getting angry. "You weren't there," she told Julie. "You didn't hear his story. I did, and he was telling the truth!" she screamed.

Cursing under her breath, Julie stalked into the kitchen. "It figures," she muttered.

"Hey, wait a minute!" Kirsten followed. "What was *that* supposed to mean?"

"Like you're such a good judge of character these days!" Julie replied without looking back.

"I *know* you want to elaborate, Julie," Kirsten said. She couldn't stand when Julie got her holier-than-thou attitude. "Go ahead. Say what you've been thinking for months. Say it. Get it off your chest. I want to hear it!"

"Well, first Paul Stone, and now Leslie Fenk?" Julie explained. "You don't exactly have a great track record when it comes to surrounding yourself with quality people, Kirsten. I mean, how many times are you going to fall for this guy's bullshit? And Leslie—do you know what people are saying about you two? That you guys are more than just buddies."

"Oh, come on. You don't believe that. You're just jealous!" Kirsten fought back.

"Of that slut? Yeah, right!" Julie's words cut deep. "You just hang with her so she can get you high! You're pathetic!" Julie spat with finality, turning off the kitchen light, hurrying past Kirsten and going upstairs.

Kirsten felt as if she had been punched in the stomach. And she was about to punch back. She spun around and caught up to Julie on the steps. She grabbed her arm and got directly in her face. "You know what, Julie? I think you're jealous that I'm starting to make new friends," she said.

"Oh please." Julie rolled her eyes.

"And you are definitely jealous of what Kyle and I had," Kirsten added.

"Yeah, right!" Julie huffed, but there was something in her eyes that told Kirsten she might be right about this one. She went with it.

"I mean, what do *you* know about love? The last guy who liked you—I mean, really *liked* you—was Kenny Dwiggler! In seventh grade!"

Julie's face twisted with pain. She pulled away from Kirsten and ran upstairs.

"All those one-night stands don't count!" Kirsten cried. She knew how to hit where it hurt.

Julie broke into sobs as she slammed her bedroom door.

As she listened to Julie cry, Kirsten felt instantly sorry for what she had just said to her friend. *When did I become such a world-class bitch?* she wondered, but before she had a chance to follow her friend upstairs, Julie swung her door back open again.

"I am so sick of dealing with your *shit*, Kirsten. I've been there for you every day for the last *eight miserable months*, but I can't do it anymore, okay?" she said.

"Julie, I—"

"No. Sam was my friend too!" Julie interrupted. "And you're in love with her *killer*?"

Those words were like a slap. Kirsten sank onto the steps. Intense feelings of shame and anger and fear overwhelmed her.

"I don't want to see you here when I wake up!" Julie shouted before slamming her door again, this time for good.

Kirsten moved to go upstairs again, but then stopped

herself. *I'd better let Julie cool down,* she thought. *Nothing I can say—no apology—can fix this right now.*

She gathered her things and opened the door of the Pembrokes' farmhouse.

The sun had risen and was now shining bright above the trees. It was a beautiful morning. Her thoughts turned back to Kyle as she walked across the gravel driveway. His story had sounded so real, so convincing. She wondered where he would go. Where could he run to?

But that didn't matter anymore.

I have *to patch things up with Julie,* Kirsten thought as she turned up a long, straight road, heading for the Jitney stop in the nearest town. *I can't push away the one true friend I have left. . . .*

18

As Kirsten knocked on the large, stately door of 523 East Seventieth Street on the Upper East Side of Manhattan, she heard Dr. Fitzgerald's voice in her head: "Maybe the best way to get over Sam is to help other people get over Sam."

Sam Byrne lived in a quaint brownstone on Seventieth and Park. The place was some kind of registered historical landmark. Sam was *old money*—the kind of first-generation, *Mayflower* money that afforded you prime real estate in the snobbiest area of Manhattan. Kirsten knocked again and then she just waited, seemingly forever. Just as she turned to leave, the door slowly opened.

Kirsten was surprised to see Sam's stepfather—"Rolf from Düsseldorf," as Sam always called him—staring out from the entryway. The Byrnes' live-in housekeeper, Maria, usually answered the door. And Rolf Knauerhase was not looking his usual personal-trainer handsome self. His wavy sandy-colored hair was a mess, his piercing blue eyes seemed to have a dull haze over them, and he was dressed in nothing more than a pair of wrinkled pajamas.

"Hi, Rolf," Kirsten said, trying not to grimace. She usually loved talking with him. She and Sam used to always make fun of his German accent, but all in all, he wasn't a bad guy. But today was different. There was a strong smell of whiskey on his breath as he embraced her a little too long.

"So gut to be seeing you, Keersten," he croaked, trying to fix his hair and make himself look more presentable.

"Great to see you, too," she said as Rolf led her inside.

A flash of memories came back to Kirsten as she stepped into the marble foyer: hours of hide-and-go-seek . . . tossing Barbie dolls off the top of Sam's grand staircase . . . the stress of getting ready for their first fall dance at Woodley. . . .

Kirsten glanced up at a white sheet that was hanging limply over the large painting of the Byrne family that dominated the foyer. "Is Bobbi here?" Kirsten turned back to Rolf, trying her best to smile.

"Um . . . no," Rolf replied, but he didn't sound too convincing.

"Okay . . . ," Kirsten said awkwardly, not knowing exactly what to say. "Um, could I see Sam's room?" she finally asked. "I, um, just want to see it—like, for a minute."

"Sure," Rolf said, his eyes surprisingly sad at the mention of his stepdaughter's name.

Kirsten was blown away by how affected Rolf was. She

was so wrapped up in her own sadness that she nearly forgot that other people missed Sam too. Rolf pointed the way up to Sam's room—a way that Kirsten knew well—and shuffled off toward the kitchen.

Wow, Kirsten thought. If Rolf was leveled by Sam's death, she could only imagine what Sam's mom, Bobbi, must be going though.

I should have come to see them sooner, Kirsten thought. She felt selfish as she walked up to Sam's third-floor bedroom. She hadn't been thinking about anyone but herself for a long time.

The door to Sam's bedroom was already halfway open, and Kirsten quietly entered it. The room clearly hadn't been touched since Sam's murder. Books lay everywhere, makeup lined the windowsill, and Sam's iMac was framed with pictures of the Three Amigas. There were even a few outfits tossed casually across the bed—rejects for their big night out at the Party Room.

The last night at the Party Room.

She burst into tears. Being back in Spammie's room brought a tide of emotions. She noticed Sam's well-worn copy of *Leaves of Grass* sticking out from under a pillow on her bed—the book that she and Sam had read with religious fervor. Kirsten found herself smiling, and she wiped away her tears. As she picked up the book, several papers fell out of it. Notes or something.

Curious, Kirsten unfolded one and started to read it. It was a to-do list.

1) Bio: Chapters 3–5

2) Cal-study!!!

3) Peer Leadership meeting w/ Dean K. @ Wood

4) Yoga w/ Jules and Kirsten!

Kirsten smiled at Sam's manic handwriting. She remembered how simple their lives used to be. At one point they were both just normal high school girls, living normal high school lives. It was nice to have these memories. Good memories.

"You okay, Kirsten?" a weary voice said from behind her.

Kirsten jumped back, flustered by the sudden interruption. She quickly slipped the book and notes into her Coach tote and turned around.

Oh my God, Kirsten thought when she saw Sam's mom standing in the doorway. The woman who had been like Kirsten's second mother now seemed like a total stranger. She was a rail. A skeleton, almost. Bobbi's hair was dull and gray. Her skin looked flaky and raw without her usual makeup. "Hi . . . um, Bobbi," Kirsten started nervously.

"Please stay as long as you like, Kirsten," Bobbi said. "I'm glad you're here." She looked lifeless without her daughter. She looked lost.

"I am so sorry I didn't come sooner. I . . . I—" Kirsten felt herself starting to cry again. She didn't want to, but the moment was just too intense.

"I am too," Bobbi said sadly, looking over Sam's room. "She was . . ."

"Incredible," Kirsten finished her sentence. "She was the greatest friend you could ever ask for."

"And daughter," Bobbi agreed softly, sitting down on the edge of the bed.

Kirsten reached out and put her hand on Bobbi's shoulder. And if a smile can be defined as an infinitesimal rising of the corners of one's mouth, Sam's mom smiled.

Then Kirsten let out a long breath she hadn't even realized she was holding. And she stood there, holding Bobbi's shoulder, letting the tears come, and wishing that she had visited a long time ago.

Later that day, Kirsten was sprawled out on her canopy bed and reading the notes that she had carefully laid out on her duvet. *Leaves of Grass* had practically burned a hole in her purse while she was sitting in Bobbi Byrne's library drinking tea and trading memories about Sam. She didn't know why she took the book, but Kirsten had been dying to sift through the notes she had found.

Now, reading the miscellaneous flirtations and gossip and lists, Kirsten felt as if she were with her friend again. She even found herself laughing out loud.

God, I miss you! she thought as she read and read and read.

Sam not only had notes she had received, but ones she had written herself.

Kirsten scanned through a series of back-and-forths between herself and Sam from when they were in Mr. Costas's bio class together, then she saw a few notes between Sam and Brandon.

As Kirsten unfolded another paper, she remembered how Sam had broken up with Brandon and how badly he had taken it. And how terrible Brandon had looked just a few nights ago. Then she read the note:

Brandon—

I saw Jones again. I had to. I know you'll be angry w/ me, but I had to. I have to keep seeing him. I just have to.

Kirsten furrowed her brow. *Sam never mentioned any Jones guy to* me. She rushed through the rest of the note. She couldn't believe what she was reading. Apparently Sam was seeing this Jones guy on the side. And Brandon knew about it! *How come Sam never said anything about it?*

She scanned the next note:

I can't go on like this. It's got to stop, Brandon. Don't go to Volume again, please. I'm telling you

> *for your own good. Stay away from Jones. He's really pissed and I don't think I can control the situation anymore. It's major. Trust me, this isn't like at Talcott, B. Just do me a favor and keep your butt OUT of VOLUME!!! Okay?*

Kirsten read the last two notes again. Although the scraps of information that she could pick out were sketchy at best, she felt as if she was seeing a whole new chapter of Sam's life. Kirsten had never heard of this Jones guy. Volume? Was it a bar? Kirsten had never been there.

Kirsten wondered if this had something to do with why Sam broke up with Brandon. Now that Kirsten thought about it, Sam had never actually said why she'd dumped him. What did she mean—"This is major"?

Kirsten couldn't make out the story, but something had been going on between Sam and Brandon right up to the day Sam broke up with him, and maybe the night she disappeared!

Who is Jones? Why didn't Sam tell her about him?

The warm feelings of nostalgia drained out of Kirsten as she realized that her best friend—her *sister,* practically—had kept a secret from her. By the looks of it, an *enormous* secret.

"What a total mind game," Scott said the next day as he examined the fractured face of Mademoiselle de Avignon at the Museum of Modern Art.

"That's one way to describe it." Kirsten tilted her head and squinted at the huge Picasso painting.

"It's like he's looking at people through some kind of kaleidoscope or something," Scott added.

"Either that or he was on some heavy drugs," Kirsten joked. She smiled at Scott, glad that he had agreed to hang out with her that day. Julie was still way too angry to speak to, and Kirsten needed to chill with a friend, so she'd called Scott.

As they moved to another of MOMA's permanent collections, however, Kirsten grew quiet. Even though she was having fun with Scott, she couldn't get her mind off the weird notes Sam had written about Jones. She wanted to talk to Julie about them, but of course that wasn't happening anytime soon. And what was Kirsten going to do about that, too?

"You all right, Kirsten?" Scott asked, breaking the silence.

"Huh?" Kirsten replied.

"I said, Are you cool?" Scott led her into another room of paintings. This time they stopped in front of a Magritte—the one with the dark house and the light sky. Scott pushed further. "You can tell me anything—you know that, right?" he said, putting an arm around her shoulders like a comforting brother. "You know, bartenders are practically therapists."

"Is it that obvious I'm upset?" Kirsten asked, smiling weakly.

Scott nodded. "Kind of," he said. "What's going on?"

"Well, Doctor . . ." Kirsten took in a deep breath, and everything spilled out. She told Scott all about the huge disaster in the Hamptons. Her embarrassment with Brian at that party . . . driving home and almost getting into an accident . . . and the huge fight she'd had with Julie the next morning.

"Man," Scott said. "That sucks."

"I know," Kirsten said flatly. "Julie was so mad at me, and we were so mean to each other. But I was worse than Julie was. Much worse. I didn't know I had it in me."

"But what *started* it all?" Scott asked. "What was Julie so mad about?"

Should I tell him about Kyle? Kirsten wondered. But then again, she knew that she could trust him. Scott had been a big support for her ever since Sam died. And one thing that she had always appreciated about him was that he never judged her. Never rolled his eyes when she freaked out over something insignificant . . . never told her she was imagining things, like her other friends had. . . .

"You don't have to tell me if you don't want to," Scott said.

But Kirsten realized that she did want to. She wanted to talk to someone objective. "Kyle came to see me," she finally admitted, staring deeper into the painting in front of them, getting lost in the bright blues and whites. "Out at Julie's beach house."

"Jesus . . . ," Scott said.

"And I think . . ." Kirsten hesitated. "He told me this story, and . . . well . . . I think he might be innocent."

Scott swallowed. "How come?"

Thank God for Scott, Kirsten thought. She appreciated the

fact that he was keeping an open mind. But she knew she couldn't tell Scott about Kyle's secret—about what had happened to that girl Gina. Not yet. Not until she knew more.

"I—I just do." She turned her head away from him as they walked on to a Mondrian painting—tiny squares dancing around in a never-ending maze. Then Scott completely surprised her.

"Maybe you're right," he said. "I mean, if this guy was *really* a killer—and he wanted to kill you . . . he had the perfect shot out there at Julie's. But he didn't do it, right?"

Sam smiled at Scott. "Exactly."

"But if Kyle's innocent, who's guilty?" Scott asked.

"I don't know," Kirsten murmured as she ran through all the possible scenarios. If Kyle truly *was* innocent, then who would have had the motive to kill Sam? And, when you thought about it, Kyle didn't have a reason to kill Sam, either, but the police were very willing to blame him for it—maybe it *was* a copycat, as Kyle had said.

Scott put his arm around Kirsten again and drew her in close, making her feel safe. He was strong, protective, and kind. Kirsten was so lucky to have him as a friend. "If we could just think of who else might have a reason to do it. . . ." He sighed, exasperated. "I wish I could talk to Kyle. Maybe I could help you guys figure it out."

"Too bad you can't. I told him to get out of town. He's probably long gone by now. So, I guess we'll never know what happened." Kirsten said, but her mind kept thinking about it—going back to the last night at the Party Room. *Who was there? Who was there?* She kept asking herself.

There was Kirsten, and Julie, Carla and Sarah, Emma . . . and almost every senior from Woodley. Scott was at the bar . . . Kyle later admitted he was at the Party Room that night . . . and Brandon was there too, of course. Kirsten remembered he was acting like a jerk and trying to take pictures up Sam's skirt. But Sam just ignored him, and then she met this guy . . . an older guy with reddish hair.

"Erik the Red!" Kirsten yelled out her nickname for the guy. "I've completely forgotten about him. The one who left that night with Sam! Remember? He was cute, but very dangerous looking." Kirsten rambled, reminding Scott about the details of Sam's disappearance. "He turned out to be a dealer. I found him, and when I asked him about Sam, he freaked out and ran. The police forgot all about him when the evidence pointed to Kyle—and so did I! But that guy is probably long-gone too." And Kirsten wasn't sorry about that. This guy was very shady—and he wasn't happy about her having tracked him down.

"Wait, who?" Scott squinted as he thought of something. Then a flash of recognition: "Did this guy have *red* hair like Seth Green?"

Kirsten nodded. "Uh-huh."

"Oh my God, Kirsten!" Scott said. "I remember him . . . and . . . and . . . I saw him last night at a place called Volume!"

19

"'I saw him last night at a place called Volume!'" Scott's words echoed in Kirsten's mind the next day as she poured a few of Leslie's pills into her hand. She popped them into her mouth and leaned over the faucet in the WXRJ bathroom. Kirsten drank greedily and swallowed them down.

So I can concentrate . . . focus, she chanted to herself. She hadn't been able to sleep all night.

As Kirsten straightened, she splashed a handful of water on her face and tried to shake off her thoughts. Now she wished that she hadn't told Kyle to leave town. She needed to find him somehow—to talk about that guy Sam left with. But right now she had to work.

After a few more minutes of deep breathing, Kirsten walked out of the ladies' room and down the hallway toward Studio Five. When Kirsten entered the studio, she was shocked to see Kate Grisholm already there, throwing minidisks all over the tech room.

"There you are, Kirsten!" Kate said, exasperated.

Uh-oh, Kirsten thought. *I must've lost track of time in the bathroom.* She looked down at her watch. "Sorry, I—"

Kate raised a hand to stop her. "You know, when you first came here, I thought you were going to be my star intern, but now . . . what's going on with you?"

"I . . . ah—" Kirsten stopped short. She had nothing to say to defend herself. She'd been doing an awful job lately, and she knew it.

"I had to come in *two hours* early today to reorganize this place. You left it a total mess on Friday!"

"I'm sorry," Kirsten mumbled, her hands beginning to shake. *Maybe I should have taken three instead of four pills this morning,* she thought.

"There are *a lot* of people who would gladly take this job!" Kate said as she rose from Kirsten's chair.

"I'll do better. I promise!" Kirsten pleaded as Kate stormed off toward the main studio, leaving Kirsten to file the rest of the mini-disks by herself.

Before she closed the tech room door, Kate shot Kirsten an icy glance.

A warning.

Kirsten knew she was hanging on to this job by a thread. Only minutes remained before *Love Stinks* would begin. There was no way Kirsten could get all the work done.

"Good morning, sunshine!" Brian smiled, swinging open the door to the studio.

"Is it?" Kirsten said flatly, shoveling mini-disks into random piles.

Brian bent down and immediately started helping Kirsten. "Looks like you and Kate are best friends now," he joked, trying to lighten the mood.

Kirsten laughed and nudged him with her arm. "Thanks."

Then, with blinding speed, Kirsten filed the last DAT and got ready to man the phones for the show. When a still-frustrated Kate Grisholm took her seat in front of the main headset, Kirsten was ready to give her a thumbs-up.

The engineer cued the intro music, and the show buzzed to life. Kirsten exhaled and smiled. She *loved* her job. She couldn't stand the thought of losing this opportunity.

As she finished her prep work, Brian just looked on in admiration. "Know what, Kirsten?" he said. "When you're actually *here*, you really kick ass at this!"

"Thanks," Kirsten said, taking in the compliment. But she had to explain. "I've just had a lot on my mind recently."

She remembered the rainy night. Their conversation outside Julie's. How she had turned Brian down. How he had taken it so well.

"It's all right, Kirsten," he assured her. "I know all about it."

Huh? Kirsten stopped working suddenly. "Know all about

what?" she asked, afraid to hear the answer. Why should he be bothered with the madness of her life?

"Well," Brian began. "I ran into some tweaked-out guy named Brandon last night while I was bar hopping with a few friends. He told me about the, um, *murders*. And about your old boyfriend."

No! Kirsten's mind screamed. Brandon Yardley kept finding ways to mess with her life. She knew she should talk to him about that Jones guy, but Kirsten didn't want to go there with him. "Listen to me, Brian," Kirsten snapped. "Brandon Yardley is psycho. Seriously. Don't believe a word—"

The phone rang.

The first caller! Kirsten remembered. She was getting distracted again. She had to focus. She couldn't afford another mess-up!

Before Kirsten could answer the phone, Brian picked it up. *"Love Stinks,"* he said, winking at Kirsten. "It's for you." he said, handing the phone to her.

For me? Kirsten thought. A sudden shiver ran up her spine. *Is it Kyle? Did he call me again? I want to talk, but how am I going to explain the call to Kate?*

See you later, Brian mouthed as Kirsten turned to her work. Brian then turned to leave. He'd been gone from the mail room for *way* too long.

"Love Stinks," Kirsten repeated into the phone.

"You can say that again, baby!"

Not Kyle, Kirsten realized. *Leslie Fenk.*

"Hey, sexy!" Leslie sang into the receiver, a sultry R&B song whispering in the background.

"Leslie, you can't call me on this number," Kirsten whispered, ducking out of Kate's line of sight. "Why didn't you use my cell phone?"

"I will next time, okay?" Leslie said. Then she started to giggle. "Stop that, Danny!" she whispered to someone in the room. She was calling to invite Kirsten and a guest to a party she was hosting that very night in the super-chic meatpacking district.

After a pause, Kirsten decided to go. She knew she should really go check out that bar where Scott saw Erik the Red. But Kirsten decided to blow it off. She needed to relax more than ever. "I'm in," she said.

"Good. Don't forget to wear something trasheee!" was the last thing Leslie cooed before she screamed and laughed and hung up the phone.

She might be crazy, but at least she's fun, Kirsten thought. *And a party is just what I need. But who would want to go with me to a Leslie Fenk party? Definitely not Julie.* She glanced out the window of Studio Five and spotted Brian depositing mail in the station manager's in-box and got her answer.

"I had no idea it was going to be like this," Kirsten whispered to Brian as they passed a sign that said WELCOME TO LESLIE

FENK'S WONDERFUL WORLD OF SEX PARTY! Then a sign that listed a set of do's and don'ts for the party, such as: "Do feel free to get naked at any time within the course of the evening," and "Don't feel as if you have to take part in the action—some people just like to watch."

Brian didn't say anything as he gaped around while they entered the dimly lit loft on Little West Twelfth Street.

Kirsten was embarrassed, to say the least, and she was going to kill Leslie just as soon as she could find her! The girl had conveniently left out the part about this being an X-rated theme-park party in her invite.

She took in the scene. Strobe lights. Incense. Velvet-covered couches. A group of scantily clad blondes standing by a curtain of metal beads, smoking skinny cigarettes and pretending to look unaffected by the scene.

There's sheer, and then there's topless, Kirsten thought as she watched them practically devour Brian with their eyes while they walked by them.

"Ooh, he's delicious," one girl said, licking her bloodred lips and staring directly at Brian.

"Mmm . . . ," another one, reaching out and grazing her fingers across the front of his black Armani T-shirt.

"Uh, *excuse* you!" Kirsten pulled the slut brigade off her dazed but not *entirely* upset date as they walked through a curtain of metal beads and found themselves in a completely foreign environment: trip-hop blared loudly from invisible speakers, and kids on Ecstasy lay in corners of a large, cushioned room.

"I'm sorry." Kirsten turned to Brian, but before he had a chance to respond, someone grabbed Kirsten's butt! Hard! "Hey!" she shouted, and spun around.

It was Leslie, dressed to maim severely in shiny leather pants and a Gaultier bustier, and looking completely gone on something. "Hello, my pretties!" Leslie yelled, even though she was hugging both Kirsten and Brian already. "Welcome to my naughty little fiesta!"

"Thanks," Kirsten began. "And I brought—"

Before Kirsten could even finish her sentence, however, Leslie's tongue was halfway down Brian's throat. Kirsten frowned. *Thanks a lot, Leslie!*

"Don't be so naive!" Kirsten could hear Julie's voice now, mocking her and being 100 percent right.

When Leslie and Brian finally separated, Brian turned to Kirsten with a surprising smile. He didn't mind! He hadn't minded *at* all.

"What the hell are you doing, Brian?" Kirsten cried.

But Brian's expression changed. "Sometimes you gotta just go with the flow," he murmured.

"Come on, Kirsten. Don't be so uptight," Leslie cooed. "I'm sure there's plenty of Brian to go around. Want to see?"

Kirsten's stomach turned. "I don't think so," she said.

"Leslie wants to see . . . Leslie like-y," she purred, dragging her new boy toy away.

So that's it, huh? Kirsten shook her head in disbelief. That was the cost to enter the Leslie Fenk Club: one perfect male for the sacrifice. *Well, once a Woodley Bitch, always a Woodley Bitch.* She held her purse tight and walked up to a stainless-steel bar in the far corner of the party. She'd have one drink, and then she was out of there.

As Kirsten ordered and finished her drink in one fluid motion, she thought back to her fight with Julie. More than ever, she wished it had never happened. She had been such a *maniac* that night. Now she needed a real friend. A true friend.

Kirsten wrestled her cell phone out of her too-small purse and speed-dialed her friend. *Please pick up, please pick up,* she chanted to herself as the phone rang.

Straight to voice mail.

Julie was still screening Kirsten's calls.

"Julie. It's me!" Kirsten knew she sounded desperate, but she didn't care anymore. "I'm sooooo sorry, girl. I'm a total bitch, and I—"

Suddenly, a tall, model-esque girl ran a hand across Kirsten's face, dusting her with glitter.

Kirsten whipped around, startled. She hung up the phone and shouted, "Can I help you?"

"Hi there." The girl leaned in close to Kirsten's face. "You're really pretty."

"No offense, but that's not my thing." Kirsten pushed the girl away from her—a little too hard. The waif-ish model skittered across the floor, sailing into a pack of older guys.

Kirsten looked around for Brian, who was nowhere to be seen. People groped one another everywhere, grinding in corners, French kissing on the dance floor. Freaked and suddenly claustrophobic, she ran out of the loft as fast as she could!

"Taxi!" she screamed as she hit the street. She tried to calm down now that she was outside, but she noticed that everyone in line for Leslie's party was gawking at her.

Why is everyone looking at me? she wondered, looking down at her outfit: Just a simple black French Connection miniskirt, a Scoop tank top, and a pair of strappy Manolos. *What are you staring at?* Kirsten wanted to scream. *This city is crazy,* she thought as she flagged down a passing livery cab. *And Brian's another lost cause.*

Kirsten climbed inside and gave the driver her address. It was definitely time to go home.

As the cab raced uptown, jostling Kirsten from side to side, she sank into the backseat and wondered how she had ever gotten involved with Leslie Fenk. Julie had been so right about the girl. And now, Kirsten wished more than anything that she could have her best friend by her side. She missed Julie . . . and she missed Sam, too.

"Why couldn't it just go back to the way it was!" she screamed out the open window. "Why do there have to be so many freaks in this city!" she said, ignoring the odd look the driver was giving her.

Then she sat back and watched the city blur by. It was never going to go back to the way it was, she realized. Julie might never forgive her and, well, Sam was gone. And though Kirsten wished she had the power to make that not so, she knew she could do nothing to change it.

There was only one thing that she *could* do. Now that she believed Kyle was innocent, there was a killer out there. Sam's killer. Someone who had gotten away with murder. Maybe if she could find out who he is—she'd be able to move on. To make this awful time in her life just a bad memory.

But she had to decide on one thing first. *No more pills. No more booze,* Kirsten thought. *Just the truth.* She had avoided things for far too long.

Just as she had resolved herself to action, the cab raced by a brightly lit bar. She couldn't believe her eyes. The sign outside said VOLUME in small neon letters.

Volume! That's it! Kirsten remembered. Volume was the bar she had read about in Sam's letter! *The one where Jones was hanging out.*

"Stop!" Kirsten heard herself scream. The cabbie immediately slammed on the brakes. She paid him and rushed out onto the street. *To do what?* Kirsten asked herself. She didn't have a plan. She just *knew* that she had to find Jones.

He'd have answers. He had to.

Taking in a deep breath, mixing courage with craziness, Kirsten walked under the neon sign and entered Volume.

The place was a dive in every sense of the word. The walls were lined with peeling yellow wallpaper. There was no top shelf behind the bar. Even though the ban on smoking had been on for years, Volume smelled like an ashtray. A couple of junkies congregated near the back bathrooms, looking for a fix. And that was about it.

"Drinking or just looking?" someone muttered behind Kirsten.

Kirsten spun around to find herself face-to-face with a female bartender. She was an Amazon: well over six feet tall, wearing heavy gauge earrings and an alligator-skin choker. The bartender had a tattoo of a small black spider under the corner of her right eye.

Kirsten gulped down her fear. Maybe running into a random bar at one in the morning wasn't such a great idea. . . .

The black spider danced as the bartender repeated her question: "Drinking or just *looking*?"

"Jones," was the very first thing out of Kirsten's mouth.

Did I just say that? Kirsten yelled to herself in disbelief. She was in total blurt mode, when nothing could stay in her subconscious for more than a few seconds.

Just as Kirsten was about to hurry out, the Amazon spoke again. "Jones doesn't operate here anymore," she said curtly, strangling a bottle of Seagram's.

Kirsten skin burned with excitement . . . and a little fear. *She knows Jones! But what did she mean by "operate"?*

The bartender stared at her suspiciously, and Kirsten tried to conceal her emotions by biting her upper lip. Inside, however, she was crawling with questions. "Is Jones a dealer?" she burst out again.

The bartender's expression changed: It turned darker, angrier. "Are you *crazy*?"

"Um, well . . . I, uh . . ." Kirsten's mind raced for something to say.

"Look, little girl!" The Amazon marched out from behind the bar to confront Kirsten. "I don't know *who* you are, but I suggest that you take your designer outfit out of here!"

Kirsten froze. She needed to know more, but she also wanted to get out of Volume alive. She just stared at the bartender. "I was just wondering if—"

"I SAID GET THE HELL OUT OF HERE!" the woman screamed, waving to a gigantic bouncer near the door.

Rocking back on her heels, Kirsten knocked over a stool. As she heard the bouncer running toward her from behind, she slipped past the Amazon, avoided a skanky drunk, and ran out of Volume. Just in time to avoid being *thrown* out.

Back outside, Kirsten caught her breath and tried to gather her thoughts: Jones had clearly worked—or *operated*—at Volume. He must've been a dealer there or something, Kirsten assumed. Then her stomach soured. What was Sam doing, going out with a dealer? She had been crazy and liked to party, but not *that* much.

"Looking for Jones, huh?" a voice muttered. Suddenly, *somehow*, a short, skinny man had materialized right next to her. He stared at her jeans skirt, eyes darting from side to side. "You looking for Jones?" he repeated under his breath, drawing closer to her.

Ew. *Too close.* He stunk like a brewery, and need a shower big-time.

"Yeah," Kirsten said as she backed up a little and folded her arms across her chest. She stood tall and tried to look as tall and as confident as possible.

She knew she was in way over her head, but she had to continue.

"I—I—I know where you can f-f-find him," the small man whispered mysteriously. He then looked down the street and waited. And waited. And waited.

After far too long, Kirsten suddenly realized what he was waiting for: money. Cold, hard cash. If she wanted more info, she'd have to pay for it.

Kirsten reached into her purse, pulled out her wallet, and stuffed a twenty into his shaking hands.

"He's at Stop Light tonight. It's a club. Three blocks up, on Tenth Avenue," the skinny man rattled. "Bouncers in the back room. Tell 'em you're on 'the Guest List.'" And with that, he scuffled off down the street and around the corner.

Kirsten shook her head back into clarity and exhaled slowly. She had a choice to make—possibly even a life-or-death choice. She could track down Jones right now and try to solve the mystery, or she could go home to safety. But she would risk never finding Jones again.

Screw it! Kirsten decided. *I'm going.*

She fished her cell phone out of her purse and called Julie one more time. One last time. Kirsten needed her friend now more than ever. The phone rang four times and then went straight to voice mail again.

"Hey! It's Julie P.!" the message started. "Your favorite person in the whole entire world! Please leave a message at the—"

BEEEEEEP.

Kirsten swallowed and spoke in a hushed tone: "Julie. It's Kirsten. I need your help. Seriously. Tonight, if you can. Please. At the Stop Light. Tenth and, like, Thirty-Sixth. Okay? See you there." *What are you doing, Kirsten?* she thought. *Julie's not going to all of a sudden forgive you and show up because you said "please." The way things are going, she probably won't ever talk to you again!*

She sighed and checked out the street toward Stop Light. At this time of night, this part of Tenth Avenue was dark and empty, aside from the occasional staggering drunk. Disregarding a whistle coming from a dark archway across Tenth Avenue, Kirsten held her purse tightly and set off.

She walked quickly up the three blocks to Stop Light. As she hurried, she passed empty storefronts and cheap diners, shuffling homeless men and walls of black garbage bags lining the curbs. Kirsten shivered as she looked across the Midtown wasteland.

When Kirsten arrived at the club, she paused and stood outside for a moment. Now that she was actually there, what the hell was she supposed to do? She took a few seconds to come up with a plan. She'd go to the back room and see if she could find him.

What sort of guy would Sam hide from me? she asked herself as she entered the place, passing a sleeping bouncer. Once inside, Kirsten squinted to adjust her vision. It was dark in there, and she barely made out a bar lining one wall, a collection of weird photographs on the other—faces, limbs, feet—and a small linoleum dance floor in the back. A huge working stoplight illuminated the dazed pupils of the few scattered regulars who were staring at her.

"Excuse me," Kirsten said politely as she stepped around a man swaying near the bar, literally crying into his beer.

She walked toward the back room, scanning the place for someone who looked like a dealer. Everyone was pretty much sloshed and silently slumped in their own worlds. People seemed to be moving in slow motion.

As she walked farther and farther into the club, Kirsten felt a dull tremor overtake her body. She couldn't quite place it, but something was wrong with this place. She had a bad feeling. Really bad. What was wrong with her? She shouldn't be alone in a place like this. Maybe she should get out of there.

Before Kirsten could turn around to leave, she heard a word. One simple word that changed the course of everything:

"Jones."

Jones! Kirsten silently shouted as she twisted back around. *Was someone talking about him?* To *him? Was Jones there at that moment?* Kirsten shook with fear as she looked around the bar.

Through the darkness and intermittent flashing lights, Kirsten could make out what looked like a drug deal going down near the back exit. A guy who was facing the back door was handing a small plastic bag to a chattering woman. "Jones, Jones, Jones!" she repeated over and over, rubbing her hands on a greasy pair of jeans.

Then the woman raced past Kirsten and into a nearby bathroom. The dealer shook his head and turned around.

Kirsten's knees buckled and she dropped to the floor when she saw his face. . . .

Saw his red, flaming hair.

20

Jones is the red-haired guy. The last person to see Sam alive. He is Sam's killer! Kirsten screamed inside. She picked herself up from the grimy floor and scrambled backward. Then, a hand grabbed her shoulder!

In a desperate panic, Kirsten looked up. It was only an elderly man staring down at her, looking concerned.

"You all right, little lady?" he slurred through a toothless grin.

Kirsten shot up to her feet and pushed by the elderly man—no time for thank-yous— and ran out of Stop Light.

On the way out, Kirsten ran directly into the bouncer. He was clearly awake now. Before the huge doorman could fully grab her by the wrist, however, Kirsten wrenched free and tore uptown.

I have to tell someone! Kirsten said to herself, supercharged with adrenaline. She reached for her cell again and immediately called Scott at the Party Room.

"I saw him!" Kirsten yelled as soon as Scott answered the phone.

"Who?" Scott shot back, clearly recognizing the terror in his friend's voice.

"The red-haired guy! His name is Jones!" she screamed as she ran though screaming traffic.

"Jesus, Kirsten!" Scott yelled back. "You can't catch him alone! Who the hell do you think you are?" Kirsten could hear the Party Room buzzing on the other end of the line.

"But—"

"But nothing! That guy is a killer, Kirsten! Get the hell out of there and call the cops!" Scott demanded.

"Okay!" Kirsten hung up and tracked down a yellow taxi waiting at the corner of Thirty-Eighth Street and Tenth Avenue. She swung the door open and slid inside, not even looking back to see if Jones was on her trail.

Then, in her second cab of the night, Kirsten sank back into the torn seats and calmed herself. Remembering Scott's advice, Kirsten picked up her phone again and dialed a different number. This time, Detective Peterson answered.

"Did he see you?" Peterson asked in his clipped, official tone after listening to her.

"I don't *think* so," Kirsten answered, watching the Upper East Side whiz by outside.

"Are you sure?"

"Well, not totally," Kirsten admitted. "Everything happened so quickly. He *might've* seen me . . . but I don't think so." *What was I thinking?* Kirsten said to herself. She could still see Jones's terrible, menacing face.

"Stop Light is *not* the place for a high school girl," Peterson spoke firmly.

"I know that, but I had to do *something*!" Kirsten snapped back.

"No!" Peterson was now shouting into the phone. "That's our job! That's my job! I just want you to go home now. Do you hear me?"

"But don't you need me to ID him or something?" She wanted to stay involved.

"No thanks, Kirsten. We'll handle this thing. We've got a file on this Jones guy and we'll get him," Peterson assured her. "Until then, just go home and—"

"I'm already there," Kirsten said as her taxi pulled up in front of her apartment. She paid the cabbie and walked quickly into her lobby.

"If we need your help, we'll call you, okay?" Peterson said. "Kirsten?"

"Yes?" she asked.

"Don't worry about this guy," he said. "We'll get him."

"Finally." Kate Grisholm stuck her head into the tech room, surprising Kirsten as she cued the *Love Stinks* outtro music.

What now? Kirsten frowned, turning toward her boss.

She'd been trying her hardest all day. Sweat clung to Kirsten's body even though air-conditioning pumped through WXRJ. "I'm sorry?" she asked tentatively, trying to smile at Kate.

But then a smile spread across her boss's face. "Finally, the *real* Kirsten Sawyer is back!"

"Oh!" Kirsten breathed a sigh of relief.

"Great work out there today," Kate added. "Really. You nailed it. You handled the callers beautifully, and hey, you even saved my butt when I accidentally hung up on the guy with the stocking fetish!"

Kirsten beamed. It felt good to do something *right* for a change.

"Thanks," was all Kirsten could say, relaxing back into her chair.

"No. Thank *you*." Kate smiled, shutting the door. She turned off the overhead lights in the main room, gave Kirsten a final friendly wink and walked out of Studio Five.

Kirsten felt tears welling inside, but this time they were different. They accompanied a deep feeling of accomplishment. True to her promise, Kirsten had managed to stay off drugs for two days now. And she hadn't had a drop to drink, and she had even stopped taking the sleeping medication her psychiatrist had prescribed for her.

As Kirsten smiled to herself, she caught Brian passing by the tech room door. "Brian!" she called out.

No response.

Kirsten frowned curiously and hurried out of her chair. She hadn't seen Brian since the whole Leslie Fenk incident and she was *dying* to ask him about it. "Hey! Brian!" she called out again as she swung the door open.

As she stepped into the hallway, however, Kirsten saw Brian practically *running* away! Even from at least ten yards away, Kirsten could make out a purple ring of hickeys around Brian's neck!

She laughed out loud. *Guess he's not in the sharing mood,* she thought, turning back to close up the studio. As Kirsten locked all the doors and walked down the long WXRJ hallway, she smiled again. It had been a tough workday, and now all she really wanted to do was get a long night's rest. She planned on staying in, curling up to bad TV and, of course, a cup of Mom's cocoa. Her parents were off antiquing upstate again, but she found herself craving her mother's famous cure-all.

Kirsten rode the elevator down and strolled out of the lobby. She grinned when she caught herself whistling. *I'm whistling while I work!* Kirsten laughed again. *How cheesy!*

As she walked out into the busy Times Square traffic and headed to the subway, an elderly woman approached her. "Got some change?" the woman rasped, scratching the back of her neck.

Usually oblivious to street people, Kirsten stopped and actually *looked* at this woman. She was pulling a shopping cart down the sidewalk, singing to a grimy collection of teddy bears. "Sure." Kirsten smiled.

Although she only had a few teeth in her mouth, the old woman managed a smile back. "Don't worry, be happy!" the woman sang as Kirsten reached for her wallet. She had a fragile, sweet voice.

Don't worry, be happy, Kirsten thought. *Good advice.* But as she handed the woman a few dollars, something flashed into the corner of her eye.

A tie-dyed shirt.

Kirsten accidentally dropped the money on the ground and she turned to face the distraction. Down the block, across the way, Kirsten saw someone jump through a shadow. Advancing.

Was it Jones? He'd been wearing a tie-dyed Phish shirt the night Sam was murdered. Kirsten's heart pounded, and she felt her body suddenly stiffen, her happy mood deflate.

"You all right, sweetie?" the homeless woman asked as she gathered Kirsten's donation from the sidewalk.

Kirsten couldn't speak. She scanned the streets for Jones. *Is my mind just playing tricks on me again?* she wondered. Then she saw the figure again. Coming closer!

"Hey! Get out of here!" someone shouted behind Kirsten. "You're not wanted here!"

Kirsten turned her head just enough to see Noel, one of the doormen at WXRJ, coming over to shoo away the homeless woman.

"Was she bothering you?" Noel then asked, noticing Kirsten's grave expression.

"No, not at all," she said, distracted, but relieved that Noel had shown up.

Down the street, making his way through broad daylight, Jones was running away.

Kirsten sat in the Seventy-Ninth Precinct waiting room, holding her breath against the foul smell of urine that wafted up from the holding pens. Her heart was still racing.

Not even an hour ago, Jones had been tracking her—waiting for just the right moment to take her out.

Peterson finally popped out of his office, shirtsleeves rolled up, eyes sunken with fatigue. "All right, Kirsten," he said, waving her inside.

Kirsten stood up, still a little shaky, and followed the young detective inside. She sat down in a chair facing Peterson's cluttered desk and looked around the office: piles of reports stacked everywhere; a series of awards collecting dust on one wall; a picture of Peterson with a newborn baby.

"Jake's two now," Peterson suddenly announced. He leaked a tired smile. "I work so much, I'm not sure he even recognizes me anymore."

Kirsten frowned. In all her time dealing with the detective, she'd never once thought about his own life.

Peterson moved in front of Kirsten and sat against the edge of his desk. "So how close did this guy get to you?" he asked as he flipped open a notepad.

"Maybe half a block. Or a bit closer . . . ," Kirsten answered. "As soon as he saw the building's doorman come over, he took off."

"Sure." Peterson concluded. "Out in broad daylight like that? Jones was taking a real risk in going after you."

Kirsten felt another shiver overtake her. "I guess he did see me the other night."

"I'll say he did," Peterson exclaimed. "You marched right into a serious drug dealer's point of operation, asking all sorts of things about him? Of course he's going to come looking for you, Kirsten."

"I had no idea what I was getting myself into," Kirsten admitted. She knew she had acted rashly the other night, but she didn't realize how far Jones would go.

"Hey, don't beat yourself up about it, Kirsten." Peterson moved toward her, placing a hand on her back. "Truth is, you did something brave."

The young detective smiled at her; Kirsten melted inside.

"Look, your placing Jones at Stop Light will make busting him much easier for us," Peterson continued. "I just don't want you—"

"Acting like a maniac," Kirsten finished his sentence and smirked. She was happy that Peterson was finally taking her seriously—and also happy to let the police take over.

Peterson smiled. "We won't let anything bad happen to you, Kirsten," he said. "You can count on it."

"Thanks again," Kirsten said to the policeman who rode in the elevator with her up to her apartment.

"No sweat, Ms. Sawyer." The cop nodded.

The elevator door opened into the foyer of the penthouse apartment.

"I *promise* to stay home tonight." Kirsten smiled, trying to put the cop at ease. "No more tracking drug-dealing killers on my own, okay?"

"Good to hear," the officer said. "Have a nice night."

Kirsten stepped out of the elevator and waved to the officer just as the elevator door closed. She tossed her purse on a nearby chair and turned toward her bedroom.

An unfamiliar feeling crept over her for the first time in a long time. A warm feeling. The muscles in her face and neck felt looser.

I feel safe! Kirsten realized. *Finally.* She felt happy. Comfortable. Although she'd come close to danger, she had also come closer to the truth. Now it seemed as if it was only a matter of time. . . .

As Kirsten approached her room, she thought about Kate's words of encouragement today. But as she faced her door, her throat tightened.

The door was slightly open, and she *distinctly* remembered shutting it that morning—pulling it tight as she hurried off to work. Her parents weren't home, and their maid had cleaned the apartment yesterday.

Am I just overreacting? she asked herself as she slowly backed down the hallway.

CRASH!

Something fell in her room!

Someone's in there! Kirsten filled with panic, but she resisted the impulse to scream. Maybe she could slip out in time. Maybe the police officer was still double-parked outside. She hurried to the elevator, pressing the call button a million times.

But it was too late.

Someone emerged from her bedroom—letting the door slam open against the wall!

"Noooo!" Kirsten cried.

21

Brandon Yardley burst out of Kirsten's bedroom, his eyes wild. "What did you find?" he yelled, rushing at her, his body swaying and banging into the walls of the narrow hallway.

"W-w-what are you talking about?" Kirsten stammered, backing away from the elevator—away from Brandon—and toward the kitchen. *How did he get in? I'm not even safe in my own house!*

"I followed you to Sam's house the other day!" Brandon yelled, clearly agitated and unstable. "What were you doing there?"

"Nothing!" Kirsten protested, but inside, her mind was racing. Maybe if she could make it to the kitchen, she'd be able to grab the biggest knife and scare Brandon out of there.

"I don't believe you!" Clearly Brandon wasn't into reason right about now.

"She was my best friend, Brandon! Ever think I just wanted to visit her parents?" Kirsten asked.

"How sweet!" Brandon said. "So you didn't *find* anything? Or should I say find *out* anything?"

Before Kirsten could round the corner and slip into the kitchen, Brandon reached out and grabbed her wrist.

Okay, Kirsten thought as she winced in pain. So Brandon knew that she knew. All of a sudden, Kirsten went limp. She relaxed, giving in to Brandon's tugging, even falling into his arms. *Time to switch strategies,* she thought. Instead of avoiding Brandon, she was going to use him. Brandon was going to tell her everything she needed to know . . . about Jones . . . and Sam. Everything!

"What's going on with you?" Brandon said frowning.

"Okay, you got me," Kirsten said quietly, demurely, as she looked into Brandon's saucer-size pupils. "I *did* find something at Sam's house. Something about *you*."

Time to play, she thought.

"Tell me!" Brandon demanded.

Kirsten prayed that her plan would work.

"Why do I have to say anything?" Kirsten asked. "You know what was in those notes, Brandon. The ones you thought were so *secret*. You know, the ones where you and Sam were talking about Jones."

"The notes!" Brandon cried.

"Yup." Kirsten looked into Brandon's eyes. "And I know *all* about it. All about you and Sam and Jones! Sam told me *everything*."

"No!" Brandon slammed his fist against a wall. "Sam promised me she'd let it all go until . . ."

"Well, it looks like she broke that promise," Kirsten replied. She was improvising everything. Buying time. Trying to get him to say more.

"I knew it!" Brandon cried. "Right before we broke up, Sam said she was going to tell everybody at Woodley. I knew that you'd be the first person she told. You guys were inseparable!"

"Of course we were," Kirsten said.

Brandon stalked into Kirsten's living room as if he had lived there his whole life.

Stay a while, Brandon, Kirsten thought. He slumped into her father's favorite chair and ran a hand through his hair. "Look on the bright side. At least there are no more secrets." She sat on the ottoman directly across from the chair.

"I've been trying to get to you for *days*, Kirsten!" Brandon groaned.

"What do you mean?" Kirsten asked. "I haven't seen you for a while."

"Yeah," Brandon grinned. "But I saw *you*! I was here the other night, Kirsten." He let out a low, weird laugh. "In your bedroom!"

Of course! Kirsten realized. It was *Brandon* who had broken in the other night!

"You shouldn't leave a spare key under your doormat, Kirsten." Brandon smiled. "There are a lot of nut-jobs out there."

And I'm looking at one, Kirsten realized. He looked terrible. His eyes were surrounded by purplish yellow circles and his hands moved around in his lap, stuck in a constant nervous dance. She had to either get Brandon back on the topic of Jones or out of her house. "So, did everything turn out okay . . . with Jones?"

"Are you crazy?" Brandon cried. "What did Sam tell you?"

Kirsten shrugged. "A lot," she said. "Did you ever go back to Volume?"

Brandon shook his head. "No," he said. "I didn't."

"Look," Kirsten said, leaning closer to him. "I don't want to judge you, but it's kind of hard knowing only one side of the story. Now I want to hear *your* side, Brandon. It's only fair," she said. *Did it work? Is he going to tell me what I need to know?*

Brandon was quiet for a long time. Then he let out a long, weary sigh. "It was all about the drugs. You know how corny all those health classes were? Well, I guess maybe the teachers knew what they were talking about. Drugs . . . suck," he admitted.

"Tell me about it," Kirsten chimed in, encouraging Brandon to continue.

"They literally *suck,*" Brandon said. "They suck your ambition. They suck your identity. Shit, they even suck your blood!"

Kirsten nodded her head, doing her best Dr. Fitzgerald impersonation.

"Anyway." Brandon cleared his throat with a shuddering hack. "Jones was my dealer, right?

"I was into coke pretty bad back then, and I owed his people a ton of money. I tried to ask Jones for more time, 'cause my dad froze all my credit cards, but Jones wasn't having it. He *never* let anyone off the hook. He made me one of his runners as 'punishment.'"

"Right, sure," Kirsten chimed in, pretending to know the story that Brandon was beginning to unfold.

"And I have to admit, I kind of liked it. At first it was cool, you know? Being a dealer. I got to know everyone, I made a little pocket money on the side, and I got girls. *Lots* of girls." Brandon smiled for a moment, then went on. "But eventually I just got sick of it," he said. "I was sick of hiding from cops. And I was helping people snort their *lives* away, you know? Kids!

"When I tried to get out of the game, Jones told me that he'd expose me. He'd tell my parents! He'd get me kicked off the JV basketball team at Talcott!"

"I remember hearing about that," Kirsten lied.

"Yeah!" Brandon yelled. He was worked up now. "At first I did what Jones said, and kept dealing, but then one day I said, 'Screw it!' I told my parents all about my problem and my dealing. They notified the police about Jones, and he was arrested. Luckily, my dad hushed things up at Talcott, seeing how everyone was studying in the *Yardley Library*, after all!" He grinned.

And so did Kirsten. The story was becoming clearer.

"I had to leave the school, but my record was *spotless*. That's when I started going to Woodley—and by senior year, I was dating Sam. I wasn't dealing anymore, but I was still doing a ton of blow. Sammy even got into it for a while."

How could I not know that Sam was into coke? Kirsten wondered, but she quickly corrected herself! Sam had given her a hit of E that night at the Party Room. Sam had been more of a partier than Kirsten ever knew. She nodded her head as if she'd heard it all before.

"But when she saw how crazy it made me," Brandon continued, "she dumped my ass. I was heated, but honestly, it was a smart move for her. I was a mess. I guess I still am."

Brandon looked up at Kirsten and made an attempt at an apologetic smile. In that moment, he looked so vulnerable. So weak. Inside that big, tough body was just a little boy.

"And you know the rest . . ." Brandon trailed off.

"Wait!" Kirsten heard herself shout. She held her tongue. If she sounded too eager, Brandon would realize that she didn't know a thing.

"I know *Sam's* version, but it didn't make *you* look so good," she said. "What do you have to defend yourself for, Brandon?" Kirsten asked.

Brandon squinted at Kirsten. He seemed suspicious.

"I just want to know," Kirsten added.

Brandon nodded. "I know, I know," he said. "When Jones

got out of jail, he tracked me down and said that I owed him money. He gave me just one week to pay them off. Or else they'd KILL ME! Even though Sam and I were over by then, she felt bad for me and tried to pay off Jones. And that's why she was seeing him. That's why she was with him that night in the Party Room."

At last, Kirsten thought. *The mystery is coming together!*

Kirsten tried to conceal the wide smile spreading across her face. She had something! Something concrete that could help her find the real murderer—Jones!

"But she never came home that night, so Jones is still out there . . . and he's looking for me," Brandon said as he slumped farther into the chair. "I know it."

"You don't have to worry anymore, Brandon." Kirsten reached out to him. He seemed so scared now. "I've told the cops about Jones already."

"You what?" Brandon suddenly jumped out of the chair. The color drained from his face.

"I told them to arrest Jones." Kirsten furrowed her brow. "We'll finally learn what happened to Sam. And once he's in jail, you'll be off the hook."

"No!" Brandon yelled. "They'll never catch him. And when Jones finds out that someone turned him in again, who do you think he'll go after first?" Brandon cursed over and over, slamming his fist into his open palm. "I'm a dead man!" he cried.

22

"A dead man!" Brandon cried again. His gaze darted around the room as if he wasn't sure what to do next. Then he tore out of there and into the elevator.

"Brandon, wait!" Kirsten said, but it was no use. The elevator doors closed.

Minutes later she could see him from her living room window, racing out of the building and flagging down a cab.

Oh my God, she thought. She had played Brandon perfectly, but had she also sentenced him to death?

And Jones was still out there. Somewhere.

Oh, Sam, Kirsten thought. *Why did you get involved in all of this? Maybe if you had stayed away from Brandon and Jones, you wouldn't have died. Or maybe if you had told me that you were in trouble, I could have helped. Maybe you'd still be alive today.*

But now Kirsten had someone else to worry about: Brandon.

When does this story end? Kirsten wondered. *When does a new one begin?*

She walked groggily into her bathroom and splashed water onto her face. It was late already. Time to crash. *For a week.*

Kirsten looked at her reflection in the mirror and inspected the lines across her forehead, the glazed look in her eyes. She looked like a thirty-year-old, even though she still wasn't old enough to buy her own smokes.

Whatever, she thought, walking into her bedroom and changing into a pair of silk pajamas. She crossed to the window, pushed it open, and sat carefully on the ledge. She hugged her knees as she stared down at what looked like a sea of yellow cabs and wondered if Brandon had made it home all right.

Kirsten craned her head slightly out of the window and took in a deep breath. *I guess it's time to go to bed,* she thought. As Kirsten stepped back inside her room, something down on the street caught her eye. She noticed someone standing in the middle of the street, wearing a baseball cap and sunglasses.

Sunglasses at night? Kirsten thought. *Why?*

From her vantage point it almost looked as if the guy was staring back at her. In this gigantic city, two random people could still cross sightlines from such a great distance.

Wait! Maybe it isn't random!

The figure across the street waved.

To who? To me? Kirsten wondered. Unsure of what she

was seeing, Kirsten blinked her eyes. When the stranger took off his sunglasses, however, all doubt vanished. Kirsten immediately recognized the figure from twelve stories up:

It was Kyle!

Without thinking, Kirsten threw on something and hurried downstairs. Now that the truth was out there, she had so much to tell Kyle! She couldn't wait!

After a quick elevator ride, Kirsten hurried out onto the street, looking everywhere for Kyle. It was colder than she'd expected. She shivered in her simple white T-shirt and shorts as she approached the corner, expecting to see Kyle waiting for her.

She turned the corner and looked for him everywhere, but he was gone.

Fear crept back into her mind. Maybe it *wasn't* such a bright idea to go running out into the middle of the night for a wanted man.

Just as Kirsten started to leave, confused and worried, Kyle stepped out from the shadows. She softened when she saw him smile. Then, without thinking, she reached out and hugged him. Grabbing Kyle hard, holding on as if her life depended on it, Kirsten whispered, "I thought I'd never see you again."

Kyle, surprised by the hug, stepped back a little. "I didn't think you wanted to see me." He frowned. "I didn't know whether you believed me."

"I was afraid, Kyle," she confessed. "You'd lied to me before. You were wanted by the police."

"So why'd you come down this time, then?" he pressed.

"Because I know something." Kirsten smiled.

Kyle's face brightened ever so slightly. "Tell me. . . ."

"The red-haired guy—that guy who left with Sam that night—"

"Uh-huh." Kyle was hanging on to her every word.

"He was extorting Brandon, and when Brandon tried to put an end to it. Sam tried to help him and—"

"He put an end to her," Kyle finished her sentence.

"Exactly!" Kirsten cried. At least Kyle had some kind of lead now. Something that might clear the name Paul Stone forever.

"Shh, Kirsten," Kyle reminded her, glancing around to check the street. The new evidence might clear his name, but until then, he was still a wanted man.

Just then, a police officer turned the corner. Kyle suddenly pulled Kirsten in close. Then he leaned in and kissed her to avoid being detected.

Kirsten relaxed into Kyle's soft lips as her mind swirled and her heart pounded in her chest. She had nearly forgotten how Kyle's kisses felt. And her long embrace with him felt like a welcome excuse to forget everything except being close.

So much so that Kirsten was disappointed when the cop finally shuffled across Eighty-Fifth Street. She pulled away from Kyle to catch her breath and stop a spark from quickly turning into a fire.

"Maybe after all this—" Kyle began awkwardly, looking down at his feet.

"Maybe," Kirsten cut him off. "But not yet, Kyle. Not now."

"Okay." He looked at her with calm, understanding eyes.

A siren started up down the block, and Kyle jumped. He glanced over his shoulder for a moment and then slipped a folded piece of paper into Kirsten's hand. "Here, take this. . . . I'm hiding at the Lisbon." He leaned in quickly, this time giving her a sweet kiss on the cheek. "I'll be in touch," he whispered and, with that, he disappeared back into the shadows.

Romance can wait, Kirsten thought. *But how long will it take before the nightmare is over?*

As she walked back into her building, thinking about *that kiss*, her cell phone rang. She pulled the phone out from her pocket and stared at the caller ID, which said UNKNOWN NUMBER.

Who's this? she wondered, and answered the phone.

It was Peterson.

He never sleeps! Kirsten thought.

"Good news. We have Jones in custody," he said.

"Oh my God!" Kirsten screamed. She was blown away. "I'll come down to identify him!"

"No need." Peterson laughed. "We got enough drug charges on this goon to keep him off the streets for a *while*,

Kirsten. That'll be enough time to investigate Sam Byrne's and Emma Harris's murders."

"Yes!" Kirsten wanted to reach right through that phone line and hug the detective.

"And you'd better *believe* that Jones isn't posting bail. That's how he gave us the slip last time!"

Peterson went on—something about trial dates for Sam's case—but Kirsten couldn't hear anymore. She broke into a flood of tears.

"Thank you!" she sobbed into the phone line as Peterson went on. "Thank you!"

Finally the past could stay in the past.

Finally it was over.

PART THREE

23

"Love Stinks!" Kirsten Sawyer cheered from the tech room at WXRJ. It was the day after the police had arrested Jones, and Kirsten was brimming with new energy. Now that Sam's and Emma's killer was behind bars, she could get back to her work in a serious way. "How may I help you?" she asked a caller on the phone.

"I was hoping to talk to Kate," a distressed voice answered back.

"Absolutely. That's why we're here, sir. I'll just need a name and the nature of your call," Kirsten said, switching his line into the studio.

"Kevin," the caller said, seeming to relax a little. Then he told her that he wanted to ask Kate if it was possible to love your kitty *too* much.

"All right, Kevin, I'm going to transfer your call, and the next voice will be Dr. Grisholm's. . . ."

Swiveling around in her chair, Kirsten entered "crazy for

kitty" into the computer and smiled as she breezed through her job like an old pro. *This is how work should go every day,* she thought. Now that she was off the pills and the killer was off the streets, she could behave like an actual human being.

Kate smiled at her and took the call.

Kirsten leaned back in her chair and pictured Kyle standing outside her building again. She closed her eyes and imagined their kiss. Now she had even better news to tell him. Yesterday he had given her a sweet letter that included his cell phone number and address. But this was something that she wanted to tell him in person. *I'll go to the Lisbon as soon as I can,* she decided.

As Kirsten thought about the *next* kiss she and Kyle would share, she spotted Brian entering the tech room with his head down. "Hey there, surfer boy." But before Kirsten could even finish her sentence, Brian grabbed a microphone stand and darted back out.

Kirsten ran into the hallway only to watch Brian hurry away. Even though his hickeys were fading, his ears were bright red.

She laughed out loud. He had been avoiding Kirsten all day, ducking her at the water cooler, pretending to be reading a magazine in the mailroom. He had even faced the back of the elevator on the ride up to work!

Kirsten was blown away by Brian's transformation: He had come to New York pretty naive, but Leslie Fenk had turned him quickly to the dark side. And her little surfer boy seemed a little embarrassed about it.

As Kirsten shook her head and walked back into the tech room, her cell phone rang the song "Rock Your Body."

It was Julie's cheesy Justin Timberlake ring! The girls had programmed the same ring into each of their phones so they'd know when the other was calling. Kirsten was dying to talk to Julie, but suddenly she felt nervous. *What do I say?* she wondered. *How can I patch things up?*

Kirsten flipped her phone open anxiously, careful to move out of her boss's line of sight. "Hello, Julie?"

"Hey," Julie replied softly, sounding still bruised from their fight.

There was a long pause. An eternity. Finally Kirsten decided to clear the air: "Julie, I am soooo sorry. I never meant to—"

"Kenny Dwiggler was a hottie!" Julie broke in with her shrillest voice and familiar laugh.

"Yeah! A total hottie!" Kirsten played along. "And I'm a total bitch," she added more seriously.

"The biggest in all Manhattan?" Julie asked.

"Now don't get carried away, slut!" Kirsten laughed.

It felt good to joke around with her friend again. In fact, it felt amazing. Kirsten leaned back in her chair and smiled. "So when do I get to see your beautiful face?" she asked. She couldn't wait to see her best friend. They had so much to talk about.

"Tonight?" Julie smacked gum on the other line.

"Just tell me where and I'm there," Kirsten said.

"Duh!" Julie cried. "The Party Room!"

Three hours and twenty-seven minutes later, Kirsten and Julie were once again attached at the hip, gossiping on the back couches at their favorite bar.

"'Dear Kiiirrssssten,'" Julie *ooh-la-la*-ed as she began reading Kyle's note to Kirsten—the one he had slipped her on the street.

"Just read the damn note, Jules!" Kirsten laughed. She was so happy to be hanging out with Julie at the Party Room again. Just like old times. She had just finished telling Julie all about Jones and her latest meeting with Kyle. Now she was excited to share Kyle's sweeter side. . . .

"'In the blur of the past few months,'" Julie read on, "'I've never stopped thinking about you. I'm sorry I brought you into all this, Kirsten, but I'm not sorry that I fell for you.'" Julie looked up from the note and squeezed Kirsten's arm. "And the panties are off!"

"Slow down, Pembroke. I'm a good girl." Kirsten winked.

"But why's he staying at the Lisbon?" Julie asked, reading the address Kyle had scribbled on the bottom of the note. "It's such a dump."

"Really?" Kirsten was surprised. Kyle had plenty of money.

"It's right near my yoga class in Midtown," Julie added. "I think you can actually pay for your room with crystal."

"I guess the crappier the place, the easier it is to hide," Kirsten suggested. She took the note back from Julie and folded it into her purse.

"Whatever you say, daaahling," Julie drawled in her old, overly done rich-bitch voice.

She was back. Julie was back! Kirsten suddenly sprang forward and hugged her friend.

Julie let out a fake "oof!" and squeezed her right back.

The two friends shared a long, much-needed hug until Scott came by, festive as ever, balancing two gorgeous drinks on a round cork tray. "Pomegranate Martinis for the VIPs in the back," he said.

"Now we're talking!" Julie shouted.

Scott passed Kirsten her drink, but she put up her hand. "No thanks, sweetie. I'm taking a break from the booze for a while. Just Diet Cokes and Pellegrino for me for now."

"Whoa!" Scott looked a little surprised, then said, "Your wish is my command."

Kirsten winked at Scott. "Thanks, genie."

"So you're not drinking with me?" Julie asked as Scott left to get Kirsten a kinder and gentler drink. Julie picked up the two martinis. She tilted her head and frowned as she stared at the drinks, then at Kirsten. "You sure?"

Kirsten nodded. She hoped that this wasn't going to

be a problem for Julie, because they were older—almost in college—and she didn't want to have to deal with the whole peer-pressure thing.

But then Julie broke into a giggle and took two large sips from each martini. "That just means more for me!"

Kirsten laughed as her friend went to town on the drinks.

Julie put the martinis down and grabbed Kirsten's hands. "I'm proud of you. You look great. You've really pulled yourself together, girl."

"Yeah, Kirsten," Scott agreed as he bussed empty glasses from the surrounding tables. "Sometimes you have to back away from all this craziness and find your limits."

"Thanks, guys," Kirsten said sweetly. It meant a lot to her to have her friends' support.

"But just 'cause you're on the wagon doesn't mean you can't party!" Julie smiled as she pulled a flyer out of her purse.

Kirsten looked down at a glossy photo of the Brooklyn Bridge with the word BROOKNASTY stamped in bright yellow across the bottom. "What's this?" she asked.

"Oh, I don't know . . . ," Julie said, "only the biggest dance party of the entire year! It's in Brooklyn. Right on the water. Tomorrow night!"

"Oh yeah, Brooknasty," Scott chimed in. "Big bash. Very cool. Too bad I'll be working!" he said as he hurried back over to the bar.

Julie watched Scott walk away for a moment, licked

her lips, and then spun back to face Kirsten again. "Listen, Kirsten: Everyone we now know, ever *knew*, or ever dreamed about knowing is bound to be there," she continued, pinching Kirsten's side. "It's must-see TV!"

"Well then, we're there, baby!" Kirsten grinned as visions of fabulous outfits danced in her head. Why not? Detective Peterson had Jones, and soon Kyle's name would be cleared. It was definitely time to celebrate, right?

24

I love it!

I really do!

I really, really love it!

IREALLYFUCKINGLOVEHOWGODDAMNSTUPIDYOU-COULDBE!

Thought they had me for a second, but they don't! They NEVER WILL!

Calm down. Control. Keep cool. Refrigerate after opening . . .

I'm not going to lose it now.

Do you think I'm crazy or something?

But here, my friend, here is my final question:

Do you really think it's that easy?

You actually think this story wraps up like some nice little present sitting under a Christmas tree?

Think again.

I just need to change direction. And watch my back.

Just need to think. And find some fresh air. Breathe a little.

Then ATTACK!

I'll finally settle this thing once and for all.

But that's the problem with all of you. You don't want the truth. It's too ugly. Too complex. You want everything so damn simple and happy and right.

But I've got news for you: There's a lot that's wrong. A lot I gotta make right.

You might think the story is over—but trust me, it's not.

It hasn't even started!

25

THUMP, THUMP, THUMP!

Bass reverberated through the moving bodies. A jazz trumpet rose above the sweaty dance floor, mingling with the wide Manhattan skyline.

It was Saturday night in Brooklyn, and the party was hot! Ridiculous.

A live house-music band played furiously, with the Chrysler Building as a backdrop and some five hundred pulsing people as the foreground.

Brooknasty is right! Kirsten thought as she let go of Julie's hand. She laughed and threw her head back, watching stars dance in the hazy sky above.

The party took place in a large, roofless warehouse, surrounded by high metal walls. Kirsten felt as if she were in some postmodern coliseum. The spectacle of the day didn't have to do with fighting or lions, though, just raw beats and sex.

The music rolled through Kirsten's entire body as she slid from person to person. She released all her inhibitions and spun around. Julie was now a few yards away, dancing with some college guy, and also having the time of her life.

Although Kirsten was getting farther and farther away from her friend, she didn't fight the movement of the crowd. The band switched to a salsa number—something fast and furious. Kirsten found herself being swept up by a Latino hottie who wore an old guayabera and gave her a wide, disarming smile.

Why not? Kirsten decided in an instant, letting him spin her around and around. They snapped into a solid salsa stance, and he led her through a dance routine that cleared the floor around them.

Thank you, dance class, Kirsten thought as she kept up remarkably well. When he placed a hand behind her back, she grabbed for it. With dexterity and grace, he whipped her through a long, winding move. The crowd cheered for them.

"Alejandro," he said politely as he dipped Kirsten at the end of the song. He thanked her "for the pleasure" and walked away.

Kirsten smiled at the fun-loving partyers around her and then looked up for Julie, but all she saw was an ocean of dancers. She headed toward the bar to find her friend, slithering her way though the swaying, grinding bodies on the dance floor.

And speaking of grinding, Kirsten ran directly into Leslie and Brian. Leslie was running her hands up the front of Brian's shirt, kissing him sloppily on the neck and face. *No shame in their game.* Kirsten laughed to herself, happy that she had never hooked up with Brian. She tried to avoid them, but Leslie noticed her out of the corner of her eye.

"Kirstennnn!" Leslie called. Her eyes were as wide as saucers, and her pupils were dilated. Clearly the girl was gone on something. "I want you to meet Byronnnnn. My new boyyy-friennnd!"

Was Leslie for real? Was she *that* bad a friend? Was she *that* big a bitch?

Brian looked up, eyes smoked-out, mouth pasty from dehydration. He had on a strategically ripped Diesel T-Shirt and a Von-Dutch trucker hat. "Already know her," he mumbled, turning back to tongue Leslie some more.

Kirsten just shook her head and kept dancing toward the bar. She thought about Brian's metamorphosis—from nice to nasty. He was a completely different person all in a matter of weeks.

As Kirsten scanned the party for Julie again, she noticed an elevated section near the back. *Must be the VIP section,* she realized as she saw hipsters juggling bottles of Cristal, bouncers checking IDs, supermodels, deejays, and some rock-star wannabe with red hair—

Wait! Kirsten gasped. How many guys had hair like that?

Air escaped her lungs faster than she could breathe it back in. She stumbled back, reaching out to the people around her to steady herself. There, standing in the middle of the VIP section, was a guy with red hair and sunglasses. It couldn't be, but . . .

JONES!

How? Kirsten's mind reeled. *He's supposed to be in jail! No bail. That's what Peterson said.*

This wasn't fair! Just as Kirsten's world was building back up, it came crumbling right back down again! Why was he out of jail?

Kirsten instinctively ducked into the crowd and made her way toward the ladies' room. Someone in the crowd elbowed her accidentally, and Kirsten crashed into someone's drink.

Beer and sweat all mixed together in one long smear down the front of Kirsten's dress. Not caring about how she looked, however, she pushed the rest of the way to the bathroom. Her heart pounded as she cut the long line of women waiting outside the bathroom, and she slid into a stall.

"Bitch!" a chorus of women rang out, but Kirsten didn't care.

Jones was out there. Free, somehow.

She wanted out of Brooknasty—and she wanted it now!

Where the hell is Julie? she wondered.

26

Where the hell is Kirsten? Julie wondered as she pulled herself out from between two moshing frat boys. "Ever heard of 'excuse me'!" she yelled at them. *I am so over this place.*

The last time she saw Kirsten, she was dancing with some Latin cutie. Julie had gone to the bar for a drink, and when she'd turned around, Kirsten was nowhere to be found. Now the scene was changing, and the crowded dance floor was turning aggressive, almost hostile.

"Ugghh!" Julie yelled as someone flung a soaked T-shirt in her face. *Brooknasty is just straight up nasty!* she decided as she wiped sweat from her hair. *And where the hell is Kirsten!* she wondered again.

"Kirsten!" she shouted out, but she couldn't compete with that jangling guitar line blaring over the speakers. *I just want to go home already,* she thought. *This is too much.*

And to make matters worse, Julie couldn't find Kirsten

anywhere. They hadn't been separated for that long, but in a place like this, time was relative.

A tall, skinny guy rushed up to Julie and grabbed her by the waist. "Dance with me, baby!" He stared into her eyes. His breath smelled like sewage, and he looked like a zombie—an extra from *Evil Dead II*.

"No thanks!" Julie yelled as she pushed him off and continued toward the VIP section. At least there she could wait in style. But as the music picked up tempo, Julie suddenly felt the urge to go outside—*really* outside. Even though she could see the sky above, she felt too . . . boxed in.

Gotta get some air, she said to herself, but she didn't want to leave the party alone. "Kirsten!" she yelled one final time.

Now she was *really* starting to feel claustrophobic. A hot tingle overtook her face, and each of her breaths became labored, uneven. Ever since the time when she was four and had got stuck in a Barneys elevator for six hours, close spaces hadn't quite agreed with her.

Julie found her bright pink cell phone and tried Kirsten's number. The problem was, however, that she couldn't even hear her *own* phone ringing. As music blasted, she strained to listen to the call.

Nothing.

Lost at sea, Julie joked to herself as she looked across the massive dance party. Finally resolved to do *something*, Julie took a deep breath and plowed her way to the bar. She knocked into a stand of anorexic Brearley girls without saying a word to them. She'd make it up on the tennis courts.

Plus, Julie didn't have time to be social right now. She was starting to feel strange. Her stomach sloshed with acid, and she felt a burning in her throat. She wondered if the three hot dogs she'd wolfed down at Gray's Papaya earlier had anything to do with it. No matter how rich her family was, Julie swore she'd never stop eating those skinny, salty dogs.

That is, until tonight.

As Julie felt the sickness surging in her stomach, she spotted a velvet curtain leading somewhere. *Anywhere is better than here,* she thought as she made her way to the dark red exit.

Finally reaching the high metal wall, Julie pushed through the curtain and stumbled out into an alley.

Outside. Ahhh. After taking a huge, greedy breath of air, Julie opened her eyes and looked around: She was standing alone at the edge of an abandoned, bottle-strewn lot.

SLAM!

Julie felt her heart drop to the concrete as she spun back around. A large door banged closed in front of the velvet curtain she had just exited.

Where did that door come from? she wondered. The soft velvet entrance was now barred with a thick metal door. *Weird.* Julie scrunched up her face in confusion. She rushed back to the door and pulled on the handle, but it wouldn't open.

What? Julie suddenly panicked. The door wasn't budging, and she was trapped on the wrong side.

"Hello!" she screamed, half annoyed, half scared. She banged on the metal door with all her might, but no one came to open it. *They probably can't hear me!* she thought, banging again and again and again until her hands started to ache.

Julie frowned and rubbed her hands. The night was going from bad to worse. "And I looked so cute tonight," she said out loud, glancing down at her poofy Carrie Bradshaw skirt. Now it looked more like a dead lily. "What a waste."

Julie hugged herself and breathed into her hands. She was wearing practically nothing, and it was starting to get chilly out there. "Hello!" she shouted to no one in particular. She listened to her voice echo across the abandoned lot. A new, more intense shiver washed over her as she suddenly felt vulnerable. She was all alone.

Stop being such a wuss, Julie scolded herself, but she couldn't help it. She didn't like the creepy quietness. She gazed around and spotted a small shack sitting at the far end of the lot. A dim light flickered inside. *Hel-lo* . . . There was hope. Finally.

Left with no alternative, Julie started off toward the structure, stepping over rusted nails, bicycle tires, beer cans, and shattered fifths of Thunderbird. She hoped there was someone inside the shack—a security guard or something—

someone who could help her get back inside the party so she could find Kirsten.

"Hello?" Julie's voice squeaked as she neared the building.

No answer.

She peeked inside the shack through a dirty window and spotted a lone red candle dripping on the center of the floor, but no one was inside.

Weird, she thought, getting the sudden feeling that maybe coming out there hadn't been such a bright idea. She backed away from the house.

Then someone rushed her from behind. "Arrrrrhhhhhh!" he yelled as he knocked her to the ground, facefirst.

"No!" Julie screamed, suddenly recalling all the self-defense classes she had taken at the 92nd Street Y. She moved to kick her attacker, but failed as she got caught up in something.

Oh my God! Julie realized. He was wrapping her around and around in a red cloth. Then dragging her . . . dragging her into the shed.

"Let me go!" Julie screamed again, and tried to claw her way out of the cotton web, but there was no escape.

As a hood pulled tightly over her head, the last thing Julie saw was a red-haired man. . . .

27

"Julie!" Kirsten yelled again, her voice hoarse. *Where are you?* she wondered. Despair was beginning to set in. Even though it was already one in the morning, the party was just building up momentum. The crowd had multiplied so much, there was no room to move *anywhere* anymore, let alone find someone. Club kids filled the dance floor with shrill whistles and bouncing neon necklaces. The band had been replaced by a bald female deejay. She was spinning techno music and bopping her body to a rambunctious beat.

It was on.

The party roared like a growling beast.

And somewhere out there, Jones was lurking.

Kirsten trembled now. All the fear that had seemingly dissipated over that last couple of days came rushing back into her body. She hoped that Julie was just off being her usual self, making out with some guy in a dark corner somewhere—and not in trouble.

Kirsten *prayed* that this was the case.

After a serious struggle, Kirsten made it to a far corner of the party and stepped outside through a thick velvet curtain. Feeling the coolness of outside air, she found herself standing in a dark, empty lot.

Finally able to hear herself think, Kirsten dialed Julie's phone again.

Still no answer.

Kirsten's arm dropped to the side. She let her phone ring for a while, waiting for Julie's voice mail to activate. *Useless,* she thought, but just as she turned to go back inside, she heard something. Or at least *thought* she heard something.

Kirsten stood still and listened intently. Faintly in the distance she could make out . . . "Rock Your Body."

It was Julie's Justin Timberlake ring.

Filled with another gust of energy, Kirsten spun around to see where the ringing was coming from. Across the large abandoned lot, she saw a dark metal shack of some kind. It seemed as if the sound was coming from that direction!

Why are you out there, Julie? Kirsten wanted to ask. *And why aren't you picking up your goddamn phone?!*

Kirsten's mind burned, and she started out across the lot, trampling through the refuse. As she neared the shack, her heart practically imploded when she heard a muffled cry for help coming from inside.

Julie's in trouble! Kirsten was sure of it. She ran faster and faster toward the door. Her shoes fell off, but she kept running, right into the metal siding, breaking down the door and tumbling inside.

That's when she saw Julie, tied up in a chair, eyes wide with fear! "Julie!" Kirsten hurried to free her friend from the cocoon of tattered red cloth. A stream of blood ran from Julie's nose into her shirt collar, collecting in a dark, shimmering puddle. Her face was scratched as well, and a jagged cloth stretched from one swollen cheek to the other.

Kirsten ripped the gag out of Julie's mouth.

"Red-haired guy!" Julie's voice was garbled with panic and blood. "Grabbed me!"

Kirsten held Julie's hands tightly and stared directly into her eyes. Wild, flitting eyes. "Where is he?" she asked Julie. She needed her help now. *Both* of their lives depended on it. Jones could be anywhere. She shot a quick glance toward the door, then turned back to Julie. "Where is he?"

"Gone," Julie finally gasped. Then she looked down, taken over by racking sobs.

"What is it, Julie?" Kirsten begged. "Are you okay? You can tell me."

"He told me he'd KILL ME, Kirsten!" Julie sucked in short breaths between sobs. "If I didn't—"

But then Julie's voice cut off. She hung her head as if she was defeated.

"If you didn't *what*, Julie?" Kirsten asked, her heart pounding with adrenaline.

"If I didn't tell him where Kyle was hiding!" Julie broke into a fit of sobs again. "So I did!"

Kirsten could feel her heart sliding away, melting into acid in her chest. They had to get to Kyle—fast! She finished untying Julie and practically dragged her out of the chair. Out of the shack.

Faster! Faster! her mind screamed as she began running. She tugged on Julie's arm to help her keep pace. Kirsten then reached into her purse, pulled out her cell phone, and speed-dialed Kyle with her free hand.

Got to warn him! she repeated over and over in her mind, numb to the glass and metal that poked and cut her bare feet.

Kirsten strained to listen to her phone. After a series of crackles and stalls, she barely made out a voice. "Kyle, is that you?" she cried out desperately.

She stopped to listen, letting her terrified best friend catch her breath for a minute. Julie moaned now, her legs buckling under the stress of what she had just been through.

The phone connection was awful. And there was only one power bar left on Kirsten's phone.

"Kyle! Can you hear me?"

And then, finally, the best sound Kirsten had ever heard in her seventeen years on the planet came over the line: a garbled "Yes."

"Run, Kyle! Get out of there. Just leave. Right now! Get the hell out of the Lisbon!" she cried.

More static.

Julie was leaning against her now, pulling Kirsten down.

"Kyle! Did you hear what I said?" she screamed into the phone. "Go!"

" . . . figured it out!" Kirsten heard just the smallest fragment of what Kyle was saying.

Had he heard her at all?

" . . . know who the murderer is . . ."

Before Kirsten could ask any questions, the line went dead.

She speed-dialed again, but her battery failed.

In a moment of sheer rage, Kirsten chucked her phone across the street. Then she snapped back to life and physically carried Julie the rest of the way across the lot. She found a small but workable tear in the large chain-link fence surrounding the property.

"Hello! Help!" Kirsten yelled out for her car-service driver as she guided Julie through the jagged opening.

Julie moaned again as she sprawled out across the sidewalk on the other side.

"Julie!" Kirsten cried. She had to get her home. She scraped through the rusty opening herself, grabbing high above her head to stabilize herself.

She felt something strange—something soft and silky—and she looked up:

There, hooked right to the fence, was a wig. It was the exact color of Jones's hair.

28

"Pick up, pick up, pick up . . . ," Kirsten murmured as she called Kyle for what seemed like the hundredth time on Julie's cell phone. But he didn't pick up, and the phone rang and rang as the black Lincoln ripped uptown, skidding over potholes, revving across intersections toward The Lisbon.

Kirsten's driver would drop her off first and had agreed to make sure that Julie made it safely into her East Eighty-Fourth Street townhouse.

Kirsten hung up the phone and pressed redial.

Still no answer.

Her mind reeled as she squirmed in her seat and glanced at Julie. *Who did this to you?* she asked silently. Then she envisioned that hideous red wig hanging from the chain-link fence in Brooklyn. *And what was the deal with the wig? And what would he want with Kyle? Has he confused him with Brandon?*

Kirsten didn't know. All she knew was that she had to find him—or at least make sure that he got away.

Finally, the car skidded across Forty-Second Street and slammed to a halt right outside the Lisbon. Kirsten shoved a hundred-dollar bill into Julie's palm and raced into the lobby of the hotel.

It was totally empty. Quiet, except for Muzak playing in some far-off room.

"Hello!" Kirsten shouted, looking around frantically for a desk clerk. She didn't know what room Kyle was staying in.

Kirsten yelled out again. She didn't have time to waste! But her words rang through the dingy waiting room. The Lisbon was a dump. Sweaty wallpaper peeled onto shabby plastic couches. A cracked-out tenant mumbled to himself under a "choking victim" poster.

"What?" a voice finally cracked, and Kirsten spun around. A small Asian woman had materialized from behind the front desk. She frowned at Kirsten.

"I'm looking for someone who is staying here!" Kirsten said.

"Congratulations," the woman drawled, unmoved by Kirsten's urgency.

"He's around my age. Dark hair? Hazel eyes?"

The woman didn't budge.

"I don't know . . ." Kirsten tried to focus, but she was

losing it. "He might be registered as Kyle or Paul Stone. . . ."

The woman's face was still blank.

"He's been staying here for a few nights now? He's . . . very quiet," Kirsten added.

"Maybe I know this kid," the woman finally muttered, slowly nodding her head.

"Well, can you *please* tell me which room he's in?" Kirsten pleaded. She was desperate. "It's a matter of life and death!"

"Sure, but I'm very old. Memory's not too good." The woman smirked.

Kirsten threw her final twenty at the woman. There was no time for bartering.

"10A!" the Asian woman said.

Kirsten flew into the elevator and jabbed at a worn-out button. *10A, 10A, 10A,* she chanted to herself as the elevator crept to life. She could hear the metal cords winding as it slowly pulled upward.

Come on! Kirsten thought as the doors opened on the seventh floor.

"Going down?" an elderly man in Bermuda shorts and black socks said, smiling a toothy grin.

"NO!" Kirsten cried. She didn't have time to be nice. She pushed the tenth-floor button again, and the doors closed. When the elevator door opened just a crack on the tenth floor, Kirsten instantly slid out and ran down the hallway.

10A, 10A, 10A! Kirsten squinted in the dingy light as she

checked each door. Finally she spotted Kyle's room at the very end of the hall and broke into a run.

She noticed that Kyle's door was slightly open. *This is not good!* she thought.

She felt her body slowing down. Everything became eerily quiet. And although Kirsten was *dying* to walk through that door, she couldn't bear to do it.

Why is his door open? She felt a shiver spread up into her spine. But inside the pit of her stomach, she knew the answer. She knew. . . .

And when she pushed the door to room 10A open wide, her worst fears were confirmed. "Kyle!" she screamed, running to the limp body sprawled in the center of the room.

A pool of blood had matted his wavy brown hair and soaked a large, neat oval into the dirty tan carpeting. His eyes were open, staring . . . still staring at some unknown horror that Kirsten did not want to imagine.

Then she saw the gun.

It was on the carpet, next to his right hand.

"Noooo!" she cried out, pulling the gun from his hand. She bent over his body and pressed her ear close to his bloody mouth. His body was still warm. *Maybe he's still alive. Maybe he's breathing!*

But he wasn't. Kyle was dead.

Dead!

Kirsten had tried to warn him, but she was too late! Why? Why was this happening? Why did the people she loved keep dying?

I can't do it. I can't go through the pain again! she thought, hugging Kyle's body. She squeezed her eyes shut as tears streamed down her cheeks. *No, no, no, no!*

A few minutes later she opened her eyes and pulled away from him. Something strange caught her eye. It was Kyle's left hand . . . balled into a fist? Why?

She leaned over him and realized that he was holding something! Gently she pried open his hand, and a crumpled photo fell onto the floor. She picked it up and studied it.

It was picture of Kyle . . . a little younger, about seventeen or eighteen . . . and there was a girl in his arms . . . petite . . . beautiful blond hair . . .

Is this Carolee? Is this what she looked like? Kirsten wondered. *But why is he holding this?* She couldn't figure it out right then, but she knew that she'd have plenty of time—the rest of her life, maybe. She slipped the photo into her pocket.

Right now I have to call the police, Kirsten thought, standing up and glancing at the gun still in her hand. *I have to report a murder.*

"NYPD!" a uniformed officer yelled as he and four others rushed into the room—shoulder to shoulder, guns drawn.

Kirsten gasped. *Talk about perfect timing!*

She relaxed when Detective Peterson followed the

initial push-through. "Detective!" she cried, crossing the room. "Thank God! I'm so glad to—"

"Drop it, Kirsten!" Peterson said, quickly drawing his gun and pointing it at her.

Kirsten glanced at the gun in her hand. "This? No, you don't underst—"

"He said drop it!" a uniformed officer said as they all surrounded her.

Kirsten gulped and did as she was told. Her mind swirled as the detective locked her wrists into a pair of handcuffs and arrested her for the murder of Paul Stone.

last call

PART ONE

PROLOGUE

It's over.

That's what I've been telling myself.

Completely over. Done. History.

It was a perfect summer. Not a bad fall, either. Peaceful. And now it's February in New York, snow on the ground, chicks in sweaters, meat in the freezer and spices in the cupboard, and I should be in a great mood.

Hey, what's past is past and what's dead is dead.

Memories can't hurt you.

So why am I feeling it again? What's wrong with me?

WHY AM I FEELING IT?

Is it because they're back? That must be it. They're back for winter break. Back from three months of taking drugs and screwing each other at Harvard and Yale and Princeton and Brown, where they never would have been accepted but for Mom and Dad's seven-figure donations. Yes, that must be it. They're back, and their smug faces are reminding me of the . . . the . . .

Incidents.

Preppy Murders. That's what they called them. Well, guess what, they're not MURDERS if they happen for a reason.

Carolee . . . Sam . . . Emma . . . I had to kill them. DAMN IT, THEY HAD TO GO! Sometimes justice requires sacrifice. And the sacrifice has been made. Three times. More than enough, thank you very much.

No, not enough. One more. The prize—Kyle—the one who liked to pretend he was so innocent. I enjoyed putting him down most of all.

BUT IT WAS SUPPOSED TO BE OVER AFTER THAT—NO MORE!

So why do they ruin it? Why do they bring it all back? They remind me. They taunt me . . . HELLO? WAKE UP, PAL. WHAT ARE YOU TALKING ABOUT? THOSE KIDS ARE MEANINGLESS. I shouldn't give a shit about the ones who are here. The ones who remind me . . . . I got RID of the bad ones—the ones who made trouble.

It's something else. Something else is getting me juiced. So what is it?

I know.

It's the cops. I'm seeing too many cops.

Are they after me? How can they know? THERE'S NO ONE LEFT TO TELL THEM A GODDAMN THING. Except . . .

Except . . . for her. For Kirsten.

She'd better not be stirring up bad feelings again. She

should let it rest if she knows what's good for her. . . .
No, she knows. She knows what will happen. Taught by example.
No, it's paranoia. It's got to be.
Paranoia is the enemy, pal. Paranoia means lack of control. And it's all about control. CONTROL is my middle name.
So I'll nose around a little if I have to. Just enough to be sure it's all okay.
And keep a lid on.
Calm down.
Remember, it ain't over till it's over.
And it's over.
Isn't it?

1

"Shake it a little," Kirsten Sawyer said, smiling at the way her new college roommate was teetering on Kirsten's fabulous stiletto-heeled footwear.

"Shake it?" Lauren Chaplin said, pausing on the sidewalk outside their dorm. She turned uncertainly, her pool of ink black hair falling like a shadow across her alabaster forehead. She looked like a small child about to enter kindergarten for the first time. "I have scoliosis. You know, curvature of the spine. It's kind of hard to shake."

"It'll make it easier to walk on those shoes," Kirsten replied.

Lauren sighed. "Does everyone in New York wear Manilas?"

"Manolos," Kirsten corrected her. "You don't have to wear them if you don't want, but they look so hot on you. They make your legs look killer."

"Okay, I *said* I wanted to try them, and I *will*," Lauren said, taking the challenge like the future hotshot lawyer she wanted to be. She began walking again, this time moving her shoulders in an odd up-and-down jerky motion, as if testing some new form of personal outpatient electroshock treatment. "Is this right?"

"Um, better . . . ," Kirsten said as encouragingly as she could. *She'll get it,* she told herself. *Give her an A for effort.*

She liked Lauren. Compared with Kirsten's New York friends, Lauren seemed from another planet—innocent, eager, hardworking, fashion-clueless—and totally refreshing. Totally able to laugh at herself. She was definitely taking the edge off Kirsten's dreaded return to the land of reality.

Arriving in Manhattan in the dead of winter was tough enough for any normal person, but it was a thousand times worse when you'd spent the last few months on a sunny Greek island with nothing but a stack of books, an iPod, some cold drinks, and miles and miles of clothing-optional beaches. Return from that qualified as Severe Reentry Trauma.

Kirsten had only met Lauren, like, five hours ago—in line at registration, along with the few other odd freshmen who had deferred starting college until second semester. To feel good about her first day, Kirsten had dressed in what seemed like the perfect outfit for an NYU freshman—Coach tote, Marc Jacobs pants and sailor coat—nothing too flashy, just a little visual cue that said, "I'm a native New Yorker." But something felt weird. All around the room she could feel people staring at her. Was it her island-bronzed skin, the fiery red sun streaks through her chestnut brown hair . . . outfit envy? Or was it something worse? Did they recognize her? That couldn't be true. They couldn't know who she was. As her good mood began to slip fast, it took all her strength to not bolt for the nearest travel agency—when a voice behind her piped up, "Hey, that's a neat outfit."

It was the phraseology that did it.

"Neat?" Kirsten replied, as if testing a new word in a particularly tricky ancient dialect.

During her entire life on the Upper East Side of Manhattan, right up through four years of the exclusive Woodley School, where hot fashions and cool lingo changed by the week, Kirsten had never, ever heard the word "neat" in the same sentence as "outfit." She turned to see Lauren's face, smiling and nonjudgmental, framed in the hood of an L.L. Bean anorak. They got to talking, and within minutes Kirsten knew that Lauren had grown up on a farm in Wisconsin, started NYU late because she'd been working with a local environmental law firm on a project that went till January, and was determined to (a) score the grades to go to Yale Law School, (b) find her first boyfriend, and (c) learn how to dress like those girls on *Pretty Little Liars*—in that order. Which wasn't exactly the most auspicious beginning of a friendship, until Kirsten opened her mouth to describe her own personal history—and Lauren hung on every mundane detail as if she were in the presence of a master storyteller. She was a great listener, laughing and friendly, sweet and cheery. The cheeriness was key, since Kirsten had felt an acute cheer deficit in her life.

Lauren had been assigned as her roommate, part of a three-girl suite in a temporary dorm called the Better Ridgefield Hotel—which, to Kirsten, was totally cool. And they made a pact: Lauren would tell Kirsten about what life is like on a farm, and Kirsten would show Lauren how to dress like a New Yorker.

Which was why Lauren was, at the moment, struggling up the steps of the Better Ridgefield in Kirsten's sexiest pair of Manolo heels, hanging on to the metal banister for dear life. The grungy green backpack that was hanging from her shoulders was way wrong, accessory-wise, but one thing at a time. "I'm getting . . . the hang . . . of it," she said through a brave grimace.

"Just pretend it's easy," Kirsten said, opening the front door.

They walked slowly toward the first-floor lounge, down a musty hallway that smelled of fresh paint and cheap carpet. There was nothing "Better" about the Better Ridgefield, as far as Kirsten could tell. Until this year it had been an abandoned hotel, but the school had bought it for temporary housing while a new dorm was being completed. They had renovated it fast and cheap, and it looked it.

The lounge was a converted old apartment with the walls knocked out, decorated with thrift-store sofas surrounding an old TV. Kirsten's eyes went directly to a hunky blond god on the sofa. Part of her wanted to wink at Lauren—"watch this"—and seduce the guy in seconds flat, but that wasn't really her style. So she sat casually on a thick, padded armchair and smiled hopefully. She did not expect Adonis to do a sitcom double take at the sight of Lauren carefully placing one fabulously clad foot in front of the other—or to leap up from his six-foot slouch like a giant cocker spaniel and offer her the spot next to him. "I'm Brad," he said with a smile that could have wiped anyone's slate clean.

Lauren sat, blushing, in the romantic light of a flickering car commercial.

Go, girl, Kirsten thought with a sigh. *Ah, the transforming power of six-inch heels.*

Just like that, Brad had his arm around Lauren, and Kirsten tried to keep her eyes on the TV while some other guy, sitting in an armchair, smiled at her. "You're from the city, aren't you?" he said. He had short brown hair and freckles, and he was built like a linebacker.

"How'd you know?" Kirsten replied.

"I can always tell," he said, which might have been a harmless observation, but sounded vaguely like an insult and made Kirsten wonder what the *hell* it meant. "What's your name?" he continued.

Before Kirsten could react, a thin guy wearing an orange knit hat rose from an armchair. His face was angular and rugged, with high cheekbones and a firm jaw. He looked kind of familiar, but Kirsten couldn't figure out why. If he put on a few pounds, maybe rearranged the features a bit, he'd actually be kind of handsome—like that 1950s star with gorgeous hollow eyes, whose perfect face was put back together after a car accident and always looked slightly *off*, slightly ravaged . . . what was his name? Mom had rented some of his movies in Greece. *The Young Lions. The Misfits.* Cliff something. Montgomery Clift. That was it.

"Shhhhhhh!" he called out, his eyes glued to the television. "Yo, people. It's starting! Watch this! *Watch this!*"

The linebacker-guy smiled. "Film geek," he remarked. "Tisch School."

But Kirsten wasn't listening, because the screen was filling up with images of a TV movie, and an earnest voice intoned, *"Next on this station . . . ripped from today's headlines . . . murder and privilege in the Big City . . . it's a lethal combination. . . ."*

There it was, on the TV screen, the Party Room. Her favorite hangout of all time, only more crowded, more crazed than it ever really was—and there, at the bar, tossing her head back with a loud, sexy laugh, was her best friend, Samantha Byrne. Only it wasn't Sam, not really, it was an actress playing Sam, and next to her were two other actresses, both trash-talking and juiced to the gills: one a dead-ringer for Julie Pembroke; and the other—*oh God*—the other looked just like Kirsten, and she felt herself doubling over, as if hit in the stomach, because this trailer "ripped from the headlines" was advertising a TV movie *based on Sam's murder*!

But it was different, weird and exaggerated, as if lifted from a bleak, distorted place in her own mind, the place that held the recurring nightmare she'd had for months, the scenes racing by in quick jump cuts: Sam arguing with her ex-boyfriend, Brandon Yardley . . . Sam walking out of the Party Room arm in arm with Jones, the red-haired drug dealer—the man Kirsten still believed was her murderer . . . a moonlit night in Central Park, Sam with bare shoulders lying in the grass, smiling dreamily into a guy's face . . . not Jones, but another actor—another way-too-familiar face—and then a pair of hands grabbing her wrists and tying them with a blue-and-gold-striped Talcott school tie . . . grabbing a large rock and bludgeoning her head over and over and over. . . .

Kirsten felt a shock that seemed to fry her nerve endings, her brain suddenly numb but her body moving as if it had a life of its own . . . toward the door, away from the TV, away from the memory she'd hoped to put behind her, now flooding her mind like an open wound. And she was vaguely aware of a voice, the guy with the orange hat, hooting with derision at the trailer, calling it cheesy—but "cheesy" wasn't the word Kirsten would have chosen for something like this, something that seemed to mock and stab at the same time.

As she exited the building, the February cold hit her hard.

"Kirsten?" Lauren's voice called from behind her. "Kirsten? *Ow!*"

Kirsten turned.

Lauren stood in the doorway, her backpack slung over her shoulders, pulling off the Manolos. "These things are killing me. Wait up. What happened? Why did you leave like that?"

"I had to go . . . to the bathroom," Kirsten said absently as they crossed the street.

"You're lying."

"How do you know?"

"Because you passed the bathroom and we're now outside in the middle of the street in February without any coats—and I'm barefoot." Lauren paused. "It was the movie, wasn't it?"

As they turned onto MacDougal Street, passing small groups of briskly walking students, Kirsten tried to summon an answer. But what could she say? Lauren was so innocent. She had no idea. How do you explain murder and grief to someone who couldn't possibly understand? Lauren was supposed to be part of Kirsten's *new* life—a world away from the murders.

"Kirsten," Lauren said softly. "I know. I know who you are."

Kirsten stopped in her tracks. They were near the corner of Washington Square Park south and MacDougal, and a light snow was beginning to dust the dog run just inside the park. "You do?"

"They have newspapers in Sheboygan, you know," Lauren replied with a sarcastic lilt. "TVs, too," she added. "I recognized your name from the moment I got the roommate assignment. But don't worry: I won't say a thing if you don't want me to. And we don't have to talk about it—ever."

No, Kirsten thought. She had to talk about it. She had to get it out in the open or else it would be hanging between them for the rest of the year. She exhaled a cumulus puff into the air. When she spoke, the words seemed to come from far away. "The movie has it all wrong, I'm sure," she said. "We weren't that drunk. And Sam . . . she didn't let herself get that out of control. Never. She was wild, but not stupid. Well, not until that night, anyway. She left the bar . . . with a guy named Jones—a drug dealer—she was . . . *involved* with him somehow. . . . He killed her in Central Park . . . at least, I think he did. I don't know for sure. The killer, whoever he was, had killed another girl two years earlier, Carolee Adams, in the same exact way: beaten and stabbed, with a Talcott school tie bound around her wrists. Then he came back and killed again. First Sam, then another girl, Emma, who idolized Sam; tried to be just like her. . . ."

"Why them?" Lauren asked. "Why Sam?"

Kirsten shook her head. "All I know is, Kyle had said he had it all figured out. But that was right before . . ."

"Wait. Kyle?" Lauren spoke up. "Who's he?"

Kirsten sank onto a park bench. How could she explain who Kyle was? Their relationship was so complicated. "I met Kyle at the Party Room one night—and before I knew it, I was in love with him," she told her. "He said he went to

Bowdoin College and was in New York visiting a friend. At least that's what he told me, but it wasn't true. His name was really Paul Stone. I'll always know him as Kyle, though."

"Oh, wow," Lauren whispered. "I know that name too. From the papers. But isn't *he* the one the police said committed those murders? And if Kyle and Paul are the same guy . . ." She wrinkled her nose. "But then you said the other guy did it. What was his name? Jones?"

"Kyle was not the killer! That's what everyone thinks, because his Talcott tie was found on Carolee, but he didn't do it. I know it. He was framed. He'd left that tie in some bar. Someone must have taken it—and when it was traced to Kyle, the papers were all over him, printing these ugly mug shots and calling him names. He was convicted in an unfair trial—and he was eventually let go on a technicality. But by then he and his family were ruined. That's why they came to New York—to find the real killer and to clear their family's name," she said. "So maybe the killer got scared. He knew Kyle was on his tail. The only way to get rid of him was to kill again—to murder someone the same way that Carolee was killed. Of course, the world knew Paul Stone was free from jail. The minute someone recognized him, Paul/Kyle would be arrested—this time, they'd throw away the key. So that was the reason for the murders. *That's* why the killer went after . . ." Kirsten couldn't finish the sentence. Her numbness was giving way to tears.

"It's okay, you don't have to talk about it anymore," Lauren said gently, her voice comforting and reassuring.

"Kyle . . . knew he was in a race," Kirsten said haltingly. "He had to get the killer while he had the chance, before anybody realized who he was. He had lost weight, changed his look—but he wasn't going to fool everyone forever. The thing is, he told me he knew what really went down, Lauren. I think he knew who the killer was—but now we'll never find out!"

"I know, I know," Lauren said, nodding sympathetically. "The pressure must have been so great. Suicide is such a senseless thing—"

"*It wasn't suicide. He was murdered, Lauren!* Don't you see? It's the perfect crime: Frame someone who's already been in jail—someone the public hates—and if he has the guts to try to figure out your identity, kill him and make it look like suicide. Who's going to investigate any further? Case closed."

Lauren was silent for a long time. "So . . . you think the killer's still out there? This Jones guy?"

"That's the only bright spot in the whole story," Kirsten said. "He's in jail—not for murder, though. For dealing drugs."

"You're very brave," Lauren said.

Kirsten smiled. "Yeah, right. That's why I ran away to Greece—and I'd still be there if my mom hadn't gotten tired of feta cheese, olives, and men who spit when they talk."

"Someday, after I graduate Yale Law and I've set up a litigation practice involving the fair and equitable representation of women and minorities, I will represent you in your case against this guy—pro bono. And we'll put him behind bars forever."

"I may take you up on that," Kirsten said. "Even though I barely know you—"

Lauren grinned warmly. "If you want to know me, take me shopping. You were the one who said shopping is a way to discover a person's deepest soul, right?"

"You're learning, girlfriend," Kirsten said with a sly laugh, slowly feeling her sense of humor return. She couldn't let herself dwell on the murders any longer. The whole thing had almost driven her crazy! No, she had to let it go—let go of the guilt—let the police handle whatever investigation was left. It had taken months in therapy to get to this point, but she could finally say that she was at peace with herself now.

Lauren slipped on the Manolos again and stood. "I'm freezing and stressed from this conversation and I desperately need some spearmint chai with lemon to calm my nerves. And so do you. Come on." She yanked Kirsten up and gamely walked with her, a little less wobbly than before, to the student union building.

Kirsten felt spent and sad and torn apart, but the cold was beginning to seep in now, and she really did need something to drink. Something stronger than tea, though. Visions of Scotty the Hottie's Hot Rum Toddies danced in her head—a killer winter drink patented at the Party Room by Scott, the hunkiest bartender in town.

That's what she needed. And she'd ask for one tonight. This evening Julie was coming over from Barnard to meet her, and together they planned a night of barhopping like old times. Just the thought of it cheered her up.

The student union's lobby had a huge, vaulted atrium, ringed with balconies that seemed to go up forever. On one side of the main floor were filigreed metal tables with comfy-looking chairs, spilling out from a grill / refreshment area.

Lauren dumped her backpack on the table, pulling out a sheaf of papers. "We can coordinate our schedules and maybe collect some data about our instructors before we choose classes, okay?"

Kirsten glanced at the pile. On top was the revised roommate assignment list they'd received that morning. One of the names had changed.

Jan deVries.

Kirsten Sawyer. Lauren Chaplin. ~~Clarice Moravec.~~

That was weird. Kirsten knew the name Clarice Moravec. Vaguely. From the TV news—the sports part, during which she usually bolted for the fridge. "Isn't Clarice an athlete?" Kirsten asked. "Like, basketball or baseball or something?"

"Basketball," Lauren replied. "A point-per-game average of 29.3 and double digits in both assists and rebounds. How disappointing. She would have been an asset to the suite.

Let's just hope Jan is as nice as we are. I'll get the tea."

As Lauren scooted over to the counter with tiny, clackety footsteps on the tile floor, Kirsten stretched, arching her neck back and gazing up at the levels of the circular atrium. *This semester with Lauren is definitely going to be interesting,* she thought.

That's when she saw something plummet down the center of the atrium. She thought at first that someone had dropped a laundry basket.

But laundry didn't have arms and legs.

Laundry didn't scream.

"Oh . . . my . . . GOD!" Kirsten murmured, instinctively leaping up from the table at the same moment that the falling clump—*not a clump, a GIRL, a HUMAN BEING*—hit the floor tiles with a sickening noise like a sack of giant cantaloupes, and then bounced—actually *bounced*—which was the most shocking and sickening thing of all. Kirsten felt every meal she'd had over the last two days fighting to rise up through her chest as screams pierced the air, as people began rushing back and forth, surrounding the body, the lifeless remains of someone alive a moment ago—and a sudden howl rose up around her so loud and jarring that Kirsten didn't even realize it was her own.

2

Limp.

Broken.

Motionless.

A doll tossed out of a crib.

Dead.

The thoughts ripped into Kirsten's brain in a nanosecond, but it seemed as if time had stopped, and the image before her was morphing . . . her brain trying to match it to another image in her memory, as if that would somehow make sense out of the horror . . . the senselessness . . . and now she saw another corpse, the only other real dead person she'd ever seen besides . . .

Kyle.

Splayed out, his eyes open and pleading, his legs twisted at odd angles, his fingers folded around a photo—a photo she immediately took because he seemed to be offering it, like a gift, the only thing she could have that was his, a piece of him she'd keep forever that no one else could touch—and Kirsten wondered if the girl in the atrium had anyone who loved her, who loved her so deeply that they would *need* to remember her every minute of every day. . . .

And she became acutely aware of the power of death, unexpected death, and for a moment she was grateful and relieved to not know this girl, to not have to suffer the unbearable ache of personal loss—and the cold perverseness of that thought was, finally, what got her moving.

She had to get away. Anywhere else. Outside in the cold air. Away from the noise. The reminders. The death.

No more death.

She staggered through the crowd, clutching her backpack, fighting against the streams of students running every which way. The quiet atrium was a chamber of shrieks, sobs, and the hollow guttural sound of kids puking—one girl against a potted plant, a guy by the window. *Where did they all come from? There weren't that many people here a minute ago.*

She tried to run, but the crowd was too thick. Too many obstacles. And now the police were arriving. Clanking heavily through the open glass doors, their guns and cop paraphernalia bouncing on their belts. Forcing the students to step aside.

Lauren. Where was Lauren?

Ignoring the instinct to avert her eyes, she looked back. The body was blocked from view by a clutch of onlookers. On their periphery Kirsten recognized the guy from the lounge, the skinny film geek with the orange knit hat. He was circling the crowd, holding a camera high above everyone's head, his lens aimed downward toward the dead girl, snapping pictures.

Pictures!

A girl was lifeless and crushed on the floor, a girl whose proud parents at that moment imagined she was alive and healthy but were about to get news that would forever rock their world . . . and this pervert was *taking pictures*!

"Kirsten! Oh my God. Kirsten! Did you see what happened? Someone jumped!"

Lauren was heading for her, shoes in one hand. *That's right, she had gone off to get us tea.*

Before Kirsten could respond, a bewildered-looking guy wandered over from the front door, wrapped in a down coat and scarf. "What happened?" he asked.

Kirsten pointed upward. "A girl fell from that balcony—like the sixth floor or something."

Scattered around all the balconies, students had gathered to gawk. At the place where the girl had jumped, more or less, stood a guy, conspicuous with a shining, shaved head—too old to be a student, probably a teaching assistant. Kirsten's eyes drifted past him and scanned the other faces, all unfamiliar, all frozen with shock. But something about the bald guy—his posture, his body language—was different from everyone else. He seemed distracted, looking around for something on the floor, then glancing disinterestedly downward. . . .

And that was when Kirsten got a good look at his face.

He seemed familiar. She knew him. Somehow.

He wasn't unattractive. His eyes seemed dark and powerful, with a piercing coldness she could feel intensely, even at that distance.

And it was in that glance, in that split second when his eyes rested a little too long on hers, that she realized who he was.

The hair was gone, but the face was the same. If she imagined him the way she'd last seen him—with a shock of flowing red hair, a drugged-out smile—she knew.

She knew, and she was scared out of her mind.

It was Jones.

"LOOK!" Kirsten blurted out. A cop thundered past her, and she grabbed him by the sleeve, pointing upward. "Look! That guy!"

The officer glanced up—but Jones's face was gone. Disappeared behind the balcony wall.

"Didn't you see him?" Kirsten pleaded.

"Who?" the cop and Lauren asked at the same time.

"The bald guy. His name is *Jones*!" Kirsten said. "He was a suspect in Sam Byrne's murder. A drug dealer. He was put in jail, but now he's out. He was on the balcony where the girl fell. He pushed her—I know it. *He's a killer!* Ask Detective Peterson. He was in charge of the case. Do you know Detective Peterson?"

The cop squinted. "Are you sure it was the same balcony? Did you see where he went?"

"NO! I don't know!"

It was useless. They were staring at her as if she were crazy.

Maybe she *was* crazy. Maybe she needed to follow her original instinct to *go*.

She made a break for the door, pushing her way through and feeling again the shock of February's cold against her perspiration-soaked body.

What was Jones doing out of jail? And why did he push that girl? Who was she? All his victims so far had been linked—Sam, Carolee, Emma—all part of Kirsten's Upper East Side crowd. This girl wasn't one of them.

Was this girl involved in a drug deal gone bad? Was that the reason he killed her? She turned up MacDougal, shivering, pulled out her cell phone, and punched Detective Peterson's number.

"KIRSTEN! HEY, WAIT!" Lauren ran up alongside her, her breaths puffing in the frigid air. "Are you okay?"

Kirsten put her fingers to her lips, shushing her friend. On the other end of the phone, Peterson picked up right away. Just like the old days. "Peterson."

"It's Kirsten. Kirsten S—"

"Sawyer. I can tell by the sound of your voice. How was Italy?"

"Greece. I'm at NYU now, but listen. Something

happened . . . a girl . . . she fell from a balcony in our student lounge. She was pushed—"

"Pushed? Did you see this happen? Are you sure?"

"No—yes! I don't know!" Kirsten said. "The thing is, I saw *Jones*. He's out. He was on the balcony. Why would he be there? Maybe this girl was involved in drugs. Maybe she didn't pay him or something? I don't know. But he shouldn't be out of jail—*you have to get him*!"

Peterson took a few seconds before answering. By the time he spoke, Kirsten and Lauren were on the steps of the Better Ridgefield. Kirsten's lips were shaking with the cold as she stepped into the warmth of the foyer. The place seemed empty. It looked like the whole school had rushed over to see what had happened.

"Hang on a second, Kirsten," Peterson said. "I'm getting a report." For a moment, his phone went silent.

Kirsten turned to Lauren. "This is the detective I was in touch with during the time when—"

"Hi, Kirsten?" Peterson's voice interrupted. "Okay, here's what the officers radioed in. I can't divulge the girl's name, but apparently they have a suicide note. Of course, this isn't conclusive, but I think—"

"And they haven't found Jones? They didn't say anything about him?"

Peterson paused a moment before responding. "I don't think you have to worry about Jones."

"What do you mean? He's out of jail. The only way I wouldn't worry is if he was dead!"

"Exactly."

"He's *dead*? Oh my God. Is that what you're saying?"

"Is it possible you may have seen someone who looked like him? He's a pretty common physical type. And if he was high up—"

"Well, um . . ." If Jones was dead, then she *couldn't* have seen him. Duh. But the resemblance . . . could it possibly have been someone else? A look-alike? Maybe it was Santa Claus. At this point, in her state of mind, Kirsten couldn't trust anything she was seeing.

Can I help? Lauren mouthed.

Kirsten shook her head.

"Look, I'm so sorry you had to go through that, Kirsten," Peterson said. "It must have been rough. This time of year is the worst for student suicides. The cold. The bleakness. The grade pressure. It's all too common. Seasonal affective disorder, they call it."

Seasonal affective disorder?

He was so smug. So confident.

He'd been just like that when she'd reported Kyle's cause of death. Suicide, he'd proclaimed. Like he'd seen it a million times.

Kirsten and Lauren were in the dorm lounge now. Mercifully, the TV was off, leaving an eerie silence, but

Peterson's voice was breaking up on the cell phone. "Not all suicides are really suicides, you know!" she said, slipping the phone from one ear to the other. "You said *Paul Stone* was a suicide, Detective Peterson! Where was *his* suicide note?"

"Kirsten, not all suicide cases leave notes," Peterson's voice crackled over the cell phone. "Stone had nothing on him. No clues. We had to piece things together forensically—"

"Not *nothing*. Maybe he didn't have a suicide note, but he did have—" Kirsten stopped herself.

A *photo*, she'd almost said.

But Peterson didn't know that. No one knew that Kyle had had a photo in his hand when he died—because Kirsten had taken it. And she couldn't tell Peterson about that. She wasn't supposed to *have* it. It was evidence. Stealing evidence is against the law. She wasn't even sure why she'd done it. It just sort of *happened*.

"Kirsten? Are you there?" Peterson asked.

"Um, bad signal," Kirsten replied.

"What were you going to say?" Peterson pressed.

"I—I forgot," Kirsten said.

"You saw Stone's body before anyone else did. Is there anything you need to tell us? I*s there something you're keeping from us, Kirsten?*"

3

Soft amber light glowed from the windows of the brick houses lining the uptown side of Washington Square Park. From inside, people stood watching the snow—a tweed-jacketed man smoking a pipe, a child holding a yellow toy truck. They were like pictures from another era, all coziness and warmth.

Kirsten wanted to cry.

Peterson hadn't believed her about Jones. He'd treated her like she was a dumb kid, and in the end, when he'd kept asking if she knew anything more, she'd just stumbled and stammered and made excuses. Which just made him impatient, but at least he'd dropped the subject.

What good would it do to mention the photo now, anyway? It was just a dumb picture of Kyle in a bar, with Carolee—that's all. Well, not so dumb. It had hurt to see it. It had hurt that his last action in life was to clutch a picture of his old girlfriend. Who needed to see that? Maybe that was why

Kirsten had taken it—so no one else would discover it. No one else would see how much he cared for Carolee. Which seemed immature and stupid, and if she'd really thought it through, she might not have done it. But she hadn't thought at all. She'd just taken it. The point was, it didn't really matter. As evidence, it would have been useless.

After the call, Lauren had tried to comfort Kirsten. But it was already time to meet Julie, and as sweet as Lauren was, *Julie* was the one who could always make her feel better. Kirsten checked her watch. 9:02. She was supposed to meet Julie at 9:00 under the Washington Square Arch.

A cab was waiting by the curb. Its rear window slowly slid down and there she was, leaning out, waving, her sunny face framed by a halo of blond hair grown long and tied back in a way-too-mature-looking ponytail. "Hi! You look terrible!" Julie called out. "Let's do something about it. Hop in."

Kirsten opened the door and slid into the cab beside her friend. "Puerto Vallarta, please," she said to the cab driver, who returned a blank stare.

"Second Avenue and Eighty-Fourth," Julie said. "The Party Room."

The cab headed west, navigating the one-way streets that would take them east and eventually uptown.

"Guess his sense-of-humor chip wore out," Kirsten muttered.

"Are you all right?" Julie asked.

"A girl just fell off a balcony and died, so close to me that I could practically feel her last breath," Kirsten said, sinking back into the seat. "Otherwise, I'm great."

The last vestige of Julie's salon tan vanished along with her smile. "Did she . . . kill herself?"

"Supposedly," Kirsten replied.

"What is supposedly supposed to mean?"

Kirsten exhaled loudly. Outside, a bicycle messenger going the wrong way swerved out of the cab's path and calmly flipped a middle finger to the driver. "I thought she was pushed," Kirsten said. "I looked up to the balcony, and near where she'd jumped, I saw Jones—or someone who looked like him. He was staring down at the body, and then he looked into my eyes—and I knew. It was Jones. The trouble is, it wasn't. Jones is dead. Peterson just told me."

"Oh," Julie said. "So, it was just someone who looked like him? Or—"

"Or what?" Kirsten asked. "Or I'm *crazy*? Yeah, maybe that's it, Jules. That makes the most sense to me. . . ."

Kirsten's voice choked in her throat. Julie was watching her with such concern, her face so open and sympathetic, and her expression brought back a flood of memories, of times when Julie was there for her—the sand-throwing bullies on the playground outside the Metropolitan Museum of Art, the humiliations of Ms. Baudry's dancing school, the junior high crushes, the horrible night after Sam died. . . . She let her body tilt ever so slightly toward the center of the seat, and Julie took the cue, wrapping her in soft, Burberry-clad arms as Kirsten sobbed.

"Sssshhh," Julie said. "It's hard coming back home. You are being so brave. Hey, awful things happen. Kids commit suicide. Frankie Federman had to be pulled back from his bedroom window after he was wait-listed at Harvard—"

"He lives on the second floor!" Kirsten said, pulling back. "And this is *nothing* like that."

"Kirsten, how far away was Jones? How many stories high?"

"I don't know. Six? Seven?"

"It's a long way up, right? No one's eyesight is *that* good. *You* think back, Kirsten—remember when you were seeing Kyle's face and Jones's face, like, everywhere? It was the pressure. Listen, you have a responsibility to yourself. To your own mental health."

"You sound like my parents," Kirsten said.

"But unlike them, *I* have your best interests at heart," Julie replied with a grin. "As soon as we get to the Party Room, I'll get Scott to pour some of his magic for us—on him. Just for fun, okay?"

Kirsten nodded.

"And guess what?" Julie added. "Sarah's home from Vassar, and Carla's coming up from Princeton. It'll be like Old Home Week."

Kirsten stiffened. Sarah Goldstein and Carla Hernandez had been two of her best friends all through grade school, middle school, and high school. They'd all cried together over Sam's death, too. But as Kirsten had stayed involved with the investigation, they'd drifted away. They'd wanted to leave it all behind. Soon Kirsten even stopped getting e-mails and IMs from them. "Do I owe them money or something?"

"Stop it. I've talked to them both. They feel guilty. They realize they were stupid and uncaring, but they didn't mean to hurt your feelings. They know that now. They want to bury the hatchet."

"In my head or my back?" Kirsten asked.

Julie gave her an exasperated but tolerant look, and Kirsten decided it was time to glide uptown in silence, open the window, and let her own sour vibes out. She was feeling prickly, but in truth, she couldn't wait to see her old friends again.

The funky East Village streets gave way to the glass giants of Midtown, and soon the taxi was speeding up Third Avenue lane-to-lane through slow traffic as only New York City cabbies can. Somewhere above Fifty-Ninth Street the neighborhood abruptly changed, and the streets were alive with kids dressed in Ralph Lauren, men still in suits walking pugs and poodles, and, of course, The Ladies with Face-lifts That Launched a Thousand Plastic Surgeons. Kirsten felt at home. "Welcome to the Upper East Side," she said under her breath.

As they circled around and came back down Second, Julie

pointed to a small redbrick building sandwiched between two boxy high-rises. "There," she said to the driver. "The place with no name and all the kids in front."

The Party Room didn't need a marquee or advertising—especially if you went to The Woodley School, New York's A-list prep school and venerable breeding ground for celebrity kids, old-money trust-fund babies, and Wall Street offspring. Woodley's graduating class each year was a snapshot of the future Power Elite, and at night, the Elite went to the Party Room. If you were a Woodley kid, if you knew one, if you *wished* you were one—which covered just about everyone in New York—then you knew where the Party Room was. On the outside it looked like nothing, a relic from another time, a building too small to attract a toss of Donald Trump's bad hair. Inside, however, was another story. Inside was a cavern of perpetual good times that swallowed your cares as you swallowed some of the best drinks in New York.

Julie and Kirsten got out of the cab and ran the slow sidewalk gauntlet of hugs, kisses, "You look greats," and "How's colleges" from people they knew and people they'd never seen in their lives. If you were a regular, if you were one of the Woodley chosen, then people just knew you.

The front door was open, and Kirsten caught that familiar sweet smell of oak wall paneling and pine floorboards soaked in generations of old beer and liquor. There was nothing like it. They descended the too-steep stairs, which were rumored to have been built when the place was a stop on the Underground Railroad (and which, by ninth grade, you learned by bitter experience to take *slooowly* on the way out). An old DMX song, driving and loud, pulsed up from below.

"We're HOME!" Julie sang, opening the door at the bottom of the stairs.

That was the door, Kirsten thought. *The door that framed Sam when you last saw her the night she'd been attacked by that Neanderthal, drug-addict ex-boyfriend, Brandon Yardley, and then left with . . . him . . . Jones . . .* Kirsten took a deep breath. *Brute Mental Force, kid. Block those thoughts. Now.* Screwing a smile onto her face, she stepped inside.

The place hadn't changed a bit. The monster speakers were tilted down from the corners, flanking a plasma TV that at the moment was showing a basketball game to a small bunch of non-dancing guys who were bellowing over a touchdown or whatever. But most of the kids were shaking and baking, interrupting themselves only long enough to give Kirsten more hugs and welcomes.

She felt better already—and twice as good when she spotted Scott, sexy and rugged as ever, behind the bar along with Kevin, the second bartender. Kirsten waved at Scott, and he smiled back, his dimples even deeper than she had remembered, which, despite the age difference between them (he had to be twenty-seven, at least), nonetheless induced the great desire to get horizontal with him. It was an occupational hazard of every girl who came to the Party Room, and it got worse with each drink.

Kirsten suddenly realized that since her return from Greece, the topic of hot sex hadn't really reared its, um, head. Which was a shame. But tonight's crowd at the Party Room assured her that things were headed back on the right track.

"Some hotties here tonight," Kirsten said, eyeing a perfectly round ass that led upward to a glorious chiseled face that would have made Kirsten's pulse run wild if she hadn't suddenly recognized him as Gabe Garson's snot-nosed little brother, all grown up.

"At last, dear Lord, the girl shows signs of life," Julie replied. "Mostly high school kids, though. Personally, I am not into cradle-robbing."

"Speaking of cradles," said Scott, wiping a spot on the mirror-smooth bar top, "may I see your IDs, college girls?"

As usual, Kirsten and Julie both whipped out their trusty fake ID laminates, procured one drunken evening in a shop near West Fourth Street, and vaguely waved them over the bar.

As usual, Scott pretended to look. He was already pouring. "Hey, welcome back, Kirsten. We missed you."

A pair of hands closed over Kirsten's eyes, and she recognized the unmistakable mix of chocolate and Angel perfume, which could only belong to one person. "Sarah?" Kirsten said.

"I am *soooooooo* sorry," Sarah Goldstein squealed, releasing her hands and then spinning Kirsten around. She was dressed in basic Prada, which Kirsten couldn't imagine anyone outdoing until she saw Carla in her vintage Pucci dress—and the three girls hugged and apologized and caught up and swore eternal friendship. And just like that, all four of them were up and clearing the dance floor like old times. Once again, Kirsten watched the boys' jaws drop at the flash of Carla's man-killer legs, and the bounce of Julie's devastator 36Ds, and Sarah's dance-moves-just-this-close-to-the-act-of-sex-itself. Watching the massive scramble for the best view was as fun as ever. Kirsten laughed. Some things would never change.

Out of the corner of her eye she spotted the back of a pair of broad shoulders making their way across the floor; thick, dark hair; gym-sculpted arms; a super-thin waist, with khakis; a button-down shirt; and a cotton sweater tied around his neck.

Athletic prep. Very sexy—and most likely *not* a high-school kid.

Definitely Kirsten's type these days. She danced away from her friends, accidentally on purpose bumping into the new guy from behind.

He stumbled a bit and turned. "Kirsten?" he said.

It took Kirsten a moment to recognize him. The lines of the face were thinner, the hair shorter. But the sharp-ledged brow was the same, and so was the thick-lipped grin that spread across his face like a cloudburst on a spring day. "My God," Kirsten said, "what happened to you?"

If there was any doubt, the braying-horse laugh cemented the guy's identity as Brandon Yardley. Ex-Boyfriend of Sam Byrne. Woodley's Drug King. Flunky for Jones the Dealer.

"I've turned over a new leaf," Brandon replied. "Funny, huh? Scares the crap out of my dad. He thinks I'm pulling something."

"The last time I saw you, you were—"

"With Jones. That asshole. I can't believe what he did to me. If I ever see him again . . ."

"You won't," Kirsten said softly. "Jones is dead."

"You're kidding, right?" Brandon gave her a funny look, and a blond girl Kirsten vaguely remembered, someone's little sister, sidled up to Brandon and pulled him by his sleeve toward the door. "Oops. My public calls. See you!"

Kirsten watched them go, shaking her head.

He was wearing deck shoes, no doubt from Brooks Brothers, but *deck shoes*!

And they were paid for by drug money. Earned through a partnership with a drug dealer. Jones. The man who may have been responsible for Sam's death.

Drug money had killed her best friend, and now drug money had bought Brandon respectability. How ironic.

Kirsten suddenly wasn't in the mood to dance any-more. She crossed the room and joined Julie, who was now sitting by the bar, sipping on what looked like a very deep martini.

Scott began pouring Kirsten a drink. Kevin, the other bartender, had cranked the music up a notch, and behind them the place was going insane. In the midst of it all were Carla and Sarah, dancing up a storm.

Scott slid a lethal-looking concoction across the polished bar top as she told them all about Brandon's new look.

"Here's your Evian," Scott said. "Sip slowly, and it'll go down like water."

Kirsten took a sip and nearly fell over. "Wow. *Fire* water," she said.

"Sam was so right to dump Brandon," Julie remarked. "A shit head in Brooks Brothers clothes is still a shit head. I still can't figure out what she saw in him."

Kirsten swirled the liquid in her glass and watched it flow thickly back down the side. "Sam did not have luck with guys. . . ."

"But no more dark thoughts, remember?" Julie said. "What's over is over."

"*If* it's over," Kirsten murmured.

"Don't start, Kirsten," Julie warned. "Don't spoil the night. The police analyzed all the evidence they had for the killings. I'm sure if they found anything else, they'd reopen the case."

Julie sounded so confident.

Maybe it was the drink, or maybe it was the encounter with Brandon—or just the nagging guilt that had been cooped up for so long. But at that moment, Kirsten couldn't keep her little secret inside. "But they didn't have all the evidence," she said softly.

Julie gave her a look. "What do you mean, Kirsten?"

"I kind of took something," Kirsten admitted, immediately wishing she could take it back.

"What?" Julie said, sitting forward and nearly spilling her drink.

Kirsten took a deep breath. "It—it was a picture, that's all. Of him and Carolee at some bar. He was holding it . . . and I took it. I—I know it was stupid, but I don't know, the picture didn't seem all that *important*."

"Do you still have it?" Julie asked. "This could be serious, Kirsten."

Kirsten downed the rest of her drink. "It's in a drawer somewhere. I haven't looked for it. Do you think I'll get in trouble?"

"Is the Pope Catholic?" Julie replied.

Scott, who'd been busy filling an order, leaned over the bar toward them. "Hey, hey . . . let it rest," he said soothingly, sliding refills toward the girls. "What was it—a snapshot? Chances are, it wasn't that important. If you turn it in now, it'll look like you withheld it for a reason. Just between us, if I were in your shoes? I'd burn that picture."

Kirsten felt the blood rushing to her face. She hadn't meant to let Scott in on this too.

Julie stood up from the stool. She did not look convinced. "Time to change topic. Let's dance."

Behind her, Sarah and Carla were slow dancing with a couple of guys who looked like they'd won the Lotto. An R&B ballad was playing now, a smooth Usher tune.

"You go ahead. I'll catch the next song." Kirsten turned back to the bar, where Scott was now filling a munchies bowl.

"Why aren't you dancing?" he asked. "I can see, oh, about two dozen 'Will-I-get-lucky-tonights?' salivating for you on the dance floor."

But the song was bringing back a vivid memory. "Two summers ago," Kirsten said, absently moving some pretzels around in the bowl, "Carla's big sister's driving us out to the Hamptons in her convertible, and we get stuck in traffic—Route 27, I think—and we're *sooooo* bored . . . and *this* song comes on. Well, Sam stands up in the backseat and starts singing along at the top of her lungs, wearing only her new bikini. So, like, every guy for miles is gawking, and this flock of ducks waddles over from the side of the road and starts *quacking* at her, and Sam bursts out laughing and screams, 'They *like* me! They really *like* me. . . .'" Kirsten's voice trailed off, and she fought back tears. "It's a stupid story. I guess you had to be there."

"Maybe I should switch the track," Scott said gently.

"Hey, help me pick out another CD. I have a bunch of new mixes in the vault."

Kirsten loved that Scott still used CDs. "Okay," she said. "Thanks."

Scott asked Kevin to take over and then he slipped out from behind the bar. Holding her drink, Kirsten followed him around the side, to the wall just before the restrooms. He took out a key and opened a locked door, revealing a deep pantry lined with shelves. On one side were liquor bottles and cartons of munchies, and on the other were stacks of CDs.

Scott handed Kirsten three of them. Most had labels written in loopy handwriting with hearts and sweet messages.

"Fans?" Kirsten said.

Scott leaned over Kirsten's shoulder. "One of these kids is into hip-hop and house, the other mix is more pop and R&B. They all think it's funny I like CDs. But the sound's better. And I'm old!"

Kirsten held up the hip-hop CD to Scott. It was current—all new hits from this year. "Well, none of this will bring back memories of Sam, I guess."

"I guess I *am* old—I don't know half of these groups," Scott said with a smile. "Hey Kirsten, it's okay. Look, I know how it feels to have someone really close to you die. It changes you. Kind of turns off a light in your soul. What you're feeling is so totally normal. I can't lie to you—you will never stop thinking about her. You'll never feel the same again. But life is all about change. Slow change. You learn how to deal with stuff like this. You do. Trust me. And you move on, and life gets beautiful again—only the colors are slightly different, that's all."

Kirsten brushed a tear from her eye. Scott was such a good friend. Even if the clientele was getting too young at the Party Room, she knew she'd never stop coming here. Because of him.

As he took the CD, his fingers brushed against hers. They were blunt fingers—you would guess Macho Road Worker rather than, say, Sensitive Pianist—but the nails looked manicured, which was so *Scott*. He was full of surprises.

She caught a scent of cologne, an old-fashioned kind that she'd smelled once on Julie's hunky brother Chad, causing her and Julie to run into the bathroom and read the label, which had no recognizable designer logo but contained the words "bay rum." It was the smell of Man Unafraid, Kirsten had decided—and without even thinking, she found herself slowly inhaling, leaning toward Scott . . . and closing her eyes.

The CD fell from her fingers, clattering against the tiled floor, but she didn't care. It didn't matter what was playing. It could have been "Happy Birthday." She stood on tiptoes, and now she felt his soft, warm breath against her cheeks as she moved her lips closer.

She smelled his skin now, rugged and slightly bitter beneath the cologne, and now the musky-minty scent of his breath. She felt his arms close around her, firm and comforting.

His lips were full and wide and surprisingly soft, and she could have stayed like this for hours, drinking him, breathing him, feeling his warmth course through her body, if he hadn't gently pulled away. "Kirsten?" he said.

"Mmmm," she replied, slowly opening her eyes.

He was smiling, but not the way she wanted. Something in the odd angle of his lips, the slight tightness in his face, the distance in his eyes that hadn't been there a moment ago. "Look, maybe this—"

A voice broke the spell. "Yo, Scott—this chick just asked me for a long, slow, comfortable screw against the wall! Can you believe these—"

Scott dropped his arms, and Kirsten sprang away.

It was Kevin, standing in the closet doorjamb.

"Uh," Kirsten squeaked.

"Um, I, well . . . ," Kevin said.

Scott scooped the CD off the floor as if nothing had happened. "Hate to disappoint you, Kevin, but that customer wasn't coming on to you—it's the name of a drink. One shot each of sloe gin, Southern Comfort, Galliano, vodka, and orange juice. . . ."

As the two guys left, Kirsten leaned against the wall.

Shit. Shit. Shit.

She had come on to him. Cornered Scott—good old

Scott—in a closet behind the bar, in the middle of his shift, and tried to hook up with him. *What were you thinking?* she asked herself. *Ladies and gentlemen, let's give it up for the winner of the American Idiot Award.*

He was never going to look at her the same again. He knew now. He knew she was hot for him. From now on, he'd always be a little wary, a little cautious. Unless . . .

It wasn't as if he'd hated it, Kirsten told herself.

He hadn't jumped back and yelled at her. It took two pairs of lips to kiss. He'd put his arms around her.

Kirsten allowed herself a slightly guilty smile. It had felt good. It had felt *sooooo* good.

It was something she'd been dying to do for ages.

She composed herself and stepped out of the closet, wondering if anyone besides Kevin had noticed. The first song of the new mix blared over the speakers. Everyone was dancing now.

She jumped onto the floor, joining a group that included Julie, Carla, and Sarah, everyone moving, shaking—letting it all go. No more cares. No worries. She tossed her head back and soon she was floating, not feeling a thing except the music.

And something else . . .

Eyes.

She was being watched.

Of course you're being watched, she told herself. *You're at the Party Room. You WANT to be watched.*

But this was different. A feeling that made the hairs stand on the back of her neck. As if the crowded room had suddenly become an abandoned street, and someone was following her . . .

As she spun around, dancing, she tried to take in the whole room, to see if anything was different and strange. The place was jumping as usual. Nothing different.

Nothing.

It was paranoia. That's all.

Relax, she told herself. *Shut out the world.*

"If I Close My Eyes" was playing now, one of her favorite tunes, drawing *everyone* onto the floor . . . Reina wailing her heart out about lost love . . .

Kirsten closed her eyes.

Click.

She swayed, swinging her hair, thinking about the new year ahead . . . about the moment she'd just spent in the back room with Scott . . . about what she'd say to him . . .

Click.

Click. Click. Click.

Her eyes sprang open at the sound. Someone ducked behind a group of dancers.

"WHAT THE *HELL*?" Scott's voice boomed across the room. He jumped over the bar like an Olympic athlete and ran through the crowd, clearing the dance floor.

"Did you see that?" Carla said. "He was taking pictures."

"Pictures?" Kirsten said. "Who?"

"What a perv," Sarah replied. "He comes up close to you, Kirsten, pretending to listen to his cell phone. Then he's holding it over you, like he's trying to see down your shirt."

Kirsten heard a guy cry out at the door. Scott had someone by the collar, pushing him, shouting into his face. She ran closer for a better look.

She recognized the orange knit hat before she saw the face—the guy from the NYU lounge. The film geek who had been taking pictures of the dead girl in the atrium. "I know him," Kirsten murmured. "He goes to NYU."

"How'd they let someone like *that* in?" Sarah asked.

"They must have had to fill a quota for jackass creeps," Sarah said.

Kirsten felt nauseated. She'd only seen this guy from behind—he'd never looked her in the eye.

Or had he?

Who was he? Why was he here? What made him think he could take pictures of her boobs?

And what was he going to *do* with those pictures?

"YOU COME NEAR HER AGAIN—YOU EVEN LOOK IN HER DIRECTION—I'LL PUT THE HURT ON YOU, BIG-TIME!" Scott boomed, grabbing the guy by the shirt and pants and throwing him upstairs.

Kirsten's mouth fell open. She had never seen Scott like this.

"Hmm . . . ," Sarah said with a raised eyebrow. "Uh, what exactly happened between you two in that back room?"

Kirsten felt herself blushing.

"Uh-huh," Carla said, and nodded. "Once a Woodley girl, always a Woodley girl. We don't miss a thing."

"Details, Kirsten. We need details," Julie said. "Did you hook up?"

"No!" Kirsten protested, unable to stop grinning. "And there are no details!"

"A likely story, given that big, fat grin on your face," Carla said.

"He's always been into you," Sarah added. "Anyone can see it."

"He *has*?" Kirsten asked.

"Duh," Carla said. "Don't play Miss Innocent."

"But if you don't want to . . . hey, I'd do him," Julie volunteered, giving Scott an appraising eye.

"Leslie did," Sarah piped up. "She says he's great in bed."

Julie groaned. "Leslie did *not* do Scott."

"She has the condom to prove it," Sarah replied.

"EWWWWWWW!" they all shouted.

Try as she might, Kirsten could not wipe the smile off her face.

Me . . . and Scott? she thought. *Hot Scott?*

It was a concept.

4

Kirsten floated up the front stairs of the Better Ridgefield Hotel. As she inserted her passkey in the front door, she glanced at her Movado: 1:27 a.m.

Pushing the door open, she shuddered a bit. The guy with the orange cap was in this building, somewhere. She imagined him pacing his bedroom, smarting from Scott's treatment, deciding what to say to Kirsten. But she wasn't scared. Not really. If he had the slightest reading on an IQ chart, his first words would be "I'm sorry." Better yet, he'd say nothing—ever—if he *really* knew what was good for him. Scott would be watching.

She smiled. The martini was still flowing through her, making everything seem so mellow.

Scott . . . my hero . . . She giggled a little at the thought of him.

The rest of the night he'd taken a lot of teasing about his

outburst, but had shrugged it all off with a bashful grin. And he'd been so sweet to her—no funny "our lives will never be the same" looks after their encounter in the back room, no come-ons—just solid, normal, hunky, delicious Scott.

Where would this lead? Kirsten wondered. She and Scott had become good friends over the past several months, but did he care about her in *that* way? Was it possible?

Maybe. Maybe not.

Be realistic, she told herself. *Scott was there for you when you had trouble dealing with Sam's death, but you don't really know that much about him. You don't even know where he lives, or if he has a girlfriend!*

Well, whatever happened between them, Kirsten would always remember that hot moment, no matter what. Her heart thumped hard in her chest just thinking about it as she tiptoed down the hallway to her room. She unlocked room number 103 and pushed open the door, stepped inside, and flicked on the living room light.

It would take a little while to get used to the smell. Not rotting garbage or anything. More like IKEA-type particle-board dressers and desks. They had a certain "I'm really cheap but hey that's what you get when you live in the dorms" kind of smell.

Kirsten's dad had offered to buy her a $3 million pad down in Tribeca when she announced that she'd been accepted to NYU, but Kirsten had turned him down. She'd *wanted* to live in the dorms—to be like a regular college student. So here she was, tripled up in a dumpy suite in a dumpy "hotel" with two other girls. At least the place was a decent size, as far as dorm rooms went. Most of suites at the Ridge had three or four bedrooms surrounding a small living space and a private bath, and there were a few singles scattered on the upper floors—probably reserved for seniors.

She and Lauren had nearly sanitized the room that morning, but everything looked totally different now. Piles of stuff were stacked against the walls—comics, food containers, books, and about a dozen sealed boxes.

The New Roommate had arrived, and she was a slob.

Each of the three bedroom doors off the living room were decorated with multicolored woodblock letters: LAUREN, KIRSTEN, JAN. That was a new touch. Not Kirsten's style, exactly. All that was missing was a little needlepoint thingy that said HOME SWEET HOME. But hey, the effort was nice.

Lauren's door slowly swung open, and the dim light of her bed lamp filtered into the common room. She was dressed in a snowflake-patterned flannel nightgown, which looked soft and cozy and boxy and exceedingly ugly. Lauren's hair was loose and messy around her shoulders, her face preoccupied and grim.

"What are you doing up so late?" Kirsten asked.

"Homework," Lauren replied.

"Homework? We haven't had classes yet!"

"I got the course description for Intro to Constitutional Law. Sounds pretty neat. Thought I'd get a head start. Did you have a good time? Were you able to forget Chloe Pepper for a while?"

"Who?" Kirsten asked.

"The girl who jumped," Lauren said. "That's her name. It was in the papers."

"Oh. Yeah." Kirsten took a deep breath. The night had been so full that she had stopped thinking about the girl's death for a while. And now the awful images were coming back, spoiling the lingering good feelings and making her feel somehow guilty, somehow disloyal to this poor girl whose name she'd just now learned.

She walked into her room and dropped her pack onto her bed. "Sorry, I guess I kind of disappeared this evening."

"That's okay," Lauren said, and exhaled. "It's been a rough day. Some way to start a college career, huh? I practically had to beg my parents to not send me a ticket home. They were horrified. The late newspapers have jumped on the story—the *Post* called it 'Sorority Sister Suicide.'"

Suicide. In a headline. That made it sound so official. As if any other possibility had been ruled out. "Do they *know* it's a suicide? I mean, have they had a full investigation?"

"I don't know. I tried not to think about it all day. I went for a swim, lifted weights, took a jog around the park. Anyway, then I got back here and found out that the movers lost my special mattress from home." Lauren pressed down on Kirsten's mattress with two hands. "Yours is much firmer than the piece of crap they gave me. I have scoliosis—I think I told you, right? You know, really bad curvature of the spine? Until they deliver my mattress, I'll deal with my futon and hope I don't do any permanent damage."

A thump sounded from the other bedroom, followed by a muffled yawn. Slowly the third bedroom door creaked open.

"Oh, that's another thing," Lauren said softly. "Our new roommate is here. Kirsten, meet Jan."

Kirsten stood up, put on her best smile, and stepped into the living room.

Out of the other room, rumpled and yawning, walked the last person on earth Kirsten had expected to see.

Jan was not a she.

Jan was a he.

And Kirsten knew exactly who he was.

Even without the orange knit cap.

5

"You?" Kirsten said.

She couldn't believe it.

Him. Here. Not only in her dorm.

In her room!

He was just standing there with his ravaged, "haven't figured out how to be handsome" face, looking like a little kid caught with his hand in a cookie jar.

This couldn't be happening. Not after a day like this.

"Um, I can explain . . . ," Jan replied.

Kirsten backed away, into her room. "You're—a guy. And . . . and you're . . ."

"A pain in the neck?" Jan said. "A geek? A busybody? A wiseass to Upper East Side bartenders who threaten his fragile masculinity? Guilty on all counts. Plus, I have a name that could also be a girl's name. This has not only warped me from birth, but also messed up the housing office, which is why they put me here. But despite it all, I'm kind of sweet and quirky and harmless in a loose-limbed way. And I'm a really good cook, so I do have redeeming values."

A talker. A big mouth, too-clever-for-his-own-good, talker. On top of everything else. One more notch on his belt of detestable qualities.

She hated guys like him.

"You were at the Party Room," Kirsten said. "Taking pictures. And this morning, when that girl died, you were taking pictures of *that*. Who the hell *are* you?"

Jan did a little showbiz shuffle and bowed low. "Jan deVries at your service. Worshipper at the altar of Tarantino, Kurosawa, Scorsese, Wise, and Welles, in roughly that order. My life mission: to boldly go where no filmmaker has gone before, to never stop trying to capture the essence of the human condition on film—digital or celluloid."

"Will you ever stop talking?" Lauren said.

Jan blushed. "Just tell me to shut up. I'm used to it."

"I'm going to bed," Lauren said, turning back into her room. "Classes start early tomorrow, if I can drag my aching back to them. Good night."

She shut her door, and Kirsten was alone in the room with Jan. She knew she had to *do* something, but her instincts were short-circuiting, undecided between ignoring him and shoving him out the window.

His gray-eyed gaze was darting around the room. With his left hand he nervously twirled the ends of his curly hair, which fell in knotty brown ringlets over face. And that maddened her too, because there was something familiar about the mannerism, as if he was imitating someone she knew. . . .

"You're mad at me, right?" he asked. "You are. I can tell. I mean, there I was, being a paparazzi at the Party Room, and now here I am, in the weirdest coincidence of the century, and you feel threatened and hate my guts, and frankly I don't blame you."

"Coincidence? I don't think so," Kirsten said, folding her arms across her chest.

"No, really. I swear," Jan said. "First of all, we've never met before, right? Um. Hi, by the way." He gave a little wave and a smile, but Kirsten just stared at him. "Anyway, the likelihood of me traveling to the Party Room to see you is virtually nil. And second, you see before you a guy whose admitted misfit-loner qualities have allowed for the development of superior Web skills, for whom Googling a list of New York City hot spots is very easy—and which action would, as you can imagine, lead him to Second Avenue and Eighty-Fourth Street. And once I was there, being the camera freak that I am, naturally I'd be looking for interesting subject material."

"Cell phone pictures of my tits?" Kirsten asked.

Jan turned beet-red and muttered something unintelligible about interesting angles.

Kirsten sighed. This guy was just a geek. She couldn't imagine him trying anything. And the idea of him skulking around to find the hottest club in New York—and choosing the Party Room—didn't seem so far-fetched.

She felt too sorry for him to be mad. He was annoying, but threatening? Uh, no. Probably gay, too, Kirsten figured, which was kind of a relief. "I don't exactly know how to feel," Kirsten said. "Let me sleep on this. Maybe tomorrow I can go yell at the housing office. We were originally supposed to have a girl roommate—Clarice Moravec."

"Really? I heard she was coming here. She's famous. Did you see the documentary *Hoopskirts to Hoopsters: A History of Women in Basketball*? I didn't. Anyway, she probably got the penthouse suite at the Plaza. That's what colleges do with athletes."

"There's your great American exposé," Kirsten said, turning to go back to her room. "I get credit for the idea. Night. See you at Sundance."

She shut the door behind her and began getting ready for bed.

The fire engines blared up Sixth Avenue at around 2:15. One of the piles in the living room crashed noisily to the floor shortly afterward. A cat started wailing in the airshaft about a half hour later. Kirsten had to pee just before 3:00.

She was finally getting to sleep when Lauren began snoring . . . seriously.

Kirsten sat bolt upright. This was ridiculous. Putting on her robe, she shuffled into the living room and knocked on Lauren's door. "Hey . . . pssst, Lauren? You're rattling windows."

She heard a series of snorts, and Lauren fell quiet. But now Kirsten was wide-awake. In the corner near the bathroom was a tiny box-shaped refrigerator that Lauren had brought. Kirsten pulled it open, took out a bottle of Diet Coke, and began pacing. *It's college life,* she said to herself. *Get used to it.*

Jan's fallen pile of junk was all over the middle of the room. Papers with tiny scratchy handwriting . . . elaborate illustrated sci-fi scenes . . . and underneath them was a manila envelope that had come open, with some photo contact sheets sticking out.

Kirsten knelt over and began neatening up. Out of pure nosiness, she pulled out one of the contact sheets. In red grease pencil, various images were circled—mostly neighborhood scenes: the West Fourth Street subway entrance, narrow little Minetta Lane, the Porto Rico coffee importer . . .

And Lauren.

Kirsten brought the sheet into the bathroom light and scanned the various images. Lauren, in a telephoto shot, descending the subway stairs (or rather, Lauren's cleavage, which was about all that fit into the frame) . . . Lauren again, lying in a bikini on a beach chair beside an indoor pool . . . Lauren lifting weights, her chest bulging with the effort . . . jogging under the Washington Square Arch . . . She looked totally unaware. The photos must have been taken over the weekend.

Guess that takes gay out of the picture, Kirsten thought as she sifted through some of the other sheets. More girls. Each sheet a portrait of some other girl, some NYU student.

Kirsten's first instinct about him had been right: a jerk. A red-blooded, heterosexual perv. Someone who followed girls around. He must have thought he'd died and gone to heaven when he got Lauren as a roommate.

Kirsten's eyes caught one of the faces—dark hair, big doe eyes and full lips . . .

She knew that face.

On a hunch, she held the contact sheet side by side with a copy of today's *Daily News* that was lying on the floor. On the front page, beneath a headline that screamed "COED LEAPS TO DEATH," was a smiling freshman-register photo.

It matched exactly the face on the contact sheet.

Chloe Pepper.

"Oh . . . my . . . God," Kirsten murmured. He *knew* Chloe. He had been stalking her when she was alive. Then, when she died . . . *there he was*. Snapping away with his camera. And only moments earlier he'd been in the lounge, watching TV.

Coincidence?

Jan's life was a little too full of coincidences, wasn't it?

Showing up at the Party Room.

Being on the scene when Chloe jumped.

Ending up as Kirsten and Lauren's roommate.

Kirsten riffled through the sheets until she got to the last one—and she nearly screamed. There she was—Kirsten—stepping out of a cab on Fifth Avenue. Swinging with Julie on the swings in Central Park. Laughing at a corny joke that her doorman, Hector, had told in front of her house. But these were taken two weeks ago. Before she'd gotten to NYU. Before she'd ever seen his stupid orange knit cap bobbing around the city.

Kirsten's heart raced. Who *was* this guy?

Her hands were shaking as she shoved the contact sheets back into the envelope.

She felt defiled. Violated. Sleeping in this room was out of the question. She would crash for the night on the floor of Julie's dorm room at Barnard, then make a huge stink at the housing office in the morning.

She quickly righted the fallen pile, keeping the manila envelope hidden under all the other stuff. She grabbed a toothbrush and some makeup from the bathroom, and a change of clothes from her not-yet-unpacked suitcase. Then she ducked into Lauren's room and prodded her roommate awake. "Lauren," she whispered. "Jan's been taking weird pictures. You're in a lot of them, and so am I."

Lauren sat up, grimacing. "Whaaa? Pictures? So what?"

"It's, like, peekaboo stuff—legs and cleavage. Totally sick. I'm spending the rest of the night on the floor at my friend Julie's. Come with me. Tomorrow we can go to the housing Nazis."

"Oh God, no sleeping on floors for me, but thanks. Hey, can I use your mattress while you're gone? It's much better than mine."

Kirsten nodded, and Lauren got out of bed.

"You're not creeped out?" Kirsten asked her.

"I have mace and pepper spray and a black belt in tae kwon do," Lauren replied, shuffling sleepily toward Kirsten's room. "He tries anything with me and he's toast. Night."

"I'll call you to check up," Kirsten said. "What's your number?"

"I don't have a cell. The school is supposed to give us a landline tomorrow. Leave your number on my nightstand, and I'll call you and tell you what it is."

She disappeared into the room and shut the door behind her.

A few hours later, squinting in the morning sun, Kirsten was back at NYU. It was 9:00 a.m., but she'd had only about forty-five minutes of sleep on Julie's dusty dorm floor. She and Jules couldn't stop talking all night—and Julie was full of tactical advice for what to do next.

Which was why, at this ungodly hour, Kirsten was headed into the school athletic complex for the girls' varsity basketball team practice. Here, Kirsten intended to find out if Jan deVries really was the coincidence king.

They had found the practice schedule online. The girls, it

seemed, had to practice at the crack of dawn, while the boys got a midday time slot. Figured.

Tup . . . tup . . . tup-tup-tup-tup-tup . . .

The thumping of basketballs and squeaking of sneakers on the gym floor sounded like some nightmare hip-hop track as she pushed the door open.

She focused on a girl who must have been six feet five, standing at the side of the court. She wore a knee brace and paced back and forth, shouting things like "Screen!" and "Pick off!" that seemed to have nothing to do with basketball. Her last name, MORAVEC, was emblazoned on the back of her shirt.

Before Kirsten could call out the girl's name, a big orange ball came bouncing toward her, fast. She cried out in surprise, shielding her body with her arms, and felt a sudden jolt. When she looked down, she had the ball in her hands.

"Nice grab," the girl said.

"Um, thanks," Kirsten replied, handing her the ball. "Are you Clarice?"

The girl's smile tightened. "Sorry, I can't do interviews during practice. I mean, I'd like to, but my coach—"

"No, no. I'm not a sports reporter," Kirsten interrupted. "You were supposed to be in my room."

Clarice cocked her head. "Are you Jan? Hey, I owe you some thanks."

"Me? No, I'm Kirsten Sawyer."

"Oh. Well, it's because of someone named Jan that I got

this great single on the top floor of the hotel. So thank her for me."

"Jan got you a single?"

"Well, she gave the housing office some big sob story—she was arriving late, she had to room with someone from New York, she had a room on a high floor but was afraid of heights, blah, blah, blah. I mean, hey, it would have been nice, but I did get lucky, I guess." Spinning around, Clarice launched the basketball into the air, and it went through the hoop with a soft *swish*. "Oh, did you have something you wanted to ask me?"

"No," Kirsten said, turning away. "You told me everything I needed to know. Thanks."

She gritted her teeth and marched out of the gym. Everything she and Julie had guessed had been true: Clarice hadn't backed out of the roommate group after all. *Jan* had arranged the situation—pretended to be a girl and fooled the administration somehow.

Coincidence, my ass, she thought.

She didn't know what Jan's deal was, but she did know something:

He was *not* going to get away with it.

6

Pot roast.

Is it weird that I like pot roast?

WHO ON EARTH COOKS POT ROAST ANYMORE?

Use "brisket cut" only, oh yes indeed, sliced thinly and on the diagonal—and if not the diagonal, pal, it SUCKS because you learned the hard way, didn't you? It's TOUGH and CHEWY that way. The slicing has to be just right, not to mention the proper searing of the meat on the bottom of the pot.

Meat . . . Flesh . . . It's all one and the same, isn't it? WE ARE ALL FLESH, AREN'T WE?

God, it's amazing how pot roast can turn you into a feakin' philosopher.

Does she think about these things?

Does she know that when you come down to it, we're all nothing but carbon and hydrogen, protein and sugar, hair and FLESH? That the only thing that separates us from an inorganic slag heap is a SOUL, and we have an OBLIGATION to that soul, and if we break it we have no privilege to keep it?

Oopsy. We're hot and ready. . . .

Into the pot goes the beef—tsssss—up comes the bubbling fat—blub, blub—and now, ladies and gentlemen, the secret blend of spices, an old family recipe . . .

Now, as long as we're being goddamn Schopenhauer here, take this cow—the one we're cooking—she had a soul once too. A MOJO behind all that MOOING. But once ol' Bessie outlived her usefulness, it was time to move on. Pot roast, baby.

Onions, garlic—tsssss—now it starts to smell. The SMELL is half the fun.

Does she know about me? About what I've done?

She MUST!

But she can't.

Then why does it FEEL that way?

Like she's on to me.

Okay, think.

THINK!

Figure out where things could have gone wrong. Because they shouldn't have. There was never any room for mistakes.

I covered the bases.

Everything was under control.

SHE SHOULDN'T KNOW.

Oh, damn. Where are the scallions? I HAVE TO HAVE SCALLIONS!

Ah. Here we go. Tssssss . . .

Okay. Okay. Don't get crazy.

Make a plan. A RECIPE.

Investigate.

Give her the benefit of the doubt. For a while.

Because if she thinks she can outsmart me, she's got another thing coming.

I may be out of practice, but I still have the ability.

And the talent.

And the desire.

And the CONTROL.

And the red peppers. Always the red peppers last. TSSSSSS . . .

See, WHEN I decide it's time, she goes.

And there will be nothing she can do about it.

Except scream.

7

E-mail. That had to be how Jan had fooled the housing people, Kirsten thought. He sent an e-mail. That way, they didn't have to hear his voice, didn't have to know he was a guy.

Kirsten walked into the administration building, stomping the brown Greenwich Village snow off her shoes, and headed for the housing office. *Why?* Why did he do it? Was he really that obsessed with girls? With *her*? Was he some kind of Internet voyeur porn freak waiting for just the right moment: "HEY, FELLAS!!!!! CLICK ON THIS LINK TO SEE REAL COLLEGE COEDS WALKING AROUND TOPLESS AND MUCH, MUCH MORE XXX ACTION! THROUGH THE KEYHOLE!!!!" There were plenty of other girls in his pile of contact sheets—dozens of them. He could have chosen to sneak into any of their roommate groups, so why Kirsten and Lauren?

The housing office was closed until ten.

Kirsten checked her watch: 9:21. She hadn't stopped at the Ridge yet to check on Lauren, but chances were good that she was already at breakfast. The thought of food made Kirsten's stomach rumble. Her appetite had come back big-time. She headed back outside, zipped her coat, and walked toward the cafeteria.

About a block away, she spotted Jan leaving the cafeteria building.

Kirsten froze. The sensible part of her wanted to run. The other part wanted to heave a block of ice toward Jan's temple. He was listening intently to his iPod, hands deep in pockets, a camera hanging around his neck.

"Hey—Jan!" she called out, but he was walking away from her and oblivious.

She had to give him a piece of her mind. Right now.

His stride was long and quick. She tried to match his pace but got stuck at a red light on Bleecker Street while he darted into the student activities building.

By the time she got into the lobby, he was gone. Above the front desk was a list of meetings and clubs: All-University Gospel Choir . . . Baha'i Club @ NYU . . . Club Anime . . . Inter-Greek Council . . . Photography Club . . .

Photography. That's why he'd be here.

On the desk was a sign-up sheet with the heading DARKROOMS. Jan's name was at the bottom, next to Room 7.

"Where are the darkrooms?" Kirsten asked.

The girl behind the desk, a serious type wearing far too much black and engrossed in a graphic novel, pointed absently to her left. "Basement," she said. "Through the door, and then downstairs."

Kirsten pulled open the basement door, stepped downstairs, and followed signs to the darkrooms. She rounded a corner to a long hallway. At the opposite end, a door flew open.

Jan barged out, clutching a stack of photos. He turned, heading toward the other end of the hall. He was picking up his work. Actual film. So weirdly retro. Carla used to do that when she was in the Woodley Photo Club—leave wet pictures to dry overnight and then get them the next morning—at least until she got in trouble for locking herself and Trevor Royce in the room for *way* too long.

Kirsten ran down the hallway after Jan. She could hear him rushing up another set of stairs. But as she passed Room 7, she stopped, getting a different idea. She casually jiggled the door handle. Locked.

Then she glanced over her shoulder and pulled out her trusty American Express Platinum card from her Prada backpack and slipped it through the crack between the door and the frame. *Click.*

Too easy, she thought as she pushed the door ajar, and she made a mental note to check her dorm room lock when she got home.

Inside was a small room lit with a dim red bulb. In the near-darkness she could see a sink, a huge photo-enlarging machine, and ledges about waist-high that held rectangular pans containing foul-smelling liquid. Photos and clippings of all sizes had been taped to the wall, strips of film hung on clothespins from a line, and several stacks of accordion folders had been lined up next to the pans.

Kirsten leaned in toward the taped-up images, her elbows resting on the accordion folders. As her eyes adjusted to the light, the images became clearer. Smiling faces . . . a night in the Party Room, wild dancing, Julie and Sam and some guy Julie was seeing last year . . .

A wave of queasiness rushed through her. Just what was he doing with these pictures? How did he get them? Kirsten wasn't sure she wanted to know the answers as she stared at the horrifying collage in front of her.

Some of the taped-up images looked as if he'd photographed them himself, but many of them were old, ripped out of newspapers and yearbooks. Stuff he had carefully collected. An old yearbook picture of Sam, arm-in-arm with her old boyfriend Julian, laughing . . . Emma Lewis, flirting with Brandon, back when Emma was in her I-am-Sam's-clone phase, before she was strangled too . . . and there, in another photo, was Carolee Adams among a swarm of admirers, her head thrown back, revealing a slender, swanlike neck—the neck that had been crushed one night in the park four years ago, the grisly butchery that had started the whole chain.

"Ohhhhh." The sound escaped from her throat as she stared . . . stared at the happy, smiling pictures of girls who were now dead. She tried to sort it all out. Clearly, Jan was a freak. That's why he had lied his way into her room. But, why? What was he going to do? Did he have some crazy plan that involved her?

She moved on to another set of familiar faces. Talcott kids she vaguely recognized who'd long since graduated—a group of friends and a kid with thick brown hair who could only be . . .

Kirsten squinted. *Kyle!* Back before he'd gone to jail. Back when he was a student at Talcott.

Was Jan so obsessed with the murder case? Fixated with the thing that had torn her own life apart? Some wackos collect famous people's shoes—Did Jan have a "Preppy Murder" fetish? That had to be what this was all about. And the fact that she was rooming with him made her ill.

Kirsten backed away from the wall. A top-sheet from one of the accordion folders had stuck to her elbow, and she pulled it off: ADAMS MURDER, it read.

She turned the folder open-side up and skimmed through the yellow legal sheets with handwritten notes, more newspaper clippings and photos—all related to Carolee's murder. She glanced at the labels on the other folders: BYRNE MURDER, LEWIS MURDER, AUTOPSY PHOTOS. Sick.

Kirsten lifted the last folder. Swallowing hard, she looked at the top photo.

It was Sam.

Sam. Naked and ghostly pale, her eyes open as if daring the photographer to shoot, a blue bruise over one side of her face and her soft beautiful auburn hair matted by blood.

It was Sam. Dead.

Kirsten let out a gasp and dropped the folder, let it fall on the counter, spilling out more images of her best friend, side, front, close-up, full-body. And the obvious questions of *How did he get these?* and *Why does he have them?* and *Who the hell is this freak?* were lost in the jangled sparks that were short-circuiting her brain.

As she backed out of the room, the images on the wall seemed to taunt her with their frozen smiles, the four faces circled in red grease pencil . . . Sam . . . Emma . . . Carolee . . .

All the dead girls. He'd circled all their faces. Plus one—one other face that Kirsten hadn't noticed before, circled bold and thick.

She ripped it off the wall for a closer look. And in the first split second of recognition, her mind's chaos rallied into a stubborn wall of denial, trying to convince herself that the face *wasn't* circled, because it made *no sense* for this face to be circled, only *dead* people were circled and the person *inside* the circle wasn't dead, but as alive as . . . as . . .

. . . as she was.

It was *her* face.

Her own face marked like the others. Circled. Like a target.

Carolee . . . Sam . . . Emma . . . me, she thought. *Marked for death. Like the last in a line of victims.*

"No . . ." The sound welled up from deep within, hoarse and rasping. She clutched the photo to her chest, not wanting to let go of it, as if taking it away would prevent her own . . .

Her own what?

Murder.

She turned, pulled open the door, and lunged for the hallway. But she couldn't go far. A tall figure blocked the door.

Jan.

"Out of my way!" Kirsten crouched, leaning her right shoulder into Jan's chest.

He gasped, leaping back into the hallway. "What the—?"

Kirsten tore off toward the staircase.

"Wait!" Jan shouted.

But Kirsten was taking the stairs three at a time, racing across the lobby, scattering visitors and students. She burst out onto the street, still holding the photo, nearly falling on a patch of pitted ice. She didn't stop until she reached the housing office. It was open now, and a mild-looking lady with cat's-eye-shaped glasses sat behind the reception desk. "I need to speak to the freshman housing person," Kirsten said breathlessly.

"You'll have to sign up for an appointment," the lady began.

"Don't tell me to wait. I will not leave until you have given me a new room!"

A couple of surprised faces peeked over cubicles, and the lady rose quickly from her seat. "Let me get someone who can help you." She disappeared into an inner office for a moment and then stepped out, gesturing Kirsten inside, where a balding man dressed in a tweed jacket looked up from a computer.

"I understand you have a conflict," he said with a tight smile, "and I sympathize. But I'm afraid it is late in the year, and roommate groups are no longer as fluid—"

"My roommate's name is Jan deVries," Kirsten interrupted, trying desperately not to shake, "and he's a *guy*. Somehow, you let him room with two girls. But, what's worse, he's a pervert and possibly a murderer—and if you don't switch me, I will have the police on you before you can say 'tweed coat.'"

The man tilted his head as if trying to decide if Kirsten was crazy. "These are serious accusations."

Kirsten placed the photo—the one she'd taken from the darkroom—on the man's desk. "He did this," she said.

The man leaned forward—and Kirsten immediately realized what an idiot she was being. It was a picture of her face, circled in red. Out of context, it meant nothing. "I got it in—"

she began. In where? A darkroom that she broke into, raiding someone's private materials? How would she explain *that*? "Never mind," Kirsten said.

"Well, he has a good photographic eye," the man said noncommittally, then began tapping on his keyboard. "You are right. You shouldn't have a male roommate. That is actionable. But, as I suspected, the database is coming up blank on open rooms. There's quite a crunch. Look, I will talk to Jan and see if I can get him a temporary transfer—and I'll put in an expedited request for a single for you next week. That's the best I can do," he said, handing her a sheet that read REQUEST FOR ROOM TRANSFER.

Kirsten took the sheet. Her hands were shaking.

"We're very sorry," the man said with a wan smile. "It was a clerical error."

By lunchtime Kirsten had been to French and Intro to European Art History but hadn't retained a thing. The words "clerical error" had taunted her all morning. She could see the headlines now: "College Coed Killed in Clerical Error."

The guy at the housing office had treated her like crap—like she was just another pesky, dreary kid. And so had Peterson, when she'd called him.

He's about had it with my phone calls, Kirsten thought. *He probably thinks I'm a certified nutcase by now.* She sat in a corner of the cafeteria, facing the door in case Jan came in, fiddling with a plate of congealed pasta al pesto. She was so distracted, she didn't even notice when Lauren slid into the seat next to her.

"Hey, how was Barnard?" Lauren asked. "Meet any neat-looking Ivy League guys?"

Kirsten jumped. "You scared me. You're still here, thank God. You'll never believe what I found out about Jan."

"I think he likes you," Lauren said, setting down her tray.

"*What?* Oh my God, don't say that. You have no idea what you're saying—"

"He's not so bad," Lauren said. "And he was a perfect gentleman last night."

Kirsten felt sick to her stomach. "That sounds like something from an old movie. What was he a perfect gentleman *about*, Lauren? You and he didn't . . ."

"Do it? Oh, please, no!" Lauren said with a funny giggle.

"Because if you ever get that idea into your head, if you ever even think about it, I will personally drive you back home to Kansas—"

"Wisconsin."

"Whatever. Look, he is worse than any of us imagined. . . ." Kirsten carefully went through every detail of her discoveries in the living room and the dark room, plus her encounter with Clarice Moravec.

Lauren listened closely, sipping from a bowl of split-pea soup. "That *is* kind of icky."

"'Icky'? It's a little more than that, Lauren," Kirsten said.

"Okay, but I guess I'm not so sure why you're so freaked out," she said. "I mean, let's break it down. Let's look at it objectively. He likes to sneak pictures of girls. That puts him in a big club with, like, oh . . . the majority of guys I know. Besides, I knew he was taking those pictures of me. He was kind of obvious."

Kirsten raised her eyebrows. "You *knew*? And you didn't kill him?"

Lauren smiled. "I kind of enjoyed it," she admitted. Then she tilted her head. "Does that make me an exhibitionist or something?"

"Uh, *yeah*," Kirsten said.

"Really?" Lauren's face fell. "Is that bad? I posted some pictures of me on the Web, too. On this dating site."

Kirsten was seeing her roommate in a new light. "Like, *sexy* pictures?" she asked.

"Um, I guess it depends on what you call 'sexy,'" Lauren replied with a sly grin.

Kirsten groaned. Pure little Lauren the Lawyer wasn't as innocent as she seemed. "God, Lauren, one kinky roommate is bad enough, but *two*?"

"Look, let's stay on point here. I do think it's strange that he circled the faces. That's kind of weird. But did you look at all the pictures? Are you sure there weren't *more* faces circled, faces that didn't fit the pattern? I mean, photographers like to mark their best images with circles—for cropping, for reproductions. Did you *really* look? Did you go back and rule out all the possibilities?"

Kirsten couldn't believe this. Lauren sounded as if she were deciding a case for the Supreme Court. "You couldn't pay me enough money to ever go back there. And you wouldn't do it, either, if you saw a copy of your best friend's autopsy photo."

Lauren grimaced. "That must have been so awful to see. He probably got it over the Net, you know. People do that. Once, when I was doing a report on the Civil Rights era, I found the autopsy photos of John F. Kennedy, with, like, half his head missing. He looked like he was smiling. *That* was weird."

Kirsten dropped her fork and held back a sudden small upsurge of half-digested pasta. "Please, Lauren."

"What I mean is, I'm thinking that Jan may be doing some kind of project. Something involved with the murders. That's why he's collecting all that stuff. I mean, he *says* he's a documentary filmmaker, right? So it would make sense."

Kirsten nodded. It was a reasonable explanation. But it didn't really hang together. "The thing is, if he was shooting a documentary, why would he keep it a secret from me? He could just ask me for info. But, instead, he goes through all that devious stuff to room with us!"

Lauren thought about that a moment, then sat up with

a start. "Oh! Speaking of Jan, I almost forgot!" She reached into her pocket and pulled out an envelope. "I saw him on the way here. He told me to give you this note."

"A note?" Kirsten said warily. "What's in it?"

"I didn't ask," Lauren replied. "Read it."

Swallowing hard, Kirsten opened the envelope. Reluctantly she unfolded the note.

Kirsten,
I know what you took.
We need to talk.
Do NOT, under any circumstances, show or tell anyone what you saw.
Or we are both dead.

8

"Uh-oh," Lauren said ten minutes later, unlocking the door to their room and peering inside. "He bounced."

"He's *gone*?" Kirsten said, though she really wasn't so surprised.

Lauren pushed the door wide open. All of Jan's stuff—piles of papers and suitcases and books—had disappeared.

"See what I mean?" Kirsten said. "He's running scared. You read the note. 'I know what you took . . . we are both dead.' How do you explain this, Counselor?"

"Maybe the housing office cleared him out. What did you tell them—that they put you together with this generation's Charles Manson?"

Kirsten shook her head. "Not quite. The guy didn't believe anything I said about Jan anyway. He said he was going to *talk* to Jan. Made it sound as if he'd be taking him to the Plaza for high tea."

Their footsteps echoed hollowly as they stepped inside.

The room felt twice as big as before. Jan's bedroom door was open. His room was totally empty.

"Lauren, when you saw Jan before lunch, did he say anything about this?" Kirsten asked.

"Nope. But he was in a rush. I guess he was in the middle of moving. God, this *is* starting to get kind of creepy." Lauren walked into Jan's room and tried the mattress. "Ugh. Soft. How come *you* got the only good one?"

"Now what?" Kirsten asked, sinking into the living room sofa with a deep sigh. "Am I back to looking around corners, into shadows?"

"Kirsten, I admit, if I were you—if I'd seen what you saw, and if I were as close to the murders—I'd be on the first plane home," Lauren shouted from the other room. "This is totally weird. But my gut tells me this guy wouldn't hurt a mosquito. You've spoken to him. You know what he's like. 'Don't tell anyone, or we're both dead. . . .' This is a guy who probably scripts his life dialogue from bad movies. Hey, at least we don't have to room with him anymore."

Kirsten paced, trying to settle, trying to think *straight*. Lauren seemed so rational, so feet-on-the-ground. But Lauren wasn't the one who'd gotten that note.

"We need to talk . . ."

Talk about what? What did Jan mean? And when were they supposed to talk? *Where was he?*

Lauren walked out of the cleaned-out room with a smile.

She put her hand gently on Kirsten's shoulder. "I have an idea. You need some R&R, I need to find an ATM, and we both need to celebrate our expanded room situation. So how about taking me shopping for a new image?"

This was *not* what Kirsten had expected at a time like this. "Um, I gave you a new image already. Or at least some practice getting one. And there's an ATM on Sixth Avenue."

"'ATM' as in, 'rich boyfriend.' Like, M-I-T—Mogul in Training? Don't tell me you didn't know that?"

"Uh, yeah . . . but I'm not exactly thinking about shopping right now," Kirsten said.

"I thought you always thought of shopping!" Lauren said, smiling. "Look, Kirsten. Don't let Jan ruin your life. If he wants to talk to you, he'll find you. Then we can both give him a piece of our minds. Meanwhile, my parents sent me some money, and I want a neat new look—like, all-American but sexy. I want guys' eyes to pop out when I pass by." She grabbed her shoulder bag and headed for the door. "So if you don't want to come with me, fine. I'll just have take myself to Joyce Leslie. Where's the mall in this town, anyway?"

Kirsten took a deep breath. "I may be totally screwed up about my life, Lauren. I may be hallucinating and seeing conspiracy theories and misjudging everybody. But I will *not* allow you to go to the mall. Wait up."

• • •

Henry Higgins.

That's who Kirsten felt like. The guy from the old movie musical *My Fair Lady*, who rescues a girl from the gutter and teaches her how to dress and talk.

Well, it wasn't that extreme. Lauren was upbeat and optimistic and so enthusiastic about clothes—and after a while, Kirsten actually began having fun. Much more fun than old Henry H. ever did.

Gently convincing Lauren not to use the word "neat" was Step One. Getting her a decent pair of jeans—a pair of low-rider Sevens from Intermix—was Step Two. This was made difficult by the fact that on the way out she kept trying to pull the jeans up, asking, "Can you see my butt?" every few feet and not accepting "That's the point!" as an answer.

Giggling like kids with their first credit card, they ducked into Stella McCartney's place in the meatpacking district, Anna Sui in Soho, and Barneys uptown—just for ideas—and then they zoomed to the trendy stores on the Lower East Side so that Lauren could buy the same styles at half the price.

By the end of the day, Lauren had her outfits organized into Smart Tart outfit, Future Big-Bucks Attorney outfit, Keep-It-in-Your-Pants-I'm-Not-Interested outfit, and last but not least, her Slut outfit. Plus, a handful of cute, sexy camisole tops that Lauren didn't want to buy until Kirsten forced her.

They celebrated with Frappuccinos at Starbucks, and then cabbed it back to the Ridge.

As they entered the dorm with armfuls of bags, Lauren said, "There's nothing like spending money to cure all ills."

"I never thought I'd hear you say that," Kirsten replied, bursting into the suite and dropping her shopping bags onto her bed. "Yeah, I feel human again too."

"So, what about dinner?" Lauren called from her room. "What should I wear? Something really neat. I mean, *hot*."

"Definitely one of those camisole tops," Kirsten suggested. "You will never have to worry again about sleeping alone. And I hear sex is great for your back."

Lauren lifted one of the tops from her collection. It was a soft, sexy honey color, and paper-thin silk. "I . . . I can't," Lauren said, suddenly shy.

"Why?"

"They're too . . . nippular."

"'Nippular'? Is that a word?"

Lauren shrugged. "It is now."

"Nipples, my dear," Kirsten said, "make the world go round."

Lauren howled with laughter, and Kirsten found herself laughing too. Big, free-and-easy, just like she used to.

Nothing was right about her life these days. So much needed to be figured out. But for the first time since returning from Greece, Kirsten had the glimmer of a feeling that maybe—just maybe—things could work out.

And it felt good.

9

"She convinced you this guy was harmless?" Julie asked, reaching across the bar for a handful of pretzels. "After all those freaky pictures? And you actually went with it?"

Kirsten took a sip of her Cosmo. The Party Room was pretty quiet, as was usual on a Monday night. Brandon, looking like he'd popped out of a J.Crew catalog, was dancing with a Gwyneth Paltrow's-little-sister type, whose face was starting to betray Stage Three of the Five Stages of a Relationship with Brandon, which included Attraction, Doubt, Disbelief, Anger, and How-Could-I-Have-Been-So-Stupid?

Kirsten had come in there in a decent mood, calmed down by her spree with Lauren. But the mood was starting to fade. Julie's reaction was a rude shock into reality. "Lauren is very convincing," Kirsten said. "She is going to make one kick-ass lawyer."

"Did you go to the cops?" Julie asked.

"Yup. They treated me like I was reporting a jaywalker.

The housing office, same. But at least Jan is gone from the room. That's a good thing. Oh, here's that picture I was telling you about." Kirsten reached into her bag and pulled out the shot from the darkroom.

Julie looked closely. "Why'd he circle your face?"

"He also circled other faces in other photos—Carolee's, Sam's, Emma's . . ."

"Oh, you've got to be kidding. That is so morbid. You don't need to call the cops, you need to call a psychiatric facility. I can't believe he did this."

Scott leaned over the bar with a raised eyebrow. Kirsten felt suddenly warm all over, and she couldn't help a huge smile from taking over her face. A dozen clever, sexy opening lines formed in her head, all jockeying for position, but they all got stuck, so she opted for, "Hi, Scott."

"What's that you got?" he asked, nodding at the picture in Julie's hand.

"You'll never believe it," Julie said, starting to hand it over to him.

Kirsten grabbed the picture. "Forget it. You don't want to know," she said. Actually, she didn't think Scott needed to get involved in this. He'd already had to deal with too much of her drama since she'd come home, and it wasn't fair.

"Aw, come on. You guys know I don't allow printouts of Internet porn in here," Scott said with a sly grin. "Unless you share it."

"Oh . . . my . . . God," Kirsten murmured. She put the photo back in her pack, slowly watching an orange hat moving through the crowd until it turned into Jan.

"Who's that?" Julie asked.

Kirsten was already off her stool and halfway across the floor, headed for Jan. "What the hell are you doing here?" she demanded. *"What was that note all about?"*

"Oh. Hi, Kirsten," Jan said nervously. "Sorry to spoil your night, I didn't want to come here, especially if Conan the Barbarian Bartender is on duty, but we have to talk. Look, you didn't have to go to the housing office. I can explain everything."

"You can explain what? Autopsy pictures of Sam? What do you do with them, Jan? *What do you do with pictures of dead girls in the darkroom?"*

At Kirsten's outburst, a group of kids jumped away.

"Shhhh . . . listen, it's not what you think," Jan said.

"Oh. That's right. You like live girls, too. I guessed that when I saw the pictures of Lauren's breasts. That must be why you fooled the housing office and forced them to get rid of Clarice. You could keep all your little fetishes alive—sleep in a suite with two *live* girls, and hey, it gets better. One of them knows all the *dead* girls you've been salivating over. You need help, Jan. You're *sick*!"

"Look, I did a stupid thing, I admit. It's this cinematic technique of mine. Total immersion. I believe a filmmaker has to be close to his subject. Live and breathe the same air. I'm a . . .

student of the Byrne killing. I recognized your name in a list of the incoming class. I believe serious crimes need serious film studies—not like that awful TV movie Hollywood made."

"That is the biggest crock I've ever heard. You're a serious student of NYU, Jan—not the Byrne killing. Sam Byrne doesn't need a wacko like you poking around her autopsy photos and spying on her friends. You . . . you get your skinny ass out of here right now, and if I ever see you again, I swear I will make your life miserable."

Now Julie was by Kirsten's side, taking her hand tentatively. "Is this the guy?"

"Look, Kirsten," Jan pleaded, "after what you did to me this morning, you could at least listen. You and I . . . we want the same thing. The trouble is, you don't even know it. And if you don't wise up—if you don't listen to me—you are going to be in deep shit. Trust me."

"Don't you threaten her!" Julie said.

"What do you mean, 'after what I did to *you*'?" Kirsten shouted at Jan.

Scott emerged from behind her, his jaw set firmly. "Yo, my man, I thought we had a little talk last time. Did you forget?"

Jan shook his head, backing away. "Nope. As I recall, you told me to get out of your bar, I told you it was a free country, and you replied you would give me a free kick in the balls if I ever came back."

"Guess it's time to collect," Scott said, grabbing Jan by

the collar and pushing him toward the exit.

"Maybe we should finish our drinks and go," Julie said, gently leading Kirsten back to the bar.

By the time they got there, Scott was charging back in. He swung around behind the bar, his brow furrowed with anger as he began mixing drinks.

Kirsten felt awful. His life must have been so much easier when she was in Greece. "Sorry, Scott," she said. "I hope you're not mad. I mean, after all this time, I'm rubbing your face in the drama of my life all over again."

Scott's tense expression eased. "Hey, how can I be mad? It's not your fault. All beautiful girls have hangers-on like that guy. He'll disappear."

Kirsten found herself blushing when she heard the word "beautiful." Not that it was the first time a guy had paid her a compliment—it's just she had never heard it from Scott. But this was no time for a crush. "But this guy is fixated on Sam—on the whole murder case. He says he's making a film. So I feel like it's *not* over. Like, I came back to New York and it's all starting again."

Scott leaned over the bar and touched her hand. It felt warm and comforting and strong. "It is over, Kirsten. It has to be. All of this stuff happened in the past, and you have to move on. The killings have stopped. Paul Stone—*Kyle*—is dead."

The words hit her hard. "Kyle doesn't really have anything to do with it, Scott. Remember? We talked about that."

"Right, right . . . I know," Scott replied gently. "Sorry. Look, I know how you felt about the guy. Really. But I've been thinking. Since he died, nothing has happened, Kirsten. No murders. You have to consider that. Now, I know some of those cops on the case. They're smart guys, and they're convinced. I'm sure Stone was a great guy, but he was pretty screwed up, too, right?"

Kirsten turned away, fighting back the impulse to scream. But she couldn't be mad at him. He didn't know. He was trying to help. "No offense, Scott," Kirsten said, "but you didn't know him like I did."

"Well, that's the truth," Scott replied. "I'd never met him except for that one time he came here and started talking to you. And yeah, from what I remember, he did seem like a pretty normal dude. It's just that . . . you never *know*, Kirsten. People aren't what they seem sometimes. He *was* picked up for that other murder all those years ago . . . and two times is pretty serious, don't you think?"

Kirsten realized she must have inadvertently been giving him a poisonous look, because his voice trailed off and he smiled apologetically. "Sorry," he said. "I'm just a dumb bartender. Friends?" He leaned over the bar, arms open.

Kirsten fell into them, fast and hard, feeling his strength and tenderness, not caring who saw, not caring what kind of exaggerated juicy description Julie would give Carla and Sarah. If she could, at that moment, she'd make it every bit as juicy and more.

He gave the best hug, long and enveloping, lifting her out of her gloom and squeezing all the bad feeling away. Every pore tingled, alive and open. She felt caring and cared for, safe and protected.

"Ahem," came Julie's voice from behind her.

Kirsten let go and sat back on her stool, and Scott's smile looked so delicious she could hardly keep herself from jumping over the bar and wrestling him to the floor. "Friends," Kirsten said, answering Scott's question.

"Um, sorry to break up this little love fest," Julie said with an arched eyebrow, "but I believe we had a plan."

Right.

Julie and Kirsten had spoken earlier in the day. The idea was to start out at the Party Room and barhop through the night, hitting all the newest places on the East Side. "My coach turns into a pumpkin," she said to Scott. "See you soon?"

"You're leaving?" Scott said. "I—I'm getting off soon. I thought maybe we could . . . talk."

Kirsten gave Scott her sexiest smile. She wouldn't mind talking with him . . . and whatever else he had in mind. But Julie was already halfway out the door. "Maybe we can get together another time?" she asked, hoping she wasn't hurting his feelings. "I promised Jules that I'd go to a new place with her tonight." Scott nodded, and she slung her bag around her shoulder and paid for her drink. "See you later," she said, and headed toward the door to meet Julie.

When they reached the sidewalk and turned south down Second Avenue, Julie asked, "News?"

"No news," Kirsten replied.

"Come *on*," Julie said. "That was the hottest hug I have ever seen between two fully clothed people. Kirsten, *what* is going on with you two?"

"Nothing! I mean, just what you saw. We hugged. I like him. That's never been a secret."

"Girl, if there was any doubt in my mind that the feeling was mutual, that little incident just proved me wrong." Julie gave Kirsten a sly smile. "Umm, look, do you *really* want to do this? Because I could go ahead to the Yellow Trance *alone*, if you want to stay and . . . you know, hook up."

Kirsten laughed. "Yellow Trance?"

"Brand-new. Verrry hot, says Carla. And just around the corner."

Actually, all Kirsten wanted to do was turn and bolt back into the Party Room and hang out with Scott, but the "I don't really want to go alone" look in Julie's eyes was too much to ignore. "I'm there."

They walked a couple of blocks downtown. A crowd of kids spilled out of the Yellow Trance entrance, which was on the ground floor of a sleek black high-rise. It was an upscale, part-Euro crowd, lots of thin smokers dressed in black outside, speaking French and Russian and Japanese, with Afro-Cuban dance music blaring out whenever the plate-glass doors opened, which was often.

"Different crowd," Kirsten remarked.

"I think I heard some people speaking Greek," Julie said. "It'll bring back all the right memories."

Kirsten threw back her shoulders and headed for the front door. The bouncer unhooked a velvet rope, and the two girls entered. The bar was just inside the door, a huge slab of marble that stretched practically to the back of the place, where another door opened to a garden. It looked great, but Scott's drinks had worked their way into Kirsten's bloodstream, and the sudden rumbles in her stomach and whirls in her head meant that the first order of business would be the restroom. "Be right back," she said to Julie, who returned a knowing glance.

A group of guys, so hot looking it almost hurt Kirsten's eyes, were laughing and toasting one another at the bar, and she squeezed past them, running directly into a couple—older guy, younger girl, both dressed in black—who were slurring their words and looking totally tanked.

The girl staggered away to let Kirsten by, yanking at a halter top at least two sizes too small, and babbling incoherently. The guy was oblivious and unmoving.

Jerk, Kirsten thought, an observation reinforced by the fact that he was wearing a beret—a *beret*, how was that for a lapse in taste?—not to mention the shaved head, which Carla said was usually a sign of "sexual dysfunction guilt," only God knows how Carla would know.

"Excuse me," Kirsten said loudly in his ear as she passed, noticing the red roots that he hadn't had the good sense to shave before showing himself in public.

"Sorry," he said in a strange, gravelly voice, moving aside.

Kirsten bolted for the bathroom—then stopped in her tracks.

Red roots.

Red roots meant red hair.

Lots of people had red hair. But not too many of them shaved it all off. And spoke in that voice.

She knew him. She knew who he was.

Swallowing back the lump that filled her throat like a tennis ball, she turned back toward the bar.

He was throwing back a drink, laughing. And she got a good, direct profile.

The slightly droopy eyes and thin lips. The tiny scar above his right eyebrow. The super-broad shoulders.

How could it be? Peterson said the man was dead.

But there was no question now. This was up close, personal, and totally clear. Peterson was wrong. Jones was not dead. He was right here—as alive as she was!

Kirsten opened her mouth to call for Julie, but the name jammed in her throat—because he was turning . . . slowly . . . scanning the room like a vulture looking for a corpse.

Until his hawklike eyes met hers.

10

Idiot.

Fool.

I should have known it was too good to be true.

They never learn. Every time you think they do, they prove you wrong. They wave their stupidity in your face like a flag.

I've been watching her closely. Too close for my own good.

And now she KNOWS. Face it.

And she's stupid enough to try to DO SOMETHING ABOUT IT.

Okay then, fine.

She doesn't want to PAY ATTENTION? Fine.

She can't see what happens to the ones who mess up? Fine.

She wants to make me work hard—as if I haven't done enough, as if I hadn't taught all those lessons, put out all those fires? She thinks that's easy? FINE! FINE! FINE! I'LL DO IT!

But it's such a waste.

I thought she was one of the smarter ones. I thought I didn't have to worry about her.

Ah, well.

She's insisting, isn't she? So what choice to I have?

I'm a reasonable man. I believe in honoring people's desires.

I'll give her what she's asking for. Ashes to ashes, dust to dust.

I will be quick with her. It's the best way.

PART TWO

11

"JULIEEEEE!"

A dozen people spun around in surprise, a dozen more jumped out of the way. Julie came charging through, her eyes wide. "Kirsten? What happened? Are you all right?"

"He's . . . he's . . ." She pointed toward Jones. But he was gone. *"Did you see him?"*

"Who, Jan?" Julie asked.

"No, Jones!" Kirsten said, pushing her way through the crowd. "He's here. Follow me."

She raced to the back of the room. She would track him down. Now. *With* Julie—not like last time. Last time, when he'd had long hair, when she'd caught him at a different bar, asked him about Sam, and he'd run from her. Kirsten had chased him—alone. She'd found him on the street and managed, somehow, to wrestle him to the pavement. But he'd gotten away. He was stronger. If Kirsten had only had help . . . if Julie had been with her . . .

This time he wouldn't get away.

They were in the back of the room now, but Jones was nowhere. Kirsten pushed her way through the back exit, into the garden outside. It was surrounded by a wall at least ten feet high. He wouldn't have been able to climb over it—at least not without creating a huge commotion.

She paused in the doorway, looking around. The tables were half full. Knots of people stood chatting and laughing, drinks in hand. They circulated around, examining everyone's face, checking the shadows.

Nothing.

"Maybe it was someone who looked like him," Julie suggested.

"I am *over* seeing people who don't exist," Kirsten said firmly. She'd been there—seeing Kyle and Jones around every corner, in every shadow and footfall, raising paranoia to a 24/7 art form—and Julie knew it. But that was before Greece, back when Kirsten was interning at radio station WXRJ during the day and abusing substances at night. She was steady now, if not totally sober—and Jones was Jones. Kirsten could not have been more sure. "Trust me on this one, Jules. He was as close as you are. He recognized me. I could tell. And he ran. I don't know how he got away, but he did."

"You have to call Peterson right away," Julie urged her.

"Peterson is the one who told me Jones is dead," Kirsten

said. "He won't be any help. I'll have to get Jones myself!"

"Kirsten, don't delude yourself. He's a drug dealer, at least. Maybe even a murderer," Julie said. "We can't play hero. It's too dangerous. Talk to Peterson again tomorrow. *Convince* him that you know what you saw."

Kirsten exhaled. "Okay, okay," she said, knowing Julie was right. The adrenaline was draining from Kirsten's body, and up rushed the nausea she'd had when she came in. Only now it was worse. "I'll be right back," she said. "I—I'm not feeling too great."

"Do you want me to go with you?" Julie asked.

Kirsten managed a weak smile. "I stopped having nannies in sixth grade."

"Eighth, for me. I never got over the scars of humiliation. Hurry back, okay? I'm worried about you. And I won't be able to hold back the hotties at the bar all alone."

Kirsten adjusted her shoulder bag and stumbled to the restroom. It was empty, thank God, but the place smelled of leftover vomit and tangy disinfectant, which didn't make her feel any better. She went into the stall and closed the door. Phone numbers and crude anatomical drawings were all over the walls, and a metal toilet paper dispenser, sturdy and once intact, lay on the floor, empty and twisted.

Kirsten leaned over the toilet, which was—thankfully—clean.

Breathe . . . breathe . . . She wasn't going to puke. She *hated* puking. It was her least favorite human activity. *Mind over matter. . . . Keep it in. . . .*

Yes. The feeling was going away. Slowly. And Kirsten began thinking about Jones again. Julie was right: She would have to report him to Peterson, convince Peterson of his existence somehow.

But what was Jones doing *here*? *Tonight*? Jones was a dealer. Was he looking to sell drugs?

Or looking for me? She swallowed back her nausea and leaned against the wall. It was too confusing. *Rational. Be rational. Look at the big picture.*

He—or someone—had killed everyone associated with Sam's murder. Everyone except Kirsten.

Now Kirsten was back. In school. In New York.

And there was Jones, on her first day of freshman year . . . killing again. Killing someone who'd had nothing to do with the murder.

Why Chloe? Was she a random victim—was it just a coincidence that Kirsten had been in the atrium when Jones pushed her? And also a coincidence that he was there tonight?

No. Kirsten didn't believe in coincidences anymore. He had to have planned it all. He had to have known Kirsten would be in these places. Which meant that Chloe's killing might have been a signal. *He might have pushed Chloe to warn me—to say, "This could happen to you."*

But why? Why would he sacrifice an innocent girl when

he could have gone after Kirsten himself? Was it some kind of game? Could he possibly be that sick?

Calm down, Kirsten. You came in here to feel better. You feel better. Now take a few breaths. Put yourself together. And get out of here. She inhaled deeply, ignoring the stink. One . . . two . . . three . . .

Click!

The bathroom door opened, and Kirsten froze. Had she locked it? No, she hadn't. She'd been in too much of a rush. In another moment she heard the door shut—the quiet *thunk* of the doorknob lock . . . the rattle of a hook-and-eye gizmo.

She would wait until the person washed her hands or snorted her coke or whatever she'd come in here to do. The door of the stall rattled.

Kirsten jumped. "Someone's in here," she called out.

The rattling stopped for moment. And then the light went out.

"Hey, turn it on! I'm still in—"

She heard the stall door yank open, felt the subtle suck of stale air from the stall. Before she could stand up, an arm grabbed her around the neck. And a hand closed over her mouth as she screamed!

12

"Whfff . . . ," she mumbled, but the hand was thick. Strong.

A guy.

Instinctively she opened her eyes wide, but there was no light. She couldn't see a thing.

He was pulling her down toward the toilet, grabbing at her purse.

My bag. He wants to strangle me with the strap. He's going to kill me! Kirsten felt her knees buckle. She was sinking toward the toilet. She pushed back, but he was strong. Relentless. She reached out, grabbing for something, *anything*.

Her fingers closed around a thick piece of metal. The broken toilet paper dispenser.

She swung it up, over her head—slammed her attacker hard.

Thwack.

Contact.

She heard a startled groan. The grip loosened.

"Yeeeahh!" she grunted, swinging harder.

Thwack.

"Arrrrggghh! " he cried out.

She stood up, pushing hard with her thigh muscles. Her attacker fell backward, and she heard his head hit the tiled wall. Kirsten turned, reaching back with the twisted metal dispenser, but he shoved her aside, bolting out of the stall and through the bathroom door.

She straightened herself out, her hand dripping blood from clutching the jagged metal, and she dropped the dispenser. Holding the bleeding hand with her good one to stanch the flow, she staggered out into the dim light of the Yellow Trance.

There he was. Running through the crowd, pushing people aside, making a commotion. She caught a glimpse of a black shirt, an arm pushing someone aside.

Jones!

"Stop him!" She ran, ignoring the blood, pushing her way across the floor.

In a moment Julie was by her side, alarmed and confused. "Kirsten, what happened? Are you okay?"

"Did you see him?" Kirsten shouted, not breaking stride. "Did you see Jones? He attacked me! *Don't let him get away!*"

He was racing out the front door now. She couldn't really

see him, but she could tell where he was by the sudden movement of the crowd he was pushing aside. Then a gap. She could see a dark figure barging into the crowd on Second Avenue, running off to the left.

"Please! Somebody, stop him!" Kirsten shouted into a sea of blank, seen-it-all New York faces. She was out the door seconds later. But she ran straight into someone who had decided to step right into her path.

"Get out of my—" she began. But the words caught in her throat as she glanced up into Jones's face. "Ahhhhh!" she shrieked, jumping back and falling into Julie, who staggered backward, grabbing on to the edge of an outdoor table.

Jones took off at a sprint, up Second Avenue.

The same direction she'd seen him run just seconds before.

"That's him!" Kirsten shouted.

"How could that be him?" Julie said. "He ran away!"

Kirsten balanced herself and took off in pursuit. Jones was already to the next corner, picking up speed. Another figure was halfway up the next block, farther away, running even faster.

Jones was chasing him.

Wait. What's going on? Kirsten wondered. *Who is he chasing? The guy who attacked me? Because if it wasn't Jones . . . then who was it?*

13

"Hi, Lauren?"

Kirsten settled back into the Ralph Lauren sheets on her four-poster bed, cradling her cell phone in her shoulder. Her window looked out across Fifth Avenue at the darkened hulk of the Metropolitan Museum of Art, its roof glowing faintly with moonlight reflected off a dusting of snow.

She and Julie had totally failed to find Jones—or the other guy. As usual, Kirsten had reported the incident to Peterson, and he had gone through the motions—asking questions, giving reassurances. But she didn't expect anything to come of that.

She'd needed some stability tonight, some good old-fashioned TLC. Which was why she'd come home for the night.

"Hi, Kirsten?" Lauren's slightly groggy voice replied. "What's up? Still shaking your booty?"

Kirsten smiled. Hearing the word booty from Lauren's

mouth was, in some weird way, unbelievably uplifting. "I'm staying at my parents' house tonight."

"House? You live in a house?"

"Okay, *apartment*. 'House' is a figure of speech in New York." *Well, sort of,* Kirsten thought, considering that her family's 4,032-square-foot Fifth Avenue duplex was probably twice as large as the average house in Sheboygan and about fifty times the price. "I—I couldn't face going back downtown after tonight. I was just at a bar with Julie and—well, there was some trouble."

"Which is a figure of speech for . . . ?"

"I kind of got beat up," Kirsten admitted.

Lauren's voice rose an octave with alarm. "Are you all right? Is there anything I can do? What happened?"

"Yes, no, and it's a long story," Kirsten replied, "which I promise to tell you tomorrow, when I get back. But don't worry. I'm fine. Well, mostly. My left hand is not so happy. Look, I just wanted you to know where I was—and if you want to use my mattress again tonight, feel free, okay?"

"Thanks, I'm already sleeping on it. Well, I'm really glad you're all right, Kirsten. That's the most important thing." Lauren let out a sigh of relief. "Hey, I almost forgot. You got some good news. The housing office called. Tomorrow they're moving you to a single. I'm getting two new roommates: Ralph and Harvey. Actually, that's a joke. Two girls . . . *real* girls."

"I'm getting a single?"

"That's what you wanted, right?"

"No," Kirsten said. "Living all alone is *not* what I wanted. I like rooming with you. I just wanted them to replace Jan with a girl."

"Did you tell them that?"

Duh. She hadn't told them. She'd complained about Jan to that stuffy housing guy, and that was it. "Um, I think I blew it," Kirsten said. "Maybe we can room again next semester?"

"Only if you continue to take me shopping *this* semester. I have to keep up appearances."

Kirsten smiled. "Deal."

They exchanged good-byes. Kirsten turned off her bedside lamp. But as soon as her face hit the pillow, her eyes zinged open.

A single? In a decrepit former SRO, among a school full of total strangers? Maybe she'd have to grovel to Tweed Man again. She tried to push the thought aside, tried to force herself to sleep.

Through her double-pane casement windows, which were supposed to be soundproof, she could hear the muffled whizzing of taxis—and then the slurry voice of Frankie Federman's younger brother Chip as he got out of a limo, no doubt back from some deb ball . . . and then the flapping of wings that could not possibly have been a pigeon but was more likely one of the famous Fifth Avenue hawks returning to its nest behind a landmarked gargoyle with a tasty meal of fresh-killed rat for its offspring . . .

Stop it! Kirsten silently shouted. *Sleep!* And then she heard a thump in the front hall and leaped so high, she nearly hit the fabric draped over the posters of her bed.

Clank.

Was someone trying to get into the apartment? She slid out of bed and opened her door, hoping to hear the sound of Dad padding out of his room. But no such luck, so she tiptoed through the apartment, across the living room, hoping to get there before whoever it was actually managed to . . .

Thwack!

What was that? It came from the kitchen. Which was totally dark.

Kirsten leaned toward her parents' bedroom and called, "Dad . . . Mom?" but her voice was swallowed up in the brocade and swags and down sofa pillows and built-in oak bookshelves filled with signed first editions, and she was running now, across the living room, through the parlor with Dad's pool table, cursing the *bigness* of the place—as a low whistling started . . . and then a sweet, high-pitched voice singing in Russian . . .

Kirsten stopped in her tracks. It was Sasha, the night porter, collecting the trash.

Easy, Kirsten. Calm down. She fell into one of the antique chairs, giddy with relief—and way too edgy to sleep. At another time, before Greece, she would have gone straight to the bathroom and fumbled for her mom's endless supply of Ambien, but not now. Not anymore. *You're home . . . you're safe* . . . she chanted to herself.

She stood up, yawned, and slouched back to her room. Her closet door was ajar, and she shuddered involuntarily. The last time she'd been so scared in her own house, she'd found someone's muddy footprint in her closet. That print, of course, turned out to have been Brandon's, back when he was in one of his drug-addled phases, sneaking into people's apartments. But she had been totally freaked by that . . . and for a while, she thought the print might have belonged to Kyle—Paul Stone—the guy everyone thought was Sam's murderer. And *that* was the thing that had scared her, because for a time, she had believed it too.

Kirsten plopped down into bed and felt a jolt of guilt. Why had it taken so long to give him her trust? Because she'd been swayed by the news media, that's why. Because she was too scared to really listen to him. To *believe* in him. And if she had—if she'd helped him instead of cut him off when he really needed her, *when the killer was closing in on him*—maybe he'd still be alive. Maybe he'd be in her life right now, a living, breathing person instead of the way she remembered him now, lifeless and cold, his eyes vacant. . . .

In a horrible rush, it all came back, as if she were there—the mustiness, the metallic smell of blood . . . her own moaning, a sound so otherworldly, she hadn't even realized she was making it . . . his blood seeping into the floor of the dingy hotel room he'd been hiding in . . . her own shaking fingers grabbing the picture he was holding and slipping it into her pocket . . .

The photo. The one she took from him.

It was here. In her house. Somewhere.

The memories were unfolding, from the place they'd been locked in her brain . . . the photo . . . yes, she'd been aware of it when the police came to the crime scene, when they took her away for suspicion of his murder . . . in her frantic, desperate mind she'd been thinking *don't search me, don't take my only memento* . . . and they hadn't. They'd asked her questions, questions that for the life of her she couldn't remember, and the next thing she knew, she was home, totally cleared of any wrongdoing, lying in bed with Mom and Dad hovering and an arsenal of prescription drugs on her night table. She was in PJs, somehow having changed, and the outfit she'd been wearing was draped over her desk chair, to be washed by Marisol, the morning maid . . . with the picture still in the pants pocket. She was aware of that, she was dying to see it, she *had* to see it—*yes, now she remembered*—and when she was finally alone, she'd dug it out of the pocket for one last glimpse of Kyle alive . . . but the image of him and Carolee, looking so blissful, was like a stab in the chest, causing her to moan so suddenly and so loud that her mother came rushing back from the other end of the house, so she quickly got rid of it. . . .

Where?

In a plastic bag. She had grabbed a pharmacy bag from the floor, left from the drugs, and quickly wrapped the photo—and then, quickly, she'd hid it . . . hid it where no one would know . . .

In the back of her closet!

Yes. Under the mahogany wardrobe.

She ran into the closet—her pride and joy, which was the size of some kids' entire bedrooms—and knelt by the stately antique on which she had painted the words THIS WAY TO NARNIA as a little girl. And as she pulled away boxes and bags that had collected around the legs, she wanted more than anything else to dive inside and find herself by a snowy streetlamp in the land of a witch and a lion, because the idea of actually finding the thing she was looking for scared the crap out of her.

Her fingers closed around a thin plastic bag and she dragged it out. *Lotos Pharmacy.* This was it—exactly what she'd been looking for. The picture Kyle had been clutching when he died. With unsteady fingers, she unfolded the bag and pulled out the small snapshot. Along the white border were tiny flecks of brownish red she hadn't noticed before—*blood, Kyle's blood*—and she touched them, feeling both repulsed and somehow calmed, intimately connected with him.

The image was still sharp and bright—a bar with lots of people in it. People she knew, much younger than they were now. Maybe four years younger. But Kirsten's eyes went directly to the two faces front and center—Kyle and Carolee.

Carolee. Kirsten had never met her. But she had recognized her from the news articles about the first murder that surfaced after Sam's death. The smiling, painfully beautiful yearbook photo that had appeared daily in the newspapers. It was the same person—Kyle had good taste—and in the picture he was holding her tight. His hair was thick and unkempt, like the old photos of him in those same news articles. Their faces were flush, their smiles ecstatic. As if they'd just had sex. Or maybe it was just their tans. That had to be it. The tans.

He was in love with her. Did he ever smile like that around me? Did he carry a picture of me with him too—or was this only one? The image SO IMPORTANT that he had to grab it as the life drained out of him—to gaze at her one last time.

Kirsten felt a wave of disgust and guilt. They were dead. Both of them. How stupid to be feel jealous!

She should have given the photo to Peterson. But it was too late now. Tears streamed down her face as she slumped back to bed, propped the picture on her nightstand, and wondered how the hell she would sleep tonight.

14

Sam.

Emma.

Carolee.

Mmm, nice photos. BEAUTIFUL GIRLS.

Yes.

Look at them. Look at them closely, pal. Because for what comes next, YOU HAVE TO SEE THEIR PAMPERED, AREN'T-I-FABULOUS FACES!

Yes.

Because this work is not easy. Oh God, is it not easy.

But the pictures help. Because they're a reminder.

Yes.

BEAUTY IS FLEETING.

A goddamn profound cliché if I ever heard one.

Well, you come by it honest, oh yes you do. You discovered it yourself. Someone close to you. IT'S NOT FUN WHEN SOMEONE CLOSE TO YOU—SOMEONE

WONDERFUL . . . BEAUTIFUL—IS SNUFFED OUT.

An eye for an eye, The Man says.

DOESN'T HE?

YES!

Okay.

Okay. You're ready. You can do it. Put the pics away.

And, um, separate Sam and Emma, will ya? Emma was weird. Don't want her to do anything scandalous. Put Carolee between them. She'll make sure they behave.

Now. Move. It's time.

Time for the next one.

The LAST one.

Go.

Before you get cold feet.

This will be the hardest.

She should know how good she had it.

You've been giving her such a chance. Just watching.

You've been handing it to her. And what does she do?

HOW DOES SHE SHOW HER GRATITUDE?

You never should have let down your guard.

But you did.

You gave her the benefit of the doubt, and LOOK WHAT HAPPENED.

It's been too long, that's the problem. Too long, and you're out of practice.

You had a taste for this. You had technique.

CONTROL!

Your problem is kindness.

You should have known she'd be trouble. You should have gotten her long ago. Invited her up for some pot roast and a life lesson. Once upon a time you would have thought of that. Before you got rusty and soft.

Before YOU LOST CONTROL.

Well, no more Nice Guy.

Open door.

Step outside.

Fasten your seat belt.

It's Time.

15

"I don't care what you ***think*** you can work out with the housing office," said Gil Sawyer, Master of the Universe and, oh yes, Kirsten's father, too, as he pulled his cell phone from inside the breast pocket of his black Paul Stuart suit jacket. "I will not have you continuing to live in a former flophouse. I will not have you living in any building that does not have top-level security."

Kirsten slammed down her spoon, causing the kitchen table to shake and her granola to spill over the side. After last night's miserable sleep, she was in no mood to be bossed around. She had told her parents about Jan over breakfast, because she'd had to. The jerk at the housing office had called to report the room change, and Mom and Dad had greeted her this morning with a demand to know *exactly* what had happened. Kirsten had tried to tone it down: All she said was that Jan was a guy who had fooled the office into thinking he was a girl—but that was already enough to drive Dad ballistic. Kirsten hadn't even mentioned a thing about last night in the Yellow Trance bathroom—and her claim that a stovetop burn had resulted in the bandage on her hand had been accepted without question.

The fact that Kirsten had roomed with a guy, however, was serious. *That* got Dad into Mover-and-Shaker mode.

"Listen, Dad, I can handle this," Kirsten said. "I don't want to live off-campus, like some rich freak!"

"Hot cocoa?" her mom asked as Marisol, the morning maid, set a steaming cup and a plate of whole-wheat apple-walnut waffles on the table. "Go ahead, have some breakfast, sweetie. This is a fragile time for you. Your father wants you to have peace of mind. It will feel good to live in a full-service building—at least for a semester."

"Get me Ed Spencer at Cloverdale Realty," Dad was saying over the phone. "Coop, condo, doesn't matter . . . high floor, view . . . have him slip something to Martinetti at Butterfield Movers, because I need four men today, including anyone he knows in IT."

"I guess *my* wishes don't count, when they stand in the way of Gil Sawyer, Hot-Shot Lawyer!" Kirsten blurted out.

Her father put his hand over the receiver. "But these *are* your wishes, aren't they? You didn't want to live alone in that rat trap. You said so."

"I know—but can't you work WITH me? Can't you at least conference me in with the university so I can have some say—so I can live with real kids instead of half-dead business-people in a museum?" Kirsten bolted up from the table, put her granola bowl into the sink, and stormed off. Her father paid lip service to Quality Time, to Getting to Know Your Daughter, to Teaching the Values of the Well-Examined Life. But as a dad, he hadn't exactly been hands-on. When things went wrong, he fell back on the only things he really knew how to do well—wheeling and dealing. Denying that the word "no" existed in anyone else's vocabulary but his own.

"Kirsten?" her mom called out. "Kirsten, do you have cash for a cab?"

Kirsten grabbed her pack from where she'd left it in the living room, walked into the vestibule, and pressed the elevator button. "Why doesn't Dad just call the Taxi and Limousine Commission and buy me a fleet?" she said as the door opened and she disappeared inside.

She regretted using the subway the moment she went down the stairs. The MetroCard machines were all busted, and a hysterical guy with a potbelly and Coke-bottle glasses was cursing out the booth clerk, holding up a line that snaked almost up to the street. People in business suits were awkwardly jumping the turnstiles, shouting, "Already paid!" or "Weekly!" or "Monthly!"

Finally she squeezed onto a 4 train next to someone with garlic breath, which she had to politely endure during a ride that seemed to last for months—and then, after transferring to the 6 at Union Square and exiting at Astor Place, she had to walk clear across 8th Street to the west side, which this morning felt like a ten-mile hike.

By the time she entered Washington Square Park, Kirsten was already late for her first class. She felt like sleeping, not rushing to retrieve her books and run to class. The snow had melted, and as she hurried diagonally across the park, the city trees looked spindly and forlorn. The sound of a siren broke the stillness, and Kirsten watched the flashing light of a police car make its way around the park.

It turned onto the Better Ridgefield's block.

Kirsten squinted. The street already contained a few sets of flashing lights, but they'd been obscured by a crowd of people who had gathered at the corner of MacDougal Street. She picked up her pace, emerging from the park near the chess-for-pay players who seemed oblivious.

"What's going on?" Kirsten asked a student who was hanging on the outskirts of the crowd, but got only a shrug in return. She pushed her way through the gawkers. Soon she could see an ambulance directly in front of the Ridge. The front door was open—and a team of EMT workers was carrying away a stretcher on which a body lay, covered head-to-toe with a sheet.

Kirsten blanched.

When someone on a stretcher was injured, you saw their

face. When the face was covered, that meant they were dead.

Someone had died—in her dorm.

Oh God, she thought. *Another jumper? An overdose? Why? Why is it that wherever I go, people die . . . ?*

Where was Lauren? She wished Lauren had a cell phone, so she could know what had happened.

As she walked warily to the building, watching the EMTs lift the body to the back of the ambulance, a police officer eyed her warily. "Sorry, miss, you have to stay back."

"I—I live here," Kirsten said. "Can't I go inside to my room?"

The cop gave her a look and signaled to another officer, who was standing by the back of the ambulance as the body was loaded on. As he approached Kirsten, she read his name tag: SERGEANT P. FOLEY.

He held what looked like a purse. "You're a resident?"

"Yes," she said, suddenly feeling her legs start to shake.

Sergeant Foley nodded. "If you don't mind, can I ask you some questions?" he asked, pulling something from the wallet.

Kirsten tried to speak but couldn't.

The sergeant held an ID card toward Kirsten. "Did you know the victim?"

She didn't recognize the face at first, or the name, because her mind was shutting down, telling her it was time to turn tail and leave, hop a plane and fly to Greece—no, *beyond*

Greece, to circle the world again and again, passing the international date line each time so that she could go back in time, way back, to before any of this ever happened. . . .

And maybe she would avoid the horror of right now, of staring at a laminated card that had a smiling photo and a name she knew all too well.

Lauren Chaplin.

16

"There must be a mistake!" Kirsten said, looking toward the body, which was now being strapped into the ambulance. "Can I see her? *Can I see her face?*"

She didn't wait for an answer, running to the stretcher, hoping that it was a mix-up, that it was someone else, *anyone else*—but Sergeant Foley took her arm, pulling her back.

"I'm sorry, miss. It is the same person as the photo. She was a friend?"

"She's my *roommate*! I just talked to her last night! She was fine. She was in bed. How did this happen?"

"The perpetrator managed to break into her bedroom while she was sleeping—judging from the wounds, maybe five, six hours ago," Foley said. Then he added, as if to comfort Kirsten, "Most likely she didn't even wake up."

"Wounds? What kind of wounds?"

"A blunt object. To the head. And she was stabbed several times. As I said, she was sleeping—"

Kirsten felt light-headed. The street seemed to rise up to her in a spiraling fog. It was happening again.

The same thing.

The exact same thing.

"Tell me about her wrists," Kirsten said in a shaky voice, fearing the worst. "Were they tied up? With a school tie or something?"

The sergeant gave her an odd look. "No. Nothing like that."

There should have been something on the wrists. The killer had used the tie on Carolee and Sam . . . and he'd tied Emma with a T-shirt—Kyle's shirt.

Was this a different killer? Think, Kirsten, think.

The tie hadn't been used on Kyle, either. The ties and shirt had been a sign. They had been used to frame Kyle. But it didn't matter anymore. It no longer meant anything.

Kyle was dead. The killer was free to kill any way he wanted.

But why? *Why Lauren?*

She was killed five or six hours ago. It was about 9:30 now, so that would have been around 4 a.m. Kirsten and Lauren had talked around 2:00. *Two hours before the murder.* If Kirsten had come back instead of going home last night . . . if she'd been there . . .

A couple of other police officers had joined Foley at her side, a man named Trezza and a woman named Olsen. All three of them were leading Kirsten into the building now. They were asking questions, looking her straight in the eye, and she nodded back numbly but didn't hear a word.

The carpet outside the room had been sprinkled with talcum powder, covering Lauren's spilled blood, and a team of detectives was dusting for prints on the door frame. Kirsten and her three escorts stepped over yellow police tape and entered the room.

Lauren's bedroom door was ajar, but the cops were in Kirsten's room, searching around.

My room. Of course. Lauren was sleeping in my room tonight, not hers.

And a dark realization squeezed her like a fist.

If the killer wanted Lauren, he would have gone to her room. Her name is over her door. But he didn't. He went in and headed straight for the door labeled KIRSTEN.

"Oh my God . . . ," Kirsten said, sinking onto the living room sofa.

"Miss Sawyer?" Officer Olsen said.

The killer wasn't looking for Lauren. He was looking for me.

Sergeant Foley crouched next to her. "Did someone have anything against the girl?"

"An ex-boyfriend, maybe?" Officer Trezza asked. "Someone who held a grudge? Someone who knew her daily routine?"

Not a grudge against her. Against me.

I was to be his next victim.

If I'd come back instead of going home, I'd be on the stretcher, headed for the morgue.

The next in the line of murders—Carolee, Sam, Emma . . .

The faces passed through her mind.

The faces . . .

Circled in red . . .

Kirsten's mind flashed back to the photos, the contact sheets pulled against the wall. He had marked her.

The police wanted to know about a grudge? *Jan* had a grudge. Big-time. And Jan had the key to the room.

It was all becoming clear. Jan's act at the Party Room last night—the apologies, the sheepish look—all bullshit. He was tracking her. Scott had pissed him off by kicking him out. So Jan had marked time. Waiting. Planning. He'd had his chance at Yellow Trance, but he hadn't counted on Kirsten being so resourceful. So he waited some more, figuring that Kirsten had gone back to her dorm room. He could try again, no problem.

And so he'd sneaked in, unseen by anyone. And why not? No one suspected him besides Kirsten. Not even Peterson, who was supposed to help her.

And now her beautiful, sweet roommate was dead.

Why? Because busy Kirsten had been uptown . . . leaving Lauren unprotected . . . because no one had taken precautions, *not even the detective assigned to the case.*

"The asshole . . . ," Kirsten muttered through clenched teeth, slowly standing up.

"Miss Sawyer?" Foley asked.

"I want Peterson," Kirsten said.

"Who?" Trezza asked.

"Focus, Kirsten," Olson urged. "Your statement right now can help us."

"I will give a statement," Kirsten said, heading for the door, "to Detective Peterson, at the Eighty-Eighth Precinct."

It didn't take much time to get to the Upper East Side when you were running red lights in a cop car with a siren and flashers.

At the precinct house Kirsten got out of the backseat and barged inside while the other cops were still hauling themselves out.

Peterson was standing against the back wall, sipping coffee and chatting with another officer. He looked like Brad Pitt after a few too many doughnuts, and his slate blue eyes traveled right to her bandaged left hand. "What happened to you, Kirsten?"

"Never mind that," Kirsten said. "There was an attempt on my life in my dorm room, my roommate was killed, and I need to speak to you."

"I just got the report," Peterson said with a heavy sigh. "I didn't realize it was your room. I'm so sorry, Kirsten."

"I am too," Kirsten replied, feeling the pressure of tears behind her eyelids. "It's easy to be sorry. But Lauren is dead—

and she was in my bedroom, *using my bed*, which means she died instead of me. You could have prevented it. I told you about Jan deVries, Detective Peterson. I told you about those creepy pictures—*and you didn't listen*!"

She couldn't keep it inside any longer. On their own power her fists rose toward Peterson's chest, and she didn't care that he was a cop. She wanted to break that smug expression, make him suffer, make him hurt the way she'd hurt. . . .

He moved so fast, she didn't even see him grabbing her wrists quickly, firmly. She was locked in position, arms up like a praying mantis, and as the tears began to flow, the other officer shrank away and Peterson gently led her to a small office off a green-tiled hallway.

Inside, he offered her a chair and a box of tissues. "Kirsten, I know how you must feel. And I assure you I *am* taking this seriously. I know about deVries. The faces circled in red. The threatening letter. We're running a full background check on him. So far, all we've been able to find is the transcript from NYU—honor student, Wetherby, Massachusetts—nothing unusual. But the high school has a tough privacy policy, and they're not even taking our calls, so we're working on it. Meanwhile we *have* been taking you seriously, Kirsten. We've been tailing him—not 24/7, but enough."

"Obviously not enough," Kirsten snapped. "Obviously not last night. *He had the key to our room!* Who else could it be?"

Peterson leaned over his desk, turning around a pad of notes so Kirsten could read them. "The killer didn't use a key. The report says the lock was broken."

"Broken?"

"One good solid rap, at just the right angle, and these things snap. If deVries had a key, chances are he'd have used it."

Kirsten scanned the note . . . *blunt object . . . forceful blow . . . twenty-three stab wounds . . . great strength* . . . "If he didn't do it," she said, "then who did?"

"That's what I want to know. Think, Kirsten. Is there anyone else? Anyone you've seen who's been acting suspicious? Trailing you, maybe?"

"Of course I have!" Kirsten couldn't believe her ears. Had he forgotten all the phone calls? What kind of detective was he? "Jones. Jones. Jones. I've told you! Chloe Pepper. The back room at Yellow Trance!"

Yellow Trance. It felt like ages ago, but it was just last night. A few hours before the murder. Kirsten sank slowly back in her chair. Maybe she was right the first time. Maybe it was Jones who had come for her—not Jan. Jones knew she was an NYU student because he'd seen her in the atrium. And finding her room information couldn't have been hard. She sighed. Jan . . . Jones . . . this was all so confusing. Why couldn't Peterson bring them both in and figure it all out? Why did it seem as though Kirsten was the only one taking this thing seriously?

Peterson shifted uncomfortably. "Um, Kirsten, I told you, Jones is not in circulation. Let's take Jones out of the discussion."

Kirsten nearly jumped across the desk. "That's what you said last time. You're wrong. I saw him at Yellow Trance. He was as close to me as you are now—closer! *How can you explain that?*"

Peterson's eyes suddenly darted away, looking toward something through the doorway, out into the hallway.

Kirsten followed his glance. A man dressed in black was heading toward them down the narrow corridor, walking fast, his shaved head reflecting an eerie olive green in the fluorescent lights. Jones—he stopped in midstride just outside Peterson's office when he saw her. His black jacket billowed out, revealing a holstered gun on his belt.

Kirsten stood up, her body stiff with fear. She watched, frozen, as he reached across his chest and pulled out . . .

. . . a badge?

Kirsten's heart nearly stopped. "You're . . . a *cop*?" she said.

17

Jones stepped forward, his body now filling the doorway. He was clean-shaven, his slouched posture now ramrod straight, his druggy eyes sharp.

"Sergeant Albert Russo," Jones said, extending his hand for a shake. "I believe we've met. Don't be afraid. I'm a detective."

Kirsten thumped backward against the wall.

"A detective," she said, turning to Peterson. "You told me he was dead!"

"Not exactly," Peterson said. "I just didn't deny it when you asked. I had to. I had to protect him. He was undercover at the time. Narcotics."

"Oh God," Kirsten said under her breath. "You have got to be kidding."

"You know, I've always wanted to tell you what a bruise you gave me a while back—around the corner from Janus?" Russo said. "I mean, yeah, I was doing the slo-mo druggie act because I was working to find the neighborhood dealers—but your tackling me on Eighty-Third Street was one of the more embarrassing moments of my life."

"Dealers like Brandon Yardley," Kirsten said. "That's why you were always with him. You were manipulating him."

All Brandon's stories rushed through her mind. Jones was a BIG dealer . . . Jones had gone to jail but had been sprung, and he'd come after Brandon . . . demanding payment . . .

"Brandon was a good source," Peterson said. "Russo was using him to get to the big guys who were operating at the New York private schools."

"The kid was petrified I'd blow his cover to his dad," Russo said. "Big-shot Wall Street guy—all kinds of stuff named after him, including the Yardley Library. Anyway, the kid helped me break a drug ring—and he and I came to an agreement. He's on his way to rehabilitation, and I've been checking up on him."

"Which is why he's cleaned up his act," Kirsten said absently. She looked up. "And the night you left the Party Room with Sam?" she asked. That story was coming back to her, too. "Sam thought Brandon owed money to *you*. You were demanding he repay his debts, and she was trying to help pay it back. *That's* why she left with you the night she died, isn't it?"

Russo nodded sadly. "It was hard keeping the secret from her. I always managed to convince her not to pay. That night she seemed so confused, so angry at Brandon. I offered to take her home, but she refused. Said she could get there on her own. She didn't want to be seen with a drug dealer like me. I couldn't blame her. I should have insisted. If I'd only stayed with her a little longer . . ."

His voice trailed off, and Peterson picked up. "Anyway, Sergeant Russo has moved on to homicide. He always felt close to the Byrne case, so he managed to get the assignment—over my objections. I figured you'd run into him and recognize his face, but he thought the shaved head would do the trick." He gave Russo a raised eyebrow. "Sergeant Russo is a stubborn man."

Kirsten nodded, her mind in a flurry of thoughts knitting together months of misunderstandings. "So the day Chloe Pepper fell . . . when you were up there, on that balcony . . ."

"I'd been checking up on you—just routine," Russo said. "When she jumped, I ran up to see if there'd been foul play. But it was a suicide, Kirsten. The girl had been depressed and never went to see anyone about it."

"And at the Yellow Trance?" Kirsten said.

"I've been keeping an eye on this deVries guy," Russo replied. "Not that we've found anything, but you've had some serious complaints, and we're having a hard time tracking his records, so you never know. Anyway, I got a tip he was going to the Party Room, but by the time I arrived, he was gone."

Kirsten thought back to the struggle in the bathroom—

the strength of the attacker, and Jan's skinny body. The attacker had seemed big, but how could she know? It was dark . . . and sometimes a person's strength could be deceptive. "So," Kirsten said, "you think the attacker in the bathroom was . . ."

Both men fell silent.

Russo pulled up a chair and sat down heavily. "Tell me some more about this deVries kid," he said.

The familiar Jackson Hole late-night crowd was soothing to Kirsten. She needed soothing after a day like this. And food. She hadn't eaten since her mom had forced a lame turkey sandwich on her this afternoon. The visit to the precinct had destroyed Kirsten's appetite.

It was just after 10:00 p.m., and it had been hell convincing Mom and Dad to let her go out with Julie. All of a sudden, in their minds, she was twelve years old again. What was worse, Dad had announced that the movers were already taking her stuff out of the Ridge and into the building on lower Fifth Avenue, where the average age hovered around, oh, eighty-two. But she hadn't been able to get angry. All day she'd been haunted by thoughts of Lauren. The Chaplins were scheduled to fly in tomorrow to collect her things and take her body home to Wisconsin to prepare the funeral. What could she say to them? It was because of *Kirsten* that the killer had broken in. It was because of *Kirsten* and her decision to sleep at home that her bed was empty, which was why Lauren had been sleeping in it . . . and was murdered. How could she face the Chaplins? Would she ever get over her guilt? She didn't think even a thousand sessions with her therapist, Dr. Fitzgerald, would help her get over this.

Kirsten took a small bite of her Woulia Boulia salad, and, holding her fork delicately in her undamaged right hand, she watched Julie inhale a Santa Fe burger. "Where do you put it all?" she asked.

"With some people, it goes right to the thighs. With me, I swear it must go here," Julie said, shaking her 36Ds, "thereby also feeding the fantasy lives of Woodley boys, Columbia students, and men of all ages."

A fork clattered to the floor nearby, and a red-faced boy stooped to pick it up.

"It's hard being in public with you sometimes," Kirsten said.

"A lot of things get hard when I'm in public," Julie replied with a sigh.

Kirsten smiled. Julie was the only person who knew how to cheer her up when things were really bad.

"Now, tell me what happened after you met Officer Soprano this morning," Julie said.

"Russo," Kirsten corrected her, taking another small bite and swallowing. "We talked about the murders. All of them. Can you believe he and Peterson *still* think Kyle killed Carolee, Sam, and Emma . . . which doesn't give me too much faith in New York's Finest. I yelled at them about that. Then we talked about Jan. They pointed out that Jan's a freshman. According to common sense, and his records, he was away at some prep school when Carolee and Sam were killed, so that would rule out his being their murderer. Which means he might be a copycat. We tried to figure out if he was strong enough to have held me down like that in the bathroom—or to break the door of the suite. Peterson thinks he *could* have. He says some guys can be skinny dweebs one minute and monsters the next. But I doubt it, and so does Russo. Russo chased my attacker for a couple of blocks before losing him. He said the guy was fast . . . and built. Which doesn't sound at all like Jan. So, assuming the guy who attacked me was the same guy who killed Lauren—"

"It could have been someone else," Julie said.

"Right."

"Then who was it?" Julie asked.

Kirsten shook her head. The whole thing was so confusing. The closer they got, the further they seemed from an answer. Was there someone else who wanted to hurt Kirsten? Someone they hadn't even thought of?

The chirping sound of Taylor Swift's "Love Story," as played by cell phone, interrupted the conversation. Kirsten made a mental note to change that. It was embarrassing. "Hello?" she said, answering the phone.

There was a pause at the other end. And then a voice

said, "Kirsten? Is this Kirsten Sawyer?" The voice was muffled and distorted—a hugely bad cell phone connection.

"You have to speak up," Kirsten said. "Who is this?"

"Kirsten," the voice said, "you don't know me. My name is Rich Stone."

Kirsten swallowed hard. Julie, noticing the change in Kirsten's face, dropped her burger and was staring intently across the table.

"S-Stone?" Kirsten repeated, her pulse quickening. "As in—"

"I'm Paul's brother," the voice interrupted. "*Kyle's* brother. I need to talk to you. It's a matter of life and death."

18

"Is this some kind of sick joke?" Kirsten whispered into the phone, her voice dry and parched. "How do I know you're Kyle's brother?"

Julie's jaw dropped. "Kyle's brother?" she whispered. "How could he have a brother without you knowing?"

Kirsten held up her index finger to her mouth, shushing her. She leaned against the window, trying to blot out the clank and clatter of the restaurant.

"It's not a joke," the voice answered. "I have to speak to you. Didn't he tell you about me? Didn't he talk about his eccentric but loving family?"

It was a familiar voice. Something about the words, the rhythm, something she couldn't put her finger on. She couldn't tell if he sounded like Kyle—the way brothers' voices are sometimes similar—because the connection was so bad. "I'm going to hang up," Kirsten said.

"No! Please don't. Kyle *must* have told you things about

himself. Ask me anything about him. Test me. I'll prove we're related."

Her mind reached back. Did Kyle mention a brother? He did tell her *some* things about his family and himself—on a night that seemed like ages ago, in a dingy little room on the Upper West Side, near Columbia, where they lay awake until sunrise, talking—back before she'd found out his real identity. He was a great storyteller, making her laugh about funny incidents during his childhood. . . .

"He had a nickname . . . as a boy," Kirsten said, remembering one vivid, painful little description.

"TP," the muffled voice shot back.

Kirsten swallowed. *Yes. He's right.* "Why was he called that?" she pressed on.

"Because when he was in kindergarten, our mom thought it would be cute to dress him up as 'Prince Charmin' for Halloween. So she put him in a costume that looked like a roll of toilet paper and gave him a crown and a toilet-paper cape. And for about three years, kids called him TP. He *hated* that!"

That was true too. Kyle had described the embarrassing incident during the one night they'd spent together, and Kirsten had laughed and laughed.

"Where are you?" Kirsten demanded.

"I'm walking . . . somewhere in Central Park. Where no one can hear me. Where there are places to hide. I can't let myself be seen. He's after me now, the person who killed Sam . . . and my brother."

"You know who the killer is?" Kirsten's heart felt like a jackhammer. "Tell me!"

"Look, it's not the red-haired guy, and definitely not the kid who was your roommate—"

"How do you know about them?" Kirsten asked.

"It's someone else, and I'm determined to nail him. I have some new information that needs investigating. All along I've been *trying* to find this monster without dragging you in. But everything has changed, Kirsten. For one thing, he's on to me. I'm not sure how, but he knows I'm closing in. So I can't act alone anymore. It's too dangerous. And now you're in danger too. The killer tried to get you last night. You and I need to band together. We have no one else. Believe me, I wouldn't ask you if it weren't absolutely necessary."

Kirsten blanched. He knew about what had happened this morning. That the killer had been after her, not Lauren. How? How did he know? And what "information" did he have? Could this be it—the break? Could this be the missing link for the whole case?

Chill, Kirsten, she told herself. *Don't trust anyone. Go slowly.* "What do you want me to do?" she asked tentatively.

"I want you to meet me," he answered. "Right now. I'll tell you everything."

Kirsten was breaking out in a sweat. "It has to be somewhere public, where there are a lot of people around."

"We can't do it, then. Too risky. I'll have to go it alone—"

"Wait," Kirsten said. "Where did you have in mind?"

"How fast can you get to Central Park—the East Ninety-Sixth Street entrance?"

Central Park? Kirsten's hopes shriveled as she glanced out the window. The sun had set, and the black February night had spread over the city. The park would be empty and dark. "I'm not an idiot," she said. "No one in her right mind would agree to meet a stranger after dark in Central Park."

"Not *deep* inside the park. Near the sidewalk. The playground—you know, the one just inside Fifth and Ninety-Sixth, up the little hill? It's close to the entrance. We'll meet near the playground gate. There will be a downhill slope to your back. Right down to Fifth Avenue. If you get cold feet, you're out of there in a shot. One yell, and a thousand people hear. Not that you'll need to run. Or yell. You will want to hear what I have to say, Kirsten."

"I don't know," Kirsten said, fighting back tears.

Julie was holding on to her arm, not saying anything, just being supportive. Somehow knowing that Kirsten needed exactly that.

"Look, you have to understand the risk *I'm* taking. I'm leaving myself open to *you*. You could bring a posse of friends with you. Or the police, for all I know." He sighed. "Think about it. And come alone. I'll wait ten minutes, in a place where I can see you coming. If you're not alone, I'm afraid the meeting is off. I'll be long gone."

"Ten minutes?" Kirsten looked at her watch: 6:03.

"I can't hang around in one place. I have to keep moving. So if I don't see you after ten minutes, I'll leave. No hard feelings. You'll never hear from me again. But I hope you'll give me a chance. For my brother's—"

The line went dead. No more juice. Stupid. She had forgotten to charge it this morning.

As Kirsten pulled the phone away from her ear, Julie nearly jumped out of her seat. "Are you going to tell me what the hell *that* was about?"

Kirsten slipped the phone into her purse, her mind exploding with confusion. Was it total lunacy to want to go? Was she being a fool? There had to be a way to do this right. Some way to do what he wanted and still protect herself.

Kirsten checked her watch: 6:04. Nine minutes. "Come on, Jules. I'll tell you on the way."

Kirsten didn't know how much cash she had left on the table at Jackson Hole. But it was probably enough to insure great service from that waiter forever.

As she led Julie toward the park, she told her the whole story. They arrived, breathless, at the Ninetieth Street entrance to the park, across from the Church of the Heavenly

Rest—six blocks south of the playground. By that time the details of Kirsten's plan had fallen into place.

"Okay, you make your way to the playground along the East Drive," Kirsten said, gesturing inside the park to the path that ran around the reservoir. "Keep under the lights. Stay with the joggers."

"What joggers?" Julie said, peering into the deserted park.

Kirsten looked at her watch again. "Go fast, we only have three and a half minutes. I will run like hell up Fifth Avenue and enter the park where he's expecting me. You hang out in the trees along the path, just south of the playground—and make sure you can see me. If he doesn't seem legit, call 911. Ready?"

"I don't know if I'm—" Julie began.

"Go!" Kirsten whispered.

As Julie bounced reluctantly into the park, Kirsten raced up the bumpy sidewalk along the Central Park wall. She nearly tripped over a homeless man sprawled on a park bench. Her lungs ached from lack of exercise; her brain screamed, *Go back. Get Julie. GO HOME!*

This was crazy, insane. But she fought back the doubts. She had to trust her instincts. She had to give this a shot or she'd never know for sure.

She reached Ninety-Sixth Street at 6:14.

A minute over.

He'd be history by now. That was what he'd said.

She scanned the area for anyone leaving the park. A bus trundled out of the transverse drive at Ninety-Sixth, but that was it. No other person in sight. She turned toward the pedestrian gate in the stone wall.

As she entered the park and walked toward the playground, it was as if someone had thrown a sudden blanket over the sounds of the city. Her footsteps echoed dully in the hush, and a sharp westerly wind blasted her face. She drew the collar of her sailor coat tighter and headed off the path toward the playground gate to her left. The East Drive's distant streetlamps silhouetted the play equipment, making it look like a collection of hulking dinosaur skeletons.

Kirsten stepped inside the Cyclone fence gate, which she expected would have been locked by now. She couldn't see much in the darkness, but an orange pinpoint of light suddenly moved to her left.

Kirsten's breath caught. She moved closer. A wisp of smoke rose from the orange dot. It was a cigarette, moving up and down as a person took a drag.

A man. Dressed in a bulky, hooded, down coat.

She turned and squinted into the distant blackness beyond the fence. Another figure was moving stealthily among the bushes, and she trusted it was Julie. Julie would be here by now.

Kirsten turned back to the man and opened her mouth

to speak, but nothing came out. *Calm down,* she commanded herself. "Rich?" she squeaked.

When the guy didn't answer, she tried again, louder. "Are you Rich?"

"Not by Upper East Side standards," came the reply, "but comfortable."

The face inside the hood smiled at Kirsten. He was old—*grandfatherly*—and from nearby came a wheezy little pug that had just peed against a swing set. "Well, Stetson, shall we?" the man said to the dog. He stood up, nodded at Kirsten, and led the dog out of the playground.

As Kirsten watched them go, her spirits sank.

Kyle's brother was gone.

She'd blown it.

"We blew it!" she called out in the direction of the shadow she hoped was Julie. Kicking a rock against the fence, she began heading back toward Fifth Avenue.

And a dark figure leaped out of a shadow from behind a park bench.

"Who are you talking to?"

Kirsten gasped, jumping back. "Christ!"

"Sorry, didn't mean to scare you—who were you talking to?" The voice was whispered and muffled, just like it had been over the phone. The guy was wearing a black full-face ski mask over his face.

"M-m-myself," Kirsten said. "I do that a lot. Who are you,

anyway—and you'd better give me the answer I'm expecting or I'll scream so loud, the whole neighborhood will hear."

"Richard Stone," the guy said softly, stepping closer.

Kirsten backed away. He was between her and the gate now. She hoped he couldn't tell she was trembling. Her eyes flitted to the right. She also hoped Julie was calling the cops.

"Kirsten, you need to trust me," the guy said.

Stall him.

"Oh? Do you make a habit of jumping out of shadows wearing a ski mask?" she asked. "If you need to talk to me—if you're really who you say you are—*take off the mask*."

"Fine," he said, slowly raising his hands toward his neck. Toward the bottom of the mask. "But you have to promise to hear me out. Deal?"

"Deal," Kirsten agreed.

Angling himself into the dim light of a distant streetlamp, he peeled off the mask.

Kirsten staggered back when she caught the first glimpse of his face. "It's, it's . . . you!" she cried.

19

"You . . . ," Kirsten repeated.

The bony face . . . the narrow eyes . . . the smirk . . .

How had *Jan* managed to disguise his voice like that? How had he managed to fool her—*again*?

This was getting old. Very old.

"Sorry," Jan said. "Let me explain . . ."

Not this time, Kirsten thought. She shouted into the nearby bushes, *"Julie, call the cops!"*

Jan turned to look.

And Kirsten kicked him. Right where he lived.

He doubled over, groaning in agony. "Urrggh . . ."

Kirsten ran from the playground, around the Cyclone fence. Julie wasn't anywhere near the bushes where she was supposed to be. She was standing in the middle of the East Drive. "Did you call the cops?" Kirsten shouted.

"There was a family of *rats* in the bushes!" Julie said. "I dropped the phone in there!"

"It was Jan, Julie. He was pretending to be Kyle's brother!"

"Oh, shit. What now?" Julie asked.

Kirsten looked over her shoulder. Jan had left the playground but was still inside the park, retching against the old stone wall. "My phone's dead, but there's a pay phone on the corner."

At the sound of distant footsteps, Julie looked over her shoulder. A jogger, all bundled up in a thick outfit and knit hat, appeared from around the downtown bend of the East Drive. "Go, Kirsten. I'll flag this guy down for help!"

Kirsten took off down the path toward the exit. But Jan was closer. He stumbled into the opening, his eyes red and angry. "We had a deal. You were going to hear me out."

"Get out of my way!" Kirsten shouted.

"Don't, Kirsten," Jan said. "Listen to me, please. I *am* Rich Stone."

He was crazy. Deluded.

She lunged for the exit and tried to push him, but he grabbed her arm. He was strong. Much stronger than he looked. As strong as her attacker in the Yellow Trance.

He was the one!

"HELP!" she shouted. *"HELLLP ME!"*

Jan pulled her into the shadows, holding her tight with one hand and putting his other hand over her mouth. He yanked her around so they were face-to-face.

Against the night-blackened bricks of the wall, his eyes

seemed to float in a dark, featureless oval. "I tried to tell you," he rasped. "In the Party Room. I made a stupid mistake trying to be your roommate. I didn't want you to know then who I was, but I was wrong. I had to get you alone, where no one could hear us talk. I have something for you. Something you're not expecting . . ." Jan let go of her mouth and quickly pulled a small, dark object from his pocket.

Then his body stiffened, his eyes suddenly rising toward something over Kirsten's shoulder. "Oh my God," he muttered. "Watch out, Kirsten! Duck!"

Kirsten felt herself being shoved, hard, to the side. She landed in the grass on her hand, crying out in pain. Charging down the path was the jogger Julie had seen. But Kirsten's eyes went right to the pistol in his hand—pointed at Jan!

Jan reared back and threw something. The black object hurtled through the air and connected with the jogger's face.

"Owwwwwww!" he screamed, and immediately Kirsten recognized the voice.

It was Russo! What was *he* doing here?

He stopped in his tracks, briefly, shaking his head with the shock. Julie was over the wall and Kirsten saw the top of Jan's hat racing down Fifth.

She scrambled to sit up, grimacing. Her hand was killing her.

Russo was moving again, through the exit, running after

Jan. And Julie's arms were pulling her up. "Kirsten! Are you okay? Oh God, this was a dumb idea. I can't believe we came here. We could have been killed!"

Kirsten stared over the top of the wall, at the figure moving down Fifth Avenue. "That jogger was a cop," she said. "Sergeant Russo."

"The guy who was Jones?"

"Yes!"

"Jogging in the park with a gun? Does that make sense?"

"Nothing makes sense, Julie!"

"Well, it's a good thing he had a gun. Jan was about to shoot you, Kirsten."

"No, he wasn't." Kirsten went over to the place where Jan had thrown the black object. It lay on the Central Park grass, a solid black rectangle against the darkness. She crouched and picked it up. "He was holding a PDA. An old one. He said he wanted to show it to me."

"Turn it on," Julie urged her. "What does it say?"

"The screen is cracked," Kirsten said. "It's useless."

At the sound of heavy breathing, they both jumped to their feet. Russo was heading back into the park at a jog. "Lost him," he grumbled as he came through the entrance, rubbing the bridge of his nose, which looked red and swollen. "Are you okay?"

Julie handed him the PDA. "Are you?"

"Only my plastic surgeon knows for sure," Russo

replied, taking the device and fiddling with the controls. "Guess two things got busted. My nose and this."

"Do you always go jogging at night?" Kirsten asked.

"I'm just keeping an eye on you," Russo replied. "Lost track of you at Jackson Hole, when I got distracted by my phone. You must have left in a big rush. Thought I saw you heading for the park but I wasn't sure, so I went to check it out, looked over the wall, and saw Julie all by herself. I ran in as fast as I could." He shrugged. "I never was very good at track and field. Did he hurt you?"

"I have another hand," Kirsten said, massaging the injured one. "You know what he told me? That he was Kyle's brother! Can you believe that? He was so strong. He could have been the guy at Yellow Trance. And he's clearly out of his mind. I know you guys don't think so, *but he might be the one*!"

Russo exhaled, shoving the PDA into his pocket. "I'll show this to our IT guy. And I guess we'll be digging into the deVries records again. Come on, I'll drive you girls home."

"Wait," Julie blurted out as Kirsten and Russo began heading out of the park. "Did any of you notice what he *did*? Kirsten, he *pushed you aside* when Sergeant Russo came running with a gun. He yelled *'watch out.'* He was trying to protect you. What kind of killer does that?"

Julie was right. He'd told her to duck. If he'd been a murderer, he'd have held on to her. Put her in the line of fire.

Russo gave Julie a crooked, admiring smile. "Good question," he said.

Kirsten slouched out of the elevator and into her bedroom before her parents had a chance to see the grass stains on her clothes and the new blood flowing from her bandage. Then she quickly sneaked into the bathroom for a long soak in the Jacuzzi and a reacquaintance with her delicious H2O body lotion. Nothing like the scent of the sea to clear the brain and soothe an aching hand.

The ride home had been short, Julie and Kirsten staying silent while Russo called in a report to the precinct. From the sound of the conversation, Peterson was every bit as confused as they were.

Who was Jan? Was he the killer? A few minutes ago, she'd been convinced.

But he tried to save you. He put himself in the possible path of a bullet.

It now didn't seem possible he was a murderer.

He was trying to show her something. Maybe there was a clue on the PDA.

Maybe he really *was* Kyle's brother. . . .

She imagined the two faces, side by side in her mind. She'd never thought about it before, but there *was* a resemblance. Sort of. If you sharpened all of Kyle's angles, curled his hair, scrunched his features up.

She thought and thought until she started falling asleep, and then hauled herself out of the tub, lotioned up, and dressed for bed.

"Good night," she called out to her parents as she slipped into her room.

"'Night, sweetie," her mom said, peeking inside. "Everything okay? Nice dinner with Julie?"

"Totally fine," Kirsten lied.

"Well, tomorrow's a big day. Your new apartment is waiting. Daddy's friend Ed the real estate man made sure you got a nice view."

Kirsten nodded and forced a smile. Out of the corner of her eye she noticed her computer monitor still glowed with a screen saver slide show of the beach at Mykonos. When her mom left, she jumped up, went to her desk, and grabbed the mouse. The screen saver gave way to her e-mail program.

As she prepared to close down, she saw the latest e-mail message on her NYU account.

It was from JDVRIES.

What did he want? Where was he?

Shaking, she scrolled to the message. It was an image—a black-and-white newspaper clipping. The headline was

"Alleged Portland-Area Teenage Murderer Paul Stone Buried; Parents Claim Innocence to End."

In the center of the photo, a casket was being lowered into the ground. The hole was surrounded by friends and family members dressed in black. Three figures were holding one another, as if for dear life—a thin man with a deeply lined face, a tall woman with an old-fashioned veil, and a young man in a jacket that seemed two sizes too large. Despite the photo's graininess, there was no mistaking the tears streaking the boy's beaklike nose and bony cheeks. There was no mistaking the face, either.

"Oh God," Kirsten murmured. "It's Jan." She leaned closer, her chest pounding, and read the tiny caption underneath the photo:

Family members of the alleged murderer grieve (l to r): father Kirk Stone, mother Elizabeth, brother Richard.

Below the image was a message:

KS-

I hope you're OK.

Please be OK.

don't know who that guy was in the park today.

don't know if he was the killer or not.

I do know he followed me, but didn't get a good look at him.

I tried to get you out of harm's way. I hope I did.

As you can see by this picture, I wasn't lying. I am Richard Stone.

I'm not giving up on you. If you can, pls meet me tmw. I will wait. 6 a.m. 12th Ave. & 132nd, in the Fairway parking lot. I wish it could be someplace nicer, but I don't want anyone to see me. I wish I could make you believe me. I wish I could be sure that you wouldn't try to arrest me or get me in worse trouble than I already am.

I wish, I wish, I wish.

Kirsten, I am so in trouble.

I'll be waiting.

Be alone.

I mean it.

-RS

20

"You're meeting him?" Julie's voice came over the cell as the taxi turned under the elevated highway near 125th Street.

They were stuck at a red light. Ahead of them, enormous vaulted steel columns rose above a decrepit road lined with metal-gated auto body shops and food distributors. Kirsten felt in her shoulder bag for the envelope with Kyle's picture, which she'd tucked snugly into the bottom. And the printout she'd made of the newspaper clipping Jan had e-mailed.

She quickly told Julie all about the note from Jan.

"So he was telling the truth. Great, Kirsten. Still, that doesn't mean you should meet him alone."

"I'll be fine," Kirsten said.

"But you never know," Julie pleaded. "This guy is unpredictable and strange. You don't really know much about him. You said Kyle thought he was being framed. What if this kid turns out to be Kyle's psycho brother who did it all and then killed Kyle to get back at his parents who didn't love him enough? And now he's come to take possession of the only woman his brother ever truly loved."

"Julie!" Kirsten cried.

"Okay, so it's totally far-fetched, but it is possible—right?" Julie replied. "I mean, no one else could have known so much about Kyle: his girlfriends, his hangouts, his schedule—"

"But he was Paul's *brother*."

"Cain was Abel's brother!" Julie said, taking a deep breath. "Sorry. I didn't mean that. Anyway, you should at least let people know where you are. Like me. Just in case."

"Gotta go," Kirsten said as the taxi turned left alongside the hulking orange-painted Fairway Market building.

As she pressed off, Julie's words echoed in her mind. The theory wasn't very likely, but maybe Kirsten *was* being too trusting.

She glanced at the printout of Jan's photo—at his devastated face at the funeral. A murderer would not look like that at the funeral of someone he had killed. Julie was being overly cautious.

Oh well, that's what friends are for.

Still, Kirsten felt a little funny as the cab headed toward the Hudson River. The water was whitecapped and silvery in the morning sun. It looked like miles to New Jersey on the other shore. The current was strong. Incredibly strong.

Anything dropped into that river would be swept away,

never to be found again. Like, say, a body—if there was a hypothetical killer lurking around.

Easy, Kirsten. It's just a meeting.

Still. Julie was right about one thing: Better to be safe than sorry. Someone *should* know where she was. She whipped out her cell as the cab stopped at the STOP sign at Twelfth Avenue, near the front of the market. To her right was the now-empty display of fruits and veggies all covered with canvas, tended by a lone worker in khakis and a woolen watch cap. Just across the street, the parking lot's entrance was blocked by a chain-link fence with a blue-and-orange CLOSED sign.

Where is he? Kirsten wondered.

"What now?" the driver asked.

"I—I don't know," Kirsten said as she tapped out Julie's number.

Was Jan supposed to find me, or vice versa?

From the dashboard of the cab, a voice crackled over the intercom: "Police alert, Harlem area—car 3029, do you read me?"

As the driver picked up his intercom to answer, the passenger door to the right opened. The man in khakis slipped into the seat next to her, taking her wrist. "Please don't. You don't need to call anyone. I'm really glad you're here."

He wasn't a Fairway worker.

He was Jan!

"H-Hi," Kirsten stammered, turning off the cell.

"Go left," Jan said to the driver, his eyes intense, wary, darting every which way.

He wasn't looking Kirsten in the face at all.

This did not make her feel comfortable.

"Listen buddy, I already have a passenger," the cab driver said, covering up his intercom.

"We're friends," Jan replied. "Didn't she tell you she was meeting someone?"

In the rearview mirror, Kirsten could see the driver's probing eyes staring back. Trying to gauge if this unexpected intrusion was okay.

She didn't know how to respond. Was it okay? She wasn't sure anymore. Smiling back noncommittally, she put her cell phone away.

The driver muttered something to the person at the other end of the intercom, then turned down Twelfth Avenue.

"Did you call someone?" Jan asked.

"No," Kirsten said.

"But you were about to."

"Well, I didn't see you. I got nervous."

Jan nodded and took a deep breath. His forehead was beaded with sweat, his eyes bloodshot. "So . . . no one followed you?"

"No, Jan. No. We're alone. What's this all about?"

"I don't usually operate like this," he replied, his voice tense. "I feel like we're in some kind of film noir." As they reached the next corner, he leaned closer to the driver. "Go left again, and then left under the elevated highway."

"Where are we going?" Kirsten asked, looking at the grimy, boarded-up storefronts. "Where are you taking me?"

"Two blocks up," Jan said to the driver. "On the right—the Happy Morning coffeeshop."

It was a small, dingy place with two other yellow taxis parked in front. Jan shoved a few dollar bills onto the front seat and hurried out of the cab.

"I'll sit at the empty table," Jan said softly as Kirsten got out. "You order for us at the counter and act totally normal. I'll have a black coffee and glazed doughnut, please, and order whatever you want. My treat. It's the least I can do."

"Thanks," Kirsten said uncertainly.

The empty table happened to be the *only* table inside. The other customers—mostly men in drab uniforms—sat silently at a counter over coffee, pastries, and the *Daily News*.

Kirsten ordered the breakfast from a dour woman with hair that looked as if it hadn't seen shampoo since New Year's Day. As Kirsten walked back to the table, Jan sat staring intently out the window, shaking his right leg.

"I'm so glad you're all right," he said, not sounding too glad about anything. "I was worried that the guy in the park would hurt you. Did you manage to get the PDA?"

Kirsten shook her head. "It's dead. The screen cracked."

"Oh, great," Jan said, looking away in disgust. "Paul kept

a journal on his computer at home. I spent a month trying to crack his password—and I transferred the whole damn thing to my PDA. I wished you'd read it. He was a really gifted writer, you know. Did you know that? Did he ever tell you that?"

"Um, no," Kirsten said.

"Well, he was. He wanted to be a novelist—would have been a great one too. But he couldn't write anything too personal, anything that might tip people off. We were all living under fake names. We had to. After Paul's arrest, the whole family was disgraced. Paul lost his admission to Brown, Dad lost his job, Mom was being eased out of hers. We moved to North Dogsquat, Massachusetts, and became another family—legal name-change. Me, the family IT genius, I figure out how to alter records, make a past disappear and a new one emerge. Paul couldn't stand it. All his life he'd been, like, Mr. Confessional Suffering Writer-Poet, and now he couldn't even be Paul Stone. So Mom pulls a few strings, gets him into Bowdoin—and in the middle of his freshman year, some smart-ass kids catch on. They start calling him 'Paul' to see if he turns around. . . . He can't take it . . . but he does. . . ." Jan's voice trailed off.

Something was up. His speech was rapid, high-pitched. His fingers were tapping the edge of the table, his eyes constantly moving.

Kirsten swallowed uncomfortably. *Uppers,* she thought. *Big-time.* "Um, was this why you brought me here?" she asked.

Jan pinned her with his glance. "No! Am I boring you?"

Whoa. She eyed the door. Jan was positioned between it and her—right by the handle.

"I worshipped him, do you understand?" Jan said. "He told me *I* was the family genius—the next Tarantino, the Great American Filmmaker. And I'm, like, yeah right—we're hiding from the world in disgrace, and I'm supposed to make films? So I quit. Gave up. Took a job in a video store. I think it broke his heart to see that. I think that's the reason he came to New York. Not for his own sake. For *mine*. For his family. To clear our names. That's the kind of guy he was, *do you understand*?"

Kirsten nodded. He was freaking out right in front of her. She sat forward, at the edge of her seat, planting her toes firmly.

"On the day he died, I decided I *would* make that film," Jan went on. "But not what he would have expected—some postmodern, nihilistic shoot-'em-up, *Kill Bill Seventeen*. Hell no. A documentary—the biggest exposé of all time. The East Side Murders, *solved*. Collect the facts, let them speak for themselves—not only art, but truth! Cinema-verité. The audience tastes the blood, feels the agony of death, and then, *wham*, the primal shocker when the murderer is revealed. *In Cold Blood* meets *Titicut Follies*. . . ."

Kirsten hadn't the slightest idea what he was talking about.

He was on a roll. With himself.

He needed help. Professional help.

Go. Now. Kirsten sprang for the door.

His hand was like a lash, holding the door firmly shut. "Sorry. Sorry. I'm scaring you. I'm rambling. Sit. We're partners, Kirsten."

"No fighting about the check, lovebirds." The haggard-looking woman swooped across the floor, plopping the plates down on the table. "Out of muffins. Rye toast is on the house."

As she went away, Jan reached into his jacket pocket. He pulled out a thick envelope and spilled the contents on the table. "Recognize any of these?" he asked.

On the top was the newspaper clipping from Kyle's burial. Kirsten held it up. It had yellowed, and had ads on the reverse side. A real clipping. Nothing fake or Photoshopped.

She set it down. Underneath were all kinds of photos. A young Kyle in a jacket and Talcott tie, on his first day of school, arm in arm with his brother . . . Kyle and Jan, both much younger, under a Christmas tree, tearing open presents . . . an older and sadder-looking Kyle—the Kyle *she* knew—in a short-sleeved shirt on a snowy college campus . . .

"Bowdoin," she said.

Jan nodded. He fished around and pulled out another image—Kyle with four friends. "Recognize these guys? Their names were Moyer, Goldstein, Willett, and Schloss."

The sounds of their names took her breath away. Of

course she knew who they were. She would never forget those names, never forget the awful story Kyle had confided. . . . "They're Kyle's b-ball bros from Talcott," she said. "The guys who were with him on the night when . . .

"When everything started going wrong," Jan said. "When they all got juiced and got in a car and ran down some cute little public-school girl—"

"Gina," Kirsten said. "That was her name."

"They were tanked that night," Jan said. "All of them. My brother, too. Plus, he was upset about his girlfriend, Carolee, who was hooking up with some other guy. But he didn't do anything to Gina! It was the other guys!"

"I know. And then that same night—" Kirsten began.

"Carolee . . . ," Jan said, nodding.

"Dead too," Kirsten added. "Beaten. Hands bound with a Talcott tie. His tie. He had left it in some bar—the Zoo. Someone must have taken it."

"He was eaten up by that," Jan said. "By the idea that he should have come forward about Gina—that he should have pushed harder about his own innocence. The whole thing broke him. He didn't deserve it."

Jan's face was swollen and sad, and he wiped a tear. He turned away, too embarrassed to face her but too hurt to not let it show. It reminded her of the look on Kyle's face when he'd told her the story—and she reached out to Jan across the table. "I know how you feel."

"I loved my brother," Jan said softly.

"I did too," she replied, and leaned over to give him a hug. They sank into each other's arms for a moment, comforting, remembering the one person they missed *so much*, and before Kirsten pulled away, she closed her eyes and pictured him—pictured Kyle with his strong frame and his handsome face and beautiful wavy dark hair. As long as she kept her eyes shut, she could *imagine*, she could blot out the last year and imagine what could have happened between them, what their lives together might have been like. But just as fleeting as Kyle's image came to her, it disappeared. It was time for Kirsten to open her eyes and face reality.

"Tell me," she said. "Tell me why you brought me here."

Jan buried his face in his hands. "I—I'm feeling really messed up, Kirsten. You know? There's so much more I want to say, but I have to know . . . do you believe me?"

"I do," Kirsten said. She glanced out the window at the yellow cabs parked outside. If she needed a ride home, all she'd have to do was raise her hand in the coffeeshop and three guys would fall all over one another for the fare.

But she had to give him something first.

The photo.

He was the brother. That was certain. No matter what he'd done, he was the brother. And he deserved the picture as much as she did.

She pulled the envelope from her pack. "Jan—I mean, Richard? I took this from your brother's hands after he died. No one but me has seen it."

Jan's eyes widened as he gently took the photo, his face growing pale at the sight of his brother and Carolee, tanned and smiling. "They used to hang at this place all the time. Must have been just before . . ."

"Keep it," Kirsten said. "Maybe you can use it for your film."

Screeeeeeeee! Tires squealed outside the coffeeshop as two cop cars skidded to a stop.

Jan turned, shoving the photo into his pocket.

The front door flew open. Customers hit the floor as Russo raced in, gun drawn and grabbed Jan by the back of his collar. "What the—?" Jan blurted out. "What do you think you're doing?"

"Sergeant Russo, stop!" Kirsten pleaded. "He hasn't done anything!"

But a swarm of blue uniforms barged into the room, blocking Kirsten—and she could only watch helplessly as another officer escorted Jan outside, muttering, "You have the right to remain silent, anything you say can be used against you in a court of law . . ."

"Don't mean to scare you, Kirsten," Russo said. "But when the call came in from the cab driver, we jumped. We've been looking for you—and him—all morning. Peterson just got an item from an identity-tracking company. This guy is not who he says he is."

"I know he isn't! He's—"

But Russo had slapped the copy of a passport photo on the table.

Jan's face.

"You set me up!" Jan's hysterical voice shouted over the din. *"Kirsten—you set me up!"*

Kirsten looked closer. Under the smiling face was a name.

FRANK HARMON.

A name she had never heard in her life.

21

As she passed under the Washington Square Arch later that morning, Kirsten tried the precinct again for what seemed like the hundredth time.

It had been a horrible day. After the Happy Morning breakfast, she should have gone straight to her new apartment, but the thought of that depressed her, so she went to classes—and spent most of the time in tearful conversations about Lauren.

She missed Lauren. Lauren would have known what to make of this morning's total twisted bizarreness.

Frank Harmon?

Just when things seemed to be straightening out, *a whole new person*. It didn't make any sense!

"Eighty-Eighth Precinct," answered the voice of Trudy, the dispatcher.

"Hi, Trudy, it's Kirsten again."

"Sorry, hon. Peterson and Russo are still in conference. With that young man they brought in."

"Well, please have Detective Peterson call me as soon as he can." Kirsten put the phone away as she walked into her new building on Lower Fifth Avenue. A team of men in uniforms greeted her by name, and she rode up silently in the elevator with people who looked like their faces had been carved from granite.

She was the only one left when she got out on the penthouse floor.

Dad had proudly called her place a "furnished apartment" in "one of the finer art deco properties on Lower Fifth Avenue." Well, "furnished" was a loose term. The curtains were made of a dark maroon velvet brocade, hanging over the windows in heavy swooshes that blocked any hint of light. The carpet looked like the lifelong project of some poor Turkish slaves who had poured their blood and guts into it. Literally. And the gaudy, oversized chandelier brought back unpleasant memories of sitting through *The Phantom of the Opera* with her fifth-grade class while Herman Finkel kept trying to feel her left breast.

She half expected to find the previous owner still there, gray and forgotten and covered with dust in the closet. *Don't mind me, dear. . . .*

Dad's movers had done it all: fixed up her bedroom, made her bed, put towels on the bathroom rack, arranged her furniture. They'd even brought along a techie to set up her cable TV, desktop computer, scanner, and a wireless network for her laptop. They left her personal stuff in boxes—thank God—but she was too tired to deal with that.

She was too tired to do anything.

She collapsed onto her bed. Her laptop had been turned on and set on a swivel-table built into the wall. She swung it around, hit the touch pad to get rid of the screen saver, and found that it had been set to the home page of founder/co-owner Edward P. Spencer of Cloverdale Realtors, "For All Your High-End Needs."

Cute.

Julie had sent an Facebook message—'SUP? WHERE R U?—and she was still online.

Kirsten typed COME OVER NOW, 9 5TH AVE. U WONT BELIEVE THIS PLACE! and pressed send, when her cell phone rang. She glanced at the screen—Peterson's number!—and picked up the call.

"Where is he?" Kirsten blurted out. "What happened, Detective Peterson?"

"Russo here," Russo's voice came back to her. "Your friend Peterson is a little embarrassed. Well, no, *a lot*. See, it turns out that your pal Jan is not only Frank Harmon, but also Bill Riddly, Otis Saunders, Quincy Fielding, Barney Snipp . . . and a few others."

Kirsten sank into her pillow. "What does *that* mean?"

"Some people build model airplanes for a hobby," Russo said with a sigh, "Jan builds fake identities. On the Web. Posts them so they can be picked up by the information-harvesting services. Just made-up names. He thinks it's fun. Says he first learned the art of it when his family *really* had to change their names, and he got hooked. Jan deVries—that was the most detailed fake he created. Fooled NYU."

And you, Kirsten chose not to say. "But who is he, then?" she asked.

"Stone. Richard Stone. We're one hundred percent positive now. We've got corroboration from childhood doctors, a faxed birth certificate from the hospital, the works. It's ironclad, Kirsten."

Kirsten breathed a sigh of relief. He was legit. He *was* Kyle's brother. She began to laugh. "Barney Snipp?"

"That was my favorite too. Anyway, he gave me a lecture. Said I could have done better than the name 'Jones.' Jones was boring." Russo chuckled. "Wise guy."

"Can I speak to him?" Kirsten asked.

"We let him go," Russo said.

"To where?"

"I don't know. He's free. We couldn't keep him here. My guess is, he's sleeping. Between you and me, I think he was a little high this morning. But I wouldn't worry about him, Kirsten. He's not the guy who killed your roommate . . . or any of the others. Or the guy who attacked you at the Yellow Trance. With any luck, he'll help us find the real murderer. He had some pictures with him and says he may have some more."

Kirsten gulped. He had photos all right. Like the one she'd given him. The one she'd stolen from Kyle's body. If Russo knew about that one, he wasn't saying.

"Do you have any leads?" she asked hopefully. "On Kyle's killer?"

"At the moment," Russo replied with a big sigh, "no."

"This is my krend Fiercesten," Julie said, dancing over to the bar of the trendy new Karib Club with her usual five guys in tow. "I mean, fend Krirsten. I mean, I'm too loaded right now, so talk amongst yourselves . . . anything else is extra credit. Woo-hoo!"

She whirled away with three of the boys, leaving two with Kirsten. One had a Cheshire cat grin and a swoop of hair in front that reminded her of the Kennedy Airport terminal. The other, Kirsten had to admit, was crush material—tall, shy smile, blue eyes, soft features, a total Prince William type, only hotter. "I'm sorry, how did you pronounce that name?" he asked in a sexy British accent that nailed the image.

"Any way she wants to," Hair Swoop said. "I'm George Brent, and this is Charles Mansfield, my roommate."

"I'm Kirsten." She gave them a flip of her hair and a slow once-over. She was trying to get into the mood. She needed a break. But so much was on her mind. She hadn't heard a thing from Jan all day. Did he still think she'd set him up at the Happy Morning? He'd never had told her who he thought the killer was—and that was what scared her the most. For all she knew, he could be here. Tonight.

He could be one of these two guys that Julie had deposited.

Loosen up, Kirsten. It's been a long day. Kirsten turned to put her drink down. She lifted her arms and began to dance, moving her hips in rhythm, sending her chest in all kinds of directions, followed closely by George's and Charles's radar eyes.

"Wooooo!" shouted George, whose energy did not quite make up for his lack of rhythm. Charles was more reserved, but hot, hot, hot, in an I'm-so-cool-I-don't-like-to-show-off way.

"Are the girls in England like this?" Kirsten asked Charles.

"Wales," he said with a smile.

DZZZZZZ. Her cell phone vibrated against her thigh, and she snatched it up, poising her finger over the off button. She didn't recognize the return number, but it was a 212 area code without a nametag. Kirsten tagged all her numbers. What *stranger* would be calling at this hour?

"Hello?" she said, lifting the phone to her ear as she danced.

"I know who did it," a familiar voice said.

Kirsten put her finger in her other ear to blot out noise. "Who is this? Hello?"

"It's Richard. And I said, *I know who did it.*"

"You *what*?" Kirsten blurted out.

"Shhhh. Sounds like you're in a public place. Meet me at the Eighty-Sixth Street subway station at one forty-five."

Kirsten looked at her watch. It was almost 1:30. "You've got to be kidding. What did you find out? What happened to you today? You can't just tell me to come over there without an explanation!"

George and Charles had stopped dancing now and were looking at her with great concern and disappointment, like two fishermen watching a big catch that was about to get away.

"I'll be on the express platform, Kirsten," Richard said. "If you want to know who killed your best friend—and my brother—you will follow my instructions. Now."

PART THREE

22

There she is.

She's leaving.

Now, MOVE, pal.

But do it right.

No boo-boos.

You blew it last time. TOTALLY BLEW IT!

Oh, that hurt.

She wasn't meant to die.

WHERE WAS YOUR CONTROL, BUDDY?

You could have looked. You could have turned on the light. SOMETHING.

That was a lapse. A very, very bad lapse.

But you can't dwell.

You can't live in the past.

Because let's face it, IT WASN'T YOUR FAULT.

Oh no. If that bitch had come home the way she was supposed to . . . if she had been in her bed THE WAY SHE WAS SUPPOSED TO . . .

It would have turned out just dandy.

But she didn't. She went running to her rich Fifth Avenue mommy and daddy.

SHE SET HER ROOMMATE UP.

What kind of friend does that?

A pampered, coddled, morally bankrupt friend, that's who.

And because she set up her roommate, I missed my chance.

And because I missed my chance, she's alive.

And because she's alive, she's GETTING CLOSER.

Well, she did not play her cards right.

Because I'm calling in the chips.

Tonight's the night.

The girl has been living on borrowed time.

And when she goes, there will be none left. It will all stop.

Finally. All. Stop.

I'll miss it. Oh yes, I will. There has been some serious fun, along with the aggravation.

But when it's over, I will be able to rest again.

For the first time in years.

On your knees, little girl. Say a prayer.

And kiss your ass good-bye.

23

The headlights . . . hurting her eyes . . . the streetlamps and the screaming halogen bulbs that flanked the entrances of Second Avenue apartment buildings . . . *Second Is Diving, Third Is Striving, Park Is Thriving, and Fifth Is Arriving.* Dad's old saying; what a crock. It was all so bright against the winter blackness and it made her dizzy, so Kirsten forced her footsteps one in front of the other, her mind a jumble of loose thoughts, her feet aching in her too-tight Jimmy Choos—and around the time she reached Eighty-Ninth Street, the mojitos seemed to kick in again and she was so tight, she could hardly see straight.

Focus, Kirsten . . .

She made a right at Eighty-Sixth Street, passed the shuttered stores and the ragged, sleeping figures on the heating grates, and made a sharp left at Lexington Avenue to the subway entrance. She rushed down the stairs to get past the gentle updraft of stale urine that greeted her, and nearly tripped headlong into the puddle. At the turnstile she tried seven times to push her MetroCard through before realizing it was her driver's license.

Down past the empty local track . . . down another flight to the express level, where the number 5 train was pulling out of the station. No one was left on the platform except the dark, rumpled heap of a homeless person against the distant tiles. She hated this station. It was long and narrow, and trains came from around a curve, so you never knew in advance.

But it had a bench. Thank God for benches. She slumped onto one and waited for the choppy waters in her mind to settle. As the train's sound receded into the tunnel, a soft crackling sound came up from the Dumpster at the end of the platform. She didn't want to think about what was scurrying around in the trash.

Her watch read 1:48. Jan . . . *Richard* should be here by now.

She closed her eyes—not a smart thing to do in the subway, but she didn't give a damn.

Shhhhp . . . shhhp . . . shhhp . . .

The sound was coming from her right. The homeless guy had risen and was shuffling toward her. His feet were wrapped in tattered plastic bags held together with masking tape.

Oh, great. She stood up from her seat and edged back toward the stairs.

"Hey, Kirsten." He was sprinting now.

No. This was not real. She was drunk and hearing things, and this guy could not possibly know her name. She turned to run, but the guy was on her, grabbing her arm!

"Oh, no you don't!" She forced her bleary eyes to focus into the shadow of the man's hood and recognized his face.

"It's me, Richard," he said.

"God, you scared me!" she shouted, her voice echoing down the tracks.

"Ssshhhh, we have to be quiet," he said.

"You biter not be laying . . . better not be lying—wait . . ."

"You're drunk, Kirsten."

"You don' look much better. You have a new *identity*, huh? Homeless Guy. Or do you have a name? Pleased to meet you. Barney Snipp, I presume?"

"This is bad. How can you help me if you're drunk?"

Hold steady. Look him in the eyes. All four of them. "How'm I supposed to help you? One minute you're a good guy and I like you, the next you're in disguise and doing something creepy—and tonight you called to say you know who did it and if you're playing with me, I'll—"

Richard gently put his finger on her lips. "Sshhh. Sober up, will you?"

"You jerk." Kirsten lurched forward, wanting to hurt him, somehow, but managed only to trip and fall into his arms.

He held her tightly. "I need you, Kirsten. My brother needs you. And we don't have much time. I know who the killer is."

"Who? Who did it, Richard? Tell me!"

Richard pulled open his ratty wool overcoat. A video camera hung from his neck. "There's an old saying in show business: 'Show, don't tell.' Tonight you and I are going to show the world who did it. We're going to expose him."

"A camera? You're making a film? *Now?*"

"We're both doing it. Me *and* you. Director and star. You're going to get the killer to confess, and I'm putting it on film. This is *it*, Kirsten. The big moment. And what a setting. The shabbiness, the urban grit, the rats on the tracks, the tunnel moving into darkness—*symbolism*—sex and death . . ."

She shook her head. This had to be a dream.

This wasn't a dream.

The man with a hundred identities . . . and it all boiled down to one: the same creep she'd seen for the first time in the Ridge lounge. Movie Geek from Hell.

He made her sick.

"Wait," she said. "Let me understand this. These are roles . . . you're *staging* this . . . you're playing a bag man, and I'm—"

"You're playing Kirsten, of course. Now, I need an establishing shot. So stand by the edge, looking uptown. I'll be sitting against the wall, looking pathetic." He pulled a manila envelope out of his coat and handed it to Kirsten. "When he comes down, show him what's in this envelope."

"Who?"

"The killer."

Kirsten's alcoholic haze lifted, as if slapped right out of her. This was worse than sick. "And who's playing that role?" she asked.

Richard exhaled hard. "Someone who you—"

The sound of footsteps on the stairs interrupted him.

"Here he comes," Richard said, then closed his jacket and ran back to his place against the wall. *"Just do what I told you to do!"*

Kirsten backed away. A guy stepped down from the stairs and walked onto the platform—young and bland-looking, in an Elvis-Costello-glasses-and-Converse-sneakers way. He gave Kirsten a quick once-over and looked up the tracks.

This was the killer? The actor playing the killer?

This was absurd. Grotesque. She didn't need to be sober to know that.

Still clutching the envelope, she backed toward the stairs—and she bolted.

Tripping on the stairs. Clutching the banister. Fighting the waves of nausea and drunkenness. The lights that seemed to whirl down from the ceiling and back up.

"Hey! You can't do this! Get back here!" Richard cried. He was moving fast. Much faster than she could.

Hang on. Hang on tight to the railing and move.

If she could get all the way up . . . to the transit clerk . . . she'd be safe.

Up . . . up . . .

Almost to the landing, when a hand landed heavily on her shoulder. "Stop!" Richard said.

"Screw . . . you!" Kirsten said. With all her strength, she leaned her weight into Richard and pushed.

"Aaaaaghh!" he screamed, windmilling his arms, falling. Falling down the subway steps.

Kirsten raced upward.

She made the lower landing, the one between the local and express. *Go. Keep going.*

Her feet were more steady now. She placed her head down and raced up to the main platform, through the turnstile, and sprinted for the exit. She could smell the air from outside, wafting down into the station.

She was almost there. Almost free.

And she ran smack into someone coming into the station.

"Oh!" she screamed.

"Whoa!" he said.

She stumbled backward. A tall, broad figure stepped out of a shadow.

Scott! Dressed in his usual basic black and looking like God.

"Kirsten?" he said with a slightly baffled smile. "What a coincidence."

"Oh God," Kirsten said. "You have no idea how happy I am to see you."

She wanted to jump into his arms. She wanted to laugh and cry and kiss him and run away and go home to sleep, all of those things mixed up like a big, confusing emotional stew.

"Nice to see you, too. Is everything okay?" he asked.

"Fine! *Fine!*" Kirsten replied. Where are you going?"

"Home. Like I do every night."

"To Queens?"

"Brooklyn. But I just realized I have an errand to run for my little sister. Where are *you* going?"

"Home—to NYU!" Kirsten cried. This was perfect. Scott could be her escort onto the train. Her bodyguard. Richard wouldn't *think* of messing with Scott. Not after the way Scott had treated him at the Party Room.

She almost blurted out what had just happened, but checked herself. She didn't want Scott to go after him. She didn't want a scene. Just a simple ride home. That would be enough. Well, maybe if Scott gave her an attractive alternative to going home, that would be worth a thought. . . .

"Looked like you were going in the other direction," Scott said.

"I got a little scared, that's all. You know. The subway at night? It's deserted."

Scott smiled. "Well, not anymore. Come on. Why waste twenty bucks on a cab ride?"

As he and Kirsten walked to the turnstile, she heard a rumble from below—another train trundling out of the station. A small group of passengers began emerging from the stairwell.

The "killer" was gone from the platform when they reached the bottom, but Richard was still there, hunched against the wall and looking like a poor homeless person. His finest role. Kirsten almost laughed aloud, but she held her tongue. At the moment, Richard was probably shitting himself with fear at the sight of Scott.

At the end of the platform, Richard moved. Kirsten looked out of the corner of her eye. He was pointing the camera at them!

Incredible. He was going to film them.

She crossed her eyes at Richard and flipped him the finger.

Scott gave her a curious look and glanced over his shoulder. "That guy a friend of yours?"

Kirsten blushed. "Um . . . well, yeah. Actually he's not really homeless. He's a kid. A student. Trying to get some, um, interesting real-life experience—"

"As a bum?" Scott laughed. And that deep, rumbly, scrumptious laugh sounded three times as sexy echoing in the train tunnel. "I love college kids. Hey, is he taking *pictures* of us?"

Kirsten swallowed hard. "Just ignore him."

"Doesn't he know it's illegal to take pix in the subway these days?" Scott asked.

Kirsten could feel a gust of wind from the tunnel. Another

train was approaching. Just in time. "How far down are you going?" she asked. "Is your errand before Astor Place?"

"Errand?" Scott said.

"The one for your little sister?" she replied.

Scott nodded. "Oh, right. As a matter of fact, that's at Astor Place too."

"Cool. I could . . . um, help you run it. The errand, I mean. And then, maybe you could show me Brooklyn. It's still early. Well, not really . . ." *Ugh. Be a little more obvious, why don't you, Kirsten?*

They pulled back from the edge, letting the number 5 train roll in. As it screeched to a stop, she noticed that Richard had stood up. He was walking toward them.

Kirsten gave him a "go away" look, but he was moving faster now. His camera was down, and he was trying to say something, gesturing with his free hand. What was he *doing*?

Scott stood to the side of the door, motioning for Kirsten to enter the car. She rushed in, trying to keep his attention with a smile and a thank-you.

From halfway down the platform, Richard screamed, *"You didn't—"* But his voice was cut off by the electronic bell, the recorded "Stand clear of the closing doors" announcement, and the *whoosh* of the door.

"Don't I know that guy?" Scott asked.

Richard was standing outside the door, banging on it, holding up his camera. *"Open up!"* he shouted. *"Open the doors!"*

Kirsten hid her face in embarrassment. "Oh God, ignore him. He has been the biggest pain in my butt. He's crazy."

As the train pulled away, Richard began to run alongside it, keeping pace, pointing wildly at Kirsten.

"He's trying to tell you something," Scott said, plopping himself down on a seat. "What's that in your hand?"

Kirsten shrugged. "I don't know. He thinks he's Tarantino. He's trying to film a reenactment of the murders—and show them being solved, too. This was supposedly the climax—I was supposed to get the killer to confess. Some guy was down here, playing the murderer, but he disappeared. I had to give him this, but of course I didn't." Kirsten opened the envelope and slowly pulled out an eight-by-ten glossy photo.

She recognized it right away. It was a blow-up of Paul's photo, the one he'd been holding when he died. The one she'd given to Richard this morning. At this size, Paul's and Carolee's smiling faces seemed incandescent.

Along the bottom were the words DIGITALLY ENHANCED BY R. STONE. In the upper-right corner, a neon sign she hadn't noticed before now clearly read THE ZOO. Kirsten could recognize a couple of faces of people she knew somewhat, but not very well: Leslie Fenk's big sister, Ruthie . . . Paul's friend, Willets . . .

And someone else.

Someone she *did* know.

Someone she knew very well, but never, ever expected to see.

Scott tilted his head with a patient little smile. "Something juicy?" he asked.

She held the photo closer. To make sure.

The face was washed-out. Pixilated.

In the original photo it had been a dark blob, swallowed in the shadow of an overhanging bar-glass rack. But Richard had managed to bring out the features.

It was Scott.

Tending bar.

He had one arm on Paul's shoulder, another on Carolee's. Like old friends.

Old friends.

"Have a seat," Scott said, patting the place next to him. "Are you going to show me? What is it?"

"A picture. Kyle's in it," Kirsten said.

"That weird guy was a friend of Kyle's?"

"Um, yeah. I guess you could say that." Kirsten's mind was sharpening by the moment, and Scott's words from the night when they'd almost hooked up . . . from a conversation—a conversation about Kyle—were coming back to her,

"I'd never met him until he came in here that one time," Scott had said about Kyle. But it sure *looked* like he knew Kyle. Would he *forget* someone like that?

"Sentimental value," Kirsten said. "You wouldn't be interested. I mean, not unless you knew Kyle when this picture was taken. When he was a little younger. Back in the days when he was Paul Stone. You wouldn't have known him then, right?"

Scott shook his head. "Can't say I did."

"I mean, you *could* have known him, though—right? His hair was shaggier, and he was a little heavier. He went to Talcott Prep? Hung out on the East Side? Dated a girl named Carolee Adams? You could have known him and forgotten?"

Scott laughed. "I have a photographic memory for customers. That's what makes me a good bartender. And, I assure you, I never met that dude. Or the girl."

But he had. Obviously, he had.

She could see it right in her hand. He knew Kyle and Carolee. He knew them when they were a couple. Before Carolee was murdered.

If he'd tended bar at the Zoo, he knew *all* of them. Paul and his buds hung there all the time. They had been there that awful night—the night they drove off . . . the night those guys . . . those idiots had killed that poor girl, Gina.

Paul had left his tie at the Zoo that night—the tie that had been used to kill Carolee only hours later. He'd left the tie on the bar. *Everyone knew that.*

Scott would have known it too. *So how could he say he didn't?*

Kirsten felt the blood rushing from her face. She slowly slipped the photo back into the envelope. The train, which had been moving fast, began to slow. The conductor announced construction delays, and out the window the tunnel's vertical beams passed like dried tree stumps from some burned-out world.

She needed time to think.

This wasn't right.

Scott was hiding something.

Why?

Was he hiding the killer's identity? Did he know who took the tie from the bar? Whoever the bartender was that night would know.

"Hey, are you feeling all right, Kirsten?" Scott asked.

He was going to be with her till Astor Place. It was a long ride from the Upper East Side. She had to say something. "Can you be honest with me, Scott? Did you tend bar at a place call the Zoo?"

Scott flinched. Just the tiniest shift of muscle across his right cheek. Kirsten could tell. She knew every inch of that face. "I think I did. Yes, I did. For a while . . . there have been so many bars."

"Then you know about the night of the Carolee Adams murder. I mean, even if you weren't there—even if you were, like, a sub—you would know about it, wouldn't you? The bartenders would have talked about that."

"I guess I do remember it. I—I block things out. Especially when I'm working double and triple shifts."

"Kyle told me he left a tie on the bar the night of Carolee's murder. *Did he?*"

Scott's eyebrows lowered across his forehead like a ledge. "She wasn't the only one murdered that day, Kirsten—remember? There was another girl."

Of course there was: Gina. But that was beside the point. Why was he bringing *that* up?

"Next stop will be Fifty-Ninth Street," the recorded announcement chimed. They had a few more stops before they'd have to switch for the local. You needed the local for Astor Place. Astor Place would be kind of dead at this hour. It was a good thing she'd have company. How lucky for her that he had to run errands.

Kirsten suddenly felt the blood rushing from her face.

Errands? What kind of errands, at this hour, would a person run on Astor Place for his sister?

And the answer hit her—hard.

"Scott . . . ," Kirsten said, swallowing back her dry throat. "Who is your little sister . . . the one you're doing the errand for?"

"You wouldn't know her," Scott said. "Why?"

"Is her name . . . Gina?"

Scott stood up slowly. A smile spread across his face, and Kirsten knew the answer before he opened his mouth.

"You say the strangest things, Kirsten," he said. "I usually don't like to talk about my sister. That's one thing I reserve for myself. My personal life. That's one thing I don't like losing control over. See, to me, the most important thing is CONTROL."

24

He was the one. Of course. Scott. A killer.

He was the only one who knew them all.

He was there at the Zoo tending bar the night Kyle fought with Carolee, when he was Paul. The night he left his tie on the bar and stormed off . . . with his pals. Scott found the tie, held it in the lost-and-found for Kyle to retrieve. But then Scott got the news. The news that his sister had been killed. By a car full of boys. Boys who had driven off, leaving an innocent, bleeding ninth grader.

All except Kyle, who'd jumped out and stayed with her.

"He was the only one who'd tried to help her," Kirsten said, "who *cared* about her."

"Oh, he did?" Scott said, his face now icy cold. "Unfortunately, it doesn't fit with what I saw. I was there, Kirsten. When I heard what happened, I came running. *Do you know what it feels like to turn the corner and see someone running away from your dead sister?*"

"You saw him because he was the only one who stayed with her!" Kirsten shot back. "He held her when she was dying. When the other guys drove away."

"That's not what they told me."

"*Who* told you? Goldstein? Moyer? Those lowlife cokeheads? *They were lying!*"

Scott had backed her against the door to the next car. His breath came at her in warm, Scotch-scented bursts. "Willets . . . Schloss . . . all of them. Individually. The identical story. Your boyfriend was *driving*, Kirsten. He *aimed* at her. *'We just want to hold hands!'* That's what he said as he smashed into her. Can you imagine? He stayed with Gina *because they threw him out and drove to get help*! He felt her twitching and"—Scott's voice choked—"and he strangled her to death. Finished the job—probably so she wouldn't tell the cops!"

"That's not true," Kirsten said.

"I tend bar for all you condescending rich kids. . . . I clean your puke and give you advice, and I listen to your sob stories about the hard life in ten-million-dollar apartments and look the other way at your fake IDs and serve you drinks and hold on to your blow, and I throw out anyone who threatens your well-scrubbed, immaculate asses and smile and say thank you to your clueless cheap tips and *I protect you from the idea that anything you do might be wrong or illegal or God forbid unwise, because I am Scott the stupid, low-class bartender—and I say* SCREW YOU, KIRSTEN.

SCREW YOU AND ALL YOUR GODDAMN RICH UPPER EAST SIDE OVERPRIVILEGED SCUMBAG FRIENDS!" Scott reared back and swung.

"Ahhhhh!" Kirsten shrieked, ducking.

His fist connected with the metal wall so hard, she swore she could feel the whole car rock. "I'm sorry," he said, suddenly sounding restrained and quiet. "That . . . was very bad. That was a loss of *control*. Wouldn't you agree?"

Kirsten nodded numbly. *He's about to kill me,* she thought. *I am alone in a slow-moving subway car, somewhere south of Eighty-Sixth Street, and by the time I reach Fifty-Ninth, I will be dead.*

"Put yourself in my shoes, Kirsten," Scott said with a chilly calmness. "You're tending bar one night and you see a young guy, Paul, go crazy when he sees the love of his life screwing another guy—"

"That's not how it happened," Kirsten said. "Carolee wasn't—"

"Were you there? Or do you just *wish* you were there, waiting to get in his pants when he left the bar?" Scott cleared his throat. "Actually, you should have been there, throwing yourself at him. Then he would have been too busy to go out and kill Gina. And I wouldn't have had to . . . to . . ."

His face went slack, as if a cloud had passed across his eyes.

The train was speeding up now, just a bit.

"To get revenge?" Kirsten said, finishing his sentence. "To use his tie to kill Carolee? To frame him and ruin his future?"

"What . . . were . . . my . . . choices?" Scott asked, his voice a strangled whisper. "I loved my sister. She was smart, pretty, so beautiful. Unlike your parents, ours had no money, and I was going to put her through college. . . . *She was my life, Kirsten. He took MY LIFE! So what could I do? Kill him myself?* Have his blood on my hands and spend the rest of my life in jail? Gina wouldn't have wanted that. . . ."

"She wouldn't have wanted you to kill another innocent girl—"

"*Carolee was not so innocent!* You know who was innocent? *Gina* was innocent."

"And what about Sam? What did Sam do to deserve what she got?"

"Two years had gone by," Scott said. "I thought it was over. Your little boyfriend went to jail and was far, far away—and good riddance. Or so I thought. Then, two years later, he gets out and he has the balls to come back . . . to my bar . . . *and the asshole didn't even recognize me*!"

"So you needed to frame him again?" Kirsten cried. "*With Sam's life?*"

"He was supposed to rot in jail," Scott said through clenched teeth. "But his daddy got him out. What was I supposed to do—just sit by and watch this injustice?" he cried. "I was giving your boyfriend to the cops on a platter." Scott's voice grew distant. "But they were too stupid. They weren't going to find him before he found me. So I decided to cut off the source. I did the thoughtful thing—"

"Killing him was *thoughtful*?"

"Because it spared the lives of others! After he was gone, I could stop." Scott said. The train's pace began to slacken. They would be at the station in a minute. "Or so I thought," he added, reaching underneath his jacket.

No. What is he doing? "Scott . . . ," Kirsten began, "maybe . . . maybe I can keep your secret. Maybe we can work something out."

"Sorry, kid. It's too late for that now," Scott said as he loosened his tie and pulled a knife from his belt.

25

"You can't!" Kirsten cried, her mind racing. "You can't kill me here! There'll be people at the next stop! They'll see me. They'll see *you*!"

Scott brought the tip of the knife to her trembling jaw. "This . . . is . . . control. Like a surgeon. I can keep this a millimeter from you at will, for as long as I want, no matter how much you move. Want to try me?"

Kirsten gulped. She didn't dare nod.

"At the Fifty-Ninth Street stop we will both walk out," he went on. "Calmly. Arm in arm. Like lovers. In fact, we can keep that option open because we will be heading west to Central Park."

He lowered his knife, hiding it in his overcoat as the train slowed to a stop. The doors opened and they left, letting a tired-looking group of late-night stragglers file into the car behind them. A familiar mosaic sign on the wall said BLOOMINGDALE'S, advertising the famous department store, and

Kirsten ached for the memory of her usual reason to stop here.

They turned a corner to the stairwell, and a voice called out, "Freeze!"

Russo!

"Shit," Scott muttered, grabbing Kirsten hard and pulling her back toward the tracks.

From one stairwell, Russo and two other cops swooped down; from the other, Peterson and another cop. They crouched, brandishing their guns. "DON'T TRY ANYTHING STUPID!" Russo shouted over the screams of subway riders scurrying for the streets.

Scott's knife was out, and Kirsten could feel the presence of its tip like a baby's breath at her throat. "HE'S GOING TO KILL ME!" she cried out.

"Put the knife down," Russo said steadily.

"This is a little unbalanced, isn't it?" Scott answered back. "Put the guns down."

"It's over, Scott," Peterson said. "Last call. And you know it."

"Last call?" Scott nearly spat the words into the back of Kirsten's head. "It's not the last call. For any of us. My *sister* was the one who had last call, pal. It was last call the day she was abandoned in the gutter by that rich-bastard boyfriend of *hers*."

Kirsten screamed, feeling the knife prick her skin.

"New York's *Finest*," Scott drawled sarcastically. "Where were you when Gina needed help? WHERE WERE YOU? Protecting the streets of area code 10021 for the investment bankers and brokers and swindlers who grease your palms enough so you can buy that Weber grill for your post-age-stamp Massapequa backyard? *Last call for THAT, buddy!"* His hand was vibrating now.

The cops were silent, locked in position, and Kirsten's gaze darted from gun barrel to gun barrel.

They couldn't shoot. Could they? And if they didn't shoot, then what? Scott wasn't going to make it. The knife blade wasn't so steady anymore. She could feel the tip. The blood starting to trickle down her neck.

"S-S-Surgeon, remember?" Kirsten whispered. "C-C-Control?"

"Shut up." Scott pulled the blade lower and began stepping backward, toward the edge of the platform. "I am going to lower both of us to the tracks. We are going to walk into the tunnel, and then I am going to run. At which point, I release you and you're free—if you do as I say. *Do you understand me?"*

"Yes," Kirsten whispered back. Her chest was heaving with panicked breaths. She had to stay calm. If she did, there was a better chance that he would, too. He was being rational. Sparing her life. All she had to do was walk on the tracks.

Be calm. Say yes. Don't blow it. Beneath her feet she felt the roughness of the yellow caution strip at the very edge of the platform. Scott was leading her to a small stairway at a lip near the end of the platform, where the MTA workers go down to the tracks.

But just then she felt a breeze on her skin. A shift of wind from the tunnel itself.

"A train," Scott said.

Kirsten heard the rumble coming from uptown. They couldn't go down onto the tracks now.

Scott was frozen. Undecided.

And now, in the station, Richard Stone was racing down the stairs. Still dressed in rags. Still carrying a camera.

"Get back upstairs!" Peterson shouted.

At the sight of Richard, Scott began to shake. "Asshole . . . ," he murmured.

"Richard, get out of here!" Kirsten screamed.

But Richard was stunned. Just standing there, agape.

"Ignore him," Kirsten said. "Please."

"Get that asshole out of here!" Scott yelled.

Ca-chunk . . . ca-chunk . . . ca-chunk . . . Kirsten could hear the train approaching, by the noise on the rails. How far was it? Ten blocks? Ten yards?

Scott looked back to the track. Out to the station.

Peterson shifted his gun, ever so slightly.

Richard lifted his camera.

CA-CHUNK . . . CA-CHUNK . . . CA-CHUNK . . .

Closer. Much closer. Already creating a wind, pushing the air out of the tunnel.

"They don't listen!" Scott bellowed in her ear. "NOBODY LISTENS!" With a sudden grunt, he threw Kirsten backward.

And she tumbled . . . tumbled down, onto the tracks!

26

She hit the bottom hard.

Something snapped beneath her as she splashed into a foul-smelling puddle of unknown origins.

Dead. I'm dead.

CRACK!

A pistol shot rang out from above, and she flinched. Ahead, she saw two bright eyes. The lights of the train. Coming closer.

Kirsten screamed as a rat the size of a Volkswagen Beetle scurried across her hand and into a hole in the far wall off the tracks to safety.

Go! Get up! She scrambled to her feet. "Yeeeoooow!" she cried out in pain. Her ankle was shattered. She couldn't stand.

WONNNK! WONNNNNNK!

The train's blast was deafening. The brakes screeched.

The conductor had seen her.

He was three blocks away. Maybe two.

It can't end this way.

I can't die here!

GO!

Gritting her teeth, she reached up—to the pipes that ran along the edge of the platform, pulling herself with all her strength. Dragging her body.

WONNNNNNK!

The lights . . . like two eyes . . . widening . . . angry . . .

Could she tuck her body under . . . was there room under the platform? No. She would be sliced in half.

Scott's face, twisted into a wild grin, appeared over the edge of the platform. "Last . . . call," he said in a raspy voice.

"You can't," she said. *"Scott, help me! Help me up!"*

He continued to grin.

Move. Just move. She tried to haul herself toward the end of the platform. Near the stairs. There was an indentation there. Enough space for a human body.

But it was far. Too far.

And then she saw the hand. Reaching down toward her.

The hand covered with rivulets of blood.

Scott's hand.

"Grab it," he said.

No. He's going to kill you.

"Just grab it, Goddamn it!" Scott lunged farther over the edge and closed his thick fingers around her wrist. Kirsten screamed and struggled to shake lose, but she was rising . . . rising . . .

WONNNNNNK!

SSKKKREEEEEEEE!

The sound of the brakes was so loud, so near, so piercing, as if the train had become a part of her body. But she was out. Rolling onto the platform, crying out at the knife-edge pain in her ankle. Saved by Scott.

She looked toward him, but he was sprawled in a pool of blood. She saw the bullet entrance wound just below his right shoulder.

He looked at her with an expression she couldn't read. "I . . . loved her," he rasped, pushing himself along the platform with his legs . . . toward the track . . .

The front of the train was charging into the station now, along with the smell of burning metal. And Kirsten realized what he was trying to do. "No, Scott!" she cried out. "Don't!"

"Last call," Scott repeated. With one mighty gesture, he grabbed the edge of the platform and hauled himself over.

Kirsten turned her head away as the number 5 screamed in.

Epilogue

Kirsten set her crutches near the bar. It had been six weeks since she'd gone out at night. Six weeks since she broke her ankle in a dozen places. Six weeks of excruciating pain. Of constant physical therapy.

And relief. Incredible, blessed relief.

The murders were over. Truly over.

Kirsten's gala Spring Coming Out Party was Julie's idea, of course.

It was late March—almost spring break—the weather was finally starting to thaw, and Kirsten was feeling human for the first time in ages.

"Piña coladas all around!" Julie announced. "Today, our beloved former Woodley Queen comes back to the real world—*and is she ready to par-tyyyyy*!"

"WOOOOO!" shouted Carla, and the entire crowd—everyone who was anyone—at Rampage, the latest and greatest club on the Upper East Side. Carla raised a glass and started dancing to some new hip-hop song.

Kirsten had picked out the track. She couldn't dance yet, but she'd sure had plenty of time to watch MTV while lying flat on her back. She glanced around at the raging new place, bopping her head in time with the bass. No, it wasn't the Party Room. Nothing would be like the Party Room, but the three *amigas* had decided that they just couldn't go there anymore—too many bad memories. And besides, the Party Room was so high school. It was time for a new haunt.

She smiled at the motion, the lights on the dance floor, the scent of sex, alcohol, and teen spirit. It felt good. Really good.

All winter in the hospital and at home, Kirsten hadn't been able to move. Through her bedroom window she stared at the snow settling on the bare canopies of Central Park's trees, the school groups bouncing up and down the steps of the Metropolitan Museum, the gliding of redwing hawks over the reservoir. She'd eaten Häagen-Dazs ice cream, watched TV, read, took house calls from her shrink, attempted catching up on her schoolwork, Web-surfed, texted. Diligently. Furiously. Trying to forget.

Sleep had been rare and awful, the memories haunting her in the dark. Sam and Emma and Kyle . . . the thick streak of blood leading to the edge of the subway platform, ending at the silver bottom of the number 5 train, whose conductor had tried so hard to stop in time . . . the thick shoulders of Russo and Peterson, who attempted to comfort her as squadrons of police descended into the Fifty-Ninth Street–Bloomingdale's station she vowed to never again visit . . . the heavy, creaky clanking of the train as it was backed up slowly, back over Scott's body in order to retrieve it. . . .

At times it seemed the spring would never come, and she would be bedridden forever. Tonight felt as if she'd died and gone to heaven.

"And," Sarah announced, waving her arm to the crowd in a *very* unstable way, "to celebrate her freedom and her return to the world of—"

"Sex," Julie added.

"And just in time for spring break," Sarah said, pulling out a stack of boxes from underneath a table, "we have chipped in for a new wardrobe!"

"Oh. My. God," Kirsten said as Julie pulled out a teeny black LaPerla bra-and-panty set, an orange Yves Saint Laurent bikini, a push-up bra with Janet Jackson star cut-outs, and a pair of stiletto beach shoes.

"Yyyyyes!" shouted Brandon Yardley, his arm around the senator's daughter whose name Kirsten couldn't remember, but who smacked him so hard on the cheek that he nearly fell over.

Kirsten held each item, spreading them over her funky little Betsy Johnson dress and groaning with dismay. "I. Am. So. FAAAAT!"

"We thought of that, too," Julie said.

"Huh?" Kirsten replied.

"So we bought you, just in time for Bermuda beach season, three weeks of daily physical therapy with . . . Gay Gabe!"

And there he was, the guy once voted Woodley's Hottest Butt four years in a row, now a physical trainer at Crunch and wearing, well, just enough to cover what was necessary.

Sort of.

"How may I . . . serve you?" Gabe said, wiggling his way across the floor to a roar of laughter.

"Cruel," Kirsten said, burying her face in her hands. "So cruel."

In a moment Gabe was off dancing with Carla and Sarah, the place was bouncing, and Julie was shoving another drink into Kirsten's hand. "Happy?"

"Yeah," Kirsten said.

"Still thinking about . . . you know?"

Kirsten shrugged. "There was good news today. Peterson called me before I came here—it comes out in the *Times* tomorrow. Kyle's name was officially cleared in the murders of Carolee, Sam, Emma . . . *and* Gina. They found hard evidence to nail Scott on the first three murders—and for Lauren's. And, by the way, a cut on his scalp matched the edge of the toilet paper dispenser I smacked him with at Yellow Trance. They're pretty confident they're going to bring in Goldstein and that gang on Gina's killing, too."

"The important thing is," Julie said gently, "does it give you some closure?"

Kirsten winced. She didn't like that word. "I guess. But it's never really over. . . ." She turned her head toward the bar and shouted, "Especially if Rich decides to make that damn movie!"

"If he can get his film back from the damn police!" came a loud answer.

Richard Stone was standing behind the bar with his thumb on the blender, making what must have been his thousandth piña colada of the night. He wasn't allowed back at NYU until next semester—until the police and the campus administration gave him the okay. In the meantime, this job would tide him over.

"Anyway, with all my tip money I'm developing a different kind of project," Richard said. "A departure from the Richard Stone oeuvre. A location shoot. I think I'll call it *Woodley Bitches Do Bermuda*. What do you think? With a hip-hop score and a couple of over-the-top twists, it could be The Next Big Thing!"

"Do you know what he's talking about?" Julie asked.

"Well, it sounds like this movie is going to require a lot of tips," Kirsten said.

WHHIIIIIR . . . went the blender.

"Piña coladas all around!" Richard shouted.

Kirsten looked at Julie. Julie looked at Kirsten. They both burst out laughing.

"I think this will be the best spring ever," Julie said.

"It's about time," Kirsten said. She reached into her bag and gave Julie a wad of bills to drop into Richard's tip jar. Who knew? Maybe he really was the next Tarantino. Maybe not.

For the time being, he was a hell of a good bartender.

And that was just fine.